Haverhill

D0913326

A DIFFICULT CROSSING

VINCENT DONOVAN

ELECTIO PUBLISHING
first century principles.
a twenty-first century approach.

To the angels in our midst—both human and celestial.

"Not until we are lost do we begin to understand ourselves."

Henry David Thoreau

A DIFFICULT CROSSING

CHAPTER ONE

Christopher Maguire didn't notice a thin patch of black ice at the entrance to the pedestrian crossing. His tailbone took the brunt of the fall and he jumped up wincing in pain.

"This is a crosswalk, all right, and mine is too heavy," he mumbled.

Rubbing his lower back, he studied the faded white lines on the pavement, designed to provide a corridor of safety from a strip mall to a typical New England town square. Christopher wondered why the DPW didn't just swallow its pride and consult with the graffiti townie about his indelible paint. After being arrested for drawing a huge smiley face on the powder-blue water tower, Ralph the felon upgraded his name to Raphael. While his artistic skills were highly questionable, Raphael had a possible career track in paint chemistry as no detergent could erase the yellow happy face. Until then, men in white coveralls pushed mini-dragons spitting white paint to reapply lines with the precision of Picasso each September. Afterward, the refreshed streets would practically glow in the dark until winter. Then monster trucks spewing beachfuls of sand and salt would begin their months-long parade and slowly erase the municipal masterpieces.

An imaginary blur of planes, trains, and automobiles began racing across the horizontal lines until they collided in a giant fireball that would never make the evening news. The nightmare of the past six weeks began its afternoon matinee. *His mom and dad were sitting in the wide-body 737 enjoying a glass of champagne and toasting a romantic tropical honeymoon postponed by life for twenty-five years. They clinked glasses and watched the bubbles rise until —*

Did they hear the explosion? See the approaching torrent of flames? Squeeze each other's hands before the chaos erupted? He closed his eyes. The *Challenger* disaster two years ago punched him in the stomach. He remembered reading one account how the astronauts survived the initial explosion only to drown in the cold, deep Atlantic. *Did his parents suffer the same fate?* When he told Father Broderick about this morbid curiosity, the compassionate man of God tried to comfort him by eloquently referencing "High Flight" by John Magee and how they "slipped the surly bonds of earth to touch the face of God." Christopher opened his eyes and frowned at the pavement. *If I could see the outline of that crossing, I'd be okay. Without it, what little faith I have is fading faster than these painted lines.*

A high-pitched whistle interrupted the dark musings. Looking up, he spotted a bright orange crane inching toward a twenty-five-foot spruce in the middle of the square. The crane had supersized tires with knobby rubber teeth outlined in white frosting.

A bearded man wearing an orange hard hat reached from an extended bucket and removed the star from the top of the tree signaling the holiday season officially over.

Christopher massaged the back of his neck with cold chapped fingers that should be gloved in the winter air. Everyone seemed ready to move on except him.

As the crane beeped with a similar tone to a Saturday morning cartoon, he turned around in time to catch an orange Volkswagen Rabbit pull into a parking space in front of Billerica Drug.

The car door swung open and he watched Denise lock her prized pocket rocket. She wore the coat he bought for her birthday and he admired how her shoulder-length chestnut brown hair blended nicely with the leather. She had been watching the coat at Jordan Marsh for weeks hoping it would go on sale, and when it didn't, she put it at the top of her Christmas list. He decided to surprise her with the coat after she blew out the candles on the daffodil cake her mother baked from scratch. That was the last happy day of his former life, as the next brought an avalanche of phone calls about the plane crash and the inconsolable tears of his little sister. There were times in the last six weeks when the anguish became so intense he almost wished to trade places with any of the other 207 souls on the tragic flight.

Denise walked quickly toward him wearing a radiant smile; the same one which first caught his attention during freshman orientation at UMass three years ago, and still made his heart skip. She carried a white pharmacy technician smock in one hand and a leather clutch in the other.

"Why, this is a nice surprise," she said from ten feet away and then stopped to give him a full body scan. "I'll never understand your refusal to acknowledge winter. No gloves or hat in January?" She stared at his feet and shook her head. "Sneakers too? What are you thinking?"

He eyed her knee-high black boots and smirked. "It's my way of telling old man winter to get lost." He wrapped his arms tightly around her and inhaled citrus perfume, which immediately triggered memories of Salisbury Beach last July. They took a long stroll under a full moon to a secluded place under the dunes where the sand remained warm long into the night. They shared a bottle of cheap Chardonnay in red Solo cups and talked about the future with the understanding it would be shared. She looked forward to law school and joining her father's practice. He planned to get his master's degree and travel a bit before teaching. They still had half a bottle left, when she leaned in for a long kiss. Everything felt so right.

"I thought you were packing this morning," she said, pulling away but holding onto his hand.

He sighed as the wine and the warm beach sand disappeared. "I'm really in no rush to spend a couple weeks with the Crazy Sloanes of

New Hampshire. Plus, I don't like Kylie staying at my other aunt's house. I'll probably need a warrant to get her back."

Denise picked a piece of lint off the arm of his navy peacoat. "You could stay with us until I head back to Amherst next week." Her dark eyes narrowed and she stroked his chest. "We could snuggle and watch some old movies."

The image of the beach returned and he kissed her lips gently, so not to ruin the perfectly applied pink lipstick. "Hey, why don't you call out sick and we'll take Kylie snowshoeing this afternoon? A few years ago, my father and I went shoeing at the base of Mount Washington and got caught in a snowsquall. It felt like we were straddling the earth and sky. My dad thought it was a religious experience and saw God in every snowflake like some hippie mystic." He shrugged. "Me? I just thought it was pretty cool." He laughed. "And yes, I wore gloves."

Denise backed away and her mischievous eyes set quicker than the January sun in New England.

Christopher closed the gap and put his hands on her shoulders, eager to close the sale. "Look. I know this is last minute, but doesn't the last few weeks prove there are no guaranteed tomorrows? You have to mix things up whenever you get the chance. Besides, it would be good for my sister. We could build a snowman and get some hot chocolate in Jackson. Kylie can spend another night with me and my aunt can just deal with the delay."

He glanced at his Seiko watch, a high school graduation present from his parents. The happy family picture of that day still sat on the mantel and backed up the saying, *Acorns don't fall far from the tree.* He was the spitting image of his dad—brown hair, blue eyes, six feet tall, medium build. Kylie took after their mother—blonde, blue-eyed, with a happy-go-lucky personality.

He flashed his most charming smile. "C'mon, babe, let's live a little."

Denise frowned and glanced back at the drugstore and he watched the internal battle ensue. The length of the hesitation made him think he won, until she wrinkled her nose. The serious look that followed would become more prominent as she pursued a law profession. The image of her lawyerly father with his Shar-Pei face flashed across his mind. Luckily, Denise had inherited her Italian mother's good looks.

"Mr. Miller is scanning the parking lot right now because I'm late," she said as the opening statement.

Christopher searched the front of the store looking for the bald, unhappy man. The only thing visible were two large posters advertising Valentine cards and Tums, which made him smirk.

"As my Irish nanna used to say, don't bid the devil good day till you meet him. I know you consider missing work a misdemeanor, Counselor, but I'll happily be an accessory and move your car so you have plausible deniability. As they say, 'Don't do the crime if you can't do the time,' and unfortunately, that's about all I have now." He dug in his blue jeans pocket searching for a quarter with one hand while pointing with the other. "You can use the phone booth over at Market Basket to make the call."

Denise refolded the smock over her left arm. "I know you're in limbo, and taking a semester off to get things straightened out makes a lot of sense. But my parents are holding me accountable for half the tuition and Mr. Miller is giving me a ton of hours because Phil is out with the flu." Her face became hard like she was talking to someone in the pharmacy who wanted a refill of pain meds without a scrip. "I'll always be here for you, but I can't put everything on hold too." She bit her lip. "To be honest, I think you're starting to use what happened as a crutch to procrastinate from moving forward."

It was his turn to take a step back. "How can you say that? My parents taught me family comes first, so I'm concentrating on protecting Kylie." He rubbed his hands together and realized again the painful transition of referring to his parents in the past tense. "When my parents did their estate planning, I was only twelve at the time so I understand why they named my Aunt Evelyn as my sister's guardian—and heaven help me, Aunt Becky as mine. If I'm frustrated about anything, it's *they* procrastinated in updating their wills. My parents would want Kylie to be with me."

Her face softened. "Well, you're old enough to be out of the woods with Becky, but maybe they took a longer view about your sister. You're a great big brother no question, and legally it's a no-brainer, but can you be the best mom to a second grader? Your aunt is retired and can shuttle her to school and Brownies. I love you for putting her first, but you shouldn't have to do this alone. Plus, you'll be better positioned to provide long-term support once you get your degree and start teaching. Your aunt isn't getting any younger, why not let her help? She's family."

Her logic tasted like the vitamins his mother used to coax him to take, and he clenched his teeth the same way. The overcast sky was peppered with dark spots resembling the smudge marks he used to make in grade school after becoming too aggressive with the eraser. Continue pressing and he'd make a hole.

"Once everything gets straightened out after the investigation and the insurance settlement, we'll be okay financially. In the meantime, I would be happy for Evelyn to help out, but it has to be based out of our house—the one my parents raised us in, and where they would want us to continue living."

She reached for his hand. "Okay, I didn't mean to get into this out here. We can talk later."

The fire in his stomach remained. "Besides, my aunt is no Florence Henderson. She never married and the only things that mattered were the diplomas on her office wall and the extravagant vacations she went on. Now she's retired and I think a little bored, so she wants a new project. If she pushes, I'll get a lawyer." He smiled and kissed her leather glove. "Given how slow the wheels of justice move, I can probably hire you."

The crane made another beeping noise and he glanced back as the pine tree shed more of its Cinderella glitz. *It took over a week to put up all the decorations, and now they'll be gone in a couple hours.* It felt the same way with his parents: they fell in love, got married, built a family until one spark extinguished everything.

A cold gust rolled across the square, jingling the remaining ornaments on the tree and finding its way into his leather sneakers as a reminder he ignored winter at his own peril.

"Well, if you're going to disappoint me like this, can I at least borrow your car for a couple hours? With everything going on, I haven't had a chance to find out what's wrong with my radiator. I can't bring myself to drive my parents' car just yet." He looked at the ground. "Okay, I'll admit to procrastinating about that."

She began pulling him in the direction of the drugstore. "Sure, as long as you're not headed to the mountains because I get off at five o'clock."

"Scout's honor," he said, making the sign while calculating the mileage and time.

She let go and laughed. "You were never a Scout. Heck, you wouldn't even go fishing because you didn't want to hurt one."

He wondered what type of shiny lure Evelyn would use to try and catch Kylie.

CHAPTER TWO

The little girl manipulated a long silver spoon with the concentration of a gifted surgeon and extracted the last rainbow sprinkle from the bottom of the tulip sundae glass.

"How about some hot chocolate to melt all the ice cream?" Christopher asked, hoping to stay a while longer, even if it meant risking giving his little sister a belly ache.

Kylie's cobalt blue eyes danced and the six-week scowl momentarily disappeared. Then she giggled, probably thinking how her big brother had gone nuts in suspending all the rules which structured her young world. *And she'd be right*, he thought. Her blonde ponytail looked a bit greasy and he made a mental note to have her take a shower in the morning. He took another thoughtful sip of his third cup of coffee hoping the caffeine would delay not only sleep, but the recurring nightmares too.

The little girl looked around the deserted restaurant and he followed her gaze. In the summer, Friendly's Ice Cream was a local hotspot for Little League teams and pretty much everyone else in town, which underpinned why New England remained the king of ice cream consumption per capita in the United States. But on a blustery Monday night in the middle of January, not so much. The lone waitress, in her mid-twenties with black hair teased two feet high, busied herself shining a row of aluminum napkin holders. Christopher thought he recognized her from high school, but couldn't dial in her name. *She must have been one of those unfortunates on the fringe that drifted through.*

"So is Auntie Evelyn still coming to pick me up tonight?" Kylie asked, twirling the long spoon in the empty dish fast enough to make a ringing noise.

A dollop of vanilla ice cream on the red Formica tabletop between them caught his eye and he grabbed a paper napkin to wipe it up instead of answering the question. He promised Evelyn to have Kylie ready for a six o'clock pickup, but that deadline passed two hours ago. His aunt lived by the clock and used to cuss out his mother whenever she ran late. Last summer, she went thermonuclear when they arrived a half-hour late for a family barbecue. Looking back, he wondered if his mother made a habit of being tardy in order to tweak the nose of her big sister.

He figured by now Evelyn must have given up and retreated back to her luxury condominium in Concord, a couple of towns over. The angry call would come first thing in the morning and Concord would become home to the "second shot heard round the world" too. As far as his reservations tonight in New Hampshire were concerned, he had nothing to fear as that branch of the family lived forever in the present, hoping yesterday's misery wouldn't follow.

Kylie spun the spoon faster in the glass and the clatter got his attention. His sister's eyes looked glassy and searched his face again as if asking, *"What comes next?"* No matter how many times he told her everything would be okay, she expected the rest of the sky to fall any moment.

He reached over and slid the sundae dish to the side, but not before she gave one last spirited ring.

"Auntie will pick you up tomorrow, unless you don't want to go and I'll cancel the whole thing." *Procrastination can make good strategy, even if Denise doesn't understand,* he thought.

She nodded and began inspecting her Disney charm bracelet. "No, I want to go. With Mommy and Daddy in heaven, they can see me wherever I am," she whispered to a sterling silver Pluto.

He made sure not to bite his lip as he had a tendency to do whenever a conversation turned difficult. He wished he shared Kylie's faith and remembered his mother asking him years ago how many angels could dance on the head of a pin. *So how many, Mom?* he asked, looking up at the textured ceiling.

Suddenly, the waitress dropped a tray with a dozen plastic cups on the red-tiled floor which sounded like a rimshot after a bad joke. As he watched her pick up the glasses, he considered asking for a job application. *It would keep me busy and I could work around Kylie's schedule.*

"Auntie says I'll have my own bedroom and I can walk Tuck whenever I want," Kylie bragged. She began fidgeting in the red leather booth. "Daddy wouldn't let us have a dog because he was allergic . . . but that doesn't matter anymore." She looked away.

"But won't you miss me?" he asked, wishing immediately he hadn't.

The misguided arrow jolted the little girl. She immediately reached across the table and grabbed his hand with hers, which despite all the ice cream, felt surprisingly warm.

"Of course I will. Why can't you come and stay at Auntie's house too?"

"Because the witch never offered," he wanted to say, but took a sip of the black coffee to wash it down his throat. "Well, Evelyn has a small place with only two bedrooms and if I tagged along, where would Tuck stay?" He forced a smile. "That golden retriever enjoys stretching out on the couch and wouldn't like it very much if I made it my bed too." He looked down at his green cotton sweater, imagining all the dog hair he'd pick up sleeping on the plastic-covered floral couch. "Plus, I promised to help Aunt Becky get her house ready to sell. She says she's been building a honey-do list for twenty years, even though they've lived there for only ten." He tried to keep from frowning

thinking how her son should be the one helping, but Becky had a knack for soliciting assistance.

He gripped her hand tighter. "I promise it will only be for a couple weeks at most and a lot shorter if she doesn't have anything in the fridge for me to eat."

Tears welled up in her eyes. "But I won't see you every day!"

Given their fifteen-year difference in age, they didn't see each other much before the tragedy. But if he learned anything in the last forty-five days, perception equaled reality and Kylie needed to feel secure. "Like we've discussed, I'll call you so much you'll get sick of hearing from me," he added.

Christopher made a mental note to bring a roll of quarters for the long-distance phone booth calls, because if Evelyn lived by the hands on a clock, her sister Becky lived by the mantra "*If wishes were horses, beggars would ride.*" The Sloanes' utilities were occasionally terminated for unpaid bills, forcing his aunt to embrace an array of can't-fail-get-rich-schemes, which built many a debtor's prison in the past. Consequently, Becky leaned on the generosity of others to stay one step ahead of bankruptcy and his parents were sympathetic because at its core, the financial hardships were born out of service. Becky's husband, Aram, came home from Vietnam with a trauma no doctor would ever find on an x-ray. He died two years ago after a strange accident and his aunt had received many heartfelt condolences and a few odd ones too. She still fumed over "No-Filter" Frank Drago, who asked at the grocery store if she thought Aram was at peace. Before she could answer, he compared her husband's PTSD to whacking yourself in the head with a hammer and how good it must feel to finally stop. His aunt would have drowned the little man in a pickle barrel if a clerk hadn't intervened.

"I wish they made phones you could carry in your pocket so you could talk with your friends and family whenever you wanted," Kylie said, and rested her chin on the tabletop as the sugar rush crashed. "I could call you on the bus or when I finish my homework."

"Yeah, that would be really cool." He bit his lip. "When they had the candle vigil for Mom and Dad, I saw a black Lincoln with an antenna on the back window. It must have belonged to one of the television reporters from Boston. I can't imagine the cost."

The conversation dried up and he looked out the window and watched a bevy of snow flurries rush past the lights in the empty parking lot. January nights were long and silent and he looked forward to springtime with its nightly chorus of peepers and crickets. Last night he ventured outside after Kylie fell asleep and scanned the pinwheels of light which he rarely admired anymore. A plane flew high overhead, and he watched until it disappeared beyond the tree line. *All those people on board headed somewhere and carrying on like the future is guaranteed—until it isn't.*

Christopher bit his lip to the point where any additional pressure would puncture, which happened much too often lately. As he glanced across the table at the tired little girl, he heard his father whisper, *"Man up, will you?"* even if there wasn't enough super-glue in the world to put things back together.

He quickly shimmied out of the booth and slid in next to her. Bending his head, he reached inside his T-shirt and took off a silver necklace with a round pendant the size of a quarter at the end.

"Dad brought me here before we brought you and Mom home from the hospital and I remember devouring a Jim Dandy banana split." He chuckled, thinking how much he missed those innocent conquests. "Dad had a coffee frappe with a spoonful of chocolate jimmies added, which grossed me out because they looked like tiny ants."

Kylie laughed. "He always did silly things like that."

He nodded. "After we finished, Dad gave me this medal of St. Christopher." He pointed at the depiction of the venerable saint clutching a staff and carrying a child on his shoulders. "He reminded me how I was named after this giant of a man that helped people cross a raging river to safety. I'll never forget him telling me I may never be a giant physically, but I should try to be one where it counts," he said, pointing to his heart, "and it was my job to look after you."

He put the necklace over her head and under the ponytail. "I'll always be here and won't let anything bad happen. Remember that whenever you feel afraid." He smiled. "It's sort of like a twofer, since you have the real saint looking out for you too."

She gave him a tight hug.

"I love you," he whispered.

"I love you to the moon and back," she replied, repeating their mother's favorite saying.

Kylie sat back and straightened the chain, which nearly reached her stomach. Christopher eyed the pendant and recalled the rest of the story. One day a small child approached the giant for safe passage and he struggled mightily to carry him across the water. When they reached the other side, the child revealed he was Christ and so heavy because He carried the weight of the world.

Christopher closed his eyes. *It's up to me to carry Kylie across now.*

"There he is!" he heard a woman shout.

He opened his eyes to find Evelyn marching toward them with Denise close behind. Fifty years might separate them in age, but at this moment with slanted eyes and flushed faces, they could be mistaken for twins.

The waitress with the big hair darted behind the counter.

Christopher expected his aunt to begin yelling, but noticed the erupting volcano in his girlfriend's eyes. The three cups of coffee seized the opportunity to burn his esophagus.

"Where have you been?" Denise asked, her voice rising. "You were supposed to bring my car back before I got out of work three hours ago!"

He stood up much too quickly and whacked his knee on the table. "I thought you were working until close, so—"

"I can't believe you left me stranded like that," she said, cutting him off before an apology could be issued. "My folks weren't home and I had to bum a ride over to your house. If your aunt wasn't there waiting to pick up Kylie, I would have died from exposure."

Died? That's a bit melodramatic. The gas station is only a quarter mile away, but he kept the thought to himself.

Evelyn stepped in front of his girlfriend to get her licks in and pointed a dagger-like burgundy nail at him. "So what excuse do you have for me?" She glanced at Kylie then checked her diamond-encrusted digital watch. "This nonsense has to stop right now. It's a school night and this little girl should be getting ready for bed." The pointed finger swiveled to Kylie. "Just look at the bags under those eyes! She's sure to be sick by this time tomorrow."

He looked down at the red tile floor, expecting the water to begin rushing in any moment and quickly reach flood stage.

It would be a difficult crossing, indeed.

CHAPTER THREE

Christopher tossed and turned all night and it had nothing to do with the caffeine overdose. By mid-morning, he worked up the courage to call Denise and ask for a lift to New Hampshire. She limited her responses to three words: hello, yes, and goodbye. Hanging up, he concluded she agreed to give him a ride only to have the satisfaction of seeing him banished to the New Hampshire gulag.

Things didn't improve much when she arrived after lunch. After throwing his duffel bag in the back seat of the VW Rabbit, she handed him the car keys and retreated to the passenger side. Her one-word answers continued as he toyed with the four-speed manual transmission on the back roads. After weaving through Tewksbury, he eased the car onto Interstate Route 93 and crawled in the first lane while fiddling with the radio dial until he found "Anything for You" by Gloria Estefan and Miami Sound Machine. He smiled when he reached over to hold her hand and she didn't slap it away.

Twenty minutes later they crossed into New Hampshire and he took the first curvaceous exit into Salem and passed Rockingham Race Track, deemed in 1906 as one of the finest thoroughbred race courses in the world, now struggling to survive after a devastating fire eight years ago. The traffic light ahead remained uncharacteristically green and he downshifted as they crossed Route 28, gateway to the shopping mecca of the Merrimack Valley with tax-free shopping and cheap liquor and cigarettes.

"I feel like joining a sideshow," he mumbled, and gripped the steering wheel with both hands as they passed a one-story brick building which housed the police department and occasionally his cousin.

At the end of Veterans Memorial Parkway, he turned right on Lawrence Road and a half mile later slowed to a crawl before passing over the Spicket River on a wooden plank bridge with gunmetal-gray railings. "When I was Kylie's age, my cousin AJ had me convinced an old troll lived under this bridge," he said, pointing out the driver's side window. "I believed him until Uncle Aram told me he had a makeshift hammock down there which channeled the summer breeze nicely."

"The more I hear maybe you should take a chainsaw to that branch of the family tree," Denise deadpanned.

Christopher laughed, happy to hear a complete sentence and thinking the family tree was already morphing into something out of *Charlie Brown*. Downshifting again and braking, he let out a moan before turning into a snow-packed driveway and maneuvering the automobile through deep ruts made by other suburban adventurers.

"It's more than wishful thinking the sun will replace a shovel this time of year," he complained, as the car bounced every which way and he hit his head on the ceiling. "Just plain laziness, if you ask me."

Halfway up the driveway, he surrendered. Turning the ignition off, he eyed the white vinyl-sided ranch which looked naked without shutters. He began studying the rust-colored roof with invading patches of grayish-green moss when Denise pointed to a weathered plywood sign in the middle of the front lawn propped against a rotting wooden wheelbarrow. HAY + ICE FOR SALE it proclaimed in bright orange spray paint.

"What do you make of that?" she asked with a snicker.

"Maybe that's why they don't mow the lawn or shovel the driveway." He laughed and missed the feeling.

"You can't be serious?"

"Well, sort of. My aunt is quite the entrepreneur when it comes to making ends meet. One of my favorites is the short stint she did in real estate."

"Why?"

"Becky took a part-time job selling condos in a new mausoleum and trolled senior citizen centers and nursing homes making cold calls. When the owners stiffed her over a commission, she told everyone that behind the fancy stone façade, all the caskets are stacked in one big room like a college dormitory, but without the keg parties."

"Sorry I asked," she replied, and rolled down the window halfway. Cold air overwhelmed the green apple air freshener.

"Yeah, it creeps me out too. After that, Becky began giving private tours of Mystery Hill." He noticed new plastic sheathing covering the front windows on the house and wondered if it kept the cold out or the lunacy in.

Denise leaned forward in her seat and looked up at a line of massive pine trees behind the house. "Let me guess. The spooky hill is out back?"

"No, it's a few miles away in North Salem. The place is advertised as America's Stonehenge and built by ancient people some four thousand years ago. I remember a field trip there in grammar school and the sacrifice table drew the biggest crowd. My aunt worked there part-time until they found her giving freelance tours around Halloween." He looked away and frowned. *Would I be willing to do the same to support Kylie?*

"Meanwhile, back on planet earth, I'm working doubles most of the week," Denise said, rolling her window up. "I'll plan to drive up after work on Friday. We can grab a pizza before I head back to Amherst."

Christopher leaned over and gave her a long slow kiss like he was heading off to the front. "Sorry about last night and thanks for putting up with me." He stroked her hair and drank in her almond-shaped eyes. "Especially now that you know what's floating around in my gene pool."

She scowled, but couldn't hold it long and smirked. Opening the glove compartment, she fished out a cassette tape. "Maybe I'll listen to Michael Jackson's *Thriller* on the way back as a tribute to your clan."

He kissed her again before she got comfortable in the driver's seat. Then, with duffel bag in hand, he waved goodbye as the car seesawed backward out of the driveway.

Turning around, he found AJ silently waiting for him at the end of the driveway. It didn't look like he'd changed much in the past two years: still about five foot ten if he would stand up straight and with a midsection growing ever thicker. The shoulder-length brown hair reached the collar of a red ski jacket and was apparently still allergic to shampoo given its greasy sheen. His cousin's hands were concealed in the side pockets of baggy jeans that hung over bulky black work boots.

Christopher straddled an icy trench and shuffled forward while a worn video-loop started playing in his mind. It featured their parents playing cards at the dining room table as AJ rummaged through Christopher's bedroom to see what he could steal or break. When that got boring, his first cousin would tackle him and wrestle until he cried uncle, which wasn't long given their five-year age difference.

"Welcome to our version of the Bates Motel, Chrissy," his cousin purred, "or as the paperboy likes to call us, the house on welfare." He cleared his throat and spit. "That little punk thinks he's funny, but we always get the last laugh because we pay him by the month."

Christopher forced a smile to be polite.

AJ studied his expression. "You don't get it, do you?"

"Get what?"

"You bookworm sissies are all alike and have no common sense. Some months have five weeks so we end up getting a free month every year. Do you get it now or would you like me to write it down for you?"

Christopher took the duffel bag off his shoulder and laid it on the frozen tundra. "Thanks for explaining how to con a twelve-year-old. What's next? Laundering Canadian coins through lemonade stands this summer?"

AJ cocked his head sideways as if examining roadkill. "Ah, there's the Chrissy I know and don't love. Always the wise guy and never wanting for anything . . . well, until now. Sure looks like the Big Guy hit the reset button on you."

Christopher didn't know what to say. He hadn't entered the house yet and wanted to leave. AJ seemed to sense his uneasiness and unzipped his coat, revealing a black T-shirt with "Phuket" scripted in cursive white letters.

He knew his cousin thought you had to be related to Columbus or Magellan to travel internationally and probably ordered the T-shirt hoping to shock people not familiar with the correct pronunciation for the Thailand resort.

"So, is that where you were vacationing when we held the vigil for my parents last month?" he asked in a controlled voice.

A loud noise emanated from AJ's throat and he spit again. This time the grossness landed next to his duffel bag.

"Ma begged me to go with her, but I thought it would be a pretty lame service with no bodies. I mean no disrespect, man, but c'mon, they were shark food as soon as they hit the water."

Christopher felt a shiver run down the back of his head and looked over at a sorry-looking rhododendron to the right of the bay window, which the deer had picked clean. He pictured twisting AJ into a human pretzel to keep the plant warm for the remainder of the winter.

His cousin followed his gaze and glanced over at the bush too. "I wanted to meet your girl, but she took off like she was leaving a baby on the doorstep." He gave him a quick once-over. "Yeah, I can see why." Reaching into the side pocket of his jacket, he took out a soft pack of Marlboros and fished out a cigarette. "Remember the movie *Ten*?"

He nodded. "Sure, Dudley Moore—"

"Leave it to you to lead with him," AJ said, cutting him off. "I'm going out with Bo Derek's twin sister now and she's an easy eleven."

Christopher squinted. "All you need now is to grow a scruffy beard and you can apply for the Neanderthal-in-residence position at Mystery Hill."

AJ finished lighting the cigarette with a black BIC lighter and took a long drag before looking at him again. "How long have you been saving up that line to make fun of your country cousin? Well, sticks and stones can't hurt my bones in 'Live Free or Die' New Hampshire," he sang and then took another toke. "I'm betting the bleeding heart liberal from Massachusetts will be smoking a pack a day by this time next year." He eyed his cousin's leather sneakers. "I have some real work lined up for you. I'm sure it will be a real change of pace from sitting in your dorm room drinking beer and smoking weed."

"I don't know what got lost in translation or maybe you're smoking that hay you're selling, but I'm here to help your mother paint and get the house ready for sale." He felt his pulse quicken and he picked up the duffel bag, which he could swing as a weapon if needed. "I thought it was pretty sad she had to ask me for help, but then I remembered you flunked coloring in kindergarten. If you can get home early some night from the junk yard, I'd be happy to introduce you to a paintbrush."

AJ clenched his right fist and smiled without showing any teeth. "You know my old lady, always trying to get something for nothing. Yeah, she needs to get the house ready, but the first order of business is to finish getting me settled." He took another drag. "I moved out a month ago and can literally roll out of bed ten minutes before work. Jason gave me a great deal on a place he rehabbed. He's also running the family auto salvage business since his old man fell in love with a tramp. More than a landlord and boss, he's been like a brother to me."

Christopher shrugged. "I remember him more as the kid who liked to shoot frogs with a BB gun."

"I don't remember that exactly, but I do recall him shooting you in the butt a couple times. Now that was funny. Anyways, the apartment is small and has a good-sized garage underneath where I can run my car upholstery business on the side. The place needs some cleaning and painting and that's where my talented history major cousin comes in. Maybe you can suggest something mid-century?"

Christopher put the strap of the duffel bag on his shoulder and realized this trip was a bust. "Good luck with that. Who knows? Maybe when I need my pants hemmed in the future, I'll give you a call."

He turned around much too quickly, lost his balance, and landed flat on his back where a protruding piece of ice stabbed his tailbone, which still ached from falling in the crosswalk. Moaning, he scrambled to his feet too quickly and the sneakers almost betrayed him again as he pitched forward.

His cousin doubled over in laughter. "See you next fall, cuz."

"You're a real jerk, do you know that?" Christopher shouted back and began to slowly shuffle toward the road.

AJ flicked the spent cigarette and it landed in front of him. "Hey, Chrissy, where are you headed? I was just hazing you, man! C'mon, the house of debauchery is this way. I have a six-pack of Bud on ice."

Christopher ignored him and continued inching away, until a beige-colored K-car with a loud muffler swung into the driveway blocking his escape. Aunt Becky began waving with too much gusto from behind the steering wheel and Jackie-O sunglasses.

He gave a halfhearted wave back with no intention of stopping to explain his decision to hike back to Route 28 and find a ride home.

His aunt must have read his thoughts and opened the driver's door before he could pass. He ended up hugging it to prevent from falling again.

Becky got out and removed the black sunglasses in slow motion like a Hollywood star. In her mid-forties, she was the youngest of the three Rawley sisters and shared so many mannerisms with his mother that when the corners of her mouth worked to suppress a smile, he drank it in.

"My goodness, dear, if you hit the door any harder, Lee Iacocca could have used it a few years ago in one of his '*if you can find a better car*' commercials." She glanced inside the tired Dodge Aries. "One of those minivans sure would be nice. If I end up losing the house, I could live in it for a while." She eyed the snow. "But in Daytona."

Christopher rubbed his tailbone as his aunt closed the car door. At the vigil, she reminded him of Jennifer Beals with her dark curly hair, black dress, and wool coat. This morning, she was the definition of natural beauty with her hair pulled back in a tight ponytail with no makeup, and wearing a form-fitting cream-colored turtleneck sweater, blue jeans, and no coat. His dad looked past the good looks and thought she wasn't the sharpest tool in the shed, but his mother stuck up for her baby sister and the tough hand life dealt her. His own feelings were somewhat mixed; she could act a bit wacky at times, but possessed a down-to-earth personality he admired.

Becky gave him a tight hug followed by the same concerned look everyone greeted him with nowadays. "I spoke with Evelyn this morning. She told me about what happened last night. Ugh!"

He bit his lip, reliving how Evelyn waited silently in the kitchen while he finished packing Kylie's things. After he kissed his sister goodbye, his aunt ushered her out without saying a word.

"Well, I hope she didn't play the guardian card with you."

Becky quickly put her sunglasses back on like she didn't want her nephew reading her eyes.

His stomach churned. "Is that what she's aiming to do?"

Becky rubbed his arm gently. "Don't go worrying none, honey. My sister and I only want what's best for you and Kylie." She sighed. "I think now that the initial shock has worn off, we have to figure things out."

Stand on your own two feet, he heard his dad bark in his ears. "Look. I know there's no playbook for this sort of thing, and while I appreciate everything, some decisions aren't going to be made by committee. Case in point is Kylie. My sister belongs with me. Period."

She gave a slight nod to acknowledge she heard him. "So, who dropped you off?" she asked, changing the subject.

"Denise."

"She's a keeper." Becky looked toward the road. "Did you drop something?"

He glanced over his shoulder to where he left AJ. His cousin had vanished, though he could hear heavy metal music coming from the house.

His aunt kicked at the packed snow in scuffed white boots. "I told that son of mine to put some sand down before you arrived. But AJ lives by the Mark Twain motto to '*never put off till tomorrow what may be done the day after tomorrow just as well.*'"

The warning from Denise about his own procrastination played in his ears. He hated to admit he and AJ shared any bad habits.

She grabbed his arm and pulled him toward the house. "What are we doing talking out here? Let's go in and I'll put a pot of coffee on after I wallop my son."

CHAPTER FOUR

The first snowflakes began parachuting in on Sunday afternoon accompanied by a strong breeze; the harbinger of a nasty nor'easter. A couple hours later, the snow was ankle deep in front of the Village Store where Christopher stood admiring how the branches of a tall maple tree across the street looked outlined in Marshmallow Fluff. Throw in a horse-drawn sleigh and the scene would have been Currier & Ives worthy, though he much preferred the January thaw of the last three days when temperatures flirted with fifty degrees. Today's sudden return to winter reminded him of Shackleton's Antarctic misadventure and the endless months ahead on the *Endurance.*

His toes throbbed with pain and he stamped his sneakers in the snow. In the last week, he found AJ ran perpetually late for everything, but since Friday night, he'd lost all remaining sense of time after being dumped by his "super-hot" girlfriend, Lori. He showed up at his mother's house raving drunk at two in the morning and she locked him in their musty basement to sleep it off. Then the phone rang four hours later with Lori's father looking for his first-born daughter. By lunchtime, a Salem police officer stopped by to have a chat with AJ while he popped aspirin and chugged black coffee. As the hours passed with no word from Lori, the fear and suspicion accumulated faster than the snow.

Christopher brushed a clump of flakes off the shoulder of his wool coat and glanced back at the convenience store, which matched the monochromatic landscape with its gray shingles. In the center of the large plate glass window a neon sign blinked *C'mon In!* and he briefly weighed the invitation, but feared his cousin would blow right on by if given the excuse. He rehashed the phone call he made to Kylie from a pay phone inside as some annoying kid kept feeding quarters into a Pac-Man game three feet away. The game's incessant beeping and animated intermissions forced him to lean into the pay phone cubicle and cup his hand over his free ear.

"I-miss-you-terribly," Kylie whispered in one word. "We're baking cookies and you know how much I despise raisins. Auntie knew this, but didn't want to drive in the bad weather to buy chocolate chips. I think I'm going to barf."

"Who is this?" he asked in mock surprise. "You have a poster of those California Claymation characters in your bedroom."

"They can sing, but that's different from actually eating dry, shriveled grapes."

"Okay, but just remember to be polite," he counseled, but hoping his little sister pulled a tantrum and ground a few raisins into his aunt's cherished Oriental rugs. He fought the urge to pepper her with questions and decided an open probe would suffice. "Besides the cookie crisis, what else have you been doing?"

There was a short pause followed by a long sigh. "Not much really. She won't let me watch my shows on TV."

"Hang in there. The work up here is almost done."

A loud buzzing noise filled the line. "Kylie, the cookies need to come out of the oven. Hurry up and say goodbye to your brother."

He fidgeted hearing Evelyn's voice. "Well, I have enough quarters to last until spring if you want me to wait for you to finish baking," he said loudly, then sighed. "I'm sorry, that's wrong of me. Go help your aunt. I know how much you can't wait to sample one."

"Yuck!"

"See you soon. Love you."

"Love you more," and the phone clicked.

The wind stopped for a second to catch its breath and Christopher tilted his head back and caught a few snowflakes in his mouth like he used to do as a kid. Just as he remembered, it still tasted like wet cotton. He wondered if nature survived winter by remembering the last kiss of summer and thought about Denise. Last year at this time they were making snow angels at Winterfest and enjoying hot toddies. Now, he was standing alone in the snow and Denise ended up working additional overtime and cancelling their pizza date before heading back to school.

A set of headlights suddenly appeared tunneling through the storm and the sound of tires munching on snow grew louder as it approached.

"Well, it's about time," he mumbled. The overdue taxi slid to a stop and unleashed a strand of ice crystals from the roof of the ten-year-old, more-rust-than red Firebird, whipping his face. Opening the passenger door, he threw himself into the bucket seat and immediately detected a strong odor of alcohol which overpowered all the wetness. Christopher quickly glanced back at the Lilliputian back seat, half-expecting to find one of AJ's hoodlum friends sitting sullen and silent, but it was empty. He turned his attention back to driver and focused on the collar of AJ's red ski coat, which stood upright shielding the bottom half of his face.

"Did they find Lori?" he asked, with as much sensitivity as he could muster. Christopher suddenly felt some scratchiness on one side of his throat, which he didn't know whether to chalk up to breathing paint fumes all week or to standing in the snow for an hour. *One sneeze and Evelyn will use it as an excuse to extend Kylie's visit indefinitely*, he thought.

AJ didn't answer, but continued looking straight ahead, apparently mesmerized by the synchronized wipers struggling with growing feet of ice. Rather than repeat the question, Christopher shook his head vigorously, which sent pieces of snow flying in every direction as an exclamation point. Surprisingly, his cousin never flinched, which made him worry all the more about how much he imbibed.

"Hey, are you okay to drive?" he asked, leaning forward. "If not, I'm a pro with a stick shift." When no answer came, he took it as a signal to find another way back to his aunt's house and reached for the door handle.

AJ suddenly stepped hard on the gas pedal and the car began to fishtail. *I can suck this up,* he told himself. *It's only a short ride,* and fumbled for the seat belt.

The warm air in the cabin began to thaw more than his bottom. "I understand your worry about Lori, but you're still an inconsiderate jerk for making me wait in the snow so you could get wasted." He kneed the glove compartment for effect. "I don't know how drinking will help find your ex-girlfriend, but I don't need this drama. I have enough on my plate right now."

Suddenly, a bony hand pushed him hard against the passenger door. "So you think you can flash the poor me victim card from now on and that's supposed to trump everyone else's problems?" His bloodshot eyes shot him a quick look before returning to the road. "It will be a hoot watching a spoiled know-it-all like you have to deal with life in the trenches like everyone else."

Christopher slapped AJ's hand away. "And I'm so grateful to have you as a role model of what not to do. Sort of like Letterman's *Top 10* list." He drummed on the dashboard. "I'll save you the suspense and jump to number one, which is don't get stone drunk and not remember where you went after breaking up with your girlfriend. No wonder the cops are your BFFs now."

AJ tried to grab him again, but Christopher blocked the attempt and would have returned a hard right if he wasn't driving.

"Keep it up and I'll drop you off on Route 93 and you can thumb a ride back to your orphan house." AJ glanced at the floorboard and shook his head. "Would suit you right too, for wearing sneakers in the middle of winter. What type of fool are you? Maybe if frostbite claimed a toe or two, you'd realize mommy can't take care of you anymore." He let out a low snicker. "Maybe that's why you're sucking up to my old lady. If so, you better find another target because she's not going to baby you either. She has enough issues to worry about."

"Yeah, like where to hide the files in the cake once you're in prison." Christopher took a deep breath and grabbed the door handle, prepared to jump out at the next stop sign. In the meantime, he concentrated on the groaning metronome of the wipers as the ice streaked frozen patches across the windshield.

An uneasy silence followed and Christopher bit his lip as his frozen toes began to wake up pretty angry. He reached over to turn up the heat and noticed a brown leather wallet with a gold horseshoe clasp, sitting on top of the ashtray in front of the shifter. It didn't belong to his aunt, since hers was made of some sort of shiny material and resided permanently on the kitchen table to provide housing for her driver's license and insurance cards. Any cash or food stamps were like perpetual drifters, barely settling in before moving on.

The hullabaloo about Lori made him reach for the wallet and AJ slapped his hand away.

"Mind your business," he barked, and grabbed for the wallet, but not before Christopher noticed the initials "L.M." imprinted on the leather. AJ slipped it into the vest pocket of his coat.

"Let me get this straight," he said, taking off one sneaker and finding a dark wet sock shrink-wrapped around his foot. "Your mother thinks your ex took off in her car after breaking up with you, but forgot her wallet? I'm no Sherlock, but unless she's in the witness protection program somewhere, she must be staying with family or friends to not need any money or credit cards."

AJ moved his lips but nothing came out, as though he was chewing on which words to cuss him out with.

Christopher got another strong whiff of alcohol and guessed there must be an open bottle leaking somewhere under the seat.

"Everyone has been called and then called again," AJ finally reported in a surprisingly normal voice. He patted his chest. "Her sister found Lori's wallet in a snowbank by their mailbox. That's why I'm late, Mister Ungrateful."

Christopher remembered their conversation over a six-pack and pizza a few nights back when things turned almost normal for an hour.

"Didn't you tell me her sister is—ah, different?"

AJ let out a short laugh. "Listen to you struggling with the governor on your tongue which prevents you from saying what you really think. Yeah, Mary belongs in the same fruit bin as my old man, who pushed a bike around town for as long as I can remember." He pounded the steering wheel. "I would have developed psoriasis of the liver soon, if he didn't do us a favor by croaking."

An itchy liver? Christopher smirked. He wondered where all of AJ's dark filling came from. He felt for the St. Christopher medal under his shirt and his heart skipped a couple of beats before he remembered Kylie wore it now.

"I think you mean *cirrhosis* of the liver. And why do you always talk about your father like that?" he asked for the tenth time in the past week. "We should be grateful for his service no matter what you think about the war and how tough it was on your family. It's strange that I'm always the one defending him." He rubbed his forehead. "Isn't your name Aram Junior, for heaven's sake?"

"If I could change my name to Rumpelstiltskin, I would. All I'm saying is show me the scars, then I'll believe."

"Maybe you should change your name to Thomas then, but at least he realized his mistake." He bit his lip. *That must be my mom talking. It's certainly not me.* "Someday, when you have your head screwed on straight, you should spend some time at the Veterans Hospital in Bedford and see the effects of PTSD. It's only a few miles away from my house. Denise volunteers there."

Laughter filled the car. "Yeah, I'll be sure to pencil that in."

Christopher pulled some more on the toe of the wet sock and it felt so uncomfortable he considered going barefoot. "Yeah, I forgot you have a standing date with the Salem Police Department for the foreseeable future." He crammed his foot back into the sneaker and tried to ignore the discomfort. "How are you going to explain why you have Lori's wallet if Mary forgets giving it to you? If you wanted a memento, you should have waited until she shows up to ask for a Dear John letter instead of hiding a piece of evidence."

"Put a plug in it, will ya?" AJ punched the gas as if realizing the error. The car blew through a stop sign and continued down Cluff Road.

"Hey, where are you going? You just missed the street," Christopher said, pointing back at Lawrence Road.

CHAPTER FIVE

"Chill, will you? Better get used to the fact my old lady doesn't do Sunday dinners, and I'm not your limo service," AJ fired back.

The Firebird continued on for a couple miles before connecting with Route 38, a north-south state highway running nine miles and connecting Salem with Pelham. Five minutes later they reached a wooded section of the road where a long train of semi-trailers sat a few feet off the road. The trailers butted up against one another and had a curtain of black canvas on the undercarriages, blocking any view into Play It Again Auto Salvage. More than an interesting fencing choice, it made passersby wonder what the heck they were hiding.

AJ downshifted and stopped in front of a ten-foot section of chain-link fencing with coiled barbed wire at the top. He jumped out to unlock the gate and then plowed through a half foot of snow to an old two-story red brick building and beeped the horn twice. A small sign emblazoned with *"No Solicitors!"* in faded black lettering hung on the rusted metal door.

If an intrepid salesman didn't get bad vibes until this point, he deserves to be mauled by a rabid dog or a flying fender, Christopher thought. "So why are we stopping here?" he asked, feeling the lymph nodes in his neck. "I can't imagine there's much call for a secondhand alternator during a nor'easter on a Sunday night." A dark-colored sedan that must have kissed a tree, parked to the right of the building, caught his attention. Most of the front end was missing and the blowing snow worked on camouflaging the devastation.

AJ leaned on the horn again and then pointed to the right. "My new place is just through the woods."

Seconds later, Jason Driscoll—or as AJ liked to boast, his "brother-from-another-mother"—exited the building like he thought Carly Simon's "You're So Vain" was the soundtrack for the evening and looked around as if expecting paparazzi to appear. He sported a red ski parka identical to AJ's, minus the ski tags his cousin kept on his as a badge of coolness. The Firebird headlights illuminated Nike Air Jordan III sneakers.

"Maybe you should repeat your sermon about winter boots to your buddy too," Christopher commented.

AJ motioned with his thumb. "Okay, wise guy, get your butt in the backseat. Of course, you're welcome to walk back to Lawrence Road if you prefer."

Christopher opened the door and Jason nodded once at him. He knew that would be the extent of saying hello after their last encounter three years ago, and also covered any condolences for the deaths of his parents.

Jason didn't wait for Christopher to finish contorting himself in the back before adjusting his seat to hog more room.

"Hey, you're crushing my legs!" Christopher said and slapped the headrest.

"Sorry, man, but I'm six foot two and need the leg space," Jason replied.

"What did you hear?" AJ asked, leaning close enough to kiss his buddy.

The evil twin with no manners grabbed the rearview mirror and turned it his way to inspect the top of his blond mullet. Not happy with the dim lighting, he opened the passenger door slightly and the dome light provided the needed illumination to finish the inspection.

"Well, she met the scumbag for drinks after breaking up with you," he said to his reflection.

AJ put his hand over the mirror. "Who told you that?" he asked in an accusing tone. "I have feelers out to every bar in a ten-mile radius and no one saw them together that night or before."

Jason closed the door and rubbed the weekend stubble on his chin, clearly enjoying the suspense. "If you don't believe me, ask him yourself. Mac called me five minutes ago and said he's in the bar at Sandy's watching the game."

Christopher rolled his eyes. "Can you drop me off first, please?" He knew how this soap opera would play out, with AJ being arrested after a bar fight. Then as Becky passed around the hat for bail money, Lori would pop up after spending the weekend in Maine with her new squeeze. This would trigger a tsunami of wailing and gnashing of teeth followed by another AJ bender and still more cops.

AJ didn't acknowledge the request. He put the car in drive and stepped on the gas with too much enthusiasm. The Firebird catapulted backward across the lot and through the open gate onto Route 38.

"Hey, are you going to stop and lock the gate?" Jason asked.

AJ looked in the rearview mirror. "My three-quarters college-educated cousin analyzed the customer flow patterns and thinks we're covered tonight. If anyone breaks in, bill Chrissy."

Christopher tightened his seat belt and decided to call a cab once they made it to the combo bar and bowling alley in Windham.

The Bose speakers behind his head pulsed with Deep Purple as the rear-wheel-drive car slipped and sledded on the back roads. AJ worked the steering wheel like he was navigating high seas. Approaching a stop sign, he reached under the seat and pulled out a bottle of rum. After taking a couple long swigs, he offered it to his wingman. Jason held the bottle vertical to his mouth until a silver Camaro sped past on the other side of the road.

Christopher watched as two heads pivoted to the left like marionettes controlled by the same string.

AJ shot up in his seat like a cattle prod jolted him and navigated a sloppy U-turn. "Godfreye must think he's some type of Casper."

Christopher smiled picturing a man in his late twenties glued to the television watching cartoons about a friendly ghost.

Jason reached for the seat belt and buckled himself in. "So you're going to chase Bobby and then what? Make him admit they had drinks? What does that prove?"

"That he was the last person to see her and make him pay for knifing me in the back."

"Do you mean Bobby Godfreye?" Christopher asked, piecing together the puzzle and remembering playing 45s with the guy a few years back. He studied AJ's profile as they passed a streetlight and zeroed in on his cousin's oversized nose and unkempt hair and understood why Lori decided to trade up. Bobby Godfreye was handsome with an athletic build, and seemed to have his act together in managing a busy supermarket his father owned.

He leaned forward. "I thought you two were buddies."

AJ replied by cranking up the music.

A traffic light a quarter mile ahead proved to be an ally and kept the Camaro prisoner until AJ caught up and began flashing his high beams. Godfreye didn't wait for the light to change and took off with AJ in pursuit. The Camaro quickly abandoned the main road for myriad side streets and drove in the middle to prevent the Firebird from passing. Any other day the drivers would have more options, but the snow proved to be the great equalizer as both rear-wheeled cars struggled to stay on the road.

"Is he alone?" AJ shouted above the music.

"There's too much snow covering the back window to tell," Jason replied.

They began climbing another short hill, which curved slightly to the left when the Camaro suddenly accelerated. When AJ tried to follow suit, the car began to fishtail badly and by the time they reached the crest, Bobby was gone.

The road ahead looked dark. "Where did he go?" AJ yelled, braking hard and sledding to a stop in the middle of the road.

Jason's head swiveled and pointed behind them. "He must have banged a right on Theresa Avenue."

AJ responded by giving the car too much gas in attempting a U-turn and the Pontiac got stuck in the middle of the road straddling both lanes. Without warning, headlights came barreling over the hill and Christopher grabbed the front seat, waiting to be T-boned. At the last second, the van slid by them and went off the road and head first into a ditch.

"Who's Casper now?" AJ yelled, pumping his fist.

Jason handed the rum bottle back to the daring driver. "Talk about Russian roulette!"

AJ quickly drained the rest of bottle. "Now, let's go get that thief."

"Aren't you going to see if they're all right?" Christopher asked, pointing to the van. "We almost got killed."

"Almost only counts in horseshoes and hand grenades," AJ replied, as the car began a slow crawl back up the hill. After turning on Theresa Avenue, he extinguished the headlights.

"Are you nuts?" Christopher pleaded.

"Shut your pie hole," Jason replied, throwing an ugly glance his way.

AJ pointed fifty yards ahead to a snowy hulk sitting on the side of the road with red taillights barely noticeable in the falling snow.

They inched forward until AJ lost his cool, threw the headlights on, and accelerated.

Jason rolled down his window as the Firebird catapulted past the Camaro on the right.

"He's alone," Jason reported and shot the driver a hard look. "What are you going to do now?"

AJ braked hard and the car did a classic Bat-turn. Gunning the engine, he cranked up the music so the whole car began pulsating and raced straight at the Camaro.

Jason's tough persona immediately crumbled and he grabbed the dashboard. "C'mon, man, don't play chicken with me in the car!"

The music pummeled Christopher's eardrums as the headlights of the Camaro quickly approached. *There's no way we're going to get lucky a second time.*

A millisecond before they feasted on Bobby Godfreye wrapped in steel, Christopher put his head down and braced for the impact.

A muffled thud filled the cabin and Christopher wondered if sudden death could be this painless, and if so, maybe he had it all wrong about his parents' suffering. Then he realized the music continued to assault his ears and the car was still moving.

Looking out the rear window, he saw the Camaro had disappeared for a second time.

AJ screamed something ugly. He threw the car in reverse and backed up to where tire tracks ran down a hill, insulting scrub brush all the way down.

Jason turned down the music and pointed. "That must have been one rough ride in reverse. He's probably hiding by the boat launch now."

Christopher looked around for a house he could run to and leave all this madness behind, but nothing appeared except snow and darkness. AJ jumped out of the car and slapped the driver's side wiper blade against the windshield to break off the accumulated ice. Then he ran to the back of the car and used the arm of his coat to clean off the trunk before opening it.

Now what is he up to? Christopher wondered.

His cousin returned with a rusty tire iron and handed it to his friend.

"What's this for?" Jason asked.

"To loosen a couple of lug nuts on Bobby's tongue. He'll tell me the whole, ugly story."

"I've had enough of this madness," Christopher yelled, and kneed the back of Jason's seat. "Let me out."

The head of the tire iron drove him back into the seat. "Shut up or I'll use this on you next."

AJ put the car in drive and carefully made his way down a narrow road toward the boat launch. As Jason guessed, the Camaro sat at the end of the road with its lights off.

"We have him cornered!" AJ high-fived his buddy.

They crawled past a small metal sign with red lettering: *"World End Pond."*

"What a fitting description," Christopher commented.

Suddenly, the Camaro came alive and shot forward toward the pond, plowing through a knee-high snowbank onto an expanse of white nothingness.

Jason leaned forward. "Are you kidding me?"

"He thinks I won't follow," AJ said calmly. "Guess he really doesn't know me." The car bounced side to side before hitting the pond.

"Are you nuts? The ice won't hold, it's only a few inches thick," Christopher yelled at the two idiots in the front seat.

"I've ice fished here in April, but never caught a scaredy-cat," Jason teased, followed by a hoot and a holler from the duo in front.

AJ downshifted and the car slid hard to the right, sounding like a giant knife was trying to aggressively frost the undercarriage. AJ continued chasing the Camaro out to the middle of the pond, where the hunted suddenly slowed. Surprisingly, Bobby didn't try any magic tricks this time and came to a stop as if realizing the insanity of the situation.

"He knows he's beat!" AJ yelled.

"No, maybe he sees open water ahead." Christopher sat forward and scanned the pond through the windshield.

AJ ignored the warning and pulled on the emergency brake. The car spun like tea cups at an amusement park, before stopping a few feet away from the Camaro. The Firebird's headlights illuminated the car.

AJ grabbed the tire iron and jumped out as Jason followed.

The open door warning chimed as the wind blew the snowstorm into the car. Christopher watched the two men approach the car. AJ immediately raised the tire iron and swung like he intended to crush a fastball over the Green Monster at Fenway Park. The driver's side window immediately shattered.

Christopher fiddled with the lever on the front seat to extricate himself. By the time he got out, his cousin had dragged a dazed and bleeding man out of the car and propped him up against the front fender.

As AJ bent down to retrieve the tire iron, Christopher tackled his cousin. They rolled in the snow and Christopher quickly discovered rum and jealousy produced a toxic mix, fueling a biting, kicking, and scratching wild man.

Rolling hard to the right, Christopher found the neck of AJ's ski parka and pulled on it with all his strength to apply a choke hold.

"That's enough! You're going to kill him!" he screamed, as AJ rocked side to side.

He hoped to hold on until Godfreye escaped, but a terrific blow to the back of his head made things go black. When he came to, Christopher found himself on his back with the falling snow stinging his eyes. Jason stood on his chest with one of his expensive sneakers.

"I thought we were family, but you're a traitor just like Bobby," AJ said, leaning over, then kicked him in the side with his steel-toe boot.

Christopher gasped for air and strangely there was little to be found in the howling wind. He drew his knees up to his chest, attempting to relax the insulted abdominal muscles.

AJ and Jason started back toward Godfreye, who was nursing a bloody gash on his forehead.

"What have I done?" he asked, looking up.

"For someone guilt-free, you sure know how to run," AJ yelled. He looked him up and down as if checking out the competition. "You messed with my Lori."

"No, I didn't."

"Liar!" AJ swung a wild right at Bobby's face and missed by inches. Jason stepped in and grabbed Godfreye by the neck and AJ issued two hard punches to the stomach.

A nasty gust blew the snow sideways and Christopher heard the door chime of the Pontiac. *The car is still running*, he thought.

Finding half a breath of air, he staggered to his feet and limped toward the Pontiac. He almost fell twice before hurling himself into the driver's seat.

AJ came running too, but not before Christopher succeeded in locking the door. He put the car in first gear and laid on the horn.

In the next instant, the trap door gave way.

CHAPTER SIX

The Firebird went in headfirst and teetered like an overweight guy trying to do a headstand and doomed to fail. Black water rushed in through the floorboards, tired of being cooped up beneath snow and ice. In a matter of seconds, the water reached his knees and continued climbing northward. Christopher reached for the door handle and pulled on it hard, but it didn't budge. After trying repeatedly, he remembered locking the door and frantically searched and found the button, but the electric controls for the locks and windows must have shorted out.

The musty-smelling water continued to rapidly flood the compartment while stinging with the ferociousness of a million bees. It felt strange to be sitting while feeling like he was half-standing given the pitch of the front end. But as the water rose, the car began to slowly level off. He beat at the window with both fists, but the tempered glass held.

Someone tapped him on the shoulder and he turned to find his father sitting next to him in the bucket seat. He had on a white dress shirt, striped tie, and burgundy dress pants, which he wore whenever pitching a new client or defending his son's shenanigans in high school. He looked tanned and ten years younger, but apparently in some sort of hydrophobic coating as the cold water didn't touch him.

"Dad, help me!" he begged.

His father smiled and put his index finger to his head. "Son, do you remember the driving lessons I gave you? We went through all the different scenarios you might encounter, including this one."

He took a deep breath. "I don't have time for this," he replied, refusing to look at the apparition.

"If I recall, you said the same thing back then. Remember what I told you again and again about the headrests?"

Christopher thought hard. *They're designed for safety, but they detach so you can use the sharp ends to break a window in an emergency.*

His father laughed. "So many revelations on this side. I found out that one is an urban myth." He reached under the seat and produced a meaty-looking pipe wrench. "Lucky for you, your aunt had a clogged sink recently." He handed it to him. "Better hurry, though, you don't have much time."

The water continued rising, and grabbing the steering wheel, Christopher pushed himself up to find the last remnant of air near the ceiling. Sitting down, he hammered at the window with the pipe wrench. After a half dozen blows, the window fell away.

He made it back to the ceiling for one last breath before diving under. The coldness of the water made him want to gasp, but he fought the urge by concentrating on the bellowing in his ear and shedding his wool coat, which felt like it had a cement lining.

Feeling for the open window in the dark, he fought to push himself through the small opening. His shoulders bumped against the jagged window frame followed by his hips, but as he clawed forward, something held his left ankle. He kicked twice as hard, but the grasp only tightened. He glanced back to see if he was pulling his dad out too.

The imprisonment unlocked a flood of images of Kylie and a crushing sense of guilt. Evelyn would certainly treat her like a princess, but the anxious look his sister wore since the death of their parents would become a permanent tattoo on her expression. *Will she ever have the courage to trust anyone again after I promised to always be there?* He knew it was arrogant to equate himself with God and promise nothing bad would ever happen again. However, this stupid ending could have been prevented when he first smelled alcohol on AJ.

Christopher spun around, knowing only seconds remained before all drowning victims reach the breaking point, when the body overcome with carbon dioxide overrules logic and takes a deadly breath. Reaching for his ankle, he found a nylon strap which felt like the seat belt. He tore off his sneaker and worked on freeing his foot.

Breaking free, he kicked toward the surface with his remaining strength and his bare foot hit something smooth and hard. With each new stroke, his arms began to weaken. Although the surface seemed only inches away, it stubbornly remained out of reach, like a mirage in the desert. His thoughts slowed as the darkness surrounding him began to shimmer with a bright light.

Suddenly, something grabbed him around the waist and propelled him upward with a tremendous rush. In the next instant, he felt cold air on his face and a hard slap between the shoulder blades. He gagged as the wind stung his face, and though he tried to tread water, he began to sink again. A ghoulish-looking Bobby Godfreye appeared beside him, keeping him afloat.

"Over here!" a voice yelled again and again.

Bobby inched them toward the solid ice. When they finally made it, AJ grabbed him by the belt and heaved him up onto the ice.

Christopher lay on his back only a few feet away from the Camaro. *"This must be how fish feel after they've been reeled in; struggling to breathe, eyes frozen open, air colder than the icy water,* he thought. The gentle snow which tasted like wet cotton only a couple hours ago now pelted his face with ice crystals and tasted foul.

"Cut it out!" a voice cried above the wind.

The plea echoed in his mind and he slowly turned his head back toward the hole in the ice. Only a few feet away, his rescuer struggled to pull himself up on the ice, but Jason kept pushing him back with his foot.

"Help me!" Bobby begged.

"I already did," AJ said, kneeling down in front of him. "I'm going to let the water teach you a lesson instead of my tire iron."

Godfreye held onto the edge of the ice. "C'mon, I'm really weak."

"Weak? Is that the best excuse you can come up with? No wonder you're a glorified grocery store clerk." AJ reached in his coat and took out Lori's brown leather wallet and opened it up in front of Godfreye. "We took this picture at Hampton Beach. Check out what a great couple we make. You shouldn't have tried to ruin us." He held it close to Bobby's eyes and then threw the wallet across the ice. "A good long soak in a cold bath is a perfect remedy for someone so hot-blooded."

Bobby drifted away looking for another exit point as AJ and Jason followed.

Christopher tried to roll over to help and noticed the front end of the Camaro beginning to sag. When he glanced back he saw a red ski coat with a white tag kneeling on the ice and Bobby was gone.

He began to yell as the ice gave way again.

CHAPTER SEVEN

The hard mattress bothered the small of his back, but Christopher felt too exhausted to open his eyes and confirm, after years of complaining, that his parents had magically switched out the bedding while he slept. The old mattress with a malevolent spring that never missed an opportunity to stab him officially entered family lore last Thanksgiving. When his turn came to count his many blessings, he memorialized how the nocturnal stalker only spared his life because of its sadistic tendencies. Now with the gift of a new mattress, he knew his prankster dad would save a piece of the twisted spring to incorporate into a Freddy Krueger replica for Halloween or a hilarious Mr. Bill Christmas ornament.

Something scratched against the window of his memory and ignited a sense of foreboding. It felt similar to the momentary amnesia one sometimes experiences upon waking, knowing something of terrible consequence transpired yesterday, but the details play a momentary hide-and-seek. His thoughts immediately turned to Kylie and he found himself hovering over the little girl as they stood on a frozen pond which extended endlessly in every direction. His little sister wore a burgundy wool coat and black skirt, with her hard-to-tame hair in tight pigtails. Her delicate hands clasped a thin white candle struggling to remain lit in a cold breeze. He cupped his hands around the fledging flame to help it remain anchored to its life-giving wick, which oddly resembled the white fuselage of an airplane. As he leaned down to ask Kylie why her hands trembled so, she tilted the candle ever so slightly, and a single drop of hot wax fell in slow motion and made a terrific hissing sound as it kissed the pond. The ice immediately gave way and as the cold water pulled them under, he searched desperately for his little sister until his lungs were ready to burst. Then everything went black.

The sequence repeated itself again and again each time he woke: the bed feeling different, standing with Kylie on the pond, the hot wax melting the ice, and being swallowed by the icy water. He tried to find a path out of the repeating loop, hoping too many slices of pepperoni-pineapple pizza had fueled this nightmare.

On the seventh replay, he refused to look at the white candle in his sister's hands, and when he blinked, he found himself transported to a deserted beach. A brilliant summer sun highlighted a line of multicolored spiral shells on talcum powder sand, leading down to turquoise-blue water at low tide. He picked up one red-striped shell, rubbed off some sandy grit, and the remembrance of his parents' death came rushing back. He fell to his knees and cried uncontrollably. When he regained his composure, the tide began to quickly advance with surfer-sized waves. Crawling to the next shell with a greenish hue, he remembered Evelyn's obsession with Kylie.

An overly ambitious wave caught him off guard, knocking him over and stinging his eyes. He noticed many of the shells were migrating back to the water with each wave and he rushed to collect as many as he could.

A monster wave came out of nowhere and drove him underwater as he chased a gold-colored shell in swirling sand. Wiping it clean, he remembered Denise and how her lips tasted like sea salt after they went swimming.

He grew tired and staggered out of the water. Something small and gray caught his attention, half buried in the wet sand. Kneeling down, he uncovered a piece of a sand dollar. Quickly drying it against his shirt, he waited for the return of a new memory, but only tasted wet cotton.

The inside of his mouth suddenly felt caked with sand and he tried to locate a single drop of saliva, but found none. Threatening dark clouds rushed across the sky blotting out the sun. His sight began to dim too as if someone was playing with the venetian blind cords behind his eyes. Then everything went black.

Days seemed to pass before he finally succeeded in partially opening his right eye, followed by an additional eternity as the blurriness cleared enough to recognize a celery-colored wall. Faint pulsing sounds repeated every few seconds and he succeeded in coaxing his lone eye to make the steep climb and discovered a monitor overhead with jumping squiggly lines and flashing numbers.

A motherly face suddenly appeared and the bright light around her face glowed like a celestial being. She leaned in to study his lone periscope.

"Welcome back, honey," she cooed. Her large blue eyes looked like his favorite shooter marbles. She glanced up at the monitor and he studied her crow's-feet. His mother called them laugh lines and wondered why people tried to hide them. "They're the badges earned from good living," she said.

The nurse patted his arm. "My name is Alice and I'm thrilled you made it back to the land of the living. All I can say is you certainly gave us a good scare," she added. "You must have something special to accomplish in this life to fight the way you did."

Christopher watched her mouth move and wondered why she sounded like the time he found his dad's old record player in the attic and tried playing a Fleetwood Mac album on 78 RPM for laughs. He wanted to ask where she learned to talk faster than the guy in the FedEx commercial and how did she expect his ears to keep up?

The super-fast talker flashed a bright light in his eye and didn't seem concerned the other one continued sleeping. Then she used a stethoscope to play a quick game of checkers across his chest. He managed to nudge his tongue with his front teeth, but it felt thick like it had a shot of Novocain.

Alice began whistling a snappy tune he didn't recognize and used a black marker to write some numbers on the skin of her thick forearm before disappearing. He squinted. The fluorescent lights above felt brighter than the high beams on his dad's Buick as a monster headache began beating his temples. The pain made him nauseous and he searched for sleep even if it meant risking a return to the nightmare loop. Detecting a faint crackling noise, he looked up and watched the ceiling tiles overhead begin to droop under the weight of something behind them. He tried biting his tongue awake, but it remained dead as a single drop of cold water landed in the middle of his forehead. The ceiling continued to bow ever lower, trying its best to dam something beyond its capacity. Suddenly, there was a loud roar as the ceiling gave way and a foul-smelling waterfall swept him off the bed. He held his breath as he plummeted underwater and tried to swim back to the surface, but something grabbed his ankle and wouldn't let go.

Someone shook his shoulder hard and this time both eyes popped open. To his surprise the ceiling had been restored.

A large thin hand with dirty fingernails and oil stains in the creases of the knuckles made him blink. AJ's face suddenly filled his view and he noticed for the first time how his cousin's pupils looked like antique ink wells. *Maybe he can explain why the ceiling flooded,* he thought.

"Don't say a word until you hear me out," AJ whispered inches away from his face. "Now that you're back from la-la land, my mother will be here any second and the police won't be far behind." He glanced over at the door instead of at the dangerous ceiling. "Jason and I told the cops we were clowning around with Bobby when the ice broke and then—" He stopped and waved his hand in front of Christopher's face. "Pay attention to me, man! Just say we ended up going for an unexpected cold swim."

Christopher stared at the cigarette AJ wore like a pencil behind his left ear. He tried to capture all the words whistling by his ears like a faint breeze on a hot summer day. They were barely perceptible. He frowned and studied the ceiling.

AJ shook him to get his attention and put one finger to his lips. "Say anything else and I promise on my father's grave, I'll use my upholstery tools to sew up your mouth for good." He stepped back and nodded. "Just don't say anything stupid, and everything will be okay. It's not like they can interview Bobby anymore."

Christopher focused on AJ's cracked lips and his tobacco-stained teeth and wondered why he talked super-fast like the nurse.

His cousin watched him for a moment and then leaned over the bed railing again. "Go ahead and play mute, but remember I haven't forgotten whose side you took when it counted. I could have left you at the bottom of that muck hole, but I dragged your butt out twice." His eyes narrowed. "That should count for something. If not, I'll see to it that you're bobbing for snow cones with Bobby real soon."

Christopher sighed in confusion. *Did AJ save me after the ceiling collapsed?*

Sleep pulled on his eyelids and when he surfaced again, Becky catapulted out of a purple recliner in the corner and kissed him on the cheek. Her lips felt smooth and he recognized the signature smell of Herbal Essence shampoo.

"They say God doesn't give you more than you can handle," she began with her voice cracking. "After losing Aram and then your parents, I begged God not to take you too."

Christopher felt her words reverberate through him and focused on the first three. *After losing Aram,* and turned the words over in his mind.

He closed his eyes and found himself transported to Pine Grove Cemetery on a sunless day. A nearby maple tree began playing she loves me, she loves me not with fiery red leaves. He watched as they helicoptered to the ground.

"My son thinks it would have been better if I never came home from 'Nam," a voice nearby said in a soft voice, "and many days I felt that way too."

Christopher peered over a granite headstone and found his uncle sitting cross-legged on the matted grass in a blue suit, white shirt, red tie, and, interestingly enough, stocking feet. His black hair was neatly combed back and although his complexion was a bit jaundiced, he didn't look that bad for a dead guy,

Aram pointed to a life-sized sculpture of an angel looking forlorn as it placed a single rose on a raised ivory altar tomb a few rows over. Christopher noted the weathered stone angel was missing the upper half of one wing.

"None of us escape brokenness at one time or another," Aram said, pulling on his chin. "In my case it felt like being pulverized seventy times seven, but I still tried to put one foot in front of the other most days. That led to long walks, which proved wonderful as it made me appreciate things most miss in zipping through life. Walk long enough and kneeling comes natural too." He looked at his stocking feet. "My dear wife thought I wore out enough shoes to last ten lifetimes. Either she didn't want to invest in a rugged pair for eternity or thought I'd be more comfortable sleeping in socks." He laughed. "I wonder if a cobbler is buried somewhere nearby."

Christopher knelt down beside him and thought about offering him his sneakers.

Aram gazed at him for a long moment. "If you follow my path, you'll find many will write you off as nothing but damaged goods. In time, and with patience, you will discover a comforting freedom when all expectations disappear. No one will ask you anything of consequence, but—" he hesitated with a deep sigh, "the downside is they won't listen when you have something of importance to say."

Christopher scratched at the matted grass. "Why are you saying I'm damaged goods? I'm just trying to remember what happened after the ice broke."

He nodded. "My cross was never being able to forget." He looked him in the eye. "It will take time to sort things out. In the meantime, build a shelter with the broken pieces of yourself."

"Why?"

He grabbed his arm. "To hide from AJ and—"

"Christopher?" Becky asked in an urgent voice. He opened his eyes and sucked in his breath much too fast and gagged.

She waited until he settled down. "I know you're exhausted, my dear, but this can't wait as you will have some stern visitors shortly." She stroked his shoulder. "I have a special favor to ask." Her pretty eyes filled with tears, but didn't overflow. "AJ told me he and Bobby had . . . ah, a bit of a fight before the ice broke."

A bloody tire iron flashed in his thoughts. It grew in length like an old knotted apple tree bearing too much red fruit.

She watched his expression and bit her lip. "I've always been one to fess up no matter the consequences. Believe me, my heart aches for that poor boy and his family. But you have to understand, AJ is all I have left and nothing will bring Bobby back now. If the police hear about that fight, they will trim the puzzle pieces to make it all fit with Lori missing. If you love me and honor the lengths your mother used to go to protect me, you won't say anything."

She searched his eyes and he looked away. *AJ wants to sew up my mouth and now his mother wants to do the same to my conscience.*

Becky's face flushed. "AJ also told me you were the one driving his car when it went through the ice? Is that true?"

Christopher felt his tongue jump to the roof of his mouth. He heard enough and wanted to set the record straight, but when he opened his mouth all that came out was some high-pitched gibberish he couldn't understand. It knocked the color off his aunt's face too. *Maybe AJ stitched up my voice box while I slept!*

Panic swept over him and he looked up at the ceiling tiles, expecting Aram to peek out any moment to whisper, "Damaged goods, my boy. Better start walking."

CHAPTER EIGHT

Purple loosestrife and lily pads collaborated to begin suffocating World End pond, threatening the small-mouth bass, perch, snapping turtles, and heron that had made the location popular since colonial times. The pond drained into the Spicket River, a tributary of the mighty Merrimack, and encompassed twenty-two acres in Salem, New Hampshire.

As Christopher limped to check out the ice on New Year's Day, he scanned the front page of the *Salem Observer* and read how World End almost lost its apocalyptic identity given the civic commitment of Mr. Ned Abner. The article explained how Abner, a proactive civic-minded citizen, possessed a fervent zest to begin planning eleven years in advance for the 250th anniversary of the town's incorporation, which remarkably coincided with Y2K. A former marketing executive, he petitioned the town selectmen to change the name of World End to Tranquility Pond. Abner argued the waterway should highlight the peaceful origin of Salem "in order to separate itself from the notorious Massachusetts town of the same name." He feared World End not only represented a dreadful name of unknown origin, but was also tainted recently by the senseless accident which claimed the life of a young man.

"Poor Bobby," Christopher whispered, and interrupted his slow gait to practice sounding out the rest of the words in the article. *"Given budget shortfalls, the request was tabled until 1999. Selectman Marjorie*

Harris recommended tongue-in-cheek that in the interim, Abner could begin assessing the marketing opportunities for the return of Halley's Comet in 2061."

Rolling up the newspaper, Christopher slid it into the back pocket of his tan chinos, thinking how everyone in town talked about the *"senseless accident."* Senseless for sure, but he struggled to link it to an accident. If the newspaper interviewed him, he would have likened World End to limbo; a sullen place where Bobby drowned along with a good piece of Christopher himself. He had returned to the pond a dozen times since *that* night, and the hairs on the back of his neck still tingled whenever he approached its shoreline.

"Touch the brain, never the same." Aunt Evelyn whispered her assessment of the situation to Becky while she thought he was asleep in the hospital. Medical terminology translated the cruel saying into cerebral hypoxia. He endured months of physical therapy and still walked like a car in need of a good wheel alignment. The good doctors also worked with the speed of the Army Corps of Engineers to dam the rising floodwaters of anxiety with multicolored pills which also eased the occasional stuttering. Even so, every now and then a deluge of panic would breach that pharmacological wall, and Christopher would imagine AJ brandishing an industrial-sized staple gun to seal his mouth shut. So for added protection, whenever real or imaginary demons threatened, he learned to retreat by slipping on the earbud headphones for his Sony Walkman audiocassette player. One sound-proof pacifier in each ear silenced everything, even if he didn't bother to turn on the music.

At the end of the street, he followed a narrow rocky path to the frozen pond as king-sized feather pillows drifted across a bright winter sky. Taking a deep breath, he gingerly pressed the tip of one of his K-Mart "blue light special" canvas sneakers against the mirrored surface. He knew sneakers should be hibernating with flip-flops in the first month of the year, and though he remembered embracing such nonconformity before the accident, everyone now associated it with his changed persona.

Christopher slowly applied his weight and felt giddy for a split second before his sole broke through. Jumping backward, he avoided the rushing water, unlike twelve months ago.

"Give me a break," he yelled at the broken ice, appreciating the pun and wishing someone witnessed his ability to still be clever now and then. He averted his eyes from the growing puddle to prevent another rerun of the tragedy, and focused instead on a familiar cove tucked beside a grove of stubby pine trees a short distance away. He figured the ice might be a bit thicker over there as it spent the majority of the day in the shadows like him.

Careful not to get caught in the nasty picker bushes, he carefully made his way over to the new destination. He repeated the test, and this time the ice held, though it did emit a low moan. Reaching inside his brown nylon jacket, he quickly took out a purple inflatable life vest and put it on over the coat. After blowing into a small plastic tube to inflate the vest, he shuffled out fifty steps, pretending to be Neil Armstrong minus all the hoopla.

Growing up, he always looked forward to the first ice of the season, which usually appeared around Thanksgiving, and with luck before any snow clouded its transparency. This year had been unusual, though, as Indian summer lasted well into November. More seasonal temperatures made short visits, until an arctic blast arrived on Christmas Eve, producing a thin layer of ice with the clarity of Saran Wrap. Christopher moved slowly to his knees and pressed his nose against the cold smooth surface. The late morning light caused a glare over most of the view below, so he cupped his hands around his eyes as if peering through a store window.

The mucky bottom was peppered with dark rocks of various sizes and shapes and he looked in the spaces between them for the wallet and tire iron, representing the last links to that night. But all he found were the corpses of autumn leaves; the terracotta soldiers of nature.

A small fish suddenly appeared out of the darkness and startled him.

"Why, good morning, Mr. Perch," he said in a loud, formal voice. The little green fish with dark vertical lines shifted into neutral and

Christopher wondered who was watching whom. He wished he could remember being under the ice, wished he knew whether his parents were really waiting on the other side if he did drown. Their memorial Mass took place shortly after he was released from the hospital and the meds didn't help much that day. Family and friends gathered first at Goundrey's Funeral Home to pay respects to the hardworking couple. The receiving line stretched into the parking lot and wrapped around the building. Christopher grasped more than shook people's hands, trying to steady himself as the panic attacks outnumbered the bouquets of roses, carnations, and lilies lining the walls. When he began to hyperventilate, he sought relief in the coat closet in the adjoining hall. Sitting on the floor in the dark, he knew what Gregor Samsa in *The Metamorphosis* must have felt like when he woke up one morning to discover he was an insect. Denise found him an hour later, when his aunts became concerned. She coaxed him out with her warm smile and gentle hand, but the look in her eyes confirmed he wasn't morphing into a bug, but rather a badly bruised banana.

Christopher felt the cold smooth surface of the ice with the tips of his fingers like it represented a transparent coin that allowed one to view both sides. "Guess it's really all about location, location, location," he deadpanned. After he woke up in the hospital and some of the frightening confusion began to clear, he felt *different*, though he couldn't quite put his finger on what separated the old self from the new anxiety-filled version. He discovered quite by accident that if he cleared his mind and held his breath long enough, sometimes he could feel a small flicker of his former essence before passing out. No matter how often he repeated the painful exercise, he could not find a less dramatic bridge, nor get comfortable in his new skin.

The fish became bored and began to swim away, no doubt splitting a gill laughing at the chubby apparition above. He watched it disappear into the darkness, knowing once the snow came and turned out all the lights for a few months, he would have the last laugh.

A blue jay squawked in the distance and he remained on his knees to study his reflection. The thick mane of brown hair looked as wild as John the Baptist's while the cowlick in the middle of his forehead continued to rebel no matter who was driving the rig. When he was a boy, his mother used to tame that stubborn lock of hair with gel before he left for school, though in a pinch she would spit in her hand and work it into his scalp like a pitcher behind in the count. He thought about getting a crew cut to solve it once and for all, but feared it might make his bulging blue eyes look worse, never mind his skull had so many divots he could join a *Ripley's Believe It or Not* exhibit. The doctor dismissed the dents in his head, but given the bulging eyes and weight gain had tested him for thyroid issues last month. The report came back negative, but then again, no doctor knew what he saw.

Christopher sat up and unzipping the life vest, felt for the silver duct tape plastered across the back of the coat with CM written in six-inch capital letters. Silver highlighted his initials much better than the blue masking tape he tried last week. With some care, he hoped this version would last a couple weeks before the edges became ragged.

Something hard suddenly slammed into his right cheek and he found a dark brown acorn in his lap. A quick look toward shore uncovered the sniper as Jason Driscoll's kid brother, Ted, one of the leading troublemakers in the 603 area code. The eighteen-year-old high school dropout wore a faded dungaree coat, ripped blue jeans, and brown work boots. A grungy-looking knitted ski hat hid a mullet of blond hair he bragged incessantly looked better than Rod Stewart's to anyone who would listen.

"Hey, water-on-the-brain-man," Ted half sang, "what are you doing out there?"

Christopher wanted to rub his throbbing cheekbone, but didn't want to give the punk any satisfaction. "What did you say?" he yelled back slowly, while flashing a look of confusion which frustrated most opponents.

The teenager pointed to his ears.

Christopher stood up and let a small smile escape and looked down at the ice hoping Mr. Perch was watching this show. He thought about how best to respond, but knowing he could put the earbuds back in when he grew tired of toying with the jerk, he slowly removed them.

Ted stood on the frozen edge of the pond with both hands on his hips. "Don't you remember what happened last time you were out there?"

Christopher listened intently, since he couldn't read lips from this distance which usually helped in processing information. The words started to run together in his head, forcing a frown. He hated to be reminded there might be continuing hiccups in his wiring.

"I'm fine and appreciate the reminder," he finally replied, surprised Ted had any concern about his safety. He zipped up his life vest again and gave another puff into the plastic tube to inflate the ballast a little more.

Ted threw another acorn and Christopher ducked.

"I've been keeping every rug rat in the neighborhood off the ice until it's thick enough for hockey," Ted said, hammering the air with his index finger. "If you break through, the ice will refreeze with bumps all over it and one of us will catch a skate edge for sure. Are you trying to get me killed?"

"Only the good die young," he whispered, studying the acres of frozen water surrounding him. "I tested the ice over by the boat launch first," he commented. "It's still a bit soft over there."

The teenager looked unimpressed and pulled his hat lower. "You're the one that's soft. Now, get your fat butt off the ice before you wreck it."

Since the accident, everyone took a fancy telling him what, when, and how to do everything. He processed the request and then pointed at all the ice around him. "Seems to me you have miles of ice to play hockey on, as long as you stay away from the cat-o'-nine-tails by the road."

"Forget the weeds, man," Ted shot back. "This is where we play. Are you going to chase the puck after a slap shot misses and travels half a mile into some beaver lodge?" He let out a short laugh. "Though, you're welcome to play goalie anytime. Between being brain damaged and sporting that ugly mug, you wouldn't need to be weighed down with a face mask or pads."

Christopher looked down at his white canvas sneakers, remembering when he used to skate on Nutting Lake in Billerica pretending to be Bobby Orr. He would practice speed skating and apply the brakes hard and watch a shower of ice slivers shoot two feet high. Maybe Kylie could teach him how to skate again.

"I used to skate my-t-fine," he yelled back, as his throat tightened. He returned to his knees and began searching for the perch, thinking how unusual he must look to his new aqua buddy; maybe like one of those funny mirrors that make you look fat or skinny depending on the curvature of the glass. He didn't like his reflection much since nearly drowning, no matter the mirror.

Ted waved his arms. "Hey, nitwit, I'm talking to you. Do I have to come out there and drag you off?"

Christopher checked the zipper on his life jacket, thinking maybe he should add another fifty feet between them just to be safe.

"Why are you hanging out with him?" another voice boomed.

Ted turned around and Ray Peters came strutting down the frozen path. He had wavy brown hair and wore a heavy gray sweatshirt, jeans, and work boots to match his friend. Ray's hands were constantly cemented in his back pockets.

"Hey, CM," Ray yelled out to him. "Where's your lesser half?"

Christopher thought about the duct tape letters on his jacket. Maybe next time he would use a glue stick as added protection to keep the ends from curling.

"Yeah, where's Morbid Mary?" Ted added.

Christopher felt the acid in his stomach extend its volcanic reach and burn his cheeks. Before the accident, he only heard about Mary from AJ's rantings about Lori's odd younger sister, but in the past year he realized people's perception can be contorted like those funny mirrors too. While the accident and Lori's disappearance brought them together, most chalked it up to *birds of a feather flock together*. Regardless of the reason, he discovered a woman graced with natural beauty and unspeakable innocence. Without her, this odyssey would be intolerable.

"Her name is simply Mary," he replied with a steady voice, careful not to stutter as it sometimes still happened when he got too excited.

"Simple between the ears perhaps, but that would still be a promotion from Morbid," Ted said with a laugh. "Unfortunately, they don't make paper bags thick enough to hide the glow from that hideous smeared red lipstick, so simple won't cut it." He gazed out at him and screwed up his face. "That's why you two make such a perfect couple; like some freak equation where one plus one equals negative two. Her legs were grafted from a daddy longlegs, and you're the town freak who duct tapes his initials on his clothes like anyone cares who you are." He motioned to his friend. "Who in their right mind wears a life vest out on the ice? I mean, you can't make this stuff up!"

"Maybe Mr. Potato Head is afraid of losing an appendage and is just labeling his parts. If so, have no fear, spud-man! I'll drag your potato skin butt to safety." Ray strutted out on the ice only to break through after a half dozen steps. The teenager shot backward to avoid the rushing flood, but his hands were still lost in his back pockets and he landed on his back.

Ray moaned and jumped to his feet.

Ted howled in laughter and even Christopher couldn't suppress a grin before looking down at his sneakers to make sure the ice remained solid under him.

Ray looked red-faced and beckoned to him. "Come here so I can pull the lips off your ugly face."

Christopher let the words roll around his ears while he took a few breaths to rearm. "I think I'll stay out here because it looks like you peed your pants," he said in a slow drawl, knowing he should resist the temptation to up the ante.

Ted pointed at his buddy's wet pants and howled. "Listen to the retard make funny. Guess that proves even a blind squirrel finds a nut now and then."

Ray blushed. "Shut up," he yelled, and gave his cohort a hard shove.

Christopher held his breath thinking they might turn on each other, which would be a fortunate twist indeed. Instead, Ray grabbed Ted by the shoulder and said something out of earshot. Then they turned and ran up the path into the woods.

Christopher wondered if he could make it to the other side of the pond, which bordered a golf course. Scanning the polished ice, he caught sight of a duck a hundred yards away come in for what appeared to be a water landing.

The sound of laughter echoed across the pond and he turned back to find Ted and Ray emerging from the woods cradling armfuls of rocks. In comparison to acorns, this represented heavy artillery.

Christopher started to rock side to side to calm himself down and prepare for a painful game of dodgeball. Instead, his tormentors started bowling the rocks in every direction on the maiden ice.

"Know what we're doing?" Ray called out.

Try as he might, Christopher couldn't figure out their evil intent as none of the rocks targeted him.

"All the mothers in the neighborhood like this part of the pond for their little brats to skate on because it's shielded from the wind," he explained, sliding another granite puck.

Ted followed with a similar-sized rock which sailed past Christopher as if turbocharged. "We told you to get off the ice," Ray continued, "but you wouldn't listen. Now you're really skating on thin ice, because it's supposed to rain tonight and that will make the ice get soft before it gets cold again. Give it a few days, and you'll need a jackhammer to get any of these rocks out."

Ted and Ray laughed in unison and shared a high five.

"Can you see it now?" Ted asked. "The kiddies will be bawling and their parents will be furious when they miss watching the playoffs to drive little Johnny and Julie to the ice rink. Retard-man will be tarred and feathered by the Super Bowl."

Christopher stood still. As fast as they were talking, he heard enough to get the gist of their evil plan. "But . . . I'll . . . tell . . . them . . . the . . . truth," he stammered.

"Who's going to believe a head case that drove his cousin's car into World End?"

"You . . . don't . . . understand," he replied.

Ted threw a small stone at Christopher and he ducked. "We'll tell everyone we caught you throwing these rocks all over the pond. When we asked why, you said since you couldn't skate anymore, no one else should either."

"I even tried to get you off the ice, but I fell in," Ray said, pointing to his wet pants.

His friend chuckled. "Nice try, man, but I'm still telling everyone you wet yourself."

Ray ignored the dig and kept his focus on Christopher. "If you try and finger us, I'll have to up my game," he added and picked up a ten-pound round stone. "I know where Morbid lives and it would be a shame if she was on the other side of the picture window watching for her pathetic boyfriend when this special delivery arrived." He thought for a moment then let out a laugh. "Too bad your uncle isn't around to teach you the ropes. He could take a rock to the head any day of the week and not complain."

"What about hockey?" Christopher asked.

"Since you ruined the ice, I'll have to go to the rink too, which means better ice and babes to hit on." Ted slapped Ray on the back. "This is a gift that just keeps giving."

Christopher thought for a long moment, but couldn't think of anything to foil their plans so he sat down cross-legged on the ice. He watched as Ted feverishly hammered some of the ice along the shoreline with a short log. Not to be outdone, Ray retrieved more rocks and continued peppering the ice.

"This has been fun, but we have to run. We have a parade to ruin," Ted yelled, breathing hard from all the exertion. "Maybe you should stay out there and wait until the rain washes you back under. But do us all a favor this time and take the advice from *Poltergeist* and *run to the light, Carol Anne. Run as fast as you can! Mommy is in the light!"*

The pair disappeared into the woods and Christopher heard Ray belting out their hateful song. "Sponge and Morbid sitting in a tree k-i-s-s-i-n-g; first comes love, then comes marriage, then comes a two-headed monster in a baby carriage."

Christopher stood up and counted thirty-two rocks scattered all around him. He hoped the weather forecast proved wrong and the ice would continue to thicken so he could come back and collect the debris.

A quick check of his digital Timex watch confirmed the New Year's Day parade in nearby Haverhill would be starting in less than two hours. Surveying the broken ice at the shoreline, he searched for a safe way back to shore. The familiar tightness across his chest winched tighter. Dropping to his knees, he cupped his hands to look for the little fish, but now the glare hid everything. Sitting up, he reached into the side pocket of his snorkel coat and found a lonely peppermint Life Saver. He sucked on it hard while connecting the headphones to the cassette player and became disappointed when nothing would play. Taking a small blue notebook from his back pocket, he made a quick note to purchase generic batteries, which were always on sale at K-Mart. They weren't as good as Duracell, but he was getting accustomed to being satisfied with good enough.

CHAPTER NINE

After a brilliant morning, the sun decided to pull a thin gray blanket over its head for a long afternoon nap, leaving behind a muted glow in the sky.

Christopher hugged his life jacket and began picking his way toward the beach, careful to avoid the debris minefield. Halfway to the goal, his right sneaker suddenly broke through and in the rush to extricate himself, the other foot followed.

The liquefied ice cubes immediately reached his knees and he struggled to maintain balance on the mucky bottom. The cold water also sent scouts to terrorize his memory and in response he blew so hard into the life vest tube that it overexpanded into a gigantic grape reminiscent of *Willy Wonka & The Chocolate Factory*. Sometimes surprises like this triggered the weirdest thoughts and he suddenly feared a sudden breeze might launch him like a Zeppelin over Salem. A minute passed and nothing happened, so he began trying to pull himself out of the water one foot at a time. The ice continued to break with each attempt.

Christopher searched for a way to calm down. "Hope I squish the fish," he yelled at the overcast sky and forced a fake laugh remembering how he and his dad used to chant that line whenever the New England Patriots played the Miami Dolphins. Now his dad was gone and football too fast a game for him to follow anymore.

Abandoning the plan of making it back on top of the ice, he leaned forward and pushed like an icebreaker toward shore. The ice responded to this aggressive plan by biting the fronts of his legs like a school of starving piranhas. When he finally stumbled out of the water, he fell to his knees and crawled on the frozen sand and began shivering uncontrollably. Under normal circumstances, Aunt Becky would be waiting with a tall glass of water and a blue pill to drive the anxiety deeper than any perch could ever swim without getting the bends. But given the circumstances, he had to rally his spirits on his own. At first, he considered running down Theresa Avenue in a *Rocky*-type sprint to get warm, but his chino pants were glued to his skin and everything south of the knees felt dead as stones.

Christopher closed his eyes to concentrate and something from his undamaged long-term memory bank indicated a familiarity with the scene. Whenever this happened, he hummed a high-pitched note and sometimes it worked like Drano to unclog whatever neural traffic jam interrupted the memory flow. But after fifteen seconds of scaring away birds, his throat hurt and the gray matter between his ears felt like a dead car battery refusing to be jump started. Limping up the path into the woods, he came upon a small clearing lined with scrub pines and spotted a pile of litter beside a rotting log. The refuse felt kindle worthy and he quickly rounded up a McDonald's bag, three Big Mac boxes, and a cardboard carrier from a six-pack of Old Milwaukee beer. Building a base of pine needles on top of the *Salem Observer*, he started a small fire with a disposable lighter he always carried in his coat pocket.

As the fire started to crackle, he admired the pine trees and how they remained dressed year round.

"'To Build a Fire' by Jack London," he yelled, as the frozen memory finally thawed.

Twenty minutes later, his pant legs and socks were nearly dry, but the canvas sneakers remained hopelessly wet. With no time to stop home before the parade, he experimented stretching a gray wool mitten over one foot. Unfortunately, the mitten stopped at the ankle bone, but it would have to do.

"I wonder if Jack London ever tried this trick on the Yukon Trail," he said to himself, gathering handfuls of dry pine needles and stuffing them generously into his sneakers as insulation.

A quick check of his watch made him gasp. By now he should have walked the five miles to Haverhill and secured a prime viewing location along Main Street. Today's misadventure risked spoiling everything.

Forty-five minutes later, he was out of breath after hitchhiking part of the way, then hoofing it the last half mile to downtown Haverhill. Founded by a dozen Puritans in 1640 as a frontier town for farming, it became an industrial center and earned the reputation as the "Queen Slipper City" in the early twentieth century for its shoemaking industry. This afternoon, it looked like the entire city plus the surrounding towns were present to celebrate the new year. Twin police motorcycles drove down either side of Main Street, pushing the crowd back and making it look like a long Slinky. An army of street vendors hawked balloons, cotton candy, and popcorn.

Christopher wiped the sweat from his brow and no sooner inserted the earbuds to block out the surrounding noise to concentrate, when he felt a light tap on the back of his shoulder. Turning around, he expected to find Ted and Ray accompanied by a mob of angry parents with hockey sticks to whack his scratched and bruised shins. Instead, Mary stood in front of him, looking anxious in a light pink wool coat with big black buttons. Forgetting the awful episode in Salem, he drank in her pretty face, unfettered today from the silky blonde hair hiding under a white crocheted hat. He longed to get lost in her hazel eyes, but she never allowed him or anyone else that sublime privilege.

Mary pointed frantically at his ears and Christopher ripped the headphones off, hoping she wouldn't notice the plethora of orange sticking out of the sides of his sneakers.

"Where have you been?" she asked and continued without waiting for a reply. "I called your house and your aunt said you left hours ago. You know we have a routine! I already walked half the parade route looking for you." She pointed at her black-heeled boots. "I have blisters the size of walnuts on each foot now."

The words tumbled out too fast and with such intensity that even reading her lips, he only caught half of what she said.

Mary blushed and he wondered if she felt embarrassed for appearing so needy.

She looked away for a second then gifted him with a spectacular smile that could launch a thousand ships to reboot the afternoon. "Don't tell me you lost your gloves again," she said, noticing his red hands, but without any sympathy. Then she noticed his feet. "I'm afraid to ask if you're one of the characters in the floats."

He laughed and it felt good. "I'm really sorry to be late. It's a long story, but please know I'd turn down being the grand marshal if it meant not seeing the parade with you."

She rubbed his hands between her black leather gloves. He wanted to say something funny to make her laugh too—maybe about meeting the perch or how Ray looked after he peed his pants—but there wasn't time to even ask her to pray for no rain.

Surveying the street, he looked for an opening in the great wall of humanity.

"Can we get some hot chocolate like we always do?" she asked.

He glanced at a sandwich shop across the street, and it had a line of customers out the door.

"We'll have to get some later," he replied, looking again at his watch.

Mary scanned the street like it was the first time she noticed the large crowd. "You know I need to scrutinize all the marching bands," she explained. "Last year, Springfield had too many trumpets and they drowned out the flutes." She looked down the street. "But to do it properly, I have to be right up front. If we aren't able—"

Christopher grabbed her hand mid-rant and led her down the unbroken human chain looking for a wormhole. Suddenly, an overweight man took two steps to his left to say something to his significant other, and Christopher used his shoulder to burrow in. Mary pushed from behind and they were making excellent progress until they ran into a pair of linebackers.

"I'll never be able to see anything with those fat heads in front of us," she said much too loud.

He nodded in agreement as one of the six-foot-five goons with shoulder-length brown hair turned around to snuff out the dwarfs.

Mary didn't notice and tugged on Christopher's sleeve. "Hurry up! It's almost time."

They tunneled back out and ran down the parade route, ending up in front of City Hall. Christopher climbed a small hill near the south entrance to get a better view of possible locations to target as the sirens began crying out from the Bradford section of the city. While Mary lived to judge the marching bands, he especially enjoyed the beginning of the parade led by a string of police cruisers, fire engines, rescue trucks, and ambulances with sirens blaring. The noise was deafening and made everyone stop yakking for a good five minutes, which wasn't such a bad thing at the beginning of the year.

He scanned the crowd looking for Ted and Ray and wondered if the perch could feel the sound waves from the approaching chorus of wailing sirens.

Mary paced back and forth in front of a stone tablet and her right eye began to twitch. "What are we going to do?" she asked over and over again. Christopher didn't need this pressure after surviving the encounter at World End and trying to impress Jack London. Now, he faced the biggest test of all in not disappointing Mary.

He rocked side to side and still couldn't calm himself down. He felt like the scarecrow from *Oz* with pine needles sticking out of his sneakers, hair thick as straw, and minus a brain. His eyes scanned the stone tablet in front of him.

> *Benjamin Rolfe*
> *The Second Minister of Haverhill*
> *With His Wife, One Child,*
> *And Three Soldiers Were Killed*
> *Near This Spot By Indians*
> *Aug. 29, 1708*

I should place a marker like this at World End where Bobby and half of me drowned, he thought. *But it wouldn't tell the whole story of what transpired. Maybe something similar happened here in 1708.*

Christopher looked at Mary and she had tears in her eyes. "Okay," he mumbled to himself. "I'll do it." The headache which followed might make him throw up, but at least Mary would be happy.

He sat down and took a rapid series of deep breaths. When he began to hyperventilate, he filled his lungs and thought about what he read on the stone tablet. The seconds ticked by . . .

Two brothers of the proud Abenaki tied their horses to an outcrop of white birch trees and hurried down a frozen path along the Merrimack River. Pial calmed his nerves by studying the floating icebergs moving in a silent procession toward the sea. He felt the sticky green stripes on his forehead and regretted leaving the horses behind after applying the war paints to bestow a cloak of invisibility on both man and animal. While he wanted to taunt his older brother about having so little faith, he clenched his tongue as one misspoken word now and Simo would send him back to keep the horses company.

They cut inland and followed the trail a short distance until a cluster of cabins appeared in a small clearing, their front doors facing the east to greet the morning sun.

His brother pointed toward a large barn covered in rough pine boards set back from the cabins. "I'm sure that's where the thief is keeping our horse."

Pial couldn't contain his excitement and pointed to a tall pine tree nearby. "The day is young. I'm sure if we take a position in that tree we can wait and watch. The council will be pleased if we return with confirmation."

Simo shook his head. "I'd rather show our father what brave sons he has and return with what is rightfully ours."

Pial sucked in his breath, uneasy with this change of plans. Perhaps he believes in the magical paints after all, he thought.

His brother gave a signal and they continued moving through the thicket, stopping behind a broad maple tree with thick upper arms hovering over the barn.

"Stay here and keep watch," his brother ordered, before darting into the open and across grass heavy with white frost toward the barn door.

A dog in the middle cabin began to bark as Simo raised the crossbar on the barn door.

Suddenly, a loud yell punctuated the morning air and Pial turned to see a short white man come running out of the woods less than a stone's throw from their position. He wore a fur hat and carried a rabbit from an early morning hunt.

"Forget the horse, let's go!" Pial yelled. But his brother was already in flight, not toward the safety of the woods, but toward the white man working feverishly on his long rifle. One more step and Simo would have planted his tomahawk, but the gun discharged and his brother fell face first in the winter grass.

The white man took no satisfaction in the kill, but looked his way and began to reload.

Pandemonium followed as three burly white men poured out of the cabins yelling ugly words. Pial hugged the tree searching for any sign of life in his dead brother. The paints had failed them.

Another round nicked the bark on the tree and he abandoned the trail and ran into the dense woods. When the air became silent, he hid behind a large boulder to catch his breath. The calm lasted but a moment, as the air pulsed with angry voices. Pial didn't need to understand their language to know they *were coordinating their movements to flush him out. It would be impossible to make it back to the horses now without getting caught.*

The morning sun continued to erase the remaining shadows. A man came crashing through the brush nearby as another boom from a rifle erupted. The river provided the only escape route and he ran with all his might down an embankment. He fought through a final barricade of picker bushes which cut his face repeatedly.

Without warning, the land ended at a cliff twenty feet above the river as another round whistled by his ear. Pial took a deep breath and jumped. The water stung like a million bees and when he hit bottom he opened his eyes and a tiny yellow perch appeared.

"Christopher, why are you napping now?"

He blinked and the fish morphed into Mary's eyes, which looked almost as glassy. The face of an elderly woman with short white hair hung above Mary's crocheted hat. She yelled to someone out of view for help, but the approaching sirens swallowed her plea.

"I'm okay," he mumbled. The familiar headache arrived before he could sit up.

"Are you sure?" the woman asked, using her cane to kneel down beside him. She had a smooth face and her bright green eyes complemented the pink rouge on her cheeks.

"You look as blue as my Danny did when I lost him in the blizzard of seventy-eight," she said, studying his face.

Christopher smiled to ease her concern, but slipped one hand over his other wrist to make sure he still had a pulse.

She gripped the dark wooden cane with a sallow hand dotted with liver spots. "Let's get you over to the Hale hospital so they can check you over."

He shook his head with vigor. "Thank you, but I'm fine. Since almost drowning last year, I've had a few of these episodes," he reported in a matter-of-fact tone, because it wasn't a lie. When he first tried to take flight this way, a therapist theorized it was his way of escaping reality after a near-death experience. He tried to explain how the process allowed him to reconnect with his old self and sometimes uncover lost memories, although more often than not, just weird dreams. No matter the outcome, the resulting headaches were always terrible.

"My friend and I were so looking forward to the parade," he said, as the sound of sirens continued to grow. "Now, I'm afraid we'll have to sit way back here and try to catch a glimpse of the top of the floats."

A sweet smile replaced the concern. "I think we can do better than that, my dear." She motioned to a tall gentleman in a leather coat standing behind her.

Suddenly, people parted like the Red Sea and he and Mary were hurried through the crowd to the front by two beefy men wearing Bruins hats. Green plastic chairs appeared out of nowhere and they were invited to sit. The VIP treatment continued as two Styrofoam cups of steaming hot chocolate were delivered. Mary smiled and pointed out the tiny floating marshmallows and he urged her to hurry up and put her ear plugs in. Loud noises really bothered her.

They just finished getting settled when the first ladder truck rolled by, followed by three rescue vehicles, four ambulances, six cruisers, and four police motorcycles. Everyone forgot about him and Mary once the ambulance drivers began throwing candy.

After the emergency vehicles passed, Christopher's ears were ringing and he watched Mary laughing at the Shriner clowns as they passed by riding tiny bicycles in small circles. They wore oversized shoes without any pine needle accessories.

Ah, the things you do for love, he thought, rubbing his aching temples.

CHAPTER TEN

Despite the sugar high fueled from waves of penny candy thrown from the parade floats, Christopher's temples continued to throb from the bloody encounter of 1708. It would be a long cold walk back to his aunt's house before he could pop some extra-strength aspirin.

When the Haverhill High band marched by to close out the parade, he offered to walk Mary home, but she gave him a quick hug and took off after the street vendors, hoping to score a couple bargains. After thanking their kind benefactors, he caught a final glimpse of Mary at the bottom of the hill. She held so many Disney character balloons, he wondered how she remained earthbound.

It was nearly dusk when the leaning lamppost in front of the melancholy-looking ranch came into view. The lantern didn't throw much light with its single forty-watt bulb, but to Christopher it glowed with his aunt's affection whenever he ventured out.

"Just another tricky day," he whispered, quoting The Who as he slogged up the driveway. Suddenly the front door, which no one ever used, creaked opened.

A starched blue shirt which clung tightly around the arms and shoulders, but struggled mightily at the midsection, filled the doorway. Out of habit, he counted the three yellow stripes on the policeman's sleeve and appreciated how a sewn patch looked much better than duct tape ever could.

"Good evening, Sergeant Mike," he called out, delighted to see his neighbor and hoping he would stay for dinner and entertain them with stories about criminals who got what they deserved.

"Hello, Christopher," came the curt reply.

The stiff greeting made his stomach jump. Changing course, he cut across the frozen crabgrass and climbed three brick stairs which needed a mason with significant dental training given all the missing mortar. In brushing past the cop, he wondered if word about his weak spell in Haverhill already made it across state lines. Last time he tried the same stunt in Salem, Mary had her heart set on front row seats for a general admission concert at the high school. A humorless man called his bluff and he ended up in the emergency room.

Scanning the sparse living room which consisted of a tan corduroy couch, matching loveseat, and a black plastic entertainment center featuring a nineteen-inch television you had to whack on the top to turn on, he was disappointed to find Becky absent. She always defended him.

The sergeant read his face. "Your aunt is resting. She has a terrible migraine."

"Again?" he asked, wondering if they felt like the headaches he brought on himself. His aunt seemed increasingly prone to them since the bank stopped dragging its feet and began foreclosure procedures last month. She looked worn out and he wished he could shake her like an Etch A Sketch and redraw her with a happy face.

The sergeant adjusted his black-rimmed eyeglasses, which covered half his face and probably explained why so little ever got by him. Christopher avoided the piercing black eyes and focused instead on the policeman's hair, which reminded him of a porcupine: bristle gray and standing at attention.

"She felt it coming on a couple hours ago," he added in a slightly boastful tone, like he had displaced him as the man of the house.

He nodded. "Did she say if her sister Evelyn called? It's been two weeks since I've talked to Kylie."

The sergeant shrugged. Christopher turned and started for the hall, but a large hand grabbed him by the shoulder.

"Where are you going?"

Christopher spun around and motioned toward the end of the hall. "To see how *my* aunt is feeling. Okay?"

The sergeant tightened his grip and walked him back toward the couch. "The doctor said she needs some rest."

He broke away. "You didn't say anything about a doctor!" They locked eyes and he noticed the sergeant's looked bloodshot behind those Coke-bottle lenses. His neighbor regularly complained how he forgot to take out his contacts before going to bed and consequently, came down with a nasty eye infection. When his eyes stayed red after the infection cleared, Christopher wondered if it was caused from seeing too much pain over a storied career.

Sergeant Mike held one finger up to his lips and then pointed toward the kitchen. Four hard oak chairs around a worn table made for a perfect interrogation setting.

"While you're out gallivanting around town like Peter Pan, your aunt is here cooking, cleaning, and worrying about you," the sergeant said as if reading an indictment while taking a seat at the head of the table.

Christopher took off his coat and put it on the back of a chair. "I've never worn tights in my life and I can't fly. And what's gallivanting mean? Sounds like sword-fighting to me," he said, straight-faced.

The porcupine hair didn't move, but the eyebrows sure did. "You know what it means," he replied, with his voice rising. "I think you're a lot smarter than most people give you credit for. A lot smarter."

The way the sergeant scanned his every move when they were together made him feel like he was searching for a thread to unravel his DNA. Christopher knew most people preferred talking about themselves, so a simple question usually deflected the attention off him.

"But you're right. Now that I can read again, I do feel smarter. Did you have a busy weekend fighting crime?"

The sergeant pulled on his chin, apparently well versed in recognizing the attempted redirect.

He felt the x-ray and it made his headache spike. "No, I mean it," he countered. "Who did you bust today?"

The sergeant looked up at the ceiling instead of replying. Christopher hoped the freeze between them would be momentary, and the officer would break into a story which always helped him forget about things for a while. The coolest thing about his neighbor was never knowing what he would serve up next: an action-packed chase or working with detectives to solve a crime. Sergeant Mike also enjoyed shocking him sometimes. Last spring, for instance, when he first stopped over to say hello, the weather had been unseasonably hot. Sergeant Mike opened up his brown lunch bag and unwrapped a sandwich left in the police cruiser for a couple days. A thick slab of bologna had sweat through the Wonder Bread and globs of shiny mayonnaise clung to wilted lettuce. Manure smelled sweeter. The cop saw how much he was grossed out and slowly devoured the whole ugly mess. Then they laughed for five minutes straight.

"Remind me never to accept a lunch invite from you," he said at the time, and recorded the whole episode in his notebook. After that, his neighbor began to regularly wander over, sometimes carrying a rack of Michelob to tell tall tales while scanning the windows of his aunt's house. Usually Becky remained out of sight, but the few times she made an appearance, she wore those same Jackie-O sunglasses as if fearing the sergeant could read her eyes. The stories would continue rapid fire until he drained the last beer, and then on cue, he would pivot to how much he hated his ex-partner, who ran off with his wife.

But tonight felt different. This was about his aunt and he was too tired to play this game. He bent over and slowly removed one sneaker, exposing the bird nest of pine needles and a soggy mitten covering his toes. He didn't look up, thinking the sergeant might reconsider his comment about his level of intelligence.

"Besides the doctor, your mother also got a call from Mrs. Hinkle," the officer said like he expected him to know why.

Christopher struggled to keep his expression from changing while thinking that might be the name of the kind lady at the parade. *Maybe she called to see how I was feeling? But how did she get my number?*

"Mrs. Hinkle lives on Theresa Avenue," the sergeant continued. "She smelled smoke early this afternoon and then saw you running down the street. When she went to check things out, she noticed rocks all over the pond and a lot of broken ice. After what happened last year, she feared someone fell in and called nine-one-one."

Christopher felt a lump grow in his throat and reached into his coat pocket to fish out the headphones. The wires were knotted together and he began untangling them in case he needed to escape back to colonial times in a hurry. He'd never held his breath and passed out in front of the sergeant before. *Maybe it's my turn to provide the entertainment.*

Sergeant Mike leaped out of his chair and grabbed the earpiece out of his hands and flung them on the counter. "She's furious you ruined the ice," he said in a higher-pitched voice, and sat down in a chair next to him. "Now she'll have to take her son to the rink in Lawrence."

It took all his concentration to keep his jaw from dropping as Ray and Ted's dark vision began to come true. He wondered how Mrs. Hinkle missed seeing their dark shadows pass by.

"My guess is there's more to this story. Want to fill me in?"

The headache grew tentacles that reached his stomach and made him nauseous. The thought of being dragged down to the station and pummeled with more questions under the bright lights made him feel like he ate sweaty bologna instead of penny candy. As much as he wanted to blurt out the names of the punks, the image of splintered glass chasing Mary around the living room prevented it.

Since the accident he'd learned how to be tougher than an acorn to crack, but didn't want to lose a close friend over the stupid episode.

"Okay, I'll admit I walked on the ice and broke through by accident. But I didn't throw any of the rocks on the ice."

"Then who did?"

He shook his head twice; once for each of the jerks. "I've never been a fink." *You can ask my cousin and aunt,* he wanted to add.

"Why take the blame for something you didn't do?"

He looked down and tried to get lost in the scuffed-up red squares on the linoleum floor like Mary did whenever she found a similar grouping.

The policeman let out a heavy sigh. "There's a lot of riffraff down there, Chris. Given your history, I would think World End is the last place on earth you'd want to hang out."

Christopher counted a block of twenty-seven squares that led to the matted gray wall-to-wall carpeting in the hallway. He blinked and looked up at the hanging lamp over the kitchen table. Only three of the five candles worked and Becky ran sixty-watt bulbs to make up for the deceased twins. If he stared into the center of the bulbs long enough and then closed his eyes tight, splashes of white and yellow would pop like fireworks. He practiced that trick the day after waking up in the hospital as the memories kept dripping out of the ceiling tiles.

The snowflakes were the size of nickels and backlit by the Firebird's headlights. They pulled on my eyes, wanting to hypnotize me if only the wind would be silent. I should never have gotten in that car.

"Christopher?"

He looked up at the sergeant's lips as they continued moving and he let the words wash over him unprocessed. He wished he could find a divining rod to instruct him where to begin digging in his brain so the whole sad episode at World End would come gushing out. He was sure it would set him free. Until then, he remained in a frozen purgatory.

CHAPTER ELEVEN

The beige desk phone in the living room began ringing with the same enthusiasm as always, no matter whether a bill collector or family member was calling.

Sergeant Mike jumped up from the kitchen chair and then hesitated. "Are you going to answer that before it wakes up your aunt?"

Christopher shrugged and interpreted the ringing chime as the beginning of the next round. "Why? I thought you were playing butler for the day." He bolted for the hall before he could be apprehended. "I need some aspirin."

"We'll pick up this conversation later. And don't disturb your aunt," the policeman called after him.

It was a short runway to the bathroom at the end of the hall and he considered barging into his aunt's room before the sergeant could call in an all-points bulletin. But instead of tweaking his friend's nose, he took another three steps and closed the bathroom door behind him.

The pitted oval mirror over the white porcelain sink confirmed the reflection he saw earlier on the ice, except this later version came with bloodshot eyes and a squiggly, pulsating vein in the right temple. When he first got out of the hospital, he couldn't hold his breath for thirty seconds before his lungs caught on fire. A year later, it took seventy-nine seconds and turning almost Smurf blue before he passed out. The hangover headaches from the strange habit also lengthened in duration and intensity.

He opened a drawer and rifled through a sorry-looking crop of bent bobby pins, mangled tubes of toothpaste, and a leaking bottle of mint mouthwash before finding a bottle of generic aspirin and popped two without water. Sitting on the edge of the claw tub, he patted his red flannel shirt pocket, happy his Bigelow tea bags survived the day's ordeal. *Such delightful little packages of happiness,* he mused. He always traveled with at least two bags so he could bum a cup of hot water wherever his travels took him and have one to share.

Muffled footsteps in the hall caught his attention. He cracked the door open and watched his aunt saunter down the hall in a navy blue robe and then make the right turn for the kitchen. After counting off ten Mississippis, he tiptoed down the hall and hid beside the entertainment center.

Becky turned around from the sink with a small glass of water. "I heard the phone ring. Is Christopher staying at Mary's for dinner again?" The voice sounded a bit hoarse.

The sergeant rubbed his forehead. "No, he's here and supposedly in the bathroom, though my guess is he's hiding under his bed," the sergeant answered flatly. "Or maybe under yours after our little chat."

"You didn't mention anything about moving in with AJ, did you?"

"And have to explain why you're headed to Florida? I'd rather stick pins in my eyes than deal with your wrath." He sighed and pushed his chair back and crossed his legs. "I learned a long time ago to keep my mouth shut when it comes to you, or us."

Becky choked sipping on the water. "Us?" she asked, in a whisper-type yell. "Michael, how many times do I have to tell you the past is the past? Somehow, you think becoming my neighbor gives you permission to relive some of the wild things we did when we were young and foolish. It doesn't, and maybe you should stop listening to Springsteen's 'Glory Days.'" She took a quick drink. "You got one thing right, though. Keep your mouth shut."

A sly smile flashed over the cop's face. "I'm a patient man, Beck. I really am. The older I get, the more I think about those days. There was never anyone like you. The way we—"

Becky held up her hand. "Say another word and you can leave right now. I've had enough needy men for ten lifetimes and all this nonsense is making my migraine worse." She walked to the other end of the table and sat down. "So what were you talking about that got Christopher so worked up?"

The sergeant eyed Becky before exhaling in resignation. "Just more shenanigans at World End, I'm afraid." He rubbed the back of his neck. "I can't understand for the life of me why he's so drawn to that place. Maybe he's feeling guilty about driving AJ's car into the drink, but my cop radar says it's something more. Christopher says he doesn't remember anything about that night. Maybe that's true, but it's also mighty convenient, don't you think? We had a missing person report and a drowning within a span of forty-eight hours with people that traveled in the same circle. It doesn't take a Sherlock to come up with some possible scenarios. Problem is everyone involved is thick as thieves. But from my experience, give it enough time and one of them will break or do something stupid."

Becky stood up and leaned forward, putting the palms of her hands on the table. "Let me get this straight, Michael. You're sitting in my house—well, at least for a few more weeks, and implying my son and nephew are linked to these tragedies. You're the one that's being stupid."

The sergeant waved her off. "Don't shoot the messenger, sweetie. I've told you before, AJ continues to be a prime person of interest when it comes to Lori Martin."

She plopped back in the chair. "Well, you should leave the badge at home when you come over here." She studied him for a long moment. "You worship the past, but only the pieces that excite your male ego. I bet you don't fret much about suffocating me with jealousy."

"C'mon! Are we going to go over that again? How many times have I apologized?"

"Yeah, words are cheap, especially when I know what you want. Maybe my son is a bit like you in that department and that's why Lori broke up with him. But it certainly doesn't make him a murderer. As far as Christopher is concerned, I think he's drawn to the pond to try and recall who he used to be. He knows he's different now." She checked the double knot on her robe. "The doctors said irreversible brain damage occurs after three minutes without oxygen. He fell in twice, so who knows how long he was underwater in total." She bit her lip. "He used to be my stuck-up nephew, but there's something genuine about him now that's very special. He dotes on me every day and is forever asking about his little sister. Then there's Mary, who lights up his world."

Sergeant Mike smiled. "I'd love to dote too if you'd only let me."

She ignored the comment and shrugged. "Maybe we should all half drown. The world might be a kinder, gentler place."

Christopher closed his eyes and felt the familiar tightness in his chest.

The sergeant let out a short snicker. "Man, he's sure pulled the wool over your eyes. You think he woke up washed clean? Give me a break."

"All that water and the first thing he said when we finally understood him is I thirst," she continued, in a whisper.

Christopher closed his eyes as his ears pumped their conversation into a large stainless steel colander. He tried to grab some of the words before they drained through all the tiny holes into the dead clay regions in his brain. *The doctors said irreversible brain damage.*

The sergeant sighed heavily. "Think whatever you want, but in my opinion he's playing you."

"He will be upset and drill me with questions when I tell him about Evelyn moving," she added, ignoring the comment. "He hears okay, but like most men, has trouble listening."

The sergeant smirked. "Darling, I hear every syllable that comes out of those pretty lips of yours."

Christopher opened his eyes and studied the pair. His aunt looked lost in thought, while the sergeant wore a weird expression he never saw in his repertoire. It reminded him of a wolf with hungry eyes.

Becky got up and walked to the refrigerator. She took out a small pizza box as the sergeant stared at her backside.

"I've had a rough few years, but I can't stop thinking of that poor boy," she said. "I can't imagine what Gene Godfreye is going through these days."

The sergeant stood up and his fingers began fidgeting. "It's one thing when you lose your sister and brother-in-law in a plane accident due to mechanical issues no one could foresee. But what happened out on the ice was just plain stupid. What were they thinking? It's really a miracle they didn't all drown. I still can't believe AJ only lost his license for six months for reckless driving." He lifted the pizza box top and took out a small slice of pepperoni. "They would have tagged your nephew too, but he's never going to drive again." He took a large bite and chewed fast with his mouth open.

"I can't believe how you stuff food in your mouth without looking at the ingredients. Where's your EpiPen?"

"In my kitchen and only thirty seconds away." He curled his lip. "Though I'd risk anaphylactic shock if it meant mouth to mouth—"

She cut the air to interrupt him. "What's wrong with you today?" She headed to the oven. "Do you want me to heat up the rest for you?" She shot him a smirk. "Maybe I'll add a few nuts to straighten you out long term."

"Sure, as long as you don't get mad when I begin humming 'Cold as Ice'?"

Becky rolled her eyes. "Your wife may have left with your sleazy partner with the fake tan, but at least you two had a good run," she said, turning away. "Aram and I were only married for six months when he left for Vietnam. I didn't recognize the man Uncle Sam sent back. She nodded. "It's killing me to see Christopher go through something similar."

The sergeant took another bite and chewed slowly. "C'mon, like you didn't see that coming? Aram was always fragile growing up."

"Not fragile, just sensitive. That's what made him so attractive after going out with you. He was thoughtful."

"I'm losing my appetite," he said, wiping his mouth with the back of his hand. "I remember meeting you at Timmy Mihan's after he left for basic training." He held up the remaining piece of crust. "There was enough heat that night to burn more than pizza."

"I was furious at Aram for enlisting and made a terrible mistake."

"And here we are all these years later and nothing has changed. Your husband is gone and I'm here patiently waiting." He walked over and took the pizza box away and placed it on the counter. Becky quickly retreated to the table.

Sergeant Mike followed and hovered over her as she sat down. "So have you decided on letting your sister set up a conservatorship for the man-boy you're housing? A buddy of mine is a lawyer and said when you're ready, he could get this in front of a judge pretty quick."

"I want to honor my sister and not feel like I'm taking advantage of this sad situation to line my pockets."

The sergeant pulled a chair close to hers and sat down. "You're looking at this all wrong, Beck. With the airline settlement, Christopher and Kylie will have bank accounts that would choke a horse. Your sister is all set since she's Kylie's guardian and doesn't even need the extra money. You have the tougher assignment and should take steps to be compensated for the cross you're bearing. It's not taking advantage of anything as your nephew needs a place to live. All I'm saying is it will help pay the bills far better than selling hay and ice." He looked around. "Who knows? Maybe you could even keep this house or trade up."

Becky closed her eyes and the sergeant touched her arm. "Then do it for AJ. He may need a good lawyer soon."

She pulled away. "Yeah, to sue you and the rest of the department for harassment. My son had nothing to do with that girl's disappearance. Wasn't that clear after the dozen interviews and the polygraph?"

"That's not fair. You know I had to recuse myself when it comes to your son. I'm just saying what needs to be said, as usual."

"But I know you're monitoring everything in the background. It would be quite a feather in your cap to solve this mystery."

Christopher felt tingling in his right foot and moved it too fast and a floorboard squeaked.

The kitchen fell silent.

"Thank you, Michael, for picking up my headache medication. I apologize for spoiling your dinner hour," his aunt said in an odd formal tone.

"Ah, no problem. That's what neighbors are for," the sergeant said, standing up. "Think over the conservatorship," he said in a low voice.

Christopher tiptoed back to the bathroom and sat on the edge of the white tub again. He pulled the pocket-sized notebook out of his back pocket, which he used as a crutch for continued hiccups in short-term memory, and wrote down as much as he could remember. Next, he ran the water good and hot and after wetting a facecloth, draped it over the back of his neck for a few minutes.

Feeling a little better, he marched back down the hall and found his aunt standing as still as a mannequin, watching the headlights from passing cars through the plastic sheathing.

He coughed to break the spell.

"Did you have fun at the parade today, honey?" she asked, turning to greet him.

He nodded, not knowing where to start and wishing Sergeant Mike stayed for dinner even if he had to deal with another grilling about the ice. Now they faced another long night.

"What did you talk with the sergeant about?" he asked.

She gave a thin smile and walked past him. "It's time for your meds."

He followed her into the kitchen. "Did Aunt Evelyn call?"

She ignored his gaze and opened a fat prescription bottle. "Yes, your aunt calls like she does every Sunday at noon." She sighed. "Just like a Swiss watch, but with an attitude setting built in too."

"So will Kylie be coming to visit this week? I miss her terribly."

Becky filled a tall plastic glass with tap water and handed it to him. "You're just like your father. He would pepper me with questions too." She chuckled. "I used to call him the Shell Answer Man because he loved giving advice."

He waited for his aunt to answer his question, but none came. "So what about Kylie?"

She put the pill bottle on the windowsill over the sink. "Remember what the doctor said. Focus on one thing at a time. It helps with the memory issues. So let's finish with your meds." She handed him a pill.

He studied the green-and-cream-colored capsule the doctor explained balanced something called serotonin levels in the brain. As revolutionary as the doctor made it sound, he envisioned the pill as the equivalent of the Sherwin Williams Dutch Boy mascot pouring a can of paint over the globe. In his case, it not only covered, but dulled everything.

He pretended to pop the pill in his mouth and then hid it in his hand. It was a shame he couldn't save it for the perch to help it get through the winter darkness.

"I heard you and Sargent Mike talking," he said. "I had trouble understanding a word."

His aunt looked surprised. "You were brought up better than that. You know that spying is very rude." She played with the double knot on her robe again. "What word?"

"It was a long one but the first three letters spelled con."

CHAPTER TWELVE

The salt crystals did a decent job at keeping the ice off the sidewalk, but left it looking pockmarked and resembling a sheet of chocolate nonpareils. Christopher wondered why there weren't defroster-type sidewalks to replace the back-breaking job of shoveling, scraping, and application of chemicals. After all, if it worked so well on the rear windows of automobiles, why not apply the same technology below the surface? He pulled the blue notebook from the back pocket of his dungarees and jotted down a quick note on this sudden inspiration. But by the time he walked the last two miles to Mary's house, he preferred being the idea guy and leaving the technical hurdles of threading miles of thin wires to motivated engineers.

He hesitated before bolting up the half dozen cement steps leading to the split-level light yellow house where Mary lived with her dad and new stepmom. Few things in life were as predictable as the sequence of events which followed once he pressed the oval doorbell. First, loud chimes rivaling monastery bells would fill the house. Next, Mary would catapult out of the leather recliner in the living room and march with heavy feet across the hardwood floor to a gold-framed mirror and check her hair and makeup. A good five Mississippis later, she would holler, "Hold your horses, I'm coming!" which was odd, since she didn't know anyone who owned one. Only then would the honey-stained door fly open, rattling the three little square windows on top, and Mary would greet him slightly out of breath. Christopher always sensed a micro-burst of disappointment in those lovely eyes, because she anticipated Lori coming home someday and ringing the doorbell to announce the miracle. But in the next instant, he would watch the sun rise in her innocent face, capped with a wide smile and teeth whiter than sugar and straighter than any picket fence on millionaire's row.

For the past three months, he searched for the right words to tell her how he felt and longed to seal it with a kiss. In a precarious year, Mary had been an anchor no matter the rip currents in his life. At the same time, she was as fragile and rare as a lady slipper discovered in the deep forest.

Last week, he found the courage to confess his feelings after walking her home from the library, when suddenly, Denise barreled into his thoughts with a kaleidoscope of images before World End. It had been months since she last visited, and he compared what his long-term memory still retained versus the person he was now. The contrast brought on a strange uneasiness. He distinctly remembered cherishing their relationship and pledging his heart to her, but examining the passion reels in his mind, he recognized the stereotypical hot-blooded guy always pursuing an all-you-can-eat buffet. This new version of himself came with powerful desires too, but he had a better understanding of the difference between need and want, as exemplified by the simple pleasure in holding hands with Mary. The intense memories extinguished the impulse to confess his feelings until he spoke with Denise.

A cold breeze jolted him back to the present and he quickly climbed the stairs and pressed the doorbell. As he listened to the chimes, he hoped they could hang out on the leather couch and talk for a while or watch a movie. He enjoyed basking in what normal used to feel like.

A minute later the door flew open and he sucked in his breath to find Mary transformed into Twiggy. Last week at the library, she gushed over a black-and-white photo of the British icon from a 1966 edition of *Life* magazine. She never mentioned it again so this was a surprise. Her hair was pulled back to hide some of its length, and the front parted and combed to one side. Long fake eyelashes accented her eyes and tight black jeans with a white blouse completed the look.

"Wow! You're a ringer for Twiggy!" he said, with a laugh.

"Thanks, Chris," she replied glumly.

She struggled frequently to express her feelings and used his nickname as a code word something was amiss.

He doubled the width of his smile to try and compensate. "Why so sad?"

"Because I have no tissues." She stepped back for him to enter. "I refuse to blow my nose on toilet paper because that's just gross."

Christopher had an unused handkerchief, but hesitated to offer the gray-looking rag. "No need to fret, my dear. We can walk down to Godfreye's and I'll buy you a couple of those nifty travel packages of tissues."

She shook her head. "We never go there on Mondays."

He trotted out his sincerest smile. "I know routine is important to you, but I think we should make an exception today. I hope you're not too particular, though, because they only carry pink tissues and I don't want to ruin the retro look." He tried to corner her eyes and succeeded for a half second, before they escaped again. "We can splurge on some peanut M&M's too," he said, with a wink.

She finally gifted him a slight smile and he admired her brownish-green eyes, which could also turn gold depending on the light. If she would allow him to gaze at them long enough, he was certain he could see all the way to heaven and God might wave back. Color like that could not be found on any painter's palette.

"Can we play the Tri-State Lottery game too?" she asked, scratching a red spot on her throat which plagued her whenever she became upset. "Though I'd probably faint if I ever won the jackpot."

He frowned. "You could buy tissues for everyone in Salem with what you've wasted on lottery tickets in the past six months."

Mary's hands went quickly to her hips. "Hey, I won five dollars last week. I only need one chance to win."

"Good, because I'm running on spare change." Christopher jammed both hands into his dungaree pockets and had trouble reaching bottom. Mr. Godfreye teased he was on a see-food diet because he ate everything he saw, and the tight jeans proved him right. He fished out six dimes and a crumpled dollar bill. *I really need to talk with Becky about my allowance.*

"When can we go?" Mary asked, eyeing the hall closet ready to get her coat.

Christopher rolled up the money and pushed it back into the abyss. "Just let me rest my bones for a few minutes and we'll head out." He made his way over to the black leather couch perfectly positioned in front of the new Sony television. They liked to watch *Jeopardy!* and talk in questions for hours after the game show.

Collapsing on the couch, he felt a shiver ripple across the top of his head.

Mary noticed. "Someone just walked over your grave," she said matter of fact.

"Then I guess I'm going to be buried in the middle of the highway." He bit his lip. It had only been a couple days since stopping the pills and the side effects came without warning.

Mary paced around the room and he studied her long graceful fingers which ended abruptly with badly bitten nails, which she tried to hide under thick coats of bright red nail polish. Christopher knew her brain was wired differently, which made her special and also brought its own unique challenges. A hollow feeling filled his stomach knowing how hard she worked to lead a normal life, while he tended to exaggerate his issues in order to be left alone.

He looked away and noticed a business-sized envelope sitting on the cherry coffee table. The upper left corner bore the great seal of the State of New Hampshire with the frigate USS *Raleigh* in the center. Becky used to receive similar envelopes from Veterans Affairs, which she paraded like court exhibits in the hope of extracting money from his parents. The requests became so frequent his father was convinced she merely recycled the same letter.

Mary stopped pacing and followed his line of sight. "It's from Concord," she commented, in a matter-of-fact tone that didn't match her eyes.

He nodded. "My aunt received official letters like that filled with fancy language normal folk can't understand. My father used to describe it more colorfully."

"Well, *it* arrived this morning so my dad hasn't read it yet."

He noticed the torn top. "Did you open it?" In his family, he would have been charged with high crimes and misdemeanors for opening mail not addressed to him.

The Twiggy model pursed her lips in a pose that would have rocked any *Look* photographer. Then her eyes darted around the room like a baseball player chewing tobacco and needing to find someplace safe to quickly and discreetly spit.

"So what if I did? They're always about me anyways!" she blurted out.

He felt backed into a corner. "Okay, I guess." He looked at the envelope again. "Can I ask what it said?"

She shrugged. "They can't help me like they promised."

"What do you mean?"

She sat down next to him. "My father saw this coming a month ago after making some calls. He said they would be two-faced and act sad when they told me to get lost."

He read her lips and listened intently, but it didn't help much. "I still don't understand."

Mary picked up the letter and balanced it in the palm of her hand. "It's from the director and starts with the word 'regretfully' and it's all downhill from there." She bit the stubby nail on her index finger. "Regretfully is such a cold word. Why couldn't he just say he's really sorry, or how it stinks the independent living program was cancelled due to budget cuts."

The rapid disclosure produced a burning sensation in the back of his throat. They were counting down the days until she moved five miles up the road, which he could easily reach by bike.

She opened the letter and handed it to him. Scanning the gibberish, his eyes locked on six words: *the program has been suspended indefinitely.* At the bottom it was signed: Respectfully, Melvin Bates II.

He wondered how Melvin liked dragging Roman numerals behind him all through life. *Does he ever just sign his name* MB²? He held the letter up to the light and determined the signature was a facsimile.

"So, what will you do now?" he barked by accident.

"Well, Anne found a similar program in upstate New York and has some connections." She let out an odd laugh, and he didn't know whether to chalk it up to her projecting the wrong emotion like she did sometimes, or trying to put on a brave face. Mary's stepmother's motivation also troubled him. "*Mary has to learn to do things for herself. She can't be tethered to us forever,*" he overheard Anne lecture her new husband. He made a note to remember the remark and kept it to himself.

Mary tugged the letter out of his hand and placed Melvin Bates II face down on the coffee table. Her eyes became glassy, and her nose began to run again. Against his better judgment, he offered the grayish handkerchief.

She accepted it without hesitation and blew her nose with a loud honk that any other day he would have laughed at. She followed it up with a deep breath which seemed to revive her.

"Maybe I can stay here until someplace closer opens up. In the meantime, I can keep working part-time at the hospital," she said forcing a brave smile. "I'm a real wiz at word processing. Only problem is Anne thinks it's too crowded with the three of us sharing a bathroom, but we can make it work." She blew her nose again and then handed the wet rag back to Christopher. He held it lightly in his hand before stuffing it gingerly into his coat pocket.

"When I was growing up, mornings were a bit wild with three women, and my dad didn't need an alarm clock." She ran her index finger under one eye to catch the wet mascara before it ran. "He learned it was best to shave at night, but looking back, we had some laughs too." She looked toward the kitchen. "If I stayed, I could get dinner ready. Anne knows I'm a great cook."

Christopher didn't need to reference his notebook to remember Mary's many stories about her sweet and doting mother. She died from a brain aneurysm six months before Lori disappeared. Her father soon faced an unwinnable war on two fronts; grieving for his wife and as the days passed, the likelihood his firstborn daughter was dead too. As her father progressively withdrew, Mary ended up becoming a casualty too. She would try and get her father's attention as he sat on the leather couch, with the TV remote in one hand and a beer in the other, flipping through channels until he caught a game—any game, to limit conversation. Then suddenly three months ago, he came home from a business trip and sprang the news about proposing to Anne. In mid-December, they decided to elope so they could enjoy Christmas as a family.

"My father is planning some fun outings for us this winter," and a shadow crossed her face. "We're supposed to go to the Boston Aquarium soon. That will be tough if I'm living in New York."

He clenched his teeth and wondered if Melvin Bates II was Anne's new alias.

Mary wandered over to a cherry table against one wall and picked up her sister's high school portrait. *"I held her hand the tighter - which shortened all the miles."*

"I haven't heard you recite that one before. Is that one of Emily's too?" he asked. Mary had a passion for Emily Dickinson and saw her as a kindred spirit. She read everything she could get her hands on about her life.

Mary nodded. *"One Sister have I in our house,"* she replied, fingering the gold frame. "Everything will work itself out when Lori comes home. Maybe we can even get an apartment together. She understands all I want is what everyone else takes for granted." She kissed her sister's picture.

"I can't wait to meet her." He was always careful to refer to Lori in the present tense. Mary had a meltdown when people talked otherwise.

"In the meantime, I'll just have to wait and see how it all plays out." Mary carefully stood the picture back on the table.

Images of Lori's wallet in AJ's car took hold and he forced a yawn, fighting to stay in the present instead of letting his thoughts ripple outward. *Maybe, I should have weaned myself off the meds instead of going cold-turkey like this.*

Mary fiddled with her bangs and continued to admire her sister's picture. "Some older guy kept teasing Lori's theme song should be 'Cherry Hill Park' because she liked to tease the boys and then after dark—" She stopped and giggled.

He knew the song even though it was an oldie from the '60s. It had a suggestive storyline about a girl named Mary, which she failed to notice. "Didn't some rich guy come and take her away in the end?" he asked, treading carefully.

She shrugged. "I think another stanza of that same poem by Emily Dickinson best describes Lori. *She did not sing as we did - it was a different tune.*" Mary smiled, relishing the words. "I began packing last week and came across Lori's journal. It had a few doodles and some funny comments."

He sat up. "So, did you tell your dad?"

"No, silly, and you better keep this a secret too. There were only a few notes because my sister ran too fast to write much down. Besides, those type of things are meant to be private."

He glanced at Lori's picture. His aunt said she was the only girl AJ ever brought home and in many ways she never left. She joined them every night for supper as Becky argued her son's innocence.

"Did she mention Bobby or AJ in the journal?"

Mary flashed a stop sign. "Sister secrets."

Christopher felt another shiver fly across his scalp. Six weeks after nearly drowning, spring arrived early and a cadre of divers searched World End on a windy March day. He expected them to find Lori's wallet and the tire iron near the submerged cars. But in the end, Mr. Perch must have negotiated with AJ for a water condo in the Caribbean, because the only item recovered was his putrid wool coat. By the time the dive was over, Becky had fed him enough pills to make the whole event feel like he was watching from an easy chair behind his eyes.

That was also the first time he met Mary. Regretfully.

CHAPTER THIRTEEN

The large banner with bold black letters two feet high in the front window of Godfreye's Superette dwarfed all the other advertisements. *Here's One New Year's Resolution Worth Keeping! Win Fifty Million Dollars.*

Christopher and Mary entered the store in time to catch one of the store owner's ad hoc management lectures.

"Sam Walton should have called me before building all those mega-stores," Gene Godfreye, a thin, bald man in his mid-sixties, exclaimed to a small group waiting in line. "I would have taught him to think in square inches instead of feet." He pointed to the rafters above him crammed with Valentine teddy bears, Cupid dolls, boxes of Whitman chocolates and cherry cordials. "Believe me, it's a lot easier to shop with your eyes than running around an enclosed football field. It's a wonder they don't have defibrillators in every aisle."

Godfreye winked at Christopher to acknowledge his presence. "Instead of relying on some whippersnapper with a Harvard MBA, I designed the layout of this store myself thirty years ago. Even now, I'm always thinking about how to better utilize the space to compete with the supermarket chains down the street." He pointed at the front window. "One way is through creative advertising. For example, I let the American Heart Association put up a poster by the cigarette cartons. Do you think that's a coincidence?" He chuckled.

"I'd think that might make folks question why you carry those cancer sticks," a heavy man still married to a hideous Christmas sweater commented. He plopped down a handful of lottery forms and a twenty-dollar bill on the counter.

"I can never get through a day without some smart—" Godfreye stopped and smiled. "I'm a proud Libertarian, so I'm just highlighting the risks and letting my customers decide for themselves." He deposited the sawbuck in the register. "By the way, when your wife knit that beautiful sweater, was she thinking of you as the ghost of Christmas past or future?"

The man smacked his lips. "Either way, when I win, I'll buy this place and change the name to Malarkey Central in your honor."

Godfreye laughed as the lottery machine burped out a receipt. "Ten years ago we would have a steady line for lottery tickets with a fifty-thousand-dollar prize. Now people yawn. Everything these days has to be super-sized."

Christopher surveyed the line of waiting customers: three men and two women. All had the same hungry expression.

Mary politely nudged him. "Fifty million dollars? I want a ticket!"

"So I guess the tissues can wait then," he replied to her red nose, as she struggled to fix one of the fake eyelashes. They made their way over to a small table near the window where three men were bent over with pencils filling out lottery forms; each intent on finding the secret combination of six numbers to unlock the pot of gold at the end of the rainbow.

Christopher grabbed a few blank forms and a couple pencils, then headed toward the relative quiet in the back of the store.

Mary followed close behind before stopping in front of a row of standing coolers. She opened one door wide and let it go, watching as it hesitated momentarily before pistons in the industrial hinges engaged to gently close it. Mary repeated the trick, but this time gave the door a hard push and the hinges clicked in protest.

"Do you think these doors ever get tired of opening and closing?"

Her questions never failed to surprise him. Where others would dismiss them as random or odd observations, he enjoyed how she viewed the world and made insightful connections.

"Why do you ask?"

She held the door open and let the cool air envelop her face. "Because it reminds me how Doctor Petersen tries to open me up every week by asking the same silly questions. Then he proceeds to write down my answers, like it's the first time he's ever heard them. Last week, I told him he needs to listen more or take better notes, because next time I'm just going to say ditto and leave it at that." She gave the door another hard push and smirked when it squealed in rebellion. "*I felt a Funeral, in my Brain,*" she said, smiling. "Maybe next week I'll just quote Emily Dickinson, because she's my soul sister. If that doesn't work, I'll make a sound like the cooler door and really mess with his head."

"Why not send him on a scavenger hunt with clues to stop here?" he added in support. Sometimes on Tuesday afternoons he walked her to the appointment on Main Street. The renovated 1860s farmhouse had a large awning proudly identifying itself as the "Salem Mental Health Center." Mary would wait on the sidewalk until there wasn't a car in sight, before hurrying into the building. He stopped asking if Mary wanted him to wait after surprising her once. Her eyes and nose were the color of cherry tomatoes when she exited the building and she didn't say a word on the walk home.

"Both my aunts want me to go see another counselor so I can forget that night, but all I want is to remember everything that happened. I'm afraid whatever I do, Evelyn will use it to say I'm not fit to take care of Kylie. After what I heard Sergeant Mike say to Becky, I'm wondering about her intentions too." He looked at the cold soda, milk, and beer behind the cooler doors. *I have to continue fogging up the glass until I figure things out.*

"Well, if you end up going, watch out for the games they play. In my case, we play a silly card game where I have to read people's faces because supposedly it helps my condition. She screwed up her face. "The doctor doesn't understand this look could mean I'm happy enough, but I just ate a handful of sour Gummy Worms."

Christopher laughed. "Clearly, he hasn't lived much."

She pinched her nose. "So Mary, tell me how you're feeling with your dad suddenly remarried and your sister still missing?" She gritted her teeth.

"Well, you could blow his socks off next time and show up as Twiggy."

"And give him something else to write about to prove I'm not—" She stopped short. "I won't be labeled. Nope, never, no way! Who sets the rules about what is normal anyways? In the summer, I love admiring how the Queen Anne's lace pops up and lines the roads. But because it's wild and it chooses where it wants to grow, it's considered a weed. What colorblind, lemon-sucking, snobby committee decided white flowering wild carrots should be classified in the same category as crab grass?"

He chuckled and rubbed his chin, thinking maybe the world had everything backward.

She bent down and studied the assortment of beverages on the bottom shelf. "I sure love Yoo-hoo."

"I'm sorry, Mary, but your eyes are bigger than my wallet today. Keep it up and I'll need to win the lottery just to make it out of the store." Glancing at the lottery forms in his hand, he wished the six winning numbers would somehow magically glow. It would be neat to see the future like that. He could have saved Bobby and a piece of himself a ton of grief. Maybe Lori too.

"Do they have Yoo-hoo in New York?" Mary asked.

He looked at his lottery form. *If I had the gift of prophecy, people would glow like mood rings; fire engine red for the angry, midnight blue to signal those depressed, lime green for jealous souls.* He let out a sigh. "Color me yellow," he mumbled.

"So what about Yoo-hoo in New York?" Mary blurted out much too loud.

"Hey! What's going on back there?" the store owner yelled from the register.

"Nothing. We'll be quiet, Mr. Godfreye," he responded quickly.

Mary tugged on his arm and her eyes locked on his for a brief moment. "Yoo-hoo?" she whispered.

He nodded, then went back to studying the lottery forms without blinking. The rows of numbers blurred instead of glowing, and he thought maybe the gift of prophecy was something you had to stand in a special line to receive before birth—sort of like those Black Friday sales after Thanksgiving, where people camp out for days to snag something spectacular with limited inventory. Since he was a preemie, he probably missed the possibility of any upgrades.

Christopher forced a yawn and realized how life flowed much easier on meds, rather than dealing with random reflections spun by madcap spiders running around his mind.

"So you're positive I can get Yoo-hoo in New York?" she asked again, but only louder.

Her voice startled and refocused him. "Most definitely, my dear." He gently stroked the arm of her pink wool coat.

She looked away and pouted. "Was that so hard to answer? If you act like that when you meet with a counselor, you'll end up in New York with me." She put her hands on her hips and looked at him quick. "Know this. If I get to my new place and can't find my special chocolate drink, I'm blaming you."

The blank form began mocking him and he fought the urge to rip it up. "What's the use?" he asked, realizing what he wanted to win would never be found after guessing a sequence of numbers.

Mary began to ponder her lottery form too. "Maybe I could use my birthday for some of the numbers."

"It's on a Friday this year if you want to include the day of the week. How's that for the gift of prophecy?"

She flashed a smile. "Your birthday is next month. We could make up a combo."

He shrugged, not wanting to confess how ironic it was to be an Aquarius and terrified of water. "It feels like a long shot to have all the stars align like that."

"But that's why we love *Rocky* movies." She batted her eyes like Adrian. "We root for the brave underdog."

He chuckled, thinking how Mary was like New England weather and constantly changing. Seconds ago her world revolved around Yoo-hoo availability and now morphed into his life coach.

Glancing toward the front of the store, he caught sight of Mr. Godfreye in the middle of another monologue. He couldn't hear the speech, but enjoyed watching his arms flail around like anti-aircraft guns searching the sky for a target. The store traffic looked like it was thinning and he planned to ask for two cups of hot water and treat Mary to a cup of green tea from his special collection. The store owner always obliged, but not before rolling his eyes and telling everyone within earshot he would go broke with these freebies. Christopher knew it was all an act, and behind the bluster, a kind father still grieving the loss of his only son.

Christopher pushed a half dozen cans of cat food back on a metal shelf and laid out three lottery forms side by side. Light pencil marks on one caught his attention, and on closer scrutiny, he found someone had already selected 11-22-33 before abandoning the form. The symmetry of the numbers appealed to him and he closed his eyes and let his pencil randomly select the remaining three.

"What are you doing?" Mary asked.

He opened his eyes before his thoughts began meandering again. "I've come to appreciate how patterns and randomness might be opposites, but can be partners," he explained. His life used to have a predictable rhythm until an ice-encrusted grenade landed in the orchestra pit. "I'm trying to balance my entry."

Mary rolled her eyes. "You think too much sometimes. My dad just gets a quick-pick as he thinks any number combination has the same chance to win." She looked up the aisle. "How about the peanut M&M's you promised me?"

They were her favorite candy because if you put two pieces together they spelled her initials. *Chocolate initials beat duct tape any day,* he thought.

"Okay, Mary Martin." He gathered the forms together and they walked single file up the narrow aisle. Grabbing a yellow package of the beloved candy, he placed it on the counter and handed the lottery form to Mr. Godfreye.

The storeowner gave him a once-over and then held the single form high above his head. "I want to call everyone's attention to this young man, who didn't get writer's cramp making out hundreds of entries or withdrawing his life's savings from the bank. No, this gentleman has the courage, confidence, and conviction to spit on the odds and buy one ticket."

A short man wearing a Patriots stocking hat suddenly appeared from behind a display of bottled water fanning two dozen lottery forms. "I could forgo paying the mortgage and buy a thousand tickets and the odds would still be horrible. But my attitude is go big or go home."

"And go broke." Godfreye started to laugh, but it stopped when he watched Christopher line up a wrinkled dollar bill and five dimes on the counter.

"Oh, for the love of heaven," he grumbled, picking up the money.

Christopher quickly took out two Bigelow green tea bags from his shirt pocket. Some Saturdays, he worked stocking shelves and learned through trial and error that it was better to get all of Mr. Godfreye's bluster out at one time.

Christopher held up the tea bags and smiled as sweet as he could as the proprietor hung his head. "At times you test my Christian upbringing," he sighed, opening the cash register. "Just make sure you clean up after yourself. Okay?"

Smiling, Christopher led Mary down the aisle by the front window stocked generously with bags of potato chips, pretzels, and popcorn to the coffee and tea station.

Mary tapped him on the shoulder. "I want to hold the ticket." She opened a small burgundy clutch stuffed with lottery forms and gum wrappers.

He knew the odds of winning were next to impossible, but still feared shared custody. "Why don't I hold onto the ticket and we can check the winning numbers together?"

She looked disappointed and he quickly bent down to grab two Styrofoam cups from the stainless steel dispenser. The approaching sound of heavy boots scuffing the linoleum floor and then stopping a few feet away made him look up.

Instead of competition for the hot water spigot, he found Denise standing there. He dropped the cups as everything around him shrank into the background and the fluorescent light became harsh. Denise looked prettier than he dared remember and he stared at the dark curls which flowed over the shoulders of a black double-breasted peacoat.

"Hello, Chris," she said, with the same sultry voice and matching smile that stole his heart in another life.

His previous self would have said something cool, but he just nodded. To keep his jaw from bouncing off the floor, he looked down at his baggy jeans and mud-caked canvas sneakers. Now he understood how Mary felt in wanting to avoid people's eyes.

Suddenly, Denise was hugging him tight and his arms remained glued to his sides. He inhaled her perfume and began to tremble remembering how he once craved her more than oxygen.

She finally released him and took a step backward to get a good look. "How are you doing?" she asked, bobbing her head to try and lock onto his eyes.

"I'm . . . great," he stammered, which was embarrassing enough, but also surprising, as it differed significantly from what he practiced saying if he saw her again. After the accident, Denise practically lived at the hospital and even participated in some of the first rehab sessions. But as the weeks passed and it became apparent how much he had changed, her visits became more sporadic. At first, she blamed the demands of school, but as the time between visits lengthened, so did the silence when they were together.

Clearing his throat, he decided to try again. He reached in his back pocket for "old faithful" and flipped through the notebook. "It . . . still . . . feels a little weird," he began again. "I can picture the Spiderman lunchbox I had in first grade, but sometimes have trouble remembering breakfast unless I write it down." He stopped at a page and read for a moment. "Says right here, the last time you came to see me was on October nineteenth. The leaves were near peak and you watched me carve a pumpkin with Becky." He held up the page. "Here's the pathetic picture I drew. Looks more like a possessed squash."

Denise smiled and nodded. "Don't be so hard on yourself, Chris. I stink at Pictionary because I can only draw stick figures. Remember?" She looked away, like she was the one embarrassed now by testing his memory. "It's been too long and I apologize. Look. The reason I came to see you today—"

Christopher noticed the orphaned tea bags on the counter and gasped. "Oh my goodness," he said, cutting her off, "let me introduce you to Mary." Turning around, he expected to find Twiggy shooting him daggers and ready to knight him Melvin Bates III. Instead, the only things waiting were the empty Styrofoam cups on the floor. He walked a few steps and stood on tippy-toes to survey the standing freezers, thinking maybe she was torturing the doors again, but they were quiet.

Denise shadowed him. "Your aunt said I might find you hanging around here."

"Seldom on Mondays." Christopher rushed over to the plate glass window and caught sight of Mary running across the street.

He motioned to Denise. "If we hurry, we can catch Mary. After I apologize for being rude, I'll introduce you."

The almond eyes narrowed. "Christopher, we really need to talk in private. You can introduce me to your friend some other time."

"Okay," he said slowly, not convinced there would be another opportunity and aware she didn't seem to care his friend was another beautiful woman.

Denise led him to a quiet corner piled high with cases of beer and waited to make sure he was paying attention.

"Yesterday, I drove by your house in Billerica and saw a moving van in the driveway, so I stopped. Your aunt Evelyn answered the door and told me pretty bluntly you weren't there." She took a deep breath. "Basically, she told me to get lost. Given how long it's been since I stopped by, I understood."

"Don't take it personally. Sometimes the way she says things comes out sounding pretty harsh." He flipped to another page in the notebook and took a deep breath. "Though you're probably right. Both my aunts know how I felt when you stopped visiting." He looked up and focused on the words he'd practiced for so long. "I thought . . . you loved me."

A young and handsome Hispanic man cradling a baby in his arms walked by. Denise smiled at the baby as tears welled up in those alluring eyes.

"I love you, but—"

Christopher held up his hand. "Those first three words are like a circle; you can't add anything without breaking the bond." He stopped and swallowed the lump in his throat. "I have no trouble remembering I never added *but*."

A tear ran down her cheek and he thought about offering his handkerchief, but Mary already used it.

Denise wiped her cheek with her hand. "What can I say? I'm sorry? I know that doesn't begin to cover it. We were making plans for the future, but they also included following our own ambitions. Right? I knew things would be different and—" She stopped and took a tissue out of her coat pocket and wiped her nose. "This isn't the place to talk. Just know, I've been wandering in the desert too."

Christopher nodded and closed his notebook. "I gave you my heart, but I'm asking for it back." He rocked side to side and scanned her face. "You don't have to wander in the desert anymore."

The almond eyes filled some more. An uncomfortable silence grew which was their new normal. He turned to leave when Denise grabbed his arm. "When I got back to my car after being dismissed by Evelyn, your sister came running out of the garage. She was crying and said they were moving to Florida and you didn't know."

Christopher sat down on a few stacked cases of Miller Lite.

Denise reached in her side pocket and took out the St. Christopher medal he gave his sister. "That's why I'm here today. Kylie wanted me to get this to you. She said you'd understand."

CHAPTER FOURTEEN

The mangy black suitcase escaped its long entombment under the cellar stairs and sat by the front door like an eager dog waiting to be walked. Christopher picked it up by the chipped plastic handle and opened the hall closet and hid the forty-pound bag behind the vacuum cleaner.

"So, if they've been staying in Florida for a while, when can I visit?" he asked, rounding the corner to rejoin his aunt.

Becky pretended not to hear, apparently taking a page from his playbook as she wrestled with the top drawer of the built-in hutch. No matter how much soap she applied to grease the sliders, she seemed to be in a constant tug-of-war and usually lost. This morning, the struggle looked even more lopsided, as a dozen imprisoned papers stuck their heads out of the half-open drawer, apparently planning to join the suitcase and escape.

He knelt down beside her to offer assistance.

"I'm not discussing this again," she said, shooting him a quick look before shoving the rebel papers back in the drawer. "There's a lot going on right now with the house . . . and me. I haven't talked to Evelyn yet about her long-term plans."

"Why can't I come then? I haven't seen Kylie since Christmas."

Becky jumped up and began moving away, but not before finger-combing his crazy cowlick.

"Because this isn't a vacation, silly." She forced a smile. "That's why I'm taking the small suitcase. I'll be back so quick my old bones won't even get to thaw out."

She made a beeline for the kitchen and returned moments later with a small stack of papers to incarcerate in the overcrowded jail.

He fiddled with the Walkman earbuds. "If you're going to talk with Evelyn about my future and Kylie's, I should be there."

Becky shot him a worried look. "I'm not going down to plan your future when I don't know mine." She took a deep breath. "Between losing the house and other surprises, my new mantra is take one day at a time."

She tried opening another drawer but it was in cahoots with the others. No matter how much she rocked it, the drawer refused to yield.

"Ah, forget about it!" Becky yelled and rounded up the papers on the floor and threw them in a green trash bag in the corner. Then she took a tissue out of her jeans and dabbed one eye.

Christopher noticed how pale and tired she looked. "My mother taught me how to make a world-famous chicken noodle soup and I'll never forget the recipe. Pour the contents of the can into a pot and stir . . . Oh yeah, turn on the stove too. Can I make you some?" He tried to keep a straight face.

She smiled and gave him a quick hug. "You've come a long way, my dear, and I know you're getting better every day. Evelyn and I just want to be faithful to the promise we made to your folks should anything happen to them, never imagining any of this. Try and remember that when you're feeling frustrated. Write it down in your notebook if it helps and we can talk about it when I get back." She stuffed the tissue back into her pocket. "We never know what's around the next bend in the road, do we?" She nodded. "Thank God for that."

"Very true. But my parents would want Kylie and me together, not separated like this. You and Evelyn should write that down to remember too."

"Touché." She went back to the kitchen and returned with a can of cooking spray, unable to concede defeat. "While I'm away, take the time to make more memories with your cousin."

"More? I'm trying to forget the ones I have," he whispered to himself.

Becky applied a long spray into one crevice of the drawer. "I don't have time for this nonsense," she said, with her voice rising. She pulled the drawer hard and it suddenly gave way and tilted precariously toward the floor.

"How about I stay in my house while you're gone, or did Evelyn get rid of my bed too?"

The drawer slipped out of Becky's hand and crashed on the wooden floor with a thud. Multiple envelopes carrying eagle insignias with blue block lettering in the left corner surrounded her.

No wonder Aram couldn't forget the war; the Army wouldn't let him. Wonder if they sprinkled the word "regretfully" in each correspondence too, he thought.

Becky began scooping up the envelopes. "All you ever talk about is Kylie, but honestly, AJ has been like a brother to you."

Christopher drove his fingernails into his palms. "Seriously?"

"He saved you from drowning twice, didn't he?" she asked, throwing the pile of envelopes in the drawer. The pale face became flushed. "Plus, he never hammered you for taking his car for a joy ride before the ice broke." She shrugged. "You should never forget what he did."

"No . . . I . . . won't . . . forget," he stammered, "or you begging me not to say anything about his fight with Bobby. I can't get the image of a tire iron out of my mind."

She slashed the air with her hand. "Just shut up!" The tone was strong and she sat back on her heels and rubbed her forehead. The silence lengthened and she finally looked up at him. "Christopher, we've talked about this over and over," his aunt said in a tired half whisper. "I don't have it in me to go through it again. Just remember things can get really mixed up when you nearly drown. What you think you saw and what happened are different." She reached up and grabbed his hand. "Do yourself a favor and leave that awful night where it belongs, at the bottom of World End." She kissed the back of his hand. "Now help me with this drawer before I chuck it in the wood stove."

Later that afternoon, Christopher peered through the plastic sheathing on the front window and watched AJ pull into the driveway in a beat-up black Chevy Blazer.

His heard his aunt come up behind him, carrying the duffel bag he arrived with a year ago. It looked like it belonged to someone else now. "I put all your prescription bottles in a plastic bag," she said extra slow, betraying her earlier comment that he was improving. "I also put in a reminder not to take the blue pills on an empty stomach."

He smiled and took the duffel bag from her. Becky followed him outside in the freezing cold without a coat. When he turned to say goodbye, her eyes filled with tears.

"You better get in quick before you catch a cold. If you fly with one, your ears will explode."

"Good to know." Her bottom lip quivered.

Christopher rocked side to side trying to find a comfortable place he never could quite locate. "I thought about what you said. I know Evelyn thinks she's doing what's best, but it still doesn't make it right."

AJ revved the engine of the Chevy. Blue smoke poured out of the tail pipe and the motor made a loud rapping noise. "C'mon, man, let's go!" his cousin yelled. "I have to buy a case of STP to quiet these lifters."

She frowned and looked at the smoke camouflaging the snow and broken pavement. "Yeah, but it's complicated."

He grabbed her hand. "No, it isn't. I may never get back to who I was, but I have more than enough heart to take care of Kylie. We need to be together."

Becky looked at him differently, like she finally understood.

"My mom knew the hand you were dealt. She said you had to stuff ten pounds of poop in a five-pound bag, but never complained. I appreciate everything you've done for me, and I'll never have to write that down to remember."

The Chevy backfired and AJ let out a string of cuss words. Becky kissed him on the cheek and hugged him tightly.

"My son promised to keep me updated and make sure you're taking your meds," Becky said, backing up a step and looking him in the eye. "Maybe he'll toughen you up a bit after all my mothering over the past year." She glanced at the Chevy. "Do me a favor and work on smoothing out his rough edges. I know under all that bravado, there's still an insecure little boy looking for love."

Christopher quickly hugged his aunt and waited until she went inside before making his way over to the Blazer. He opened the squeaky passenger door and peered in.

"I bet my father had a quicker goodbye when he left for "'Nam," AJ teased. "Now hurry up and get your butt in here. My life doesn't revolve around you, believe it or not."

The oil-rich exhaust made Christopher want to gag. "You can take off. I'm not driving with you."

AJ screwed up his face like someone sucker-punched him. "What did you say?"

Christopher adjusted the duffel bag on his shoulder. "Yeah, you may have gotten your license back, but I'll never ride with you again. I'll walk or thumb a ride over to your place."

"Suit yourself, Spongey." AJ threw the truck in reverse and peeled out.

He held his breath to escape the fumes and made it to the end of the driveway before Becky yelled from the front door.

"Christopher! Where did you hide my suitcase?"

CHAPTER FIFTEEN

The two-story cement block building sat adjacent to Pine Acres Village, a manufactured home community which doubled in size over the past ten years given the rise in starter home prices. Two large garage stalls consumed the first floor, which once housed the maintenance equipment for the community before the work was outsourced. Jason made a low-ball offer on the building, which was surprisingly accepted. Then he quickly converted the second-floor loft into a small apartment with AJ as the first tenant. Christopher looked up at three small prison-like windows on the second floor. *Cement and glass are made from the same materials, just mixed and heated differently*, he remembered from chemistry class, why he couldn't fathom, but it described him and AJ perfectly.

"Well, if it isn't the Chris-meister," a high-pitched voice squealed, as he opened the door after climbing a steep set of stairs.

Christopher pictured AJ sporting a plaid sports coat and a nasty comb-over in a few years. Until then, if he wanted to come off sounding cool, he should meet the British chap who hung around Dunkin' Donuts on Route 28. If you bought him a cup of coffee, he would tell you the gruesome story how he lost a leg in the Falklands. Add a vanilla cream–filled donut and the vet would show you his stump. *Now that was cool.*

He followed the sound of race cars to a powder-blue couch with dark stains on the skirt. A badly scratched coffee table sat on what appeared to be green outdoor carpeting. AJ sat sprawled sideways on a tan leather recliner in front of a small television watching a NASCAR race.

AJ turned the volume down with the remote. "How long did it take for your legs to insult what's left of your brain about that hike?" He let out a short snort. "You better hope your settlement from the crash comes mighty soon so you can hire a personal driver." He glanced at Christopher's sneakers and shook his head. "In the meantime, cuz, I'll get on my soapbox again and recommend a good pair of insulated boots." He picked up a *Playboy* mug from a side table and took a drink.

Christopher looked around at the rough apartment with its unpainted sheetrock and plywood floors. The tiny kitchen was a few feet away and featured the same GE refrigerator his late grandmother complained about being old ten years ago. A hotplate sat next to the sink. He looked toward the dark hall and realized his aunt never said how many bedrooms AJ had and wondered where he would be hibernating until she returned. His cousin didn't roll out the welcome wagon, so he sat down on the couch and half watched the race, with its soundtrack of nervous bees. Electrical zaps started high-jumping across his scalp.

"Speaking of hikes, I saw you walking with Mary yesterday," AJ finally said, and reached for a metal ashtray next to the mug. "She wouldn't be too bad on the eyes after a few beers." He smirked. "Well, maybe a twelve-pack to get past what's missing between the ears."

Christopher felt one zap explore a new path down the back of his head and he shivered. "Why do you say things like that? She's smart and beautiful."

AJ smirked. "Well, I guess from your damaged perspective the bar is set pretty low. I bet you think Jabba the Hutt is mighty handsome too."

"Though I can see why you were looking at Mary," Christopher added, watching a yellow car pass the leader. "She has the same smile as Lori, don't you think?"

His cousin reached for a Budweiser can sitting next to the *Playboy* mug and shook it to see if it was empty. "Looks like the bank will finally get its way and kick my old lady to the curb."

Sure, change the subject, Christopher thought, searching his coat pocket for the headphones. "Your mom has a milk jug full of quarters she saved up over ten years hoping to take your father on a Caribbean cruise. When she tried to give it to the bank to apply it against the mortgage, they said it was too late. Then they offered to take it off her hands for a ten percent fee because it wasn't rolled."

AJ pushed the recliner back too fast and his feet catapulted skyward. "That's rubbish. I bet it's all pennies and leftover BBs. Either way, there's no rabbits to pull out of the hat this time because anything of value was pawned years ago."

"That's unfortunate."

"Unfortunate?" He reached down to adjust a dime-sized hole in the toe of one sock. "Unfortunate is when you lose five bucks at lunch playing cards or when you run out of smokes and the corner store is closed." He shook his head. "I can't wait to share that nugget with her."

Christopher pulled out his notebook and flipped back two dozen pages. "According to my notes, you haven't talked much to your mom since Thanksgiving when you took off before dinner." He held up the page for him to see. "Look at the funny picture I drew of the twenty-pound bird the food pantry gave us. We saved a drumstick for you, but after a week your mom laughed and said it was foul." He patted his stomach. "Man, I love turkey."

"Yeah, you and turkeys have a lot in common; like goiters and pea brains. The more you talk, the better I understand why my old lady decided to spend time with her bossy sister. How lucky am I that she dumped you here?"

Christopher unzipped his coat and felt for the medal under his shirt, not knowing how long he could continue sparring like this as the concentration required was exhausting. "She's going to help me get things figured out. Evelyn will listen to her."

AJ threw the empty beer can at him and it grazed his shoulder. "Are you so preoccupied with your sad little world of tea bags and half-wit girlfriends, you haven't noticed how bad your aunt looks?"

The feeling in his stomach felt like he flunked an exam. "Of course I have. I live with her. She gets bad headaches and looks tired a lot. Now she's fighting a cold."

"Well, aren't you perceptive! All I know is you better hope those southern doctors can fix what's ailing her." He pulled on his lower lip and went silent for a moment. "I don't know what magic bullet they have in Clearwater that she can't find in Boston. Maybe her stint at Mystery Hill told her where to look in Florida for the fountain of youth."

He felt sweaty and took off his coat. "You make her sound like she's halfway to dead."

"Well, humans are just like machines and wear out, or in your case, short-circuit." AJ fished the *TV Guide* from the side pocket in the recliner. "I was flipping through the channels the other night and came across hip replacement surgery. The doctors drilled and hammered and used small titanium screws like you find at a body shop. When they were done, they counted all the bloody gauze pads to make sure they didn't leave any inside the poor slob. Then they sewed him up, which in my humble opinion, I could have done a much better job." He let out a short laugh. "I have some purple leather downstairs and imagined sewing in a piece with the stitches just to mess with his head."

Christopher looked away, imagining his cousin sewing up his mouth like he threatened. Suddenly the *TV Guide* hit him in the head.

"Why do I try explaining these things to you? I can tell by the look on your face that you've been transported to *Lost in Space*." He leaned forward. "*Danger, Will Robinson.*" He sat back and took another sip from the mug. "Okay, I'll talk real slow now and feel free to take notes if you like. Your aunt has a major women's health issue that should have been detected years ago. But she was such a stickler for embracing 'through sickness and health,' she ignored the signs."

The terrible news about Becky was momentarily masked by the continued digs. "Are we talking about your father again?" he asked, making sure to say it even slower.

"Wow, look at you trying to be clever. Keep it up and you can sleep downstairs in the garage tonight. I'm just saying if my old lady hadn't beaten her brains in taking care of *him*, she wouldn't have let herself go. You may be waterlogged from nearly drowning in a puddle, but he was nothing but a sniveling crybaby. I watched my mother rub his back for hours trying to calm him down after a thunderstorm, and when that didn't work, he would double-up on the meds and sleep to make the bogeyman go away. I grew up watching one train wreck after another. If you ask me, my mother should have changed her name to "Glad-less.""

"Well, thank goodness you were there for her to lean on—except when you weren't, which listening to her after you stormed out on Thanksgiving, was most of the time."

A tense silence descended and Christopher slipped on his headphones and flipped the pages in his notebook back to November. Becky had recounted how she felt haunted when Aram went missing. After searching for three days, the police found him a quarter mile away in a section of woods behind Shepard Avenue nicknamed "Witches Town." The shoelaces on his work boots were connected with peculiar knots so he could barely stagger, never mind walk. He went off the path and fell down an embankment, fracturing his skull on a boulder. AJ was nowhere to be found and when he finally came home later that day, acted blasé after hearing the news.

The ceasefire ended abruptly when AJ catapulted out of the recliner and ripped the wires out of his ears. "Typical Glad-less, using me as a decoy to keep from telling you what's really going on because she thinks you're too fragile. Fragile as a rock, if you ask me. Look. All I wanted for the third Thanksgiving since he croaked was a quiet meal and to watch some football." He looked up at the ceiling. "That would be heaven compared with the years of trying to track him down after he wandered off. Man, I was even willing to say grace and give thanks for a little peace. But she couldn't let it be for one day. No, she served up the foreclosure news like an appetizer before I cracked my first beer. Then before I could upgrade to something stronger, she sucker-punched me about her health."

AJ retreated to the chair and they sat in silence again for a while. Christopher passed the minutes wondering if Mr. Godfreye would let him work more hours so he could save up for a one-way bus ticket to Florida.

"Did you catch my classy lady's ad in the *Tribune*?" AJ asked, changing topics.

Christopher and Mary saw the advertisement and laughed at the cartoon of voluptuous automobiles decked out in tailored leather dresses of different colors. But he hesitated answering as the conversation felt more like playing checkers where a king can jump around the board diagonally and he couldn't predict AJ's next move.

AJ waved him off. "What am I asking you for? You don't read anything other than the comics and probably *Dear Abby* to see how you can get to first base with forget-me-not."

His right eye twitched. "I saw the ad."

AJ's head made a chicken-like movement and he flashed a brief look of surprise. "Well, if it caught the attention of the likes of you, maybe I'm really onto something. Jason showed me some promotions he ran for the salvage yard and helped with the design. The trick is to get people's attention before they turn the page and it's critical to place it in the right section of the paper. So, I dressed up the cars to look like hot babes and ran it between the sports and automobile sections. If I get a good response and business takes off, I may run a few on billboards, though I'd probably need extra insurance when guys drive off the road."

"Do you really think all men are wired that way?"

"Of course not and you're a prime example. But speaking for most—"

"Mary saw it too and thought you should dress up the cars in leather coats and use all the cool characters from *Grease*," he said, interrupting. "I thought it was a great idea. It would target both men and women interested in getting their cars reupholstered."

AJ waved him off. "Is that the college dropout talking or the special needs guy that sweeps the floor and stocks shelves at Godfreye's? Like you and your airhead girlfriend know something about anything! Give me a break." He grunted and climbed out of the recliner and sauntered over to the small refrigerator and took a quick inventory of its contents: a small bottle of ketchup and jar of dill spear pickles. AJ slammed the door shut like Mary did at Godfreye's, except these hinges didn't protest.

Tropical music replaced the noise of racing cars and Christopher immersed himself in a lush TV commercial for Puerto Rico. As the female announcer seductively described San Juan as a slice of paradise, he looked around the sparse apartment and thought this might qualify as the entrance to hell.

AJ returned without offering him an exotic appetizer of ketchup on a dill spear. He plopped down in the recliner again and pointed a stubby finger at him. "Okay, here's the deal, cuz. I'm not gonna be your mamma making sure you take your meds or get three squares a day. If you're concerned about tracking what pill you popped last, my advice is make a note in that book you carry around like some medieval scribe. As far as cooking goes, if you can turn on the hot plate and boil water, you're good to go."

The stark green fibers on the weird outdoor carpeting caught his attention and he thought it might be fun to cut it with a lawnmower and see what happened.

AJ snapped his fingers to get his attention. "This is what I mean, Chrissy. You can't be staying here looking like a goober staring at the floor all the time. You'll scare off potential clients."

His cousin's words raced through his ears as if the continuing insults had blasted a tunnel through the mental thicket. He looked around at the impoverished setting. "What customers come up here? You work full-time at the salvage yard pulling parts off cars. Don't you fix car seats in your spare time down in the garage?"

"Ah, but this is where I do my best work," he replied, pointing at the couch. "Sometimes we talk about upholstery too."

Christopher pushed himself to the edge of the couch, feeling contaminated and wanting to take a shower.

AJ watched him. "Better get comfy since that couch also doubles as your bed six nights a week." He reached in his shirt pocket and took out a pack of Marlboros. "The gist of this little orientation is to make you understand this ain't no free ride." He lit a cigarette and took a long drag. "I'm curious why my old lady hasn't been able to tap any of your parents' money, but I'm gonna make you sign an IOU so you pay me back rent when you do get that big fat check from the airline." He stuck out his tongue and fished out a piece of tobacco with his finger. "Come to think of it, you also owe me a new car after what you did to the Firebird." He stabbed the air with his wet finger. "Until then, you're the maid around here and I expect this place spic-and-span." He climbed out of the recliner and walked over to a small rectangular mirror on the wall. "You can also vacuum the cars after I finish a job." He held the cigarette between his teeth and squeezed one nostril with two fingers to extract a blackhead.

Christopher looked away.

"Like I said, you can sleep here six nights a week. On Saturdays, you're going to have to stay somewhere else because it's date night."

"Where am I supposed to go?" he asked, opening his arms wide.

His cousin turned around. Blood seeped out of a small crater on his nose and smoke drifted out both nostrils. "That's your issue.

Maybe you should think of picking up a midnight shift at Denny's. I'm sure a college boy like you would excel at dishwashing."

"I could sleep in one of the cars in the garage," he said, thinking out loud.

"No way and stop trying to lay a guilt trip on me," AJ spit back. "Like I said, Saturday nights you're on your own. So wipe that sorry look off your face and suck it up for once." He stepped forward and held up a clenched fist. "Mention any of this to my old lady, and you'll be sleeping with the feral cats the rest of the week too."

Christopher swallowed hard.

AJ wiped the pooling blood on his nose and stretched out his arms wide. "Welcome to the party, cuz!"

CHAPTER SIXTEEN

Graphite clouds sprinted across the sky on Saturday morning as the temperatures plummeted and the winds picked up to deliver another barrage of snow.

The second Yankee Clipper of the week mesmerized Christopher as he watched the competing Boston television stations and their baker's dozen of meteorologists which Mother Nature regularly took pleasure mocking. He and his dad were especially keen on following "Storming Stan." A few summers back, Stan warned an approaching hurricane would have the impact of three Hiroshimas when it hit New England. Consequently, his dad diligently boarded up all the windows and bought enough rations for a month. When the storm drifted out to sea and the big bang reduced to a cap gun, his father sent Stan an invoice.

By early evening no one needed a weatherman, or the gift of prophecy, to look out the window and see the storm owned the night. Christopher hadn't rooted for a snowstorm since high school, but after eight inches fell, he felt confident AJ's evening of debauchery would be cancelled. He turned up the volume on the television so his cousin and half of Salem could hear the dire warnings about road conditions. Much to his chagrin, AJ sauntered out of his bedroom, looked out the window, and shrugged. Then he began his pre-game ritual by showering in some funky cologne and chugging a couple beers.

Shaking his head, Christopher slipped on his winter coat and walked slowly toward the door, feeling like an astronaut preparing for an eight-hour spacewalk with only enough oxygen for two.

"Hey, Sponge Man," AJ called after him.

Christopher turned around, hoping for a last-minute reprieve from the twisted judge. There was still time to inhale a box of macaroni and cheese and find a good monster movie on TV.

"Before I'm off as fast as a prom dress," his cousin said with a dirty laugh, "you better make a note that I don't want to see your chubby shadow until after ten tomorrow morning." He gave him a solemn salute before draining another beer.

Christopher stepped outside on the second-floor landing and though a bitter wind assaulted his face, he preferred it to the blowhard inside. At the end of the driveway, he stopped to watch the snowflakes fly overhead past the lone streetlight, and realized how few are ever counted before they join those that came before. He crouched over to protect his notebook from getting wet and made a note about what time to return tomorrow and reread the fascinating factoid he stumbled across at Kelley library last week.

Over 105 billion people have lived on earth.

Yet, he was haunted by the death of one and the whereabouts of another.

"Now what?" he complained, closing the notebook and scanning the empty street. He considered walking a couple miles to the 400 Club in Methuen to have a beer and stay warm for a few hours, but that came with risks too. Chances were good his cousin would show up and begin trolling for lonely hearts and he'd rather risk frostbite than watch that one-act play.

"Any port in a storm might sum things up for AJ, but when you're trudging around in sneakers in a snowstorm, 'Gimme Shelter' is my new theme song," he mumbled.

A couple hours later, his extremities were numb and his ears ached as the dilapidated soon-to-be-foreclosed ranch came into view. Lumbering through knee-deep snow to the back of the house, he concluded the genius who defined snow in the Cambridge Dictionary as *"the small, soft, white pieces that sometimes fall from the sky when it is cold,"* must live close to the equator and should be sentenced to spend a January in New England.

After carefully brushing off a muffin top of snow on the tarnished brass lamp next to the cellar door, he felt for the spare key his aunt *always* kept there for emergencies.

Except tonight.

He moved on and visited three basement windows, but found each one securely locked. At the last one, a desperate voice in his head demanded he break it, but all the rocks were hidden under "the small, soft, white pieces that sometimes fall from the sky when it is cold."

Where's Ted or Ray when I need them? he thought.

The wind assaulted his face to punctuate the stupidity of the plan. He tried humming "Gonna Fly Now" to keep from losing all hope, but his teeth were chattering too much to get out more than a couple notes.

Only one option remained before total panic set in, and he began snow-swimming across the yard. By the time he reached the street, his legs would hardly move and he took baby steps toward a gray house a stone's throw away.

The doorbell felt frozen so he knocked on the storm door with his fist. The house remained dark and a new round of zaps in the back of his head proved no amount of cold would freeze the withdrawal symptoms.

He pounded again, but with enough emphasis to make the door rattle.

Seconds later, he heard movement and the front lights came on which made him squint.

The black painted door flew open and Sergeant Mike stared at him like he was Frosty the Snowman, minus the black hat and corncob pipe. "What the blazes are you doing here?" he asked, opening the storm door a couple inches.

Christopher never imagined finding the career cop wearing a short silky white robe that would make Hugh Hefner blush. "I . . . forgot . . . something," he stammered, through chattering teeth. "Did my aunt give you a spare key?"

The sergeant's porcupine head swiveled to look up and down the street. "Where's AJ? Is he stuck in the snow?"

He shook his head no.

The sergeant cocked his head like a rooster, which he had a habit of doing whenever surprised, which wasn't often. "Does he know you're out wandering in the middle of a blizzard?"

"Yes, and technically it's a Yankee Clipper." He continued shivering uncontrollably and thinking, *This feels like the flu without the fever.*

"AJ should be locked up for negligence!" He hesitated for a moment and then opened the door wide. "Hurry up and get in here so I can call your cousin and melt the ice between his ears."

Christopher turned around and went down one stair.

"Where are you going?" the sergeant barked.

"Never mind. I'll stay somewhere else," he replied, over his shoulder.

The sergeant stepped out on the top landing in his bare feet and grabbed him by the arm. "What do you mean? You told me you forgot something."

No wonder the crooks crack under his interrogation. He looked at the cop's sallow feet standing in the snow, impressed with the ex-marine's ability to withstand discomfort. Maybe the truth would set him free. "Saturday is date night so I have to find another place to stay. If it were summer, it would be no big deal. But in this weather, I decided to stay at my aunt's tonight."

A confused look came over the sergeant's face before his eyebrows spiked. "Now I've heard everything!" He looked up the street toward his aunt's house. "Well, you can't stay there or you'll freeze into a Popsicle by morning." A gust of wind whipped up the snow and the skimpy robe. "And I'm halfway there already. Get your butt in my house."

Christopher didn't want to anger a friend, although it would be neat to see how long he could tough it out dressed like that.

Sergeant Mike retrieved a green bath towel and spread it out in the hall for him to stand on. Then he disappeared and returned a moment later wearing blue jeans and a gray sweatshirt. He handed him a regular-length white terry-cloth robe and Christopher jettisoned the snow-caked clothes and sneakers.

When he was done, the sergeant led him to the kitchen and pointed to the oak kitchen set. *Another day, another interrogation,* he thought.

"I have a good mind to call your aunt, except she doesn't need this garbage right now," his lifeline barked.

Christopher sat down and studied his angry red toes pulsating on the blue-speckled linoleum floor. "AJ told me she's sick." He looked up. "You knew, didn't you?"

The policeman grunted and walked over to a maple cabinet. Christopher looked around the kitchen, surprised by the lack of pictures or knickknacks that might provide additional insight into his neighbor. The empty white Formica countertops continued the minimalist theme. The only items of interest were two deadbolt locks on the cellar door.

The microwave chimed and Sergeant Mike retrieved a steaming mug and added a heaping teaspoon of Sanka instant coffee before placing it in front of him. The coffee smelled strong enough to fuel a jet plane or melt a wide swath of snow. He remembered the idea about defroster wires in the sidewalks. Maybe his brew was a better option.

The sergeant retrieved an insulated silver cup from the fridge and sat down in the chair opposite him. "You can bunk here tonight."

Christopher noticed a half dozen grounds floating on the surface of the coffee and spun the mug in his hands trying to clear a patch. The little aggregates anticipated this classic move and raced to plug the gap. Thinking maybe some milk would help, he glanced over at the two-door refrigerator, which seemed generously oversized for a family of one.

"I'll have a chat with AJ in the morning," the sergeant continued.

The image of Sergeant Mike opening the door in his short robe popped back in his mind. His neighbor looked like a funny character from a *Saturday Night Live* skit.

"Did you hear me?" the sergeant asked.

"Please don't," he said, working to suppress a laugh. "If you give AJ any grief, he'll think I ran over here to get him into trouble. That will only cause big problems for me." His cousin wielding a huge needle and thread replaced the image of a funny-looking cop.

"So that makes this okay?" The cop pounded on the table and a few drops of the instant coffee jumped out of the mug onto the highly glossed surface. Christopher examined the spill and noticed it was free of coffee grounds and wondered how they escaped this too. *Survival of the fittest?*

The sergeant jumped up and returned with a paper towel. "AJ left you in quite a jam tonight. Why would you let him get away with that?"

Christopher pictured a mummy with its lips stitched tight and took a sip of the coffee. The grounds took their revenge by locking arms and gluing themselves to the back of his tongue. He fought the urge to gag.

His neighbor looked him straight in the eye and Christopher noticed how glassy his eyes looked. "Don't go putting a halo on a guy that pulled you out of the water after getting you in the mess to begin with." He curled the paper towel into a tight ball and attempted a free throw into the sink ten feet away, which he easily hit.

"Then there's the mystery of his missing girlfriend, or as he loudly reminds everyone, his ex. If he treated her half as bad as he treats his mother and you, we should find her remains any day now."

The words sounded more bitter than the coffee. "I don't think he would hurt Lori."

He snorted. "Why? Because he had feelings for her? That makes the case even stronger, since she dumped him. The stats show the majority of people murdered know their killer. If you ask me he's nothing but an imposter."

"Imposter? I've known him my entire life."

Sergeant Mike shook his head. "There you go again toying with me, but hear me out. Last April, I went to see my brother in Chicago. It was a beautiful spring day and the sidewalks were full of people enjoying the sun during their lunch hour. All of a sudden, the pace slowed as the crowd flowed around a bearded hippie wearing nothing but a sandwich board. The sign said aliens had mastered the art of making identical copies of people and the country was being replaced by imposters."

The sergeant smiled and shook his head. "The guy was yelling that Bush and Quayle had already been replaced along with most of Congress and the only way to identify these humanoids was to watch for peculiar behavior. Given your predicament tonight, I think AJ fits the model, don't you?"

"Well, AJ may be a lot of things," Christopher began and then hesitated, not knowing whether to laugh or if the sergeant was serious. "But he's no ET phoning home to brag about reupholstering car seats and surviving on dill pickles with ketchup." He thought for a second. "Although he does wear some funky-smelling cologne."

Sergeant Mike nodded. "There you go. He's probably one of them. Cathy didn't change perfume, just her attitude. Everything seemed okay until I came home one night and she looked at me like a complete stranger." He snapped his fingers. "Poof! A week later she's shacked up with my partner. Maybe they got to him too."

Christopher slowly lifted his rear end off the chair to try and peek into the insulated cup. Given this odd conversation, something other than coffee was lighting up the sergeant. No wonder he could stand barefoot in the snow and not feel anything.

The cop noticed and winked before swallowing the rest. "After hearing about all my shortcomings from Cathy's lawyer, no alien will want me." He rubbed his hands together. "That's okay because I'm following the old adage *'Physician, heal thyself,'* with a little someone— uh, I mean something, to dull the pain. Know what I mean?"

"Not really."

"Good. Let's just say I've learned to take *it is what it is* and bend it into *it is what it was.*"

Christopher frowned, trying to understand the gibberish.

"It comes with some complications though."

"Such as?"

"Ah, wouldn't you like to know." He smoothed the sleeve of his sweatshirt and then pointed at him. "So how about you?"

"What about me?"

"Are you an imposter too?"

He shook his head. "No. That's why I always put my initials on my coat," he said quickly.

Sergeant Mike eyed him like a piece of key evidence. "I've interviewed enough people over the years to be a pretty good judge." He leaned in. "Sometimes, my boy, I think you're channeling Nellie Bly."

"Nellie who?"

"A journalist from the nineteenth century who faked being crazy to do an exposé on the awful conditions in a New York asylum."

Christopher felt his cheeks burn. "Did she almost drown too?" he asked extra slowly, thinking if they were embracing old saws, his would be *timing is everything*. It certainly summarized what transpired the night of the accident, and now tonight's sequence of events. If he had simply gone to the 400 Club first for a beer, and stayed clear of AJ, he could have bummed a ride to his aunt's house and wouldn't have been fighting hypothermia by the time he arrived. Then he would have had the patience to break into his aunt's house and look for the box of Cap'n Crunch left in the pantry.

The neighbor raked his chin with his thumb. "Nellie probably played dodgeball like you do too." He glanced at the digital clock on the white stove. "Okay, it's getting late and we can talk more about this in the morning. All I'm going to say is you have to get tougher with AJ or next time he may tell you to come back in a week. Then what will you do? Live in the woods?"

Christopher clenched his jaw. *AJ would never let me out of his sight for that long.*

"I hope someday you'll trust me enough to let me in on the story between you two. Whatever your hiding, it's going to end up eating you alive, if you keep it all in."

How about AJ's threat and Becky's plea? he thought. *Or the disconnected bits of vagueness after I fell through the ice? My dead father sitting next to me in the flooded car and Bobby helping me as AJ yelled. Then there's the repeating dreams of a tall woman with platinum blonde hair and dark eyes that keeps chasing me.* Sometimes he felt on the cusp of bringing all the wreckage back to the surface, but when he pulled too hard on the memories, the winch snapped and back down it sank.

"I would like to make you an offer," his neighbor continued.

He listened but watched as the water got darker . . . and colder.

Sergeant Mike put his large hand over his. "I know AJ's your cousin, but all kidding aside, I think he's wrapped up in what happened to that poor girl. I feel bad, because I think a lot of your aunt and the pain it may bring, but I feel worse for the Martins. Living with

AJ puts you in a unique position to help. If you see anything suspicious, please let me know and don't be afraid to snoop around a bit." He laughed. "Since you're wearing my favorite robe, you owe me."

He's trying to make me his deputy? he thought.

The sergeant inspected his coffee mug. "Don't you like my java?" He smelled the coffee and turned up his nose. "Guess I should read the directions."

Christopher smiled and decided to leave it at that.

The sergeant stood up. "Don't worry none. I'll be like fine sandpaper with AJ. But if he pulls one more stunt like he did tonight, he'll have to answer to me and I won't be as understanding as his mother."

Christopher nodded. "Fair enough."

"Okay, then the couch is yours." A concerned look flashed across his face. "How about your pills?"

Christopher smiled. "I took them before I left." It wasn't a lie as he took them into the bathroom and watched them take a couple spins around the toilet bowl before disappearing.

"Really?"

He nodded, wishing he'd kept a couple pills to help him be a better imposter.

CHAPTER SEVENTEEN

The aftermath of every winter storm belongs to a bevy of snowblowers with swirling steel teeth gluttonously devouring the white landscape like Pac-Man on steroids. This morning was no exception as Christopher awoke to an approaching roar.

He no sooner sat up on the couch when the front door flew open and the abominable snowman stuck his head in. Mother Nature had a wicked sense of humor and used the fresh wind to capture the snow discharged from the snowblower to sculpt the operator.

"You're something else," someone sounding like Sergeant Mike barked.

He looked at an empty box of Cap'n Crunch with enough orange crumbs on the hardwood floor to make finger-licking fried chicken if his neighbor had the rest of the ingredients. The scent of Pine-Sol hung in the air which his aunt used generously to mask the moldy smell which usually permeated the house.

The Yeti retreated back to the frozen desert and a minute later the sergeant entered through the back door. He shed the snow-encrusted gear in the mudroom and appeared with a scarlet nose and cheeks.

"Let me guess," he began, strolling into the room in thick white socks. "All my talk about aliens last night got you so frightened you decided to hide over here." He walked over and inspected the thermostat on the wall. "Listening to your aunt, I thought you came from good stock where your parents taught you about respect and manners." He twirled around and pointed at the floor. "For example, you don't see me tracking snow in here." He frowned at the cereal crumbs on the floor. "What I don't understand is why after rescuing you from hypothermia and making you a guest in my home, you would thank me like this?" He snaked a stark white handkerchief out of his dungarees and wiped his nose. "If you were so determined to stay over here, we could have discussed the best room to catch pneumonia in."

Christopher fiddled with the buttons on the cassette player. He woke up in the middle of the night, fleeing from that relentless woman again and afraid the ceiling might rain down like it did at the hospital. After tiptoeing into the hall to recover his things, he snuck out the back door after dealing with another set of double locks. This time he found his aunt left the bathroom window unlocked and he fashioned himself an Olympian in summoning the required strength to pull himself up and in.

"So what do you have to say for yourself?"

"I wanted to go back to my own house, but Billerica is too far," he replied to the cereal crumbs.

The sergeant assumed the classic trooper stance with arms folded. "C'mon, buddy, you can do better than that. The shift lieutenant owes me a favor and I can have him hook you up to the lie detector. I could use the opportunity and get answers to a whole list of questions."

Christopher shrugged, doubting they stocked enough sodium pentothal to get it out of him.

The sergeant glanced at the thermostat. "Lucky for you, your aunt keeps the temperature at fifty degrees to prevent the pipes from freezing." He headed to the back of the house and things got so quiet, Christopher thought he might have left.

"Okay, hurry up and get dressed," he finally barked. "I'd like to leave you here, but I made a promise to your aunt to look out for you. Talk about a tough assignment."

Christopher obeyed the order and escorted him and the snowblower down the street. He watched as the sergeant punched the entry code for his garage door, which on the Cape-style house was directly under the bedroom window. After putting the snowblower away, the sergeant said the cellar door leading upstairs was locked. Consequently, they used the front stairs and repeated last night's procedure of leaving coats and shoes in the hall, before proceeding back to the kitchen.

"Nowadays, I usually define breakfast as anything you can pour into a bowl," the sergeant confessed, opening a pantry closet.

Given the cop's macho world, Christopher expected a box of Wheaties to appear since it was the "breakfast of champions." Incredibly, the sergeant pulled out a small box of Raisin Bran instead.

Christopher inhaled a few handfuls of stale cereal before the sergeant brought over two steaming mugs of Sanka. Then he pretended to know how to scramble eggs. The non-stick frying pan proved to be as uncooperative as him, except it received a severe beating with a wooden spatula.

When Sergeant Mike placed two plates on the table, Christopher smiled to be polite.

"Want some pepper?" the proud cook asked.

"No thank you," he replied, thinking the eggs sufficiently peppered already. Upon closer inspection, however, he discovered what looked like tiny bits of Teflon flakes cemented to the yellow pebbles. The officer didn't seem to notice and hungrily attacked his portion.

"Not bad," he said, smiling, then looked toward the massive fridge. "Sorry I have no bacon." He held up his wrist and the silver medical alert bracelet. "And don't even think of asking for peanut butter. I have to be so careful when traveling. One whiff of a nut and I'm a mess."

Christopher noticed three black specks cemented on the sergeant's front tooth. "Have you ever seen *The Spy Who Loved Me*?"

"Sure. I like all the Bond movies."

"How about that character Jaws with his stainless steel teeth? Remember him?"

The sergeant smiled and the black specks seemed to glisten. "Yeah, he's unforgettable."

Christopher moved the pebbles around on his plate. He didn't want to be rude, but didn't think it was healthy to have his intestinal track mimic a non-stick pan. "Did you ever want to be a fireman?" he asked.

"No, why?"

"Just thinking of you making a breakfast like this for the guys at the station."

The sergeant poked his hand with his fork. "There you go again, trying to play me."

After breakfast, Christopher went to the sink and attacked the dirty dishes. His fears about the frying pan were confirmed as most of the Teflon was flaking off. The sergeant looked up from his newspaper every now and then and seemed pleased, except when Christopher headed to the refrigerator to put the butter away.

"Leave that on the counter," he said, sharply.

Christopher wanted to go the extra distance and make up for the comment about bad manners and began opening the refrigerator. The sergeant jumped out of his chair like he had Jimmy Hoffa on ice and wrestled the container away from him.

"I'm really particular how I arrange things in the fridge," he said with a nervous laugh. "I guess we all have a touch of OCD."

Christopher backed away and scanned the kitchen to see if there was anything else left to clean.

The policeman pursed his lips. "I'll be calling AJ and if he doesn't have a headache from binging on too many beers last night, he will when I'm through."

"Please go easy on him like you promised," he pleaded, but the sergeant's expression didn't change. "He goes out for brunch on Sundays," Christopher added, stretching the truth and hoping the additional time might cool things down.

When he was finally released from custody, there wasn't a cloud in the deep blue sky. Yesterday's storm added almost a foot of snow before ending with freezing rain. On the corner of Cole Street, he admired a huge willow tree encased in armor of crystal chainmail, bending toward the ground waiting to be knighted by the sun.

On the hike back to AJ's, he decided to stop by Godfreye's and buy one of those big sticky cinnamon buns. They came packaged in thick plastic wrapping which he enjoyed turning inside out and licking all the sugary goop from the crevices. It would make up for the weird breakfast.

When he reached the store, a red letter banner in the front plate glass window made him blink hard: *FIFTY MILLION $$$ TICKET SOLD HERE!!!*

Inside, a half dozen people huddled around knee-high piles of *The Boston Globe, Boston Herald, Eagle Tribune,* and *Union Leader.* Godfreye stood behind the counter wearing a crisp white button-down shirt, silk red tie, and black dress pants.

"Are you sure?" asked one sour-looking older man with a pointy nose and wearing a black Cossack fur hat.

All eyes turned toward the store owner, who accessorized his new threads with a smug smile. "Don't you believe everything you read in the papers?" He held up the front page of the *Eagle Tribune* and pointed to the headline usually reserved for bad or frightening news. *Newest Multi-Millionaire Minted in Salem.*

An elderly blue-haired woman pushed through the traffic jam and headed for the door.

"Hold on, Mrs. Tamock," the store owner called out loudly.

She turned around with a scowl.

"Are you going to buy that newspaper?" he asked in a serious tone. "Just because we make people's dreams come true doesn't mean we give away the merchandise now too." He struggled to keep a straight face, but his mouth betrayed him and a small chuckle escaped.

The woman blushed and started fishing in her black leather pocketbook.

"But today is your lucky day, Mabel. Other stores would have you on video and make the rest of your morning miserable, but we have a different philosophy. You forgave my son when he threw a baseball through your garage window, so keep the paper."

The woman placed a faded dollar bill on the counter and pointed a crooked finger at him. "I forgot to pay because I can't believe any winning ticket would ever come out of this menagerie of horrors." She looked over at a six-foot display of Valentine teddy bears tied to a metal pole. "Just another sign the apocalypse is near."

Snickers escaped from the other customers, but Godfreye looked unfazed. "Funny you should feel that way, Mabel. If I recall correctly, you bought twenty-five tickets from me." He pushed his lower lip out and gave her a sad puppy dog look. "I'm sorry you didn't win so you could buy me out like your hubby always wanted to do. God rest his soul."

The woman bolted for the door as a graying-at-the-temples middle-aged man wearing a dark blue suit entered the store clapping.

The store owner glanced at the *Farmer's Almanac* calendar hanging on a wall behind him. "Geez, I thought bank VPs didn't work on Sundays."

"Just stopping by to say congratulations to a dear friend."

Godfreye rolled his eyes. "Under the Blue laws, I can't sell beer until noon on Sundays. I think there should be a similar regulation about trying to close a sale before church is over too."

Everyone laughed and the banker shrugged. "You stand to make a nice commission for selling that winning ticket, Gene. How's that for straight talk?" He smiled broadly to show off his capped teeth.

The proprietor held up his right hand like a withered limb. "Not everything in here glows green," he moaned. "Do you have any idea how many tickets I've fed that insatiable machine? I'll probably use most of the commission on aspirin for my arthritic fingers and a good chiropractor for my back." He looked up at the stuffed rafters any hoarder would love. "Maybe I'll expand the inventory to include some grilling tools."

"I have one more question," the banker announced throwing a pack of Doublemint gum on the counter.

"Okay, I'll bite," Godfreye replied as he rang up the sale.

"Do you have the winning ticket too?" He pointed at the gum. "As the ad sings, that would *be double the pleasure.*"

The patrons froze like they did in the popular EF Hutton commercials.

The store owner chuckled. "If I did, do you think I would have gotten up at four-thirty this morning to make coffee for you peasants?"

"Sure you would, just to see us turn green with envy," the banker said, shaking Godfreye's hand then winking. "Lucky for you, green is my favorite color too. Tell you what. When the excitement dies down, let's chat about putting that commission money to work for you. I still have CDs paying nine percent interest."

"He's too smart for you, Olsen," a forty-something man, smelling like gasoline and wearing an oil-stained Phillips 66 hat, chimed in.

"Why?"

"Because he'll be calling *you* after he buys your crummy bank. Look how he's playing us," he said, pointing, "trading in his flannel shirt and jeans for those fancy threads."

The others laughed.

"But don't wait too long to come clean," the gas station man continued, "because we might ransack your house looking for the winning ticket hoping you haven't signed it yet."

Godfreye waved everyone off. "The truth will set you free when he or she comes forward. But don't forget they have up to a year before they have to claim the prize. I wouldn't be surprised if we don't know who it is for a bit. No doubt, the winner will seek some legal advice first. In the meantime, I'm just excited about the free advertising."

A few boos kicked up from the audience and the proprietor held up his hands to protest. "All the TV news stations will be here today and they'll be back again once the winner is announced." His gaze returned to the rafters. "The smart move would be to build on the lucky ambience of the store. I still have a few leprechaun dolls from last St. Patty's Day. I'm thinking maybe they should become permanent fixtures around the store now. That way, people will make this their new destination to buy tickets which will drive other impulse buys." He clapped his hands. "That, my dear friends, is like winning the lottery, except the payouts come over a lifetime."

Christopher had never heard the store owner so animated. As he reached for his wallet, his stomach sank when his fingers found nothing but cold denim. *"Christopher Maquire, you'd lose that head of yours if it wasn't connected to your neck,"* his mother used to say at least once a week. He considered buying a stainless steel chain to attach to his wallet to keep it from wandering away, but AJ and his ilk had the same appendage. Slipping on his earbuds, he used the silence to think whether he left the wallet on his aunt's couch or underneath the sergeant's kitchen table after nearly choking on breakfast.

Drawing a blank, he put the Walkman away and gazed at the winning numbers: 3-6-9-12-19-31. They didn't look familiar, but he recorded them in his notebook before grabbing a sticky bun and placing it on the counter.

"Good morning, Christopher," the store owner purred as he picked up the package and read the label. "I don't know what concoction of chemicals they put in these things so they don't expire for a year."

The comment made him think he should have ingested the Teflon after all. He placed two quarters face up on counter.

The owner's sunny disposition turned dark. "I told you last time they went up to seventy-five cents."

Christopher searched his pockets but came up empty. "I misplaced my wallet. Can I owe you?"

"What? Do you think I'm a bank now too?" Godfreye snapped. "I have a good mind to make you go home and get the other twenty-five cents." He waved the sticky bun at him. "It's not the money, my friend, it's the principle. I've seen this play out too often. Win a couple bucks and every Tom, Dick, and Harry have their hands in your pocket."

"But I don't know any of those guys," he said with a shrug and then waited, knowing the store owner's bark was worse than his bite.

Godfreye let out a short laugh. "Nothing like a polite beggar on a Sunday morning to remind me of the Golden Rule." He handed the package to him. "I'll put it on your tab, like I used to do for your uncle, God rest his soul. I suppose you'll want some hot water too?"

"Yes, please."

"So I'm a bank, convenience store, and restaurant, is that it?" he asked, with a twinkle in his eye while the corners of his mouth worked to suppress a smile. "If I remember right, I'm your employer too. Good grief, what have I gotten myself roped into?"

Christopher quickly retreated and made his way down the aisle to the counter holding all the self-service goodies. Selecting a large Styrofoam cup, he hesitated for a moment thinking how Denise surprised him here last, and he smiled realizing he didn't have to consult the notebook to remember. After filling the cup, he took a tea bag from his shirt pocket and using a thin wooden stirrer, drove it underwater every time it bobbed to the surface. As the water became cloudy, the stirrer suddenly morphed into a bloody tire iron punishing a bloated corpse.

The room began to spin as the zaps in his head exploded and a crushing tightness squeezed his chest. He let out a loud cry and grabbed for the counter and in the process knocked over the steaming cup. The tea bag rode the torrent like a barrel over Niagara Falls and hit the floor with a terrible plop.

Mr. Godfreye came rushing down the aisle, his cheeks red and puffy like a pressure cooker about to blow.

The dizziness remained and Christopher held onto the counter with one hand and grabbed a handful of napkins in the other to begin cleaning up the mess.

The store owner read his face and patted him on the back. "It's okay, Christopher. Tell me what happened?"

He wanted to but it would kill the kind man.

CHAPTER EIGHTEEN

Christopher knelt in the driveway and let the forty-pound black and white sheltie lick his face while he fished in his coat pocket for another dog biscuit, the only other staple beside tea bags he faithfully carried. He broke the biscuit into small pieces and watched the dog swallow each one whole and wait longingly for the next morsel.

"Mary is always telling me to stop and savor what I eat. Now I understand why." He looked up at the white colonial house and noticed a light come on in the living room. It was another reminder how short the days are in winter.

"So, Dawson, what's new?" he asked, patting the dog.

The sheltie licked his empty hand and then backed away and began barking at something down the street.

Christopher followed the dog's warning and caught sight of two wishbone legs leaning against a telephone pole a couple houses away. He hadn't seen Ted or Ray since they ruined the ice, and he hadn't been back to check on the rocks.

"Maybe I'll buy you a bone knuckle that resembles that jerk," he said, bending over to scratch the dog's ear. "Although, he'd probably taste like rotten eggs."

Dawson apparently didn't mind and jumped up and licked his face. Christopher laughed and tried to breathe through his mouth as the dog's breath smelled like the clam flats at low tide.

The sheltie sat down on the snow-covered driveway hoping for another treat, when a familiar voice cried out and he caught sight of Mary chasing Ted around a parked car.

At the same moment, the front door of the colonial opened and Dawson high-tailed it up the stairs as Christopher bolted down the street.

"Give me back my scarf!" he heard Mary yell.

"Not until you show me," Ted replied, holding the scarf high above his head.

She jumped trying to reach it, but missed. "I can't. I don't have it with me."

Ted spun around and produced a red plastic lighter from his coat pocket. "Then it's gonna go poof."

"Knock it off," Christopher yelled, arriving at the scene out of breath.

They both turned. Ted sneered while Mary looked relieved to have reinforcements.

"Why, isn't this just special?" Ted sang out, doing a pretty good impersonation of the church lady on *Saturday Night Live.* "Mr. Potato Head is here to rescue Miss Morbid Squash face. It may be January in New England, but I'm still surrounded by vegetables. Amazing!"

Rescue? Christopher gritted his teeth whenever he heard that word. Everyone around him used it to describe AJ's actions at World End.

"What do you want her to show you?" he asked, pushing World End back into the shadows while concentrating not to stutter.

Ted looked surprised anyone overheard their ruckus. "Mind your own business, Tater-tot." He glanced back at Mary. "She knows what I want." He rolled his thumb and the lighter came to life.

"Please!" Mary pleaded.

Christopher clenched his fists, trying to decide if it would be better to throw a punch or tackle him first. Either way, he wanted to see him lying horizontal and didn't care if it required taking everything this skinny Clubber Lang wannabe could dish out.

Ted dangled the scarf closer to the flame. "In ten seconds it will be gone, unless you give it to me."

Mary started to cry. "My mom made that for me."

Christopher decided to aim for the bony-whiskered jaw. "How about I buy it off you?" he asked quickly, cocking his right hand behind his back.

Ted extinguished the lighter and smiled like a grammar school bully shaking down third graders for their lunch money. "Why, that's the best idea you've ever had, Tater." He rubbed the scarf against his unshaven face. "Ah, virgin wool," he said, winking at Mary. He fiddled with the lighter, and the flame grew twice as high as before. "Twenty-five bucks for this limited time offer. Get it before it's gone!"

Out of habit, Christopher reached for his wallet; it remained AWOL, but he felt something else. A laughable idea surfaced and although a long shot, he decided to give it a try. If it failed, the ground attack would proceed.

He put his hand in his back pocket and ran his fingers along the crease of the folded paper. "I'm afraid I only have twenty dollars and it's my entire allowance for the week," he said in a sad drawl.

Ted moved the lighter north and let it scald a swatch of the scarf.

Mary started crying hysterically.

"Well, it's your lucky day," Ted said, extinguishing the lighter. "Because the merchandise is now damaged goods like its owner, it's being discounted down to twenty bucks." He held out his hand for payment.

Christopher took a half step back. "I'm . . . not . . . falling . . . for . . . your . . . stupid . . . tricks," he stuttered on purpose. "If I give you the money, you'll just burn the rest of it. Give it to Mary first, and then I'll pay you."

Ted glared at him. "Do you think this is some kind of ransom exchange like you see in the movies?" He threw the scarf in the air. "Air delivery to Morbid."

Mary jumped and caught it midair, then ran behind a black Caddy parked on the street. Christopher motioned for her to stay put. He knew how she hated the sight of blood. He did too, especially when most of it would be his.

"Now give me my money," Ted growled.

Christopher held out his left hand with the folded twenty and made a fist with the other if needed. His heart beat in his ears.

Ted grabbed the bill and stuffed it in his jeans pocket without looking and turned toward Mary.

"I haven't forgotten our discussion." The lighter came back to life. "If I find you're holding out on me, you won't be able to run fast enough before I burn you so good they'll call you Morbidly Crispy." He shot Christopher an ugly look and slithered away down the street.

When Ted disappeared from sight, Mary ran and hugged him tightly.

The wall inside of him was breached and he held her close. He shut his eyes and comforted her until she pulled away and examined the quarter-sized burn mark on the white scarf.

Christopher escorted her to another streetlight two blocks away, all the while expecting Ted to come running toward them with the lighter in blowtorch mode.

"Sorry you're out your allowance," she said.

He reached in his back pocket and handed her another twenty-dollar bill. "Here's one for you too, but before you get too excited, unfold it."

She complied and her eyes grew wide. "Twenty dollars off reupholstering?"

He sighed. "AJ had a bunch of these made up and I took a few for fun. When Ted figures it out, he's going to be pretty angry, unless he can use the coupon." He let out a nervous laugh.

Mary studied the small the portrait of AJ that replaced Andrew Jackson. "I can see why Lori liked your cousin. He is cute in a different sort of way. Maybe it's the eyes."

Christopher winced. "Five minutes ago, I risked my—" and swallowed the rest. "What does Ted think you're hiding anyways?"

"A ticket."

"To what?"

Mary reached in her coat pocket and took out a half dozen lottery forms. She studied each until she located one and handed it to him.

He studied the pencil marks in the six selected boxes and reached for his notebook to check.

Mary grabbed his arm. "I'll save you from straining your eyes. They match."

He started breathing faster. "I don't understand. We only bought one ticket."

"You bought one." She fished a wad of tissues out of her other pocket and quickly wiped her nose. "I bought a couple more when you were talking to your girlfriend," she added in a tone colder than the air.

"I didn't think you had any money. And as far as Denise is concerned, like I've said fifty times, I'm very sorry for not introducing you immediately. She just shocked me appearing like that. What we had is in the past. Now all that matters—"

She pointed at the lottery form to cut him off. "You don't believe me, do you?"

He bit his lip, not knowing what to say. She liked to sit in the magazine section of the library and fill out subscription forms for fun.

"You're just like my father," she shot back, reading the doubt. "He had a good laugh too when I told him. He asked me to buy him a new Corvette and didn't even ask to see the ticket. But I thought you were different. Funny, the only person who believes me is Ted."

"Yeah, so he could steal it from you."

She folded her arms. "Well, at least he treats me like I'm smart enough to win."

He thought about how he picked the numbers. Half were already filled in and the other half he closed his eyes to choose. "Given the odds, we're all dumb to play."

She began to walk away. "Maybe I won't show you the ticket either. I'll just keep all the money for myself and buy a house next to Michael Jackson."

He caught up to her and took her hand. "Of course I believe you, Mary," he said with as much enthusiasm as he could muster.

"No you don't."

"Sure I do, because I need to borrow twenty dollars before Ted kills me."

CHAPTER NINETEEN

The beige push-button desk phone began ringing from its precarious perch on the arm of the recliner and Christopher heard his aunt saying hello as he spun the receiver in mad circles trying to untangle another AJ mess.

"Christopher, are you there?" Becky called out, sounding annoyed.

That's the same question I ask myself every day, he thought. "Hold on," he called out, before realizing this version of Rubik's Cube might take a while to figure out. Giving up, he sat on the edge of the recliner and placed the base of the telephone on his lap so the pretzel-like cord would reach his ear. "I'm sorry—"

"Let me guess, the phone cord is all bunched up again," she said, finishing his sentence. "AJ ruined mine too with all his pacing." She let out a heavy sigh. "If you ask me, it's cruel and unusual punishment for my son to still be considered a person of interest after he passed the polygraph test, never mind all the interviews. I hate to indict the deceased, but they should look deeper into Bobby's relationship with Lori."

All this because of a twisted cord line? It seemed no matter the topic, the conversation always came back to the persecution of her son.

"You're awfully quiet," she continued. "Are you still there?"

"Yes, I hear you fine," he replied quickly. The last two phone calls had been awkward too, her voice sounding distant like they were talking into soup cans connected by a string fourteen hundred miles long. Each time, Becky had asked a few questions and made trivial chitchat until the first pause, and then quickly offloaded the phone to Kylie.

"I'm sorry," Becky added, reading his thoughts. "I shouldn't call and begin venting right after saying hello."

"That's okay. So what's new?" he asked from the worn script.

"Well, the newspapers down here sure keep themselves busy telling all the snowbirds about every snowflake they've been saved from. Though Eden has its own problems too. Last week, we had a killer frost and ironically the best defense farmers have is to give the orange trees a cold shower and insulate the young fruit in ice."

"That doesn't make them go soft?" *A similar experience at World End certainly failed me*, he thought.

His aunt either missed the correlation or didn't let on. "Who knows? Guess we'll just have to watch the price of orange juice." She struggled through a hacking cough. "Excuse me," she whispered hoarsely, when it subsided. "I also heard about the winning lottery ticket purchased at . . . ugh, I can't even say the store's name given what I just said about his son." The line went quiet for a moment. "I hope the father can milk it for all it's worth."

He nodded and studied the buttons on the phone. Like everything else in the apartment, it needed a good scrubbing.

"Any news on who won?"

He pictured Mary's pocketbook stuffed with lottery forms. "There's been some rumors, but nothing yet."

"Anyone I know?"

He frowned, not knowing how to answer.

His aunt didn't wait. "Are you taking your medication and eating well?"

"Well, I wash the pills down with a lot of water and I'm eating like a horse." The meds were in the wastewater treatment plant by now and he ate a lot of grains: Honey Bunches of Oats, Chex, Cheerios, Lucky Charms.

"And AJ? Things tolerable with him?"

Can you make the first two letters silent when pronouncing intolerable? "Well, we do our own thing on weekends," he replied, quickly wanting to reverse the focus. "And you? How are you doing?"

"It's nice to feel the warmth of the sun, but my eyes are really enjoying soaking up all the green. Winter landscapes are beautiful, but I miss living colors."

Christopher wished he could crawl through the phone line because they always said more with their eyes than with words. "Have you had a chance to talk with Evelyn yet about me and Kylie?"

A long pause followed. "There's someone here pulling on the cord that wants to talk with you."

"Becky, before you go—"

"Hey, big brother," a young voice sang out.

He smiled. "How's my favorite sister?"

The little girl laughed. "I'm your only sister, silly. Guess where we went yesterday?"

"From the sound of it, I would guess somewhere fun," although he hoped it was to a moving company to ship her stuff back home.

"Disney World. Auntie Evelyn and I had a blast on the rides."

"Did Aunt Becky go with you too?"

"No, she had an appointment, but met us for dinner. Then we went shopping and she bought some fancy scarves."

He felt for the St. Christopher medal and pressed it hard against his chest. *AJ was right, I missed all the signs.* "Did Auntie Evelyn call your school today?"

"Why? They don't have school here on weekends, though we do stay a half hour later than in Billerica."

He glanced through the kitchen window, which framed a stalactite-looking icicle. "So you started school down there, honey?" he asked, trying to control his voice.

"Yeah, and I've made so many new friends. When are you coming down to visit?"

"Even if I have to walk, very soon. Believe me." He bit a fleshy knob on the inside of his cheek and tasted salty blood.

"Well, you better leave now if you want to be here by summer," she laughed. He heard some murmuring in the background. "Auntie says I'm running up the long distance charges and have to go."

Christopher fingered the kinks in the cord and it felt like his stomach.

"Did you talk with Denise yet?" Kylie whispered, quickly.

"What?" Then he realized their conversation was being monitored. "Yes, and I won't let you down. I promise."

"Okay, love you bunches," she replied, and hung up.

He let the phone receiver bungee jump over the arm of the recliner and made a new entry in his notebook.

He was still writing when the windows began to shake with the noise of a colossal motor. Rushing to the window, he watched a mammoth yellow backhoe with leopard rust spots being positioned in the driveway. A vertical exhaust pipe spewed black smoke and he noticed a number of good-sized dents where the giant monster had battled earth.

The machine suddenly fell silent and the cabin door opened and Mary popped out, followed close behind by AJ.

He rubbed the dirty window pane to make sure the girl was indeed Mary and not one of Sergeant Mike's humanoid imposters. When she adjusted her white wool scarf, he had enough proof and bolted down the stairs without a coat.

"You're making me blush," Mary said in a giddy voice to AJ. Christopher followed them into the garage and they stood much too close for his liking.

He let out a fake cough. Mary's cheeks turned red when she saw him, but she didn't move away from his cousin.

"Did you hear Mister Testosterone?" AJ asked, pointing at the Caterpillar backhoe loader through the open garage door. "I picked it up real cheap. With a little elbow grease, I can turn a nice profit."

Christopher left them to walk out and meet the beast. On first inspection, he noticed a hairline crack running down the length of the windshield and a large dent in the front near the mud-encased treads. Peering inside the cab, he was amazed by an array of levers surrounding a badly torn black leather seat. Most of the yellow stuffing was missing.

"Your friend sat on my lap and I let her drive," AJ mentioned, coming up next to him.

He fought the urge to form a caricature of that ride in his imagination. "Well, I'm not washing and waxing this monster," he replied.

"Then you might not have lodging here next week." AJ turned and put his arm around Mary's shoulder.

Christopher stared at his cousin's arm and thought of multiple ways to amputate it. *A chain saw would do the job nicely, but that wouldn't be painful enough. Maybe a dull knife would be better? Whatever method, why is Mary letting him do that?*

AJ snapped his fingers. "Stuck in neutral again, cuz? It's too bad they can't replace that faulty transmission of yours." He smirked. "I heard about your lesson in gluttony last week."

He swallowed hard and glanced at Mary, and she intently began examining her scarf to avoid any eye contact. "I don't know what you're talking about," he said halfheartedly, knowing the weak defense would never hold.

"Well, I'm sure it's in your notebook under stupid tricks and gross eats. As your girlfriend tells the story, you lusted after a super-sized quart of chocolate milk because you were convinced the dairy overfilled it by mistake. I almost wet my pants hearing how you scraped together two bucks to buy the treasure, then hurried outside and took a huge gulp only to find out the bloated carton was rancid." He winked at Mary. "I'm sure watching a guy heave sour chocolate milk sure takes the romance out of things." He looked at Christopher. "Strike one," he whispered.

Mary kept her eyes on the scarf, but a small giggle escaped. "Mr. Godfreye almost dialed nine-one-one thinking he was having another seizure."

Christopher didn't need to reference his notes to relive the disgusting mistake. He blamed the store owner for not rotating the *real* perishables, instead of the crappy holiday merchandise he hawked constantly. Even after brushing his teeth ten times, he tasted sour chocolate curds for two days.

"So I guess the lesson is to smell before taking a sip." AJ leaned over and took a deep sniff of the back of Mary's hair, which she wore down today like a blonde goddess.

Christopher worked overtime to control his expression. "Mary, can I make you some tea?"

"I'm all set, thanks," she answered, finally looking embarrassed by AJ's actions. "Your cousin was a gracious host and made me a cup while I waited for you."

"Now, now, hon," AJ teased. "Don't go and give away all my secrets on how I charm the ladies."

Christopher breathed through his nose and his right leg began to twitch. *AJ never offered me even a cup of tap water, never mind tea. Did he find my stash of Bigelow or heat up some pickle juice?*

"Well, did she tell you she's moving to upstate New York?" he heard himself ask.

Mary's eyes grew twice as big. "Yeah, I hear it's a really nice place where friends believe in each other."

AJ clapped his hands. "Do I detect a spat?"

Christopher looked away and knew Mary would follow suit.

"I'll take that as a yes, and to be honest, I don't want to hear how Christopher messed up this time." AJ grabbed Mary's hand. "Tell you what. I'll drop by your new place after you move and you can show me around town. That will sure beat having to wait for a guy reeking of sour chocolate milk to arrive by Greyhound." He turned and looked at Christopher. "Takes the romance out of it, don't you think? Strike two."

Christopher felt the cold air weaving its way through every pore and he wanted to go upstairs and commune with the dust mites on the plywood floor. They had a lot in common; both had to gag on AJ's droppings.

AJ took Mary by the hand and walked back into the garage to an eight-foot workbench positioned against the wall. Christopher followed close behind.

"Some rich guy over on Somerset Drive wants me to replace the seats in his Jag," his cousin boasted. "Says he likes my work."

Christopher rocked side to side and started to chew even though he had no gum.

"That's great," Mary said, with too much enthusiasm.

"Yeah, it's been a banner week." He picked up a glue gun and turned toward her. "Hey, I have an idea. How about we go out and celebrate your upcoming move tomorrow night?"

She glanced quickly at Christopher. "Tomorrow night we always get Chinese food."

He smiled, thinking Mary realized she punished him enough. It felt like backing away from a high cliff with a multitude of bone-breaking boulders below.

"No, honey, you misunderstand me," AJ interjected. "Chrissy may be my first cousin, but we don't share dates. If he wants to come along, let him get his own chick." He slapped his head and winked at his cousin. "Hey, maybe you can call that girlfriend of yours, ah, what's her name? Oh, yeah, Denise. She seemed to fancy you until she had to watch you drool your applesauce in rehab." He let out a fake laugh. "After hearing about the spoiled chocolate milk caper, now I understand why." He paused and let a quizzical look overtake his face and turned to Mary "Did you meet Denise?"

Mary's cheeks turned red to match her lipstick.

Christopher felt flushed too and continued to wonder why AJ was tormenting him like this.

"She can't go out with you!" he blurted out.

AJ returned a look of feigned surprise and held up the glue gun like he about to shoot him. "I don't see a ring on her finger." He turned to Mary. "I'm not breaking up anything here, am I?"

She looked at Christopher, giving him an opportunity to confess his feelings, but he didn't realize there was only a couple seconds left on the clock.

"I would love to go out with you," she replied, with too much enthusiasm.

AJ pointed the gun at the ceiling. "Great, it's a date then."

"Your . . . father . . . doesn't . . . like . . . you . . . out . . . after . . . midnight," he stuttered. "Plus . . . he . . . blames . . . AJ . . . for—"

"Stop being a killjoy," AJ interrupted. "No wonder she's angry at you." He winked at Mary. "I'll pick you up at seven. Okay?"

She nodded. "My father and Anne are away this weekend so I can stay out pretty late," she said, shooting Christopher a dirty look.

"Great. Just make sure to wear something pretty. I always loved the clothes your sister wore. Why not borrow something from her?" He smiled and whispered something in her ear as he flashed three fingers behind his back.

"Strike three," Christopher mumbled.

CHAPTER TWENTY

Lying on the couch after feasting on ramen noodles and a peanut butter and marshmallow fluff sandwich for dinner, Christopher glanced at the television and watched an underwater camera scan the ocean floor for *National Geographic*. A pink coral reef came into view which reminded him of his present environment, where he constantly risked stepping on sharp, stony skeletons of the past. Without any meds, he considered holding his breath for dessert to see where his imagination would take him next.

Instead, he closed his eyes to find someplace happy and Mary's red cocktail dress elbowed its way to the front of his thoughts. After eloping, Mary's father and stepmother held an open house at Christmas and she invited him to stop by. He "borrowed" a blue dress shirt AJ left behind at his mother's. It was a size too big and he washed it three times to remove whatever funky cologne was infused in the fabric. When Mary opened the door with a mesmerizing smile and in a form-fitting dress accenting every curve, he dropped the holiday fruitcake he bought at the drugstore. They drank spiked vanilla eggnog in small crystal glasses and nibbled on water chestnuts wrapped in bacon. When everyone headed to the dining room for an Italian buffet, she held back and shyly asked him to slow dance next to an eight-foot Christmas tree bathed in white lights. By that point, the eggnog had mixed sufficiently with the meds to tamp down all the background noise in his head and his senses swam in blue spruce, lavender perfume, and the feel of soft cotton. "Baby, It's Cold Outside" played on the stereo and as he held her, she began to tremble. No Christmas gift this side of heaven would ever come close to those three minutes.

He held on as sleep deposited the memory on its potter's wheel. *Mary appeared wearing the alluring red dress and sat down next to him on the couch. A cold breeze blew through the room and as he turned to locate its source, AJ came running in and sat down on the other side of Mary. He leered at her with his tobacco- and coffee-stained teeth, which smelled like sulfur. Mary tried to get up, but AJ held her down and began rubbing her bare knee. He clawed at his cousin to free her, but Jason suddenly popped up from behind the couch with a blood-stained tire iron. AJ grabbed it, aimed for his head . . .*

Christopher rolled to get out of the way of the weapon and hit the fake grass hard.

"What's going on, cuz?" a voice overhead boomed.

He looked up and saw his cousin standing over him in white boxer shorts, brushing the stained teeth which haunted his dream.

AJ left him on the floor and walked a dozen steps into the kitchen and spit in the sink. "Where have you been all day?" he asked sharply.

"I worked at the store for a bit." He pulled himself back up on the couch and stared at AJ's hairy legs. They were as thin as number two pencils, but with enough cellulite to look like some buck-toothed kid chewed on them for a semester. Christopher wanted to share the funny image as payback, but knew it would boomerang since he would never grace a cover of *GQ* either.

"Hope she likes my cologne, but she's so love starved I could douse myself in the sweet smell of antifreeze and she would swoon."

Christopher jumped up and followed AJ as he drifted toward the bathroom. He used to think spying was reserved for Bond movies, not for checking on friends. Mary might consider it extreme disloyalty, but given what might transpire in a few hours, asking for forgiveness rather than permission made more sense.

AJ turned around and laughed. "Why are you shadowing me? And what's that funny look on your face?"

Christopher began to walk away in a huff, but stubbed his baby toe on a table leg and let out a yell.

AJ laughed like a monkey that hid all the bananas. "If you're going to get upset and kick something, it helps to have shoes on." He tried to slap him on the back, but Christopher hopped out of the way.

"Don't tell me you're jealous?"

Christopher grabbed a metal Lally column, wishing he could channel Samson and collapse the building on top of them to keep Mary safe. It didn't make sense why AJ was suddenly attracted to her.

"She . . . isn't . . . like . . . other . . . girls . . . you . . . know," was the best he could spit out.

AJ waved him off. "Why do you think that? Because she may enjoy being with someone normal for a change? Isn't that why Denise dropped you like a bad habit?"

Christopher started to rock side to side and looked at the floor. The pink coral reef stretched in every direction. His feet would get shredded no matter how careful he stepped.

"This isn't about me," he began again. "Mary is a rose and you're nothing but . . . a weed-whacker. You don't care what you cut down."

AJ glanced at the frosted window. "I'm surprised you didn't insult me with something from winter, given your sad history with the season." He thought for a moment. "But you have it backwards. Lori was the rose that needed tender gardening despite her thorns." He stepped into the bathroom. "Her sister is nothing but a rose bug that fed on her beauty."

Christopher lunged forward to throttle him, but AJ slammed the bathroom door and let out a howl. "Wow, you have a much shorter fuse than the prima donna I used to wrestle."

Christopher looked at his feet, waiting for the dark water to begin bubbling up from the plywood. He wouldn't hold his breath this time.

"Remember it's Saturday, so you'll have to bunk somewhere else tonight, buddy."

"I won't let you bring her back here!" He pounded on the door as AJ cranked up the radio with heavy metal music.

Not wanting to extend the torture, he grabbed his coat and left. At the bottom of the stairs, he noticed the sun hadn't done much work today as the driveway still resembled a skating rink. While riding a bicycle on the narrow icy streets in these conditions made as much sense as wearing canvas sneakers, he welcomed an activity that required full concentration. Extracting his late uncle's lime green ten-speed Schwinn from the back of the garage, he pedaled slowly down the street, careful to avoid any black ice and ignoring the horns from passing cars.

The cold made his eyes water and black dots began dancing across his field of vision from the glare of oncoming traffic. It reminded him how he used to feel after popping his meds and climbing stairs too quickly. The dark spots would appear like missing pixels on a television screen.

After a half hour of pedaling and two near collisions, his ears were throbbing and he decided to stop at Godfreye's even though it was almost closing time. Leaving his bike leaning against a telephone booth, he watched the store owner count change at the register. The new snazzy dress clothes were replaced with the proprietor's ordinary winter uniform of a red flannel shirt and jeans.

"Evening, Mister G," he called out loudly as the automatic door opened.

The store owner looked up startled, and dropped a coin. It bounced off the counter and rolled across the black and white checkered floor. Christopher pretended he was fielding a grounder and scooped it up and handed the rebel penny back to its owner.

Godfreye eyed the coin and groaned. "They're more bother than they're worth."

Christopher swallowed, wondering if he fit the description too. "They have value and can add up if you save enough of them."

The store owner stopped his counting and thought for a moment. "You make a good point. How could I make change without my copper friends?" He picked up a penny and handed it back to him. "It's also graced with the greatest president this country was ever blessed with. Maybe Lincoln is on the penny as a reminder every act, no matter how small, helps us become the 'better angels of our nature.' As you said wisely, they add up." He went back to counting. "I'll interrupt the philosophy lesson to ask why you're here. Did you forget something?"

"It's mighty chilly out there tonight." Christopher looked down the aisle toward the coffee and tea station.

Godfreye laughed. "You're about as subtle as a hockey stick to the shins." He sighed. "This time try and keep it in the cup, will ya? Hurry up, though, because I'm closing in five minutes and my dinner is waiting upstairs."

Christopher imagined baseball-sized meatballs simmering in a Crock-Pot all day and his stomach rumbled. He felt for a tea bag.

"Are you okay, son?"

Son? The term startled him and he thought of Bobby, now sleeping six feet under with that terrible gash on his head. There were so many times when he wanted to unload the burden.

The lump in his throat felt like he swallowed the penny and he looked down at the floor. *We weren't out on World End fooling around that night, sir. AJ chased Bobby out there because he was jealous after losing Lori and heard she was seeing your son. Bobby took a beating from AJ with Jason's help. I tried to stop them before the ice broke the first time.* Pins and needles ran across his chest and his throat constricted. *I don't remember a lot, but I do know your son saved me from drowning before the ice broke again. You have been so kind and I can't keep this in any longer.*

"So, where's your better half?" Godfreye asked, taking his keys out of his pocket to lock up.

Christopher looked up and rubbed his damp head. *Okay, now I need to repeat it out loud,* he thought.

The store owner read his face. "Let me guess. You and Mary had an argument?"

"We . . . weren't . . . out . . . on . . . World . . . End —" he began in a whisper.

"Hold on for a second." Godfreye opened up a metal panel on the wall next to him and shut off the lights outside. "That's okay, son, I know almost every variation of this story. When the missus and I would have a spat, things would get mighty frosty for a couple days. Eventually, I would come to my senses and realize how stupid the argument was and bring something home to apologize." He stopped as if reliving the memory and chuckled. "Lucky for me, I usually grabbed something down here and brought it upstairs. We always had a good laugh about what I found as the latest olive branch. Once it was a package of Twinkies." He let out a quick sigh. "How I miss her." He grabbed a Hershey bar from a small rack. "Give her this," he said, pushing the candy toward him. "Be sincere and it will serve as an ice breaker."

He sighed as the urge to confess about World End curled up faster than any tape he used on his coat. "But I didn't do anything wrong."

"Relationships aren't about keeping score, my friend. Given what we've both been through, I don't have to remind you how fragile life is." He checked his watch. "You have two things going for you. First, the night is still young and secondly, I won't put the candy on your tab."

CHAPTER TWENTY-ONE

Flipping up the collar of his coat, he carefully pedaled down Main Street trying to figure out AJ's game plan. When it came to eating, Mary was a grazer and would feel overwhelmed if presented with a large plate of chicken parmigiana at Pattavina's Italian Restaurant at the Methuen Mall. If his cousin decided to splurge on appetizers, she would order a garden salad and be on the lookout for baby corn. Mary refused to believe you could eat the whole tiny ear and would pick them up one by one and try to delicately nibble on the kernels, or stack them like Lincoln logs on the side of the plate. Either way, AJ would have a fit and if he tried to push a raw oyster on Mary, she would barf all over him.

"What can I do?" Sudden indigestion made him taste the peanut butter from dinner and he wondered why the marshmallow fluff never repeated. It also reminded him no matter the entrée or the amount of baby corn, AJ planned to have Mary for dessert.

He kept pedaling and the 400 Club came into view on Ayers Village Road in Methuen, Massachusetts. It was just a few feet away from the New Hampshire border and had split personalities. On the eastern end, a small windowless pub with Schlitz on draft for seventy-five cents operated seven days a week. The bigger draw was on the other side, which featured Boston-area bands on two stages Thursday through Sunday nights. Christopher learned quickly from the other regulars to pre-game at the small bar before migrating over to the music side where Michelob's ran $2.50 a bottle.

Not surprisingly, the parking lot was filled to capacity on a Saturday night. Christopher slowed his bike and watched shadows dance across the frosted windows as the sound of muffled drums rippled through the exterior stucco walls. He made his way over to the pub side and leaned the Schwinn against a telephone pole twenty feet away from the door.

A thin curtain of cigarette smoke hung in the air as he entered.

"Hey, Guvnor!" a deep voice bellowed.

Christopher scanned the faces lining the glossy pine bar before rushing down to shake the hand of a humongous man with a shaved head the size of a bowling ball. "Nice to see you, Sump," he said sincerely.

When they first met, Sump made it immediately clear he wasn't allowed to call him by his nickname because it conveyed a sense of intimacy yet to be earned. So he called the good-natured forty-something Mr. Randall until one Friday night a few months back when the giant needed some assistance to his friend's car.

Christopher took his arm and as they staggered through the parking lot narrowly avoiding a head-on collision with a parked car, the big man slapped him on the back.

"From now on call me Sump."

"Okay, Mr. Randall."

He laughed as they careened to the right. "Everyone thinks I got my nickname by working for Roto-Rooter, but that's gross hogwash. Years ago, some smart-aleck bartender was impressed how I never left a drop of beer no matter how much flowed my way," he slurred. "Some guy on the next stool said I'd be more dependable than the sump pump in his cellar. Everyone laughed, but it stuck."

The big guy slapped his arm. "So, Guvnor, what have you been up to?"

Christopher ignored the question and glanced at the Budweiser clock on the wall. The second hand swept slowly over the head of a

Clydesdale and read ten thirty. He had enough time to warm his bones before hiding in the garage at AJ's to protect Mary in case his cousin tried to bring her home.

Sump waved to get his attention. "Who's your poison?"

Christopher glanced at the man's keg-sized beer belly. "I think you mean *what's* your poison. I hear the bartender say it all time when he's asking customers what they want."

Sump raised a quarter-filled glass of beer. "Please don't connect my question with Rick who keeps me well hydrated. What I meant is you have a wild look on your face like some lassie has broken your heart or someone's stabbed you in the back."

"So you've talked to my cousin?" he replied, looking around the bar. *AJ won't bring her here,* he thought. *He'd be teased viciously by some of these clowns, no matter his evil intentions.*

Sump drained the rest of his beer and put the empty glass on the bar. "Hey, Rick, can I rent another?" he called out to the bartender, then nodded at Christopher. "You'd think by now some bright kid at MIT would figure out how to build a beer reclamation urinal instead of trying to desalinate sea water."

"You remind me of Cliff on *Cheers* sometimes," Christopher commented, "except you're a lot bigger."

"And I don't make stuff up like that know-it-all." He looked around the room. "Your eyes are casing the joint. Looking for someone?"

He shrugged and sat down on the empty barstool next to him.

The bartender put an end to Sump's short drought with a fresh beer then looked at Christopher. "What can I get you?"

Sump punched his arm. "How about a shot of Jägermeister to mellow you out a bit? My treat."

"Thanks, but I better not as I'm riding my bike tonight." He looked at the bartender. "Coke no ice, please."

Rick the bartender looked at Sump and rolled his eyes. "Listen to this jive, will ya? The Guvnor thinks I'll skimp him on the Coke." He looked back at Christopher. "Did you bring a measuring cup too?"

"No. It's just that I have enough ice inside me from riding down here."

"Did you really ride a bicycle here?" Sump asked.

He nodded.

"Are you nuts?" He tilted the glass and the suds overwhelmed his lip as he took a long drink. "What am I saying? Of course you are," he said, coming up for air. "Riding a bike in the middle of winter at night? I'm afraid your new nickname will soon be Splat." He let out a short laugh. "Sump and Splat. Sounds like a hip cartoon."

The Coke arrived with an intense sea of bubbles racing to the surface with no ice blocking their escape.

The door opened and a bearded man in a black leather coat entered.

"Hey, Frankie!" Sump called out.

The man ignored him and took the first open seat near the end of the bar. He motioned to Rick, who was washing glasses in a small stainless steel sink.

"I'm planning to take a trip south tonight, so let's start with my buddy Jose Cuervo."

Rick nodded and the man waved to acknowledge Sump. "It's been that type of day from the moment I opened my eyes this morning. One catastrophe after another. Just a minute ago, I almost ran over some punk kid riding a bike out front. Stupid idiot."

The first bubbles in the Coke were only halfway down his throat when Christopher launched himself off the stool.

"Hey, Guv, where you going?" Sump yelled after him.

The wind caught the door and he heard someone cuss at him as his worst fears were confirmed. The telephone pole where he left his bike stood alone. The wooden pole looked like it had endured multiple firing squads from staple guns and peppered with shards of metal from promotional flyers. In the center of the hodgepodge, he noticed a fake twenty-dollar bill.

"Busted," he groaned.

CHAPTER TWENTY-TWO

"Hey, moron, missing something?" a voice yelled behind him.

Christopher turned and saw Ted pushing the Schwinn. Even before he began running toward the bike, he was already tackling the bully in his mind and grinding his acned cheeks into the frozen pavement. After that, he planned to search for some yellow snow left behind from a pack of wild dogs to revive him.

Ten feet away from making good on the plan, his sneakers got cold feet and sent him airborne.

A hyena laugh filled the air. "Who said pigs couldn't fly?"

The pain in his back felt like he landed on an ice pick. He struggled to get up and only made it to his knees before Ted rammed him in the side with the front wheel of the bike. The force knocked him over and he smashed his head against the pavement.

Ted stood a few feet away straddling the bike and began clawing at the AM/FM bike radio on the handlebars. Pieces of red plastic flew in all directions. He threw a hunk at Christopher and it skimmed the top of his head.

"I heard things are picking up for you. See you next fall!" Ted yelled, and began pedaling around him like a shark.

Christopher rolled on his side and eyed the door to the bar, but knew he would never make it. He looked around for help and noticed Ted had stopped pedaling and lined up the bike like a torpedo.

"You're more stupid than I thought trying to con me like that. If it wasn't for AJ, I'd break all your ribs."

The bike came at him fast. Christopher rolled at the last second and the bike only grazed him.

Ted threw the bike on the ground and hovered over him. "AJ should be okay if I only break a couple." He kicked him three times in the side with his steel-toe boots.

Christopher gasped in pain before his lungs seized up. He thought it strange how he courted this feeling, but only on his terms.

Ted picked up the bike and inspected it. "Maybe I can get a few bucks in scrap metal," he said and rode off.

The pain mixed with the thumping noise from the club and Christopher closed his eyes. It had been months since his last seizure and he waited for the strange smell of burning toast to signal its arrival as he took small sips of air.

After a few minutes passed without incident, he slowly staggered to his feet. Holding onto his side, he limped to the back of the building and found an iron grate exhaling warm air. Taking the Walkman out of his pocket, he inspected the unit, grateful it had been spared. After he fiddled with the earbuds, an electric guitar riff filled his ears and he rocked side to side trying to concentrate on each note instead of the pain. He almost succeeded in calming himself down until a clean-cut guy about his age appeared out of nowhere and got sick in the snowbank next to him.

The air turned sour. "Hey, what are you doing?" Christopher yelled, backing away as the splatter came dangerously close to his sneakers.

Clearly inebriated, the stranger stumbled backward, his eyes half-shut. "I met the enemy tonight and it's me," he said, pointing a finger at Christopher. "But I own it."

The drunk staggered alongside the building and stopped every few feet to take a deep breath. As he reached the corner, he turned around and held his finger in the air like he was receiving an extraterrestrial transmission. "I hope you won't have to down a fifth of Jack to come to the same conclusion."

Christopher put the Walkman away and decided to ask Sump for a ride home. Staggering into the bar, he found his buddy's stool empty. He scanned the rest of the patrons looking for familiar faces. A couple of weathered-looking men wearing John Deere hats were candidates, but they were intently watching a TV in the corner broadcasting a snowy reception of a Bruins game.

His eyes began one more lap around the bar when he saw a familiar hand raise a glass and he blinked. AJ?

He stepped quickly to the left to hide behind another beefy guy in a black leather coat. Looking in a mirror on the far wall, he watched his cousin light a cigarette and take a long drag. The stools on either side of him were occupied. *Is Mary in the ladies' room?*

"Hey, Guvnor!" the bartender yelled loud enough to drown out everyone else and strangely make the TV reception better.

Christopher turned and found Rick looking almost as miserable as he felt.

"Are you trying to stiff me for the Coke you ordered?" He held a green-striped towel and twisted it into a tight noose.

"Of course not. My bike got stolen and—"

"Save it for someone who cares," he interrupted.

Christopher dug a crumpled dollar out of his pocket. "I'll tip you next time."

Rick ripped the buck out of his hand and moved on. He felt a tap on his shoulder and turning around found AJ waiting. The way his cousin swayed, Christopher thought he must be mocking him.

"Spying on me, cuz?" he asked in a heavy slur as his glassy eyes narrowed.

"No, just looking for Sump." He noticed AJ glance toward the ladies' room and he didn't want to embarrass Mary. Holding onto his ribs, he bolted for the exit.

The cold air stung his eyes as he began a slow shuffle across the parking lot. Putting his hands in his pockets, he felt the penny Mr. Godfreye gave him. *AJ is pretty drunk. How can I let him put Mary in danger? Look what happened last time he drove like that.*

Hurrying back, he found AJ sitting alone and wondered if Mary had possibly taken a field trip next door to check out the double bands. The stool next to him was free and he sat down and pressed one hand against his burning ribs.

AJ didn't say a word as he swirled a thin straw in an old-fashioned glass with dark liquid. "Since I can't make out with an American girl tonight, I decided to share the rest of the evening with some Black Russians."

Christopher watched him take a sip and noticed his leather wallet, a half pack of Marlboros, and the keys to the Blazer on the bar in front of him.

Rick came by taking away empty bottles and glasses.

"Want something?" he asked flatly, apparently still peeved.

"No, thank you," he said, with so much gusto it sounded disingenuous.

AJ glanced at him sideways. "Man, I give you credit. If I were you, I'd be guzzling anything I could get my hands on. Even moonshine. Might make you go blind, but at least you wouldn't be able to see people laughing."

Christopher took a deep breath and tried to push the comment under the ice in AJ's glass. "I came back because you shouldn't be driving tonight."

AJ laughed into his drink. "That's a great excuse. Maybe you should run for office. How about village idiot? You certainly have my vote." He stirred the drink some more. "I know why you're sitting here and I'm not going to say another word until you ask."

"I came back because when you picked me up outside the Village Store that night—" He hesitated and then swallowed the rest. *Not here, not now,* he thought. "I told you Mary isn't your type. Where is she?"

"That's why they make so many different flavors of ice cream. Not everyone likes vanilla, you know. Tonight, for instance, I found out my best friend is fond of tutti-frutti."

"What do you mean?" He looked toward the ladies' room again.

AJ fingered the glass. "Calm down, will ya? She isn't here."

He slumped on the stool. "Oh?"

AJ sighed and took another sip. "What a nightmare of an evening. Morbid gets all spiffed up and for once in her sorry life, looked almost normal. She didn't smear the blood red lipstick like I asked, although I was disappointed she didn't borrow any of her sister's clothes. But even good-looking apples can be infested with worms. The minute I pick her up, she screws up her face and says she didn't like my cologne and the smell was making her queasy. What a head case."

Christopher read his lips and parked the words in a corner of his mind to try and remember. *That's my girl,* he thought. "Her name is Mary. Some smells bother her," he replied.

AJ shot him a nasty look. "After tonight she will forever be Morbid to me. Check this out. I take her to Pattavina's and Doreen gets us a nice table in the center of the room so Morbid can see I'm not embarrassed to be with her. Then she gets confused looking at the menu with all the different types of pasta and keeps clearing her throat like she has a tic." He punched Christopher's arm. "Probably because you only buy her Happy Meals."

Christopher had heard enough and started to get off the stool.

AJ grabbed his arm. "Sit down, there's more. So, I did the gentleman thing and ordered her a nice chicken piccata with angel hair pasta and a glass of house Chardonnay. Then after three sips she complains the wine is giving her heartburn and proceeds to cut up her pasta like she's Chef Boyardee's daughter and thinks everything has to fit back in a can." He rubbed one eye. "Naturally, I did most of the talking which was okay because whenever she opened her mouth all she talked about was some poet named Emily Dickinson and you. I found it irritating she wouldn't look me in the eye and just stared at my plate."

The recap felt like passing an accident; you should look away, but the curiosity too strong. "Did you have the chicken too?"

"No, veal. Why?"

"It wouldn't matter how much you tried to romance her, with a dead baby calf on your plate."

"But it's okay to deep fry chicken nuggets? If we weren't in here, I'd smack you good," AJ slurred and his eyes began to close.

Christopher decided to ask Rick to call them a cab.

"So, I treated her to a classy dinner, which is more than she gets from hanging with you and begging for hot water and sugar packets up and down Route 28 like my old man did." He rolled his bloodshot eyes. "After that, we stopped at Smitty's in Haverhill for a drink and the place was rocking. And Morbid? She stands by the door ready to run for her life and whips out some ear plugs because the loud music bothers her. I had to drag her over to a table and order a margarita, with an extra shot of tequila to loosen her up."

"Tequila? Sump thinks it makes you crazy." His stomach sank knowing that's what AJ was aiming for.

"C'mon, man. She's already crazy as a loon! Then, what does she do, but chugs down the margarita like it's a glass of water. I asked what are you doing? That drink cost me six bucks! She says the lemon chicken made her parched. Parched? I should have dumped her right there and then. What guy wants to date a girl that uses the word parched when she's thirsty? But then the DJ cranked up U2 and after a couple shots of Jack, she could have said parched every other word and I wouldn't have cared."

Christopher looked down at his sneakers remembering the drunk. Jack was sure making the rounds tonight.

"Ten minutes later she finally mellowed out and began snapping her fingers and dancing in her chair. Someone requested 'Right Here Waiting' and I ask her to slow dance. She stops jiving like someone suddenly pulled out her batteries and stares into space like one of those catatonic zombies you see in the movies. I asked her to dance again, but much louder so the surrounding tables could hear too. She comes back to life and yells no, because she only thinks about you whenever she hears that song."

He took a deep breath and his injured ribs kicked back hard. "Really?"

AJ shot him a dirty look. "Yeah and then I go ballistic," his voice getting louder. "I'm into her for thirty-five bucks with dinner and drinks and she won't even let me get close for a few minutes?" He ran both hands through his hair. "Then it hits me. No matter how much I drink, she will still be Morbid Mary and it's Lori I want." He looked up at the ceiling and almost fell off the stool before grabbing the bar. "But that woman betrayed me." He nodded to himself. "Never again."

Christopher had heard enough and stood up. "So then you took her home?"

AJ smiled and laughed then smiled again. "No, I left Morbid in Haverhill and high-tailed it back here before last call." He surveyed the bar. "Last weekend, I made some new friends that were still thirsty after the bar closed. They crashed at my place. We had a blast."

Christopher grabbed his arm. "So Mary is stuck in Haverhill?"

"No, that's where the punch line about tutti-frutti comes in. We ran into Jason at Smitty's. He offered to give her a ride home, but asked if she liked Canobie Lake Amusement Park." He made a circle with his index finger. "I guess it's on the way home, if she prefers the scenic route."

"I don't understand. The park doesn't open until May."

"Unless your last name is Driscoll and then everything is open year round." He slapped his arm. "Don't worry, cuz. Like I said, he digs frozen fruits and nuts."

Christopher pushed him hard and he fell sideways. Before AJ hit the floor, he grabbed the truck keys and bolted for the exit.

CHAPTER TWENTY-THREE

The billboard across the street advertised a delicious-looking pupu platter at China Blossom restaurant. Above it, a digital clock read 12:30 a.m. In another half hour, the crowd would begin spilling out of the club; many arm in arm, some laughing, and a few looking hungry, but not for chicken fingers or spare ribs.

Christopher sprinted through the parking lot with his left hand pressed tightly against his side. His head swiveled searching for the beat up Chevy.

Halfway down the first row of vehicles, he stopped to catch his breath and glanced back at the bar expecting to find AJ in mad pursuit, but his luck held. Pirouetting faster than a ballerina on speed, he scanned every car within view, but came up empty. He tapped his forehead hoping to get the internal wheels moving and solve the riddle before the drunken monster arrived. Studying the parked cars, he noticed a few windshields with heavy frost indicating they had been parked for a few hours. *Since AJ arrived late, he must have parked at the far end of the lot,* he surmised.

Racing across the parking lot through a line of cars, his head continuing in ping-pong fashion, he smashed his arm on a couple side mirrors. Nearing the street, he found his hunch flawed as the Chevy remained missing. Breathing deeply made his side ache terribly, so he tried taking a series of shallow breaths instead. Rechecking a line of different-colored vehicles made him think of Mary on the musical staircase at the Boston Museum of Science. She ran up and down to tap out a funny rendition of "Smoke on the Water." The image inspired him to climb onto the trunk of a Ford LTD and crawl up the back window to the roof of the car. Surveying the parking lot from the elevated perch, he spied the rusted cab of the Blazer, with its coat hanger radio antenna, five rows over by the western nightclub entrance.

"Hey, buddy, what are you doing up there?" a deep man's voice shouted from somewhere below.

Christopher slid down the back window and skedaddled off the trunk before noticing how the windows on the next car over were all fogged up. He intended to tiptoe away, when a loud horn suddenly blared which motivated him to sprint toward the club, where he found the Blazer in a handicapped parking space. Fumbling with the keys, he unlocked the door, jumped in, took a big whiff of stale tobacco, and then froze.

The new me has never driven a car, he realized, as a rap on the window startled him.

He turned expecting to find AJ. Instead, a thin man with a long brown ponytail and wearing a leather-fringed coat circa 1968 motioned for him to roll down the window.

Christopher detached his left hand from his ribs and grabbing the window crank, turned it clockwise, which didn't accomplish anything. Frowning, he tried in the opposite direction and the window moved a quarter of an inch before getting stuck.

The squinting eyes and puckered mouth on the visitor didn't look amused. "I just called to have you towed. Shame on you for pretending to be handicapped."

He considered arguing—many would come to his defense on that point—but there wasn't time. "I'm very sorry." He looked back at the dashboard and tried to slow his thoughts down to remember, without referencing his notes, the sequence of steps from watching his aunt drive.

"Hmm, I remember Becky always put on her seat belt first," he whispered, and grabbed the harness to click himself in.

The bouncer rapped on the window a lot harder than the first love tap. "C'mon, man, get moving!"

Christopher waved like a navy pilot about to be launched off the deck of a carrier and started the truck, which immediately engulfed the bouncer in a cloud of blue smoke. Pressing the brake pedal as hard as he could, he put the shifter in reverse and moaned as he turned to look over his shoulder. Alternating between letting up on the brake and quickly reapplying it, he moved the Blazer backward in a series of jerky motions.

Just as he was getting the hang of it, he saw AJ emerge around the corner of the building to discover grand theft auto in process.

Christopher threw the Chevy in park and succeeded in locking his door before AJ arrived. World End came flooding back.

He staggered to his feet and limped toward the Pontiac. He almost fell twice before hurling himself into the driver's seat. AJ came running too, but not before he succeeded in locking the door. He put the car in first gear and laid on the horn.

In the next instant, the trap door gave way.

AJ pounded on the driver's side window. Christopher held up his hand to protect his face in case the glass shattered. The image of AJ swinging the tire iron flashed in his mind.

"Open the door!" his cousin screamed.

The bouncer watched at a safe distance, still gagging from the blue smoke.

AJ boasted about having iron fists and velvet hands, but the Blazer wasn't impressed with either. Christopher shook his head once and hurried to put on the headphones, which blocked out most of the yelling.

Becky always adjusted her rearview mirror before venturing out of the driveway, he remembered. Whether she did this for safety's sake or to check her makeup, he could never tell. Not wanting to risk missing a step, he followed suit and adjusted the mirror a hair.

"Listen to me," AJ yelled and kicked the door.

He glanced at AJ standing in the frosty air without a coat and removed one earbud. "I did once and it was the biggest mistake I ever made." He put the Chevy in drive and gave it the gas. The vehicle lurched forward twenty feet before he hit the brakes again. From here on out, he would be freewheeling and hoped his previous self would step forward and navigate the mechanical beast.

A flash in the rearview mirror revealed AJ running to the passenger side of the Blazer and a second later the door flew open. Christopher gunned it and watched in the side mirror as AJ lost his grip and bounced into the grille of a parked car.

"Too bad he missed the one with the fogged up windows. It has a terrific horn to scare him sober."

The Chevy crawled into Salem at half the speed limit, which quickly built a conga line of traffic behind him. A police cruiser passed on the other side of the road and Christopher watched in the rearview mirror as its brake lights turned red. He knew at this hour, the police were trolling for impaired drivers, as well as those without a valid license. Grabbing the steering wheel tightly, he pushed the accelerator to the floor. The Chevy shook as it gained speed and flew over a small hill. The Blazer was still building speed when he braked hard and banged a hard right. Without proper introductions, he pulled into the first driveway and spooned with a snowmobile trailer. Seconds later, the sky glowed with flashing blue lights as the cruiser flew by on Main Street. Christopher waited a few minutes before starting out again, but this time weaved his way through a large neighborhood of interconnected streets, which provided an alternate route. The side streets let him work out some of the kinks in his driving too.

Twenty minutes later, he stopped in front of the main gate of Canobie Lake Amusement Park, one of the last trolley parks which opened in 1902 and a regional gem for family entertainment. Not surprisingly, the amusement park was dark.

"Mary, where are you?" he whispered. The thought occurred to him maybe it was a mistake to take AJ's drunken comments seriously and considered driving to Mary's house to find out for himself. After all, her father and stepmom were away, so he wouldn't have to explain pulling up in the "borrowed" truck. And why not? Technically, he wasn't allowed to go back to the apartment until morning when an army of Black Russian cocktails would be lobbing mortars into AJ's head and stomach.

Preparing to leave, he clicked on the high beams and noticed the right gate did look slightly askew. Jumping out of the truck, he pushed on the gate and quite surprisingly, it swung open to a darkened parking lot three football fields in length. *So what?* he asked himself. *This proves nothing.* Aunt Becky, Sergeant Mike, and Mr. Godfreye all yelled in his ears telling him not to be stupid. *The plow guy probably forgot to lock up after the last storm, that's all.* He nodded at his logic.

Headlights approached and he jumped back in the Blazer and waited, hoping it wasn't a police cruiser. Luckily, it ended up being a small sedan and after watching it pass, his eyes settled on a shuttered ice cream stand across the street that lived off the overflow from the park. The wind had aggressively blown snow under the overhang and onto a small platform where customers waited to place their orders. At the end of the deck was a lonely AT&T phone booth.

"A pay phone!" he said out loud so all the voices in his head would shut up. Turning the Chevy off, he ran across the street and through knee-deep snow. Luckily, he had a quarter and dialed Mary's number.

"C'mon, Mary, pick up," he said over and over again, as the unanswered rings became alarm bells in his head. *After all the alcohol and battling AJ and Jason, she probably went straight to bed,* he reasoned.

He looked up at the stars and they winked back in agreement that he was kidding himself.

He raced back to the Blazer and drove through the gate into the amusement parking lot, then stopped to close it, in case a cruiser passed by. The parking lot had been well maintained all winter and he drove slowly along the perimeter of the eight-foot-high chain-link fence with an additional four-foot snowbank barrier in some places. Rolling the window down a few inches before it got stuck again, he looked for a break in the fence or footprints entering the snowbank. Finding none, he soon reached the main entrance outfitted with a few oversized shed-type buildings, where visitors entered and exited the park. Nothing looked unusual, so he continued on for another hundred feet, where the fence took a sharp left and outlined the Yankee Cannonball, a wooden roller coaster and central attraction since 1936. As the fence cut in front of its thrilling first hill, he spied a dark truck sitting parked alongside a snowbank.

Christopher considered turning off his headlights to own the element of surprise like AJ did on that fateful night, but feared what he might find. Instead, he flicked the high beams on and off and pulled alongside the cab.

"Mary?" he yelled, jumping out and slowly opening the passenger door.

The cab was empty and without a trace of anything belonging to Mary. No coat, gloves, or scarf. Two open cans of beer sat in the center cup holder.

Slamming the door shut, he inspected the eight-foot-high fencing topped with barb wire. Mary could never scale or pole vault over such a formidable barrier, and pretty boy Jason wouldn't even try. So why was the truck parked here? He looked toward the road and noticed how this corner provided a blind spot for any patrolling cruisers.

The crescent moon provided little light as he continued hiking along the fence looking for clues in the snow. After twenty more yards, his ribs throbbed and he nearly reached North Policy Street. Rubbing his hands together in the cold air, he doubled back and followed the fencing in the opposite direction back toward the main gate. Everything still looked secure so he decided to reexamine the other side of the lot. As he began walking back to the Chevy, his ears detected music. The sound was so faint, he stopped to check his coat pocket to make sure he hadn't left the Walkman on. Leaning against the fence, he held his breath and strained to listen and sure enough, could make out organ music coming from somewhere *inside* the park. Turning around, he followed the fence again as it weaved its way toward the gatehouse and thought he detected a series of small footsteps on the very edge of the snow. At the last fence post, which sat nestled up against a shed, he felt the cold twisted webs of steel and his fingers discovered a three-foot tear. Getting through the ultra-small opening required him to take off his coat and do an awkward limbo.

Once through, he pulled his coat through the opening and followed what sounded like carousel music. Hugging the edge of a sidewalk cleared of snow, he came upon a boarded up oval structure with pale light emanating from a small open door. Peering in, he rubbed his eyes in disbelief watching a menagerie merry-go-round with prancing horses, along with a deer, goat, and lion, running in circles under blinking lights without a single rider.

He ran to the revolving platform and searched every crevice to make sure Mary wasn't hiding on one of the horse-drawn carriages before racing out of the building.

After coming to this amusement park every summer since he was old enough to walk, he knew the park layout by heart. Straight ahead were his favorite rides: the Round-Up, Tea Cups, and Yankee Cannonball. The left path featured the Flying Scooters, Galaxy, and Turkish Twist. But in the middle of winter, everything was hibernating under heavy canvas tarps and he didn't know which way to go.

A loud bang straight ahead made the decision for him, and he ran past a long line of ancient rhododendrons, their large green leaves curled in the winter air. Rounding the bend, he forgot the pain in his side momentarily in finding the glass maze house eerily lit up and slowly spinning clockwise like it did all summer. A heavy black tarp remained partially attached to its base and the pale-green-tinted glass panels looked like an alien spaceship Barney and Betty Hill would recognize. As he crept closer, Mary suddenly appeared, running frantically down one glass channel. She wore the same red cocktail dress that fired his imagination at Christmas, except tonight she held her arms out in front to keep from running headfirst into a dead end. He could make out her muffled cries.

The house continued to spin and as he ran to catch up, Mary disappeared and Jason appeared, strutting slowly after her laughing.

Christopher jumped up two stairs to the revolving platform and raced into the entrance. At the first corner, he took a quick right and immediately ran headfirst into a glass wall, smashing his forehead. Jumping back, he thought it might make more sense to go into the exit instead to meet up with Mary quicker. Retracing his steps, he ran to the other side of the platform and ignored the one-way sign. As before, he made a quick turn and found another dead end. Following Mary's lead, he held his arms out in front and proceeded deliberately into the heart of the maze.

A desperate-sounding scream, which had no problem navigating the maze, made him turn around. Mary was a couple rows over, pinned against the glass with Jason's face burrowing through her long hair to get at her neck.

Christopher pounded on the glass with both fists. The tempered glass shook and startled Jason. Mary took the split-second opportunity to knee him in the groin and run away.

Jason doubled over, and for a moment looked as green as the glass. Slowly standing up straight, he shook his fist at Christopher and took off after his prey.

Losing sight of the hunter and hunted, Christopher abandoned any methodical approach and ran through the maze, trying any combination of moves only to reach one dead-end after another. He smashed his head and shoulders repeatedly.

After a couple of desperate minutes, he smelled fresh air and followed it to the exit. Standing on the spinning platform, he searched the glass panels for Mary and suddenly heard footsteps behind him. Jason's angry face flashed for a millisecond before a punch pushed his stomach back to kiss his spine.

"Consider that a down payment of what I owe you!" Jason said sharply, before jumping off the platform and disappearing into the darkness.

Christopher stumbled off the spinning top and knelt on the cold pavement, feeling like he might lose whatever remained of the ramen noodles and Fluffernutter sandwich. When he made it back to his feet, he felt like he had been hit by a truck and began a slow shuffle in the direction Jason headed. Every few steps he called out for Mary, but the pain severely limited the volume.

Passing by the large steel frame of the pirate ship ride, he prepared to call out again, when he spied a figure sitting on the edge of the pavement up ahead. It looked much too small to be Jason.

"Mary?" he asked in a hushed yell, continuing to stagger forward.

A white arm waved, but otherwise the figure didn't move.

He ran the last few yards. "Are you okay?" he asked, kneeling down and immediately noticing how her leg was bent behind her in a most unnatural way.

She reached up to hug him. "Thank God you're here." She pointed above them. "I tried to climb and hide up there, but slipped." She looked frightened to the core. "Whisper, so he doesn't find us," she said and scanned the shadows surrounding them.

He nodded. "Does your leg hurt?"

Mary nodded and bit her lip. "I landed really weird and think it's broken." She started shivering and Christopher took off his coat and wrapped it around her.

"I need to call an ambulance and there's a pay phone across the street." He began to fish in his pocket for another quarter, but all he had was the penny Mr. Godfreye gave him.

Mary grabbed his arm. "You can't leave me here!" Her eyes looked wild. "If he finds me alone—" She buried her face in her hands and began sobbing.

Christopher tried to think what his father or Sergeant Mike would do in a situation like this, but Mary's tears mixed with the searing pain in his stomach and side overwhelmed his thoughts. He tapped his forehead hard with his knuckles, but his thoughts were curled tighter than the rhododendron leaves.

Mary tugged on his arm. "I'm begging you, Christopher, don't leave me alone."

He hugged her again, hoping it would calm both of them down. "Okay, let's give this a try." He released her and positioned himself in a crouching position and tried lifting her up slowly. She cried out in pain, and he bit his lip not to join her, as his ribs and stomach strongly protested.

"I'm so sorry to hurt you," he whispered, struggling to hold her in his arms. Mary might be a hundred pounds soaking wet, but tonight it felt like he was attempting to curl Sump after he consumed a keg. He shifted his hand to get a better grip around her back and spun around. *Maybe I can hide her under a tarp where she will be warm and safe until I can get help. If I hurry, I can be back in no time.*

She read his mind. "Promise you won't leave me!"

He nodded and took the first of a thousand steps toward the Chevy, doubtful he could ever live up to his namesake and help anyone across these troubled waters.

CHAPTER TWENTY-FOUR

Every time the sliding glass door to the emergency waiting room opened, Christopher expected Sergeant Mike to appear with a radio in one hand and a legal pad in the other. Then a litany of questions would follow and he planned to answer each one extra slowly because the sergeant might be fast with a gun, but he cheated at Scrabble and had the penmanship of a preschooler. Christopher pulled out his notebook to reference the last time he made the police log, and found an entry from November 24: *Ambulance dispatched to Shriner's Circus. White male, early 20's fainted.* Mary wanted a front row seat that day too.

The glass door slid open again and when it didn't close, he looked up. AJ stood in the doorway surveying the room before committing.

Christopher wiped his sweaty palms on his pants and waved hello. He glanced at the large-faced clock on the opposite wall apparently afflicted with paralyzed hands, since they'd barely moved since he brought Mary into the ER two hours ago.

AJ's eyes narrowed as he strutted across the small waiting room and his puckered mouth looked smaller than Mr. Perch's. He sat down next to him on one of the hard blue plastic chairs.

Christopher fidgeted in his seat. "Since you have to sit here for hours, the hospital should provide comfortable cushioned chairs, don't you think?"

His cousin leaned in close enough to bite his nose off. "Maybe you should take a ticket now like they do at the deli in the supermarket. That way after I'm finished, you won't have to wait long for surgery." He grabbed him by the back of the neck. "The only reason I'm not pummeling you right now is to get my keys back while you're still conscious." He held out his hand.

Christopher grabbed it and began shaking it. "I knew you would be upset."

His cousin pulled away. "When are the ice cubes going to melt between your ears? Give me the keys."

"Oh yeah, right." He searched for them in his coat pocket, but didn't find any.

"I have a good mind to press charges for stealing my truck. Where did you park it?"

Christopher hesitated before pointing toward the glass door. "Ah, it's down the street," he replied, then moved over one seat. "You have to understand, Mary was in a lot of pain when we got here and in my rush to get her out—" He stopped and moved over another two seats. "I forgot to put the Chevy in park."

"You what?"

"Yeah, it rolled down a small hill into a snowbank. From where I stood, it kind of looked like a pillow fight because the snow went flying up in the air when it hit."

AJ slid his butt over three plastic chairs to close the gap and then punched Christopher hard in the arm. "If I find one scratch, I'll take it out of your hide."

Christopher nodded and rubbed his arm. "That's good because there's no scratches." He slid over another seat. "Just a small dent in the left front fender where it kissed the fire hydrant."

"Fire hydrant?"

"Not to worry though," he said quickly, wanting to get it all out before another punch. "The snowbank kept most of the water out." He smiled. "Good thing you're into reupholstering though. The rest is probably just electrical damage."

"That Blazer is worth five grand!" He slid over and punched him twice in the arm.

His aching ribs and stomach blunted most of the pain, but he didn't feel the need to share that tidbit. "Five thousand dollars?" he asked instead. "Are you sure you have the decimal place right and don't mean five hundred? It drove pretty rough and needs a wheel alignment."

"That's the book value and includes an upcharge for the aggravation you're putting me through. Better ask Morbid for a loan if you can't cover it."

The alcohol exuding from his cousin's pores smelled sour. "I am so sick and tired of everyone calling her by that ugly name. And why would I ask Mary for a loan? She doesn't have any money."

"Are you sure about that?"

The conversation Mary had with Ted about the scarf flashed in his mind. How did he miss the signs? AJ's talk of expanding the business, his sudden interest in someone he detested? His cousin wanted to wrap his arms around the money more than the memory of Lori.

"Maybe you should talk to Jason then," AJ continued with a smirk. "Seems he's taken with your girl and maybe he'll lend you the money. She can pay it off one night at a time."

"You're sick!" he yelled, and jumped up.

AJ followed and spun him around. "By the way, I'm here to give you some advice. Say anything about what happened at Canobie and the police will charge you with trespassing."

He felt like he was on the ice again and watching another punk bowl with rocks. "Mary will explain how I came to rescue her."

"Rescue? I didn't think you knew how to pronounce that word after I fished your butt out of World End twice. You never thanked me once."

"Thanks . . . for . . . threatening . . . me . . . not . . . to . . . say . . . what . . . happened."

AJ grabbed him by the collar, but Christopher broke away. "Your girlfriend can sing all she wants about you playing the hero. I'll tell the cops you stole my truck because you were insanely jealous after I took her out. Then you went over to her house and sweet-talked her into going to Canobie. Now she's hurt, and too afraid to tell the truth." He looked around. "Plus, they will be real curious why instead of taking her to a nearby hospital—Holy Family, Lawrence General, or Parkland—you drove her all the way to Haverhill."

"Mary thought the Hale was far enough away from her attacker . . . And I don't care what lies you try and sell . . . Mary . . . will—" He punched the air, tired of not being able to get the words out fast. "Make Jason pay for what he did."

"Jason? My best friend was with me at the 400 Club drinking Black Russians until last call. Matter of fact, he had to drive me home after you took off with the Chevy, which the bouncer witnessed."

"Rick knows Jason wasn't there."

"Oh, you mean my poker buddy who you tried to stiff for a soda?" He tilted his head back and snickered. "But don't let me stop you from running to your sergeant buddy who's had the hots for my old lady since grammar school. But before you go and have your cape dry cleaned consider this. When the cops verify my story and file charges, Evelyn will use that against you to keep Kylie for good." He smiled and leaned in close. "This time I don't want to sew your mouth shut because it will be much more fun watching your jaw hit the floor."

Christopher imagined Evelyn dressed as the Wicked Witch throwing Kylie in a dungeon while AJ and Jason assumed their natural roles of flying monkeys ready to tear him apart. He shook his head and the scene reassembled with Jason's face buried in Mary's neck.

"I have faith in Mary."

"Yeah, she's a real toughie and can take a lot of heat." He rolled his eyes. "Just like last summer when she had a meltdown and wet her pants at Denny's."

Christopher bit his lip. Mary told him some punks cornered her in the lobby and threw pennies at her which she quickly scooped up. Then they teased her and said Lori was the town bicycle and she got what she deserved. When he told Becky about it, she cornered the slugs outside McDonald's and gave them a tongue lashing.

"Earth to Christopher," AJ said, snapping his fingers in front of his nose. "I think you better book a ride in an industrial dryer to take care of that water between your ears."

A stack of *Time* magazines sat in a neat pile on a side table. They were the only weapon within reach and he grabbed a handful and flung them at his cousin. The flying magazines made a whooshing noise before they hit AJ in the chest and scattered on the floor.

AJ laughed. "Wow, talk about a paper tiger. The least you could have done is throw a plastic chair or two to get some attention from security. He turned to leave. "You're pathetic."

Christopher wished he had the phone number of the drunk who threw up on his sneakers to see if he made house calls.

The sliding door opened and Sergeant Mike appeared in baggy dungarees and a tan wool coat. The sleep-deprived expression disappeared when he saw AJ.

"I heard you were a no-show at the station yesterday."

AJ zipped up his red ski coat. "Well, I'm sick of being harassed. Nothing new to add from the last visit." He started walking toward the door.

The cop grabbed him by the arm. "We're getting mighty close to making an arrest." He searched his face. "Better keep practicing that story of yours, Junior, because the jury will frown if you start tripping over the words. You know how it goes. You start out meaning to say how she dumped you, but slip and end up saying *you* dumped her. Then, the next question will be where?"

AJ pulled away, his eyes bulging. "You're the one that should be familiar with being dumped. My old man told me all about your pitiful crush and how you stalked my old lady. I wonder if that restraining order twenty years ago is still valid?" He looked back at Christopher. "Maybe you should lend that dirty rag you call a handkerchief to your buddy, so he can wipe his mouth every time he drools over your aunt."

The sergeant gave AJ a hard push toward the door. "No, he better save it for when you cry like a baby after getting thirty to life. But don't worry none, I'll take good care of your mom. I've always been there for her."

AJ laughed and walked out the sliding door.

The cop watched him leave and cleared his throat before sitting down.

"How's Mary doing?" he asked, in a surprisingly calm voice.

"They took her up to x-ray hours ago and I haven't heard anything since. Her leg is pretty busted."

The cop looked him over. "And you?"

"I'm okay," he whispered.

"What on earth am I going to tell your aunt when she calls? She's already on a guilt trip about being so far away." He reached in his pocket and handed him his wallet.

Christopher looked inside, happy to find the ten-dollar bill still there.

"Yeah, I thought about buying breakfast on the way over." His face turned serious. "So what happened?"

He kept inspecting the wallet.

A large hand enveloped his. "Look. You don't get to call me in the middle of the night to say you're in trouble and then clam up when I arrive."

Christopher looked at the sliding door. "But if I say anything there will be, ah, consequences."

"There's consequences in every moment of life." He sighed. "Let me guess. AJ's at the center of this too." He shot him a stern look. "I don't know what evil hold he has over you, but he's the one skating on thin ice."

His mind flashed an image of Jason sucking on Mary's neck again. "Well, it started with AJ taking Mary out and then Jason—"

"AJ and Mary?" he asked, interrupting. "I didn't see that one coming. What gives?"

"The winning ticket."

"Huh?"

"Mary's been bragging about winning the lottery." His eyes felt heavy and it took an effort to talk, never mind answering questions about what, where, when, who, and why.

He watched the sergeant trying to process the connection. "So what did she win? A hundred bucks? I guess AJ could buy enough cigarettes and beer to last a weekend if he got his hands on that jackpot."

"With fifty million, he'd have enough to party with the whole state."

Sergeant Mike's head jerked back and then he let out a low whistle. "She's the one?"

"Maybe."

"You don't believe her?"

"I didn't say that."

Sergeant Mike rubbed his face hard. "I'm tired of your word games. Just give it to me straight."

Christopher rubbed his wallet. "Well, it's just . . ." He stopped, realizing she never fabricated anything. "I haven't seen it."

"And AJ?"

"He smells a big payday and knows Mary craves attention."

The sergeant reached in his back pocket and pulled out a small notepad. "You say Jason's involved too?" He looked toward the door. "His friend may figure into all this yet."

Christopher thought about Evelyn using this to keep his sister away from him, but he still heard Mary's screams as Jason held her pinned to the glass.

He took a deep breath. "AJ tells me Jason likes ice cream, but I know for a fact he loves the merry-go-round and glass houses too," he began.

CHAPTER TWENTY-FIVE

Eyes burned and temples throbbed, but Christopher had to see Mary before giving in to sleep. Despite repeated requests, none of the nurses would tell him why she hadn't come back from having x-rays and a security officer kept stopping him from wandering too far. He studied another clock in the hall and at four-thirty in the morning, he was usually dreaming about drowning at World End or being chased by that persistent mystery woman. The center of the clock had the signature *Seth Thomas* trademark, just like all the other clocks in town from the post office to the library. *How did the clockmaker continue to corner the market on time after his ran out?* he wondered.

Pacing again to the edge of the waiting room, he noticed an empty stretcher parked against the wall twenty feet away which an ambulance left behind. A blue paisley hospital nightie lay on top of the white sheet. Before the little voice in his head could say no, his legs began sprinting the short distance, and he grabbed the nightgown and continued down the hall to a handicapped bathroom. Standing on the toilet, he hid his street clothes above a ceiling tile and slipped on the nightie. He frowned at his dirty sneakers, but they would have to do. Peeking out the door, he waited until the coast was clear before crossing the hall and heading up a set of stairs.

Reaching the second floor, he walked down one hallway and at an intersection took a right and proceeded on. The fluorescent lights made him squint and he closed in on a pair of quickly moving white sneakers with little squares on the back heel resembling tiny license plates. Mary had a similar pair and knew they must be Keds.

The shoes were connected to a pretty red-headed nurse who seemed to be in an awful hurry for such an early hour.

Christopher quickened his steps to close the remaining gap. "Excuse me, is the x-ray department on this floor?" he called after her.

The nurse's head swiveled back while the Keds kept moving forward. "No, and you shouldn't be wandering around down here. Please go back to your room."

He stopped. "Okay, but what floor is x-ray on?"

She stopped and turned around. "Do you need someone to escort you back?"

Escort me back? "Yeah, any day before November thirtieth of 1988 would be wonderful as my parents were alive then." He bit his lip. "So was Bobby Godfreye and a good piece of me as well, not to mention the whereabouts of Lori Martin." Suddenly, he felt the knot on the back of his neck give way and he grabbed at the flimsy cloth before it unrobed him. "As you can see, I'm having some difficulty keeping this contraption tied. Why can't hospitals supply normal pajamas anyways?"

She studied his dirty canvas sneakers like everyone else seemed to do. "Stay right there," she ordered and headed to a phone on the wall a dozen steps away.

Before she could punch one button, he ran. In situations like this, he couldn't deny he and AJ were related. They both had a knack for attracting trouble.

He streaked down the hall holding the nightie mostly in place. A red exit sign hung over a door on the right. He flew down two flights of stairs leading to the parking garage before realizing he would freeze to death outside. Pine needles as socks were one thing, but this exceeded even his ridiculous scale.

He turned around and climbed back to the first floor, where this whole misadventure started.

Slowly cracking the door open, he moaned realizing he was on the other side of emergency wing now, and the bathroom with his street clothes a bridge too far. Hugging the cement block wall, he tiptoed forward until he spied a security guard approaching a nurses' station straight ahead. He slipped behind a cubicle curtain.

"So who clocked you with the beer bottle?" he heard a businesslike woman's voice ask from the other side.

"A buddy of mine," a man slurred. "We had a little disagreement."

"Then I'd hate to see what constitutes a fight with an enemy. Okay, let's get you out of those clothes and take a look."

Moments later a pair of blood-stained blue jeans and a white pullover sweater with dark stains across the midsection landed in a trash bin outside the cubicle. Christopher quickly snagged them and found the borrowed digs slid over the nightie easily with room to spare.

He waited for the security guard to leave the nurses' station and then bolted down the hall until he came to an elevator.

And orderly walked by pushing an empty wheelchair and gave his new suit a full scan. "The emergency room is back the other way," he said, continuing on.

"Thank you," he replied, as the elevator door opened, revealing its lone passenger to be a haggard-looking elderly gent in dark blue work clothes. His eyes were half shut and he held himself up with a mop inserted in a bucket of dirty water. A few suds clung to the side of the pail on wheels.

"Good evening," Christopher said, hoping not to be busted.

The man didn't move and gifted a small nod.

"Which floor is x-ray on?" he asked, looking at the numbered buttons.

"Third."

The elevator seemed as tired as the worker and struggled slowly to climb. When the door finally opened, Christopher looked back, expecting his elevator companion to be staring at his gruesome outfit. Instead, the janitor kept sleep-working.

A petite nurse not much older than him with puffy brown hair met him in the hall.

"Can I help you?" she asked.

"I hope so. I brought Mary Martin into emergency a few hours ago," he started softly. "She went for x-rays but never came back. I'm worried sick about her."

Her right hand flew to her hip and Christopher imitated her. "I thought I had a fast draw, but you would make a great gunslinger."

She ignored the friendly overture and looked at his gruesome clothes. "Did you fall too?"

He considered the question. *Further than I thought possible.* Nodding slightly, he looked past her at the empty hall searching for any sign of Mary. "The nurses here have been wonderful since we arrived," he added, hoping the acknowledgment they do all the heavy lifting might win some favor.

Her blue eyes lost their intensity for a split second. "Follow me. You can stay for five minutes and not a second longer. She has a long day ahead."

Christopher followed the nurse down an adjoining hall where she stopped abruptly in front of a large door and checked her watch. "Five minutes," she said without looking up, and walked away.

He found Mary asleep on a gurney in the middle of the examination room, which looked like Frankenstein's laboratory with tall glass cabinets stocked with strange-looking instruments. Mary wore the same blue paisley nightie he had on under his clothes with a thin white blanket covering her lower half. A metal stand stood as a silent sentry and his eyes followed the thin tube from the clear liquid bag to her delicate hand.

Christopher leaned over and gently kissed her forehead, relishing the softness of her skin, yet hoping he wouldn't smell any rubbing alcohol. The smell somehow attached itself to the memory of lying in a hospital bed for days and staring at window shades stained yellow by the sun. Sometimes a breeze from the heating system would catch the paper sail and tap gently against the sill, as if marking the hours since becoming lost. While he never located the genesis of the smell, it seemed like a sign no amount of rubbing alcohol could ever disinfect his troubles.

"I always loved Snow White," she whispered, with her eyes still closed.

"But I'm no prince. More like a frog, I'm afraid." A pain stabbed the back of his throat and he looked away, so Mary wouldn't see his eyes. *What would have happened if I hadn't found her?* The thought haunted him.

The nurse popped her head in the room and held up three fingers.

"My dad will be here soon and he won't be happy," Mary continued. "I need an operation on my leg."

Christopher figured they must have given her some pain meds as she uncharacteristically searched his eyes and he drank it in. "He called me Lori, you know."

"Who did?"

Mary grabbed the railing of the bed as if it would take off. "After dinner, AJ drove to some bar in Haverhill. He no sooner parked the car, when he began pushing my hair behind my ears and called me Lori." Tears began pooling in her eyes. "Then he started putting his hands all over me. I managed to push him away and get out of the car. Once we got in the bar, he kept buying drinks and urging me to guzzle them down because dinner had been too salty. I couldn't stand the loud music, the people yakking, the smell of beer, cigarettes, and perfume. It made me nauseous. When I wouldn't dance, he handed me off to Jason."

A shiver ran through him. So much to ask in the minute remaining. "You were in too much pain for me to ask on the drive here. Why did you agree to go to Canobie?"

"On the ride back to Salem, Jason explained how he worked at the park years ago and knew a secret way in. He said he and Lori snuck in once. I knew he wasn't lying because she told me about it."

"I'm sure AJ doesn't know that interesting tidbit."

"I told Jason I didn't want to go, but he drove there anyways. The gate gave him some trouble and I pleaded with him to forget about it. But he said we could park at the boat ramp and walk on the ice and get in that way."

He shivered. "Walk on the ice in the dark?"

She nodded. "All I could think about was you, but then he got the gate open and found the hole in the fence. I was freezing and he promised we would only stay for a few minutes. Once he got the glass maze spinning, he started grabbing at me like AJ did and said something very mean."

"What?"

"That if I didn't smarten up and give him what he wanted—"

"The ticket?"

Her face flushed. "No, something more valuable."

The nurse rapped on the door and pointed at her watch.

She looked away. "If you hadn't come when you did, I'd be dealing with a break no operation could fix."

His stomach jumped into his throat and he squeezed her hand. "Get some rest."

He thanked the nurse and headed toward the elevator. Rounding a corner, he saw Mary's father hurrying toward him. Mr. Martin's white hair was slicked back, which combined with the knee-length tan trench coat and untied work boots, reminded him of a flasher.

Mary's father's intense blue eyes found him first. He rarely smiled and Christopher didn't expect one this early in the day.

"What are you doing here?" he yelled and accelerated toward him.

"Checking . . . on . . . Mary," he stuttered.

"Don't you think you have done enough already?"

"You're . . . mistaken . . ." he began. "I found her—"

A hand waved in front of his face. "None of this would have happened if she didn't hang out with you, and I'll never understand why she would sneak out with that monster cousin of yours." He stabbed the air with a pointed finger. "When the police finally arrest him, I'll ask if I can plug in the chair."

"I . . . would . . . do . . . anything . . . for . . . Mary," he replied.

Something broke inside Mary's father and he pushed Christopher up against the cement wall. "Then stay away from her."

CHAPTER TWENTY-SIX

Christopher was still shaking when he reached the hospital lobby and hesitated before exiting through the revolving door, afraid Mary's father rigged it to decapitate him. The image of returning to the emergency room with his head hanging by a thread would match his new threads. Outside, the morning sky glowed with ribbons of pink and the air felt balmy with no wind.

Hiking the five-plus miles back to Salem, he followed small rivulets of water seeping out of the snowbanks and expected every passing car to be either Jason, AJ, hospital security, or Mary's father. All would be happy to run him over.

After walking two hours, he stopped in front of the Salem Post Office and watched a mailman kneel to collect a myriad of envelopes out of the big blue box chained to a heavy metal tab in the sidewalk. He wished he could put a few stamps on his coat and be shuttled south.

Inside the lobby, he approached the small newsstand and took a deep breath before extending a hearty hello to Max.

"I'm blind, not deaf," came the reply.

Christopher didn't feel in a particularly Christian mood this morning and stuck out his tongue. Max courageously embraced his disability, but at times used it as a soapbox to minimize other people's problems. Consequently, he didn't frequent the combo newsstand snack bar very often. The blind man was thirtyish and quite handsome with a chiseled jawline. He wore a black T-shirt year round to complement his blond hair and show the payoff of sleeping in a tanning bed.

"So where have you been, big guy?"

The words were meant to poke fun at his weight, and was irritating because it must have come from another party for him to know. Nevertheless, it didn't deter him from checking out the packaged white-powdered mini donuts in a rack next to the cash register. Squinting, he could see they were pretty fresh, as the expiration date was three months out. Six mouth-sized bites for a buck and a half wasn't a bad deal compared to the sickly looking bananas being peddled for fifty cents each. Then it occurred to him, the bruised fruit might be a shrewd business move. After all, what patron would dare berate him? Knowing Max, he probably got a steal on the nearly spoiled fruit which guaranteed a nice profit on every sale.

Out of habit, he reached for his wallet, but found the back pocket empty. Just his luck the first time he "borrowed" clothes, they belonged to a peasant. He hoped the hospital janitor wouldn't find his wallet with the ten bucks he kept misplacing.

Christopher placed the package of donuts on the narrow wooden counter and cleared his throat. "I'm so sorry, Max, but I forgot my wallet. Could I possibly put this on credit?" He made the request in one breath, before triggering the automatic rejection. Even though he had stellar credit with all the other merchants in town, and carefully recorded every loan, Max would have none of it. "Cash is king," he always barked.

Out of character, Max hesitated before flashing an empathetic smile. The blind never learn to disguise their looks, and Christopher was touched.

"Your sergeant buddy stopped by to get his mail and told me your girlfriend is in the hospital. I'll make an exception this one time."

"Thanks, Max." Ripping the package open, Christopher stuffed a donut in his mouth and his taste buds immediately compared it to beach sand mixed with talcum powder. The combo tickled the back of his throat and he started to gag.

"Are you okay, man?"

He nodded and then realized the stupidity of the gesture. "Yes, but could I trouble you for a cup of tea?"

"What's that line about giving someone an inch?" Max hesitated before reaching under the counter for a small paper cup and carefully filled it from a pot of hot water. Then he transferred the four-ounce cup to the counter and took a nondescript tea bag out of a metal box and handed it to him. "You're up to five bucks now."

"You're charging me three fifty for a mouthful of tea?"

"The overhead in here is killing me; rent, electricity, insurance. The papers keep saying inflation is under control, but my costs keep going up."

Christopher prepared his tea and almost gagged again when tasting the flowery concoction. "Let me guess. You got a great deal on what they fished out of Boston Harbor after the tea party." He took another tiny sip. "I'd suggest you pair this with the bruised bananas." He popped another donut in his mouth to keep his tongue from saying more.

The proprietor cocked his head and listened for a moment like he thought Christopher was a flight risk and would have to yell for the postal workers to apprehend him.

He began working the Braille keys on the register. "That's why I say cash is king and credit the court jester." He slid a paper receipt toward him to memorialize the skimpy breakfast. "I'd appreciate it if you could take care of this by the end of the week."

Christopher read the notation at the bottom. *A $25.00 fee will be assessed for late payments.* "Sure, Maxwell," he replied, knowing how much he hated it when people didn't use his cool nickname.

"So a buddy of mine saw AJ with Morbid Mary last night," Max said extra loud, apparently hoping to retrieve pieces of the dry dusty donut in his esophagus. "I thought Morbid was *your* girl."

"Her name is Mary!" he barked.

"Whatever. My friends tell me she could scare the hair off of a black cat on Halloween."

"I know who your friends are, and they're messing with you. If you could see her blonde hair and brilliant smile, you'd want to call her Marigold instead of Mary." He took another sip of the tea as punishment for sinking so low to highlight Max's blindness. The taste grew more horrid with each mouthful. "Could you top this off with a bit more water, please?" he asked.

"And I bet you expect it for free?"

"For heaven's sake, Max, it's the same cup! Even Jiffy Lube tops off fluids for their customers."

"You're comparing my tea to an oil change now?"

"Never mind." He reached for another packet of sugar.

Max listened and then chuckled. "I don't need any sugar in my tea with Roxanne in my life."

"Good for you." He and Mary had concluded Roxanne was into the gothic look with an extensive wardrobe of black accented with dark makeup. She chain-smoked skinny cigarettes and sometimes drank Manhattans with Sump at the 400.

"But it does make me wonder who the blind man is." A goofy smile lit up his face.

Christopher contemplated pouring the rest of the tea over Max's goldilocks so he could change his name to "Ginger" from the resulting burn.

Something cackled on the police scanner Max kept under the counter. "Hey, did you catch that?" Max asked. "Morbid's house got broken into early this morning. Talk about bad luck."

"Are you joking?"

"I can call Captain Dennehy and get the dirt if you like."

Dennehy acted like he was the chief and Sergeant Mike despised him. "I'm sure the captain has better things to do," he finally responded.

Max shrugged. "I'll call him later as I'm curious what's in Morbid's closet."

Christopher threw the two remaining donuts at him. They landed where his Grinch-sized heart beat and left a bullet of white on the black T-shirt.

When he got outside, he made a note to deduct a dollar from the invoice for cause.

A white and blue police cruiser sat outside Mary's house and Christopher winced when he saw Captain Dennehy in the driver's seat.

The officer motioned him over to the driver's side window. "Hello, Christopher," he said slowly.

He hated when people treated him like an idiot and considered making him repeat it, but he was tired and gave a quick nod.

Dennehy stared at the red stains on his pants. "Anything you want to tell me?"

There's a lot I want to say, he thought, but rolled out his trademark confused look instead.

The captain pointed toward Mary's house where a policeman stood in the doorway with a clipboard. "Someone really tore up your friend's place."

"Anything missing?"

"Seems most of the household stuff and jewelry is accounted for. Looks like the burglar was searching for something particular. Naturally, with Lori still missing—" The policeman stopped. "Sorry, that was kinda fast. What I said—"

"I got it, Cap'n," he replied, with a bit of attitude.

Dennehy cocked his head. "Do you know anything about this, Christopher? Maybe you saw someone hanging around here?" He began to open the cruiser door.

Christopher knew he would have to spread it pretty thick to escape an interrogation.

Closing his eyes, he swayed side to side and counted to five. "Actually," he said, holding up his index finger, "this reminds me of a story I heard recently about alien imposters replacing everyone on earth." He opened his eyes and stared at Mary's house. "Maybe an alien wanted to find out what type of shampoo Mary's father uses, because he has such a nice head of hair for a man his age. The reason I say this is because all the sightings around the world indicate aliens are as bald as cue balls. Evidently, they don't have hair clubs for aliens back home." He opened and closed his mouth a few times and made a clucking noise to amp the performance. "What do you think, Captain?" he said ultra-slow. "Maybe we're not the inferior race."

The cruiser door closed.

Who's the imposter now? he thought.

CHAPTER TWENTY-SEVEN

The ice cube trays were stacked in the back of the empty freezer and Christopher took one out and studied how the little compartments were separated by plastic fins. He used to compartmentalize things like that, before everything in his life glommed into one enormous iceberg.

He wondered if AJ found him searching the apartment, could he be charged with breaking and entering? Since he slept on the couch, maybe the police would reduce the charge to just nosing around? No doubt the sergeant would shake his head and say that argument made as much sense as the gross jars of premixed peanut butter and grape jelly Mr. Godfreye peddled.

Fridge clear, he wrote on a new page in his notebook. He glanced at the door for the tenth time to confirm the dead bolt remained engaged. Next, he scanned the kitchen window and the blanket of dust on the sill along with the whitish material resembling plaster of paris covering the lock. The only way to open that window would be to hurl a brick through it Ted style.

Methodical and *patient* were the words he found in the massive dictionary at Kelley library and described how he intended to conduct this investigation. He allotted an hour to search the apartment while AJ played poker at Jason's. Methodical required a thorough approach and he began in the kitchen. He didn't know what he was searching for as the police already searched his stuff a couple times in the past year. But what Mary told him at the hospital about calling her Lori made him want to look again.

Christopher continued the kitchen autopsy. The whitewashed cabinets and drawers were worn and with the exception of some mouse droppings in one drawer, the inventory of chipped dishes and coffee mugs along with a mishmash of utensils were sad looking, but unremarkable. Moving a few feet into the living room, he took a couple of deep breaths as if preparing for a dive and searched under the couch and investigated the recliner and side tables. The exploration uncovered multiple litters of dust kitties and three orphaned gym socks, which by their sallow color dated to Reagan's first term. Before moving on, he crawled behind the television and looked through the tiny grilles and surveyed a lunar-like landscape of dusty components.

Running down the hall, he entered the small bathroom across from AJ's bedroom. Opening the mirrored medicine cabinet, he carefully inspected a can of shaving cream to make sure it didn't have a fake bottom like he saw in a movie. He repeated the same exercise with the deodorant and toothpaste and then scrubbed his hands, feeling totally grossed out. Next, he stuffed his nostrils with toilet paper and took the lid off the toilet. The moldy tank reminded him of World End since he could hardly see the bottom of the bowl. Disgusted, he felt around all the piping and fished out a couple of bobby pins and tried not to think how they got there.

With the exploratory surgery finished, he soaped and scrubbed his hands again until they were raw, and moved across the hall. Entering AJ's bedroom, he figured Jason must have gotten a great deal on discontinued wallpaper because one wall had images of blooming hydrangea while the others featured cartoon depictions from *Star Wars*. A grungy-looking plaid blanket sat in a ball on a twin bed frame minus a headboard. Underneath the bed, he discovered the underground railroad for dirty clothes, along with a Yankees cap AJ wore in the summer to anger Red Sox nation. Sitting up, he eyed a pine bureau with missing drawer pulls sitting kitty-corner next to a window with a ripped shade. He pried the three drawers open and rifled through piles of unfolded T-shirts, sweatshirts, underwear, and mismatched socks.

Moving to the closet, he tackled a pile of dungarees outlining a strange shape. Removing the top layer, he discovered the dashboard from an old Dodge Dart Swinger. Sitting cross-legged on the floor, he examined the strange memento and the red, white, and black wires sticking out the back of the unit. The odometer read 99, 999 miles with a horizon of zeroes about to dial everything back to the beginning.

"That's the beautiful thing about old cars," his dad once remarked, when they were shopping for his first set of wheels and came upon a Datsun with a similar milestone. "You get to be reborn, but carry the scars from the past." His father's words sounded prophetic now.

His eyes traveled from the AM radio to the Swinger nameplate emblazoned across the glove compartment. The chrome letters were beginning to delaminate and Christopher was pleased to discover Chrysler engineers faced a similar challenge of affixing letters to a surface for an extended period of time.

The latch on the glove compartment didn't cooperate and he repeatedly pressed the button and jiggled it at the same time. He told himself to be patient and come back later with a can of WD-40 and let the magical lubricant do its thing. As a parting shot, he whacked the dashboard good and hard while pushing the button, and surprisingly, the compartment popped open. At first glance, it looked like another stash for junk; three crushed Marlboro boxes and an orphaned distributor cap. He reached in to explore further and something sharp stabbed his finger. As he recoiled in pain, a bevy of machine screws and an old brown wallet came along for the ride.

Christopher sucked in his breath staring at the wallet as it represented the catalyst which resulted in tragic consequences. If he hadn't reached for it on the drive back to his aunt's, AJ wouldn't have missed the turn and a whole lot of trouble would have been prevented.

Picking it up, he imagined drilling a hole in the ice at World End so Bobby could buy a Yoo-hoo, or giving it back to Lori if she was with him now. He stroked the crinkled brown leather, which felt like the skin on the ancient elephant at Benson's Wild Animal Farm. The edges of the gold horseshoe clasp were rusted and he wondered how AJ succeeded in fishing it out. He retrieved his notebook and looked back at the entry when the divers explored World End. AJ was there too, watching and chain smoking. Maybe he was calculating where the wallet went under?

A horn beeped and the pit of his stomach took a roller-coaster-sized dip. Jumping up, he scurried to the window, but the driveway remained dark so he continued examining the wallet. The currency sleeve and small coin pocket were barren, which was not surprising since AJ retained money as well as his mother. He opened the tri-fold, and Lori's license photo suddenly smiled back through a foggy plastic window. The smile was the same one he saw in every picture of her; radiant and genuine and with teeth as perfect as Mary's. He studied with new appreciation how her long dark hair curled behind her ears.

He tried to pry the license gently out of its plastic prison and momentarily had a tug of war with Mary's sister. When he finally won, a small photo of AJ took her place. It was one of those black-and-white snapshots from a booth in an arcade and preserved in a laminated sheet which helped it survive underwater. Its placement behind the license felt downright creepy, like AJ was still stalking Lori. In the snapshot, AJ's lips were puckered in a pretend kiss and he leaned forward, accenting his long nose. On the back in smudged blue ink, he signed it, *Forever and a day, I'm yours. AJ.*

However, written underneath in red marker on the laminate, he found another scribbled inscription: *Forever is now dead, like you to me!*

A shiver ran across his chest and as he hurried to reinsert the picture and license back in their shared tomb, he felt a small bulge in the middle of the wallet. Wiggling his pinky finger into a small crevice, he felt something metallic and massaging the leather, extracted a silver key with a Ford emblem emblazoned across its round top. It didn't take a super-sleuth to identify it as the combo door and trunk key to the car Lori disappeared in. Her face had been plastered across miles of telephone poles and store windows and every police department in New England kept watch for a 1985 black Mustang with a red pinstripe running down the middle of its hood. Before the posters had a chance to fade from the elements, police divers were following up on leads and searching rivers, lakes, and ponds, including World End, for the vehicle and the driver.

Christopher checked his watch, knowing he shouldn't push his luck. He returned the wallet to the glove compartment, afraid if it wasn't put back just right, AJ would know. The previous position of the cigarettes and distributor cap confounded him and he ended up guessing. So much for slow and methodical.

Suddenly the doorbell rang. If he could have crawled into the glove compartment he would have.

Running to the window, he watched a UPS truck pull away.

CHAPTER TWENTY-EIGHT

Double yellow lines ran down the center of Veterans Memorial Parkway in Salem and Christopher had an unexpected flashback on the resurfacing project last year when Butch laid down the markings for the two-lane road.

The muscular man with shoulder-length red hair sat shirtless in the August sun and bragged he didn't need sunglasses because his eyes were the size of Le Sueur peas after throwing back a "few beers" with Sump the night before.

"Get a move on," a burly foreman yelled.

Butch coughed up some white foam that looked like he was retaining the Michelob reserve for New England. The humongous painting machine inched forward applying a thick line of yellow paint.

"Don't worry about me, Guvnor," Butch shouted above the din. "Today, I'm painting like a blind man and will use the crown in the road to feel my way home."

Now six months later, Christopher was following the same center line and wondering why some memories stuck like pine sap, while others melted faster than a spring snow shower in April. The answer still eluded him when he reached the Salem police station, a modest one-story brick building challenged to serve a resident community of twenty-five thousand, which doubled most days with the influx of shoppers and patrons to Rockingham Race Track and Canobie Lake

Amusement Park. He decided to stop in and ask Sergeant Mike if he had grilled Jason yet about attacking Mary. In the meantime, he continued to debate whether to tell him about Lori's wallet. *He might promote me to partner instead of deputy with that news*, he mused, before Becky's pleading eyes interceded to keep quiet.

A heavyset cop manned the front desk.

"Is Sergeant Mike here?" he asked, studying the name tag of Corporal Heath.

Bullet eyes scanned his blood-stained pants. "No, but I can take the accident report."

He felt his stomach sink realizing there was no logic how he was wired. He could remember Butch painting lines in the road last summer, yet somehow forgot to change out of the borrowed clothes from the hospital. Looking down, he hoped the injured man hadn't reported them missing, and if so, they had they had him "red panted." He let out a small laugh.

"Hello?" the cop asked, waving his hand in front of his face.

"No accident to report, Officer. May I speak with Sergeant Mike, please?"

The policeman hesitated, waiting for a sneeze to arrive which never did. Nevertheless, he fished a tissue out of a box on top of the desk and blew his nose before looking at him again. "It's Christopher, right?"

He nodded, afraid Max had filed a complaint and he was about to be charged for assault with a tasteless weapon.

"Check across the street for your friend," the corporal said with a smirk.

Christopher turned around and looked through the glass door. "You mean Child World? Why? Is there a problem over there?"

"You never can tell when rival gangs roam the aisles packing super-soakers." He snickered and turned to answer the phone.

Who's talking crazy now? he thought.

Out of respect to Butch, he stepped over the thick yellow line as he crossed the busy street and approached a pimply-faced kid shagging carriages in the parking lot. He was having a heck of a time making headway as gray slush gummed up the carriage wheels.

He dragged a cart over. "Is Sergeant Mike here?" he asked.

"I don't think the security guys get a rank here," he replied, leaning over the stubborn train of carriages.

Christopher pointed to the police station. "No, I'm talking about Sergeant Michael Rossi of the Salem police."

The kid shrugged. "Maybe it's like the *Newhart* show where there's two brothers named Darryl."

Christopher entered the store and began cruising the toy aisles, which were pretty empty given the post-Christmas slump. He stopped at the courtesy booth and a kind pregnant woman paged Mike Rossi two times. After ten minutes, she apologized and said he must be on break.

Making his way toward the back of the store, he came upon a section stocked with enough stuffed animals to outfit Noah's Ark ten times over. A woman in her fifties with short black hair, and wearing a blue smock, worked diligently to correct any drooping animals. She heard him approach and gave him a quick look-over, like she was examining his posture, before returning to her chiropractic duties.

"I bet you have to assemble a lot of bikes in the spring," he asked, with a big smile.

Her attention remained fixated on the animals like they might bite her if she looked away. "That's the plan."

He scratched the back of his neck, trying to think how to get some traction. "In college, I remember admiring Hemingway's genius in writing a novel in six words: *For sale: baby shoes, never worn.* In here, fiction can be summed up in three: *Some assembly required.* So, if you're looking for some help come spring, I'm really good at sorting out all the hardware. You wouldn't believe how many different sizes of screws and nuts are used in building a bicycle."

"Yeah, I can see you know a lot about loose screws and nuts," she whispered low enough for him to hear, before moving away a good five feet.

Well, I tried playing nice. He rubbed his bruised ribs before patting the borrowed sweater. "Too bad I forgot my tea bags today or I could write my phone number on one of the tags so you could call me." He laughed. "Of course, the numbers would be pretty small. Do you wear glasses?"

The woman glanced over with a confused expression.

He missed being silly like this with Mary and pointed at his blood-stained jeans.

"But don't worry none, because I clean up good," he continued. "You see, these aren't really my clothes. I borrowed them from some injured guy in the emergency room the other night, because I had one of those horrible johnnies on and it came loose. Once I get my clothes out of the ceiling of the handicapped bathroom at the hospital, I'll be my old self again . . . well, not really, but that's another story." He looked down at his pants and pouted. "Since I borrowed these without asking, I need to pick up some detergent because my mother always taught me to return anything I borrowed in good condition." He rubbed his chin and glanced at the ceiling before taking another step closer. "By any chance would you have one of those industrial washing machines out back to save me a trip to the Laundromat?"

The woman skedaddled down the aisle. "Yes, please report me to security," he called after her.

The black orb in the ceiling was mounted two aisles over and Christopher positioned himself underneath it and waited. A few minutes passed and still no one came. He waved at the camera with both hands and mouthed "I know you can see me."

The store remained quiet. *How far do I have to go to make the sergeant come out of hiding?* Across the aisle, he noticed a display of sales items for vacation and picked up a package of batteries along with a throwaway camera. Holding the camera and batteries up to the eyes in the ceiling, he stuffed them in his coat pocket and waited for a code red to be announced.

Nothing interrupted the background music from butchering "Yesterday."

There's only one way to escalate this, he thought, and moved fast before his stomach could protest. A heavyset man in his early twenties and wearing an upside down smile manned the lone check-out register. Christopher knew he could outfox him if he faked to the left before the automatic doors opened.

To his disappointment, the cashier had no intention of making employee-of-the-month and remained at his station as he sprinted past with the stolen goods.

He hoofed it into the parking lot and wondered if the sergeant might be on a coffee break after all. Then he felt a kick in his stomach. What if this was all a big misunderstanding and the corporal was just having fun with him, while the kid shagging carts and the courtesy desk clerk were referring to another Mike Rossi? The white pages in any telephone book is a testament to duplicate names. If so, the real Sergeant Mike might be assembling a SWAT team to take down the half-crazed shoplifter wearing bloody clothes across the street. The woman in the stuffed animal aisle would certainly yell "Loose nut!" when he was led away.

Examining the tips of his fingers, he wondered what the police used to clean up after the fingerprinting process. His mother used generous amounts of nail polish remover on most skin stains, but that was way too feminine to go with the bars on the windows. No, if they used any cleaner at all, it would be something industrial that would likely burn. If so, at least it would take his mind off the handcuffs digging into his wrists. His mind continued running full throttle and planning where to hide tea bags in a cell, when he put on the brakes and closed his eyes. Bright yellow splashes burst in the dark and he feared the county shrink would ask him what they resembled. This time he'd have to tell him the truth. Not images of snakes or zebras, just cold Bobby Godfreye treading water next to him.

"Take another step and I'll have no choice but to arrest you," a familiar voice said from behind.

He opened his eyes and spun around to find Sergeant Mike slowly walking toward him. He was wearing a white dress shirt and a checkered blue tie held in place by a silver tie tack with handcuffs on its face. *Well, at least it's better than a blue smock.*

The sergeant's face looked crimson despite the twenty-degree day and Christopher knew only seconds remained before another highfalutin sermon would begin. "When you didn't come out after being paged, I stood under the camera for a good five minutes trying to get your attention. Then I decided to kick it up a notch and add some props in my pocket."

The sergeant put his hands on his hips. "Props? How old are you, boy?"

Boy? He was approaching the quarter-century mark and felt his face get hot. He pointed at the police station across the street. "Old enough to believe you worked over there."

"Wow, that's a mighty quick comeback for someone with brain damage." The sergeant gave a quick nod toward the station. "Maybe you should go tell the chief how you flushed me out like a prized pointer and he can throw you a bone. Then while you're gnawing on it, he can get his ukulele out and sing a ballad about a decorated officer reduced to a security gig at a toy store because of a sixty-day suspension."

Cold sweat began to form on his forehead. "Suspended?"

"Yeah, and now you're busted. You wanted to catch me out of uniform for what?" he asked, with his voice rising. "Watch me squirm because misery loves company and you wanted to see me broken too?" His mouth continued moving for a moment, but no words came out. "I'm mad your aunt told you about this," he finally managed to say.

"What are you talking about?"

The sergeant drilled a finger into his chest. "I don't care about all my buddies cackling over coffee about my troubles, but I trusted Becky."

Christopher began to rock from side to side. "I haven't talked to my aunt in days. And when we do, it's only about meals, meds, and the weather."

The sergeant looked at him sideways, weighing the testimony.

"I'm telling you the truth." He stared at the handcuffs on the tie tack. "Why were you suspended?"

A stout man with Elvis sideburns came running from the store. "Good work, Mike," he said, fixing the collar on his navy blue overcoat. "Although you should have waited until he crossed the street and then you could have marched him right into a cell."

The sergeant held up his hand. "This isn't what it looks like, Bill. He's a friend of the family and just trying to get my attention."

"A friend? Well, we'll give him special treatment and expedite the paperwork. Bring him inside."

Christopher took a step toward the store and the sergeant stopped him.

"Give me what you took."

He quickly fished the batteries and camera out of his pocket and handed them over.

The sergeant nodded. "Now get out of here and we'll talk about this later."

"What are you doing?" Elvis barked and lunged at Christopher's arm, but the sergeant intervened.

"I'll have your butt for this!"

Christopher walked away humming, "You Ain't Nothing But a Hound Dog."

CHAPTER TWENTY-NINE

The hospital lobby featured a neon sign flashing the date, time, and temperature like banks do when advertising their deposit and loan rates. But in here, the temperature stayed the same whether January or July, and few of its customers wanted a long-term relationship.

Christopher passed the reception desk and rounding a corner, came upon Punxsutawney Phil dressed in a top hat and tuxedo hunched in the middle of the corridor.

The groundhog looked up at him with dark beady eyes. "Unfortunately, winter has been extended indefinitely for you," Phil warned.

A hip-looking young orderly rushed by and apparently didn't see the sharply dressed woodchuck, and unknowingly drop-kicked the famous prognosticator halfway down the hall. The groundhog ricocheted off the wall before disappearing around a corner.

Christopher stopped and rubbed his eyes. "I seriously need some sleep." He continued on and came across a vending machine, which represented not only an oasis of sugar, salt, and saturated fats, but also a pipeline of patients for the hospital. Kneeling down, he spied three dimes and a quarter under the machine where no mop or vacuum ever ventured. Seconds later, he pushed a couple buttons and out popped a glorious package of peanut M&M's.

After a quick elevator ride to the fourth floor, he rushed into the sun-filled room, hoping her father was still home picking up from the burglary.

The bed was empty.

"I'm over here," a small voice said from the corner.

He turned and found Mary sitting in a green leather chair. Her right leg was in a cast up to her thigh and resting on an ottoman. She held a small oval mirror in one hand, while the other worked to free the stubby teeth of a purple brush from a clump of tangled hair on the top of her head. It reminded him of his mom when she used to prove familial ties with the Griswolds by mumbling in strange tongues when trying to untangle spaghetti strands of Christmas lights.

"I should never have used that cheap hairspray," she said through clenched teeth. "That's why I only buy Aqua Net."

He nodded, knowing she had a case of the brand at home. He leaned over and gently tried to extract the brush, but she pulled away.

"You're hurting me!" she snapped.

He stepped back and looked toward the hall, expecting a team of nurses to come running in thinking the worst. When no one appeared, he silently watched Mary's slender fingers methodically try a variety of options and groaning after each attempt failed. Five minutes later, she finally succeeded in freeing herself and threw the brush on the floor.

Christopher picked up the brush and noticed long strands of hair left behind in its teeth. "Look at the hair-cuffs!" he said, in mock horror.

The joke fell flat and she continued staring into the hand mirror surveying the damage.

Before he could think of something to make her smile, she sighed and turned the mirror upside down on her lap. *"Unfortunately, winter has been extended indefinitely for you,"* Phil echoed in his ears.

The silence grew between them and he sensed yesterday's hero status erased. "There's a bunch of magazines in the lobby. I can run down and get a few," he offered.

The offer of goodwill went unanswered and she stared at the white flooring with a frown.

Is she thinking about what AJ and Jason put her through or maybe she heard about the break-in? He decided it was time to use his only lifeline. "I bought something for you," he said with a smile, and pulled out the package of peanut M&M's. He slowly raised the yellow package in both hands like it was a gold bar.

She glanced at the *"melt in your mouth, not in your hands"* candy and remained silent. Christopher ignored her reaction and ripping open the package, extracted one green piece before handing it to her.

"Morsel," he said, with the same clarity he heard the announcer use at Bingo. Morsel was the first word they used to kick off a game of enjoying these multicolored chocolates, while trying to use other words starting with the letter "M" in their conversation. He always dedicated the last piece to "Mary" and she always gifted him with a wide smile.

Today's alternate reality continued when she placed the package on a plastic tray next to her, which exhibited an untouched lunch of a grilled cheese sandwich, green salad, and small carton of milk.

Christopher popped the treat in his mouth to fortify himself in the strained atmosphere. "Why are you so miserable?" he asked, not meaning to use a downer "M" word.

The meds must have worn off because she was back to her old self and refused to look him in the eye. Instead, she fished out two red candies and placed them on the lap of her pink cotton robe.

"Because being Morbid Mary means my father doesn't believe what happened at Canobie."

"Huh? What do you mean?"

"He made some calls and thinks I snuck in there with you and wrecked some of the rides. He's afraid the owners will press charges." She rubbed her forehead. "He's furious."

Christopher felt his stomach jump. *Jason has a fake alibi with AJ, and the sergeant can't investigate given his suspension.* His hands started to tremble.

"Now I'm getting a one-way ticket to New York as soon as I get out of here. So much for making our small family work." She shot him a quick look. "If my dad finds you here, it won't be pretty."

Man up, he heard his father say. *This isn't about you.* Mary always thought the red pieces were the best ones, even though they were all the same except for the food coloring. Fishing out a yellow piece, he placed it next to hers.

"I was telling Max you could change your name to Marigold," he said softly. "It's in the sunflower family and nothing is more spectacular when they—"

Without warning, she grabbed the package and threw it across the room. Two dozen colored chocolates scattered every which way on the floor.

Christopher moved instinctively to his knees to try and beat the five-second rule. Those he couldn't rescue in time, he planned to use a tissue to wipe off the germs.

Mary let out a long low growl which startled him enough to halt the gathering.

"Just leave them there!" she cried, pointing at the floor then toward the hall. "They all think I'm asleep, but I watch the nurses and the janitors sneak in here one by one. I catch them rifling through my things looking for the ticket. Let them stomp all over Morbid Mary's morsels so I can mark the thieves by the chocolate on the soles of their shoes." Her lip quivered. "Morbid Mary's morsels. That's triple credit for me!" She buried her head in her hands and began crying.

He knelt down and touched her hand. "Shhhh," he whispered. "No one here is trying to steal anything from you. Believe me, I know how medications cause bad dreams."

She came out of her hands mad. "There you go again, not believing me! Friends don't—" She pushed him away. "I hoped we were more than that."

"We are. Haven't I proven that?"

She hesitated. "What does any of it matter when I'm stuck in upstate New York and you're here?" She pulled a remote from a pocket of her pink robe and turned on the television perched high above in the corner. Feeling dismissed, Christopher walked over to the window. The winter wind blew salt and sand into small tornadoes in the parking lot below.

Looking toward the front lobby, he noticed a Blazer pull into a parking space. A figure jumped out and stood in the middle of the maelstrom.

Unlike him, AJ never seemed to cast a shadow. Even after a year of intense focus, and being a prime suspect, he still walked around free. AJ might like his work boots, but he could go bare-footed too since no sharp coral ever cut him.

"What are you doing here?" a voice boomed, and he didn't have to turn around to know it belonged to Mary's father.

The M&M's in his hands began to melt.

CHAPTER THIRTY

From a distance, the rocks resembled frozen fish with mica-colored scales glistening in the snow. After another few dozen steps, Christopher watched them change back into the ugly work of Ted and Ray. The sun would eventually free them from limbo and they would disappear below the surface like his former self.

Punxsutawney Phil messed with his head so much back at the hospital, he was surprised to find the afternoon weather unseasonably warm. Consequently, he stepped carefully on the snow-covered path to keep his sneakers semi-dry. Without a life jacket, he anticipated his heartbeat to begin racing once he reached the ice. When it didn't, he quickened his pace to cover the required distance. A few days ago even anticipating this journey would have required a handful of pills to crop dust as many brain cells as possible.

He suddenly slipped sideways and caught himself before falling, but not before feeling some slush penetrate one sock. Out of habit, he would have stopped to examine the damage, but he kept moving, afraid to slow down and become anchored like one of the imprisoned rocks. As he counted off the final hundred paces to ground zero, he expected the ice to open up and swallow him whole. But the only sound came from a couple of squawking crows in the distance.

Coming to a stop, he took a deep breath. "So this is where the B movie began." He studied the ice around him and felt an internal wave building. When it peaked, he fell to his knees and began clawing through the snow cone layer with his bare hands, needing to feel the ice on his terms.

A strong breeze kicked up and he looked up to find the pine trees along the shoreline swaying in unison.

"Stop laughing at me!" he yelled as loud as he could, but they paid no heed.

He slammed his fist against the ice and recoiled in pain. Something sharp in his coat pocket pricked his side and he remembered the cheap pen he used to write in the notebook.

Grabbing the pen, he stabbed the ice repeatedly and in short order decapitated the pen's head, which seemed cosmically proper. Doubling the effort, he continued hammering at the ice with the plastic shaft until it began to splinter and soon nothing was left but a few shards. Even after the ferocious attack, the ice only suffered a few nicks.

The palm of his hand felt wet and opening it, he found it bleeding. Not feeling any pain, he examined the ripped skin like it belonged to someone else. Extending his arm, he let the blood drip and embrace the ice like he never could.

He found himself missing Kylie intensely, and thought she might as well be living on the moon, given the distance between them. Now Mary, the other anchor in his life, would be exiled too. The familiar tightness began in his chest and hoping to outmaneuver the coming attack, he took a deep breath and held it in.

No more than fifteen seconds passed before a tickle started in the back of his throat and he fought to ignore the intrusion, waiting to escape wherever his imagination landed. But his throat would not be ignored and he ended up sneezing and coughing at the same time.

"What good does whining do?" he asked out loud, listening to the sound of his strained voice. "My first concern should be getting down to Florida for Kylie." He closed his eyes and Mary's father stood in the middle of the hospital room forbidding him from seeing Mary again. The outburst got so loud, the nurses came in to usher Christopher out.

"Maybe in time, I can find a way back to prove what really happened at Canobie," he continued, "but in the end, what good will that do? Mary will be in New York and I'll be wherever I need to be for my sister."

The pain in his hand finally registered and by accident, he extended his thumb and index finger and it looked like a gun.

"Maybe what I need is a customized litany," he said, studying the symbolic hand gun. "Say it over and over like they do in church and it will stick like flypaper in my memory.

"A gun will get my bike back.

"A gun will protect me from the likes of AJ, Jason, Ted, Ray, and all the other riffraff when I hitchhike my way to Florida.

"A gun may even get me some answers about what happened at World End."

He took a deep breath. "Let us pray."

CHAPTER THIRTY-ONE

Sergeant Mike's house sat in darkness, which wasn't unusual since he called the electric company a direct descendant of Jesse James. For Christmas, Christopher bought his friend a vanilla-scented candle so he wouldn't have to live by the glow from the TV. He also made him promise not to regift it.

After ringing the doorbell twice, he finally detected footsteps and the front door opened. Christopher wondered why the career cop didn't have a peephole to screen visitors given all the bad guys he put away over the years. The concern was lost when he found the sergeant all decked out in a shiny black tux and without the oversized eyeglasses.

The sergeant hesitated for a moment before cracking the storm door open. "AJ didn't kick you out again, did he?"

He shook his head no and continued to admire the well-dressed man. *I like this look much better than the skimpy robe.*

Sergeant Mike smirked. "You can put your eyes back in your head now. Since you seem to have an unhealthy interest in outing all my secrets, I lost more than my pride in a game of Forty-fives a few weeks back. Consequently, I'm on the hook for a benefit dance tonight."

"Where's it being held?"

The sergeant hesitated, then shrugged. "Guess I should make a call and find out the details." He jerked his head back inside the house like he was listening to something.

Christopher rocked side to side. "It's mighty cold out here, Sarge."

"Wait there a minute," he said, and closed the door.

A good five minutes passed and Christopher figured the cold solitary confinement might be payback for the incident outside Child World. He was turning to leave when he heard the returning footsteps and the door reopened.

"Okay, you can warm up in here for a few minutes while I finish getting ready." He looked down at the visitor's dingy sneakers. "I just vacuumed so you know the drill."

Christopher stepped inside on a gray scatter rug.

The sergeant brushed a piece of lint off his pants. "Like they say, a sucker is born every minute and the other night it proved to be my turn. I had a winning hand too," he mumbled and then rubbed the back of his neck. "Or so I thought. Now, I have to escort his niece who's visiting from . . . ah, Austin to the dance."

"And if you won?" Christopher asked, untying the laces on his sneakers.

"A box of wine."

"That doesn't seem like a fair bet."

"Heaven help me if she has the personality of Sparky."

"Does *she* have a name?"

There was another long pause. "Jennifer, I think."

Something seems off, Christopher thought. *The sergeant is always a master of details and it sounds like he is making this up as he goes along.*

The cop tucked in his white shirt and pointed at his suit. "I've had this in mothballs since the peanut farmer became President. Nice to see it still fits."

Christopher tried to control his expression as well as his tongue. The stories Sergeant Mike shared always included a description of himself as an emaciated rookie. Either that was a fib too, or the suit belonged to some beefy friend. Then he noticed a small red mark on the sergeant's white collar under his chin and his eyes zeroed in. *Did he cut himself shaving? ... No, it looks too bright ... Could that be lipstick? ... Is someone else here? ... If so, how am I going to pull off my plan?*

"Have you had dinner yet?" the sergeant asked, leading him down the hall toward the kitchen. "I made a killer chili today."

Christopher followed, listening and looking around. "I'm all set, thank you." *The bathroom excuse is my best option.*

The sergeant flipped the light switch and a round fluorescent bulb in the middle of the ceiling flickered before coming alive. Christopher noticed two dinner bowls and matching water glasses on the counter beside the sink. He looked down the dark hall. *Is he alone?*

Sergeant Mike caught Christopher staring at the counter and the two bowls. "I made the chili this afternoon since I got home early from work. As you can see, it came out so good I had some for an afternoon snack and then more for dinner too." His let out a heavy sigh. "Sit down and I'll heat some up for you."

"I'm really not that hungry."

The sergeant ignored him and opened the cabinet to retrieve a bowl. "I'm telling you the chili will make up for that forgettable breakfast the other day." He turned and gave him a quick body scan. "I never know which of you is going to show up; my happy-go-lucky neighbor or the helpless guy waving his crutches. But I know when it comes to eating, they both have hollow legs."

Christopher nodded. *Don't be stupid, use this opportunity*, the voice in his ears boomed. "Is it okay if me, myself, and I wash up first?" he asked.

The sergeant laughed. "So it's a trio now? I'm beginning to think you may be Sybil's brother after all." He pointed down the hall. "It's the same set-up as your house. Bathroom is at the end of the hall."

Christopher kept telling his feet to move, but they were stuck in neutral and he watched the cop continue to move around the kitchen. The hem on the suit pants surfed the top of his anklebones, probably because the material had to compensate for his expanded midsection. The sergeant opened the refrigerator and then stopped and shot him another look. For a split second, Christopher thought the veteran crime fighter, who made life and death decisions by reading faces, would see the Trojan horse.

"I just bought some nice Italian bread from Pappy's," he boasted, "and it will help put the fire out." He waved him off. "But hurry up as I haven't slow danced," he said, sounding like a teenager, "with anyone since Cathy left."

Christopher finally got his feet in gear and the walls in the hall seemed to contract as he made his way past the double-locked cellar door and down the short hall. Reaching the end, he quickly flicked on the bathroom light and fan, closed the door without entering, and then tiptoed into the master bedroom.

The light switch was where it should be, and he closed the bedroom door three-quarters of the way before flicking it on. Checking his watch, he estimated he would be safe for three minutes before the sergeant grew suspicious. The hum of the bathroom fan might buy some additional time, but not much.

He scanned the king-sized bed; a jumble of white sheets and a light blue blanket, with two pancake-like pillows propped up against a cherry backboard. *Very surprising*, he thought, figuring the officer as one of those military types with snug four-point skills. Surveying the pile of pastel silk shirts at the foot of the bed, he wondered if the sergeant collected leisure suits too.

The closet was located on the other side of the room and he rushed across the gray wall-to-wall carpeting and slid one door open. Last

September, he jotted down in his notebook how Becky sent him over with a few ears of local corn to share with their neighbor. He met the sergeant as he came home from duty and followed him into the house and watched him walk down the hall and reappear moments later without the sidearm. It had to be in here, along with others he boasted about too.

With outstretched arms he scanned the top of the closet, feeling under piles of sweatshirts and heavy sweaters for a holster and finding nothing but prescription bottles. *Is everyone medicated nowadays?* Cold sweat began beading on his forehead and he checked his watch again. The rattle of the bathroom fan continued, or was it the sound of the grains of sand rushing through the hourglass?

Falling to his knees, he looked under the bed and found nothing but three empty Budweiser cans and half a bottle of Sambuca. His ears began ringing and he knew he should abort the mission, but it felt akin to holding his breath; he needed to push through the anxiety and see where he landed. Jumping up, he ran over to the bureau on the other side of the room. The top drawer was filled with briefs, another surprise as he had him pegged as a boxer man. He quickly profiled the remaining four drawers and they held nothing of interest.

"Hurry up, Christopher, or I'll have to nuke it again," the sergeant yelled.

He counted to ten before making his way back to the door and peering down the hall. His luck was holding as a cold thought hit. Maybe the sergeant had to surrender his service pistol when he was suspended, and he kept the others locked in another room.

The gig was up and he was about to leave when he spied the cherry nightstand and knelt down in front of it. It had two drawers and the brass pulls looked worn. The top drawer slid open much too fast and almost fell out. He balanced it with his left hand as his right began a quick search of the deep cavern. It seemed to be a catch-all for everything; screws, paper clips, dental floss, empty nip bottles, loose photos. A tossed salad of junk.

He was already sliding the drawer back in, when he noticed a ruby necklace on a delicate silver chain, paper-clipped to a Polaroid of a familiar though much younger face, with long dark hair and mischievous eyes. He grabbed it and turning it over, recognized the fine cursive strokes of his aunt. *"With all my love, Becky."*

He dropped the combo jewelry and picture memento on the floor as the bottom drawer beckoned. Careful to not repeat the mistake, he opened it slowly and found the pistol sitting alone in the nest. He pulled the gun out of the holster, surprised by its weight.

Christopher started to slide the gun into the back of his pants while trying to decide whether to continue the charade and have a quick dinner or run for the door. If he could make it back to the highway, he could target one of the big tractor-trailers headed south.

The approaching footsteps in the hall made him wish he'd left the faucet running to possibly buy another minute. But then he mouthed the litany: *A gun will get my bike back. A gun will protect me from the likes of AJ, Jason, Ted, Ray, and all the other riffraff when I hitchhike my way to Florida. A gun may even get me some answers about what happened at World End.*

From now on, he would be calling the shots.

CHAPTER THIRTY-TWO

"Christopher, give me the gun."

The tone of the sergeant's voice surprised him. He expected it to be loud and angry, not low and deliberate. No doubt the career cop switched to automatic pilot in situations like this to project control and authority. His father used the same tactic years ago when trying to get through to his rebellious teenage son. However, if Sergeant Mike had the same short fuse as his late father, fire and brimstone would begin raining down momentarily. The key was watching the midsection of the cop's bulging shirt for a series of deep breaths which would ignite the dragon's breath.

"Look at me," the sergeant continued, his voice now one octave higher.

He didn't obey, afraid one look into those terrible dark eyes would conquer his resolve. "Not this time," he said. Ever since World End, he felt like a chameleon trying to disappear into the background while he worked on getting his head screwed on straight. But as he sat on the floor with the pistol, the sergeant no doubt associated him with his tormented late uncle. The cop didn't know the man he used to be, or the promise he intended to keep for Kylie. No amount of brain damage would erase that vow and he was prepared to obtain any necessary tool to fulfill it.

"Christopher!" The sergeant's voice boomed like a concussion grenade.

He shook his head hard to focus. An upsetting image took hold that the cop might misinterpret the continued disobedience and whip out a small derringer from his back pocket and shoot him between the eyes. To remove the threat, he turned the barrel of the gun so it pointed at his own stomach. The dark barrel sucked on his eyeballs. *"Look inside me,"* it invited.

The sergeant frowned and crouched down, and the pockets of his pants began to tear. "I used to marvel how you were like a mirror, always reflecting back what you wanted others to see. But now I see the real you, and you're just like all the other misguided losers I put away." He blew out a long breath. "You have the gall to knock on my door after embarrassing me at work, and I thought, he must be here to apologize. So I invite you in, offer you dinner so you don't have to eat cereal again—and instead of apologizing, you insult me this way? I should have learned my lesson the last time you arrived here cold and hungry. As they say, *fool me once, shame on you, fool me twice, shame on me."* He pointed at the gun. "I hope you do blow your brains out, because if you don't, I may put a bullet in you. This charade ends tonight."

The sergeant's words came out too fast and spilled all over him. "This isn't about you," Christopher said, fighting an out-of-body feeling.

"That's a funny thing to say as you sit in my bedroom, holding my gun, messing up my life."

A small voice in his head urged him to turn the pistol around and see whether he could make the bragging cop pee his pants.

The acidic voice hijacked his tongue. "There you go again, Sarge, practicing your police psychology which must be getting pretty rusty by now. You wow me with tall tales about fighting bad guys and I find out you're playing Dick Tracy at a toy store? Who's the master at charades?"

The words cut as quick as any bullet and Sergeant Mike's eyes grew glassy. "Would you rather hear me brag about the number of parking tickets I wrote? Salem may not be Gotham, but I made a difference in keeping the town safe from some bad dudes. My suspension came after one too many beers and running into the devil that ended my marriage." He looked up at the ceiling and took a deep breath. "I worked to control my rage for so long, then in a microsecond had my gun pointed at his head. If I had to do it over, I would have used my fists on Barry's face instead so Cathy no longer thought my ex-partner was the most handsome man on earth." He smirked. "Lucky for me, I found a way to work through all that anger."

Their eyes locked. Christopher glanced down at the gun, imagining the missile in the chamber ready to travel from one dark home to another. The trip would last less than the blink of an eye, but cause everlasting consequences. The voice in his head told him to blow a hole in the ceiling to feel the power. His mouth began to water. *Bullet or vomit, which would come first?*

He looked at the rug, planning where he would heave, and noticed the memento. "Why do you have a picture of my aunt?"

The sergeant glanced at the floor and his cheeks matched the color of the ruby necklace attached to the old photo. He bit his lower lip as if intent on tasting the words first as his eyes darted around the room, concerned other treasures might be discovered. "Your aunt and I were . . . ah, very amicable growing up." The words sounded like stiff entries in a police log and mismatched his crimson cheeks. "It's a pretty ordinary story, really. Boy meets girl, boy falls very hard for girl and gets a bit too possessive. They break up and then another guy swoops in—which is what your uncle did, after he wrapped himself in the flag." He took a deep breath to reload. "Don't believe AJ and the garbage he spews about me stalking your aunt. Yeah, they were married, but I ran into her and we had a drink. Your uncle always saw me as a threat and made a big deal out of it." He stopped and fiddled with the silver cufflink on his left arm then slowly reached for the photo. "You never get over your first love and I've gone to some wild lengths to try and replicate it."

"AJ thinks you're still stalking her because you bought this house."

"You steal my gun to grill me about my real estate choices? Maybe you are a bit touched after all." His eyes drilled into him. "Look. I worked my butt off to give Cathy everything she wanted. When we were first married, I collected aluminum cans and plastic bottles to make a few bucks so we could go out to dinner. Even after I started making decent money, I drove her nuts because I felt more comfortable in joints with plastic utensils than stuffy places that serve small chunks of food framed on large plates. Then after eighteen years of marriage, she tells me I'm suffocating her."

"Like my aunt did?"

"Say another word and I'll make sure you eat that gun." He glanced at the picture. "I used to drive by your aunt's house when I was out on patrol or to bring your uncle home after an episode. After my divorce, this place came on the market and I liked the neighborhood. Chalk it up to fate, I guess. Your uncle is gone and I'm still here for her."

A loud noise sounding like someone beating a metal drum started somewhere below them. The sergeant listened for a second then grimaced. "Great! Now the furnace is acting up." He pointed at the gun. "Okay, now that you have enough material for the soap opera you're obviously writing, can I have my gun back?"

"Why do you think AJ is behind Lori's disappearance?" he asked.

The policeman pursed his lips. "You'll need a bazooka to get that one out of me. All I'll say is he and his sidekick Jason were involved."

Christopher thought of the Mustang key.

The furnace continued making noise, but the sergeant ignored it and surveyed the cream-colored walls. "I'll have to repaint in here after you blow your brains out," he said in a nonchalant tone then looked at the unmade bed. "Maybe I'll get a new comforter too." He stood up and frowned at the bags in the knees of his trousers. "I think I still have Sunday's paper somewhere. I remember seeing a fifteen percent coupon for Bed and Bath."

Christopher pointed the gun at the cop's belt buckle. "Stop with all the jive talking because it's not going to work."

The cop shrugged. "Just taking a page from the pro. Everyone thinks you're damaged goods and I have to admit it, you play the part well."

"Why do you keep saying that?"

"Because you try to imitate your uncle riding his bike around town and making small talk with all the merchants. I guess you think by mimicking him, everyone will let you slide by. But he had a reason behind his disability, even if he was weak. You're just pathetic."

"Weak?" Christopher yelled above another loud percussion rising up from the basement. "Why do you and AJ keep saying that? My uncle was the only one in his company to survive an ambush."

"So what's your excuse?"

Images of Becky pleading while AJ threatened him with "Snitch the Teddy Bear" flashed across his mind. "World End," he replied instead.

"Really? Tell me something I don't know."

He tried to hold back the tears because he was brought up believing men don't cry. He shook his head no in reply.

The sergeant's face softened a bit. "A terrible accident. The January thaw made the ice soft and—"

"Accidents are unplanned tragedies, the shrink said," he said over the cop's voice and the banging pipes.

"That's a clinical way to put it, I guess. Let's be clear. None of you should have been on the ice." He thought for a second. "If I was your shrink, I'd sum up the story in five words: stupid stunt breeds horrible consequences."

Christopher gripped the gun harder and his teeth began to chatter.

The sergeant noticed. "Is there something else you want to tell me about what happened that night?"

"You mean to a professional crime fighter?"

"No, to the minimum wage loss prevention clerk trying to save a reckless friend." He moved closer.

Christopher waved the gun. "Get back!"

Sergeant Mike stopped. "Okay. So, what else happened? I'm thinking maybe you saw what happened to Lori?"

He shook his head. In the year since the ice broke, he arranged the flashbacks by color: red, black, and a splash of white, with wind and water as bookends.

"Why won't you let me in?"

"Because I still can't make sense of it all." He answered quickly, not wanting anything else to bubble out. He stood up slowly.

The hard look on the sergeant's face melted away. "C'mon, Chris, hand me the gun," he said, gently stretching out his hand.

Christopher put the gun to his temple to make him stop. The nozzle felt hard and cold. It was frightening to think one squeeze and it would be over. He could see Mr. Godfreye giving another impromptu talk after the funeral. *"There must have been some sort of weakness in that gene pool when it came to stress. Real shame, though, how winter claimed them all."*

A painting his mother loved in the lobby of Mary Queen of Peace church in Salem flashed in his mind: Saint Peter drowning and reaching up in desperation to be rescued after walking on water and losing faith. He cradled the gun in his hand. "I'm just trying to make things right after so many wrongs. I thought this gun could be a tool."

The sergeant began gently tugging on his hand. "When I feel like that I keep repeating what Lennon said: *Everything will be okay in the end. If it's not okay, it's not the end.*"

The words felt like salve to a burn victim, but he continued holding on.

"There's no bullets in the gun," the sergeant whispered.

The news hit him hard and he let go of the gun and collapsed on the floor, waiting to be handcuffed. *I've been played all along.*

The room remained silent and Christopher opened his eyes and saw the sergeant sitting on the bed. He looked funny and his hands were shaking.

In his palm were two bullets.

CHAPTER THIRTY-THREE

"Thanks for the lift, Danny," Christopher said to the sharply dressed white-haired gentleman as the Ford LTD rolled to a stop in front of the Haverhill Municipal Parking Garage. "It would have been a mighty long, cold walk in the dark from Salem."

"Well, I enjoyed the company. Nowadays, most people are in such a rush they use a drive-through like a pit stop at the Indy 500. Now when I was your age—" He stopped and pulled on his white goatee. "There I go again," he said, with a quick laugh, "reminiscing about horse and buggy days. Though I'll confess, when you came barreling into McDonald's, you looked like you just robbed a bank."

Christopher nodded. "Well, let's just say I had an unforgettable dinner with a friend." After the drama with the gun, Sergeant Mike made him eat a bowl of chili, which made his eyes water, before letting him leave.

As he rushed down the sidewalk, the sergeant called his name. He glanced back at the fogged-up storm door, and the cop's head looked disembodied and resembled a turnip with Chia Pet hair.

"Are you sure you don't want me to drive you back to AJ's?"

Too much had been said and he kept walking.

"Promise me you won't do anything else stupid tonight," were his *parting words.*

The old man touched his arm. "Christopher, are you okay?"

He nodded. "Aces."

"Do you know the way from here?"

"That's what I've been asking myself for the past year," was what he wanted to say. Instead, he just nodded slowly.

Danny came to a different conclusion and pointed straight ahead. "Just follow Water Street along the river for about two miles and the Hale hospital will be on your left. It's across from the stadium and you can't miss it."

"Yeah, I know. Been there a bit lately."

He shot him another concerned look. "Are you sure you don't want me to give you a lift there? It's not a summer night for a stroll. The missus is probably watching her shows by now anyways." He checked his gold watch.

"Thanks, but I really need the walk to clear my head." Zipping up his coat, he shook the good Samaritan's hand and got out of the car.

Christopher started the hike at a brisk clip, counting off the steps between telephone poles, which tonight resembled a long relay of giant crosses buried in chest-high snowbanks. Another storm or two and the mammoth snow piles in the parking lots and street intersections would begin resembling a vast mountain range and exude cold, cocky confidence to still be standing come Memorial Day. Making his way east, he remembered *"BC"* summers, as he called the *"Before Christopher"* version of himself, when he would take the bike path from Bedford to Cambridge on his bike and watch the scenery change by town. In Lexington, geraniums and impatiens dotted window boxes on small store fronts that slowly transitioned to historic homes with grand front porches where mill owners once enjoyed lemonade on Sunday afternoons after church. Nearing Cambridge, the path cut through a neighborhood of three-deckers with kids playing hoops without a net. Before heading back, he made it a ritual to find a tuff of grass poking up through a crack in the sidewalk and reward its tenacity with a drink from his water bottle.

But few pedestrians were downtown tonight with the temperature in the teens, and the sidewalks were uninhabited as he ventured further out. On his right, the river ran silent, transporting ice floes toward the Atlantic twenty miles away. Across the street a mix of new and historic houses dotted the rolling landscape. The glow of kitchen and living room lights was a sad reminder of the life he used to take for granted.

About a half mile into the walk, his legs began to drag and he had second thoughts about not accepting the ride from his new friend. He'd hoped the cold air would revive him enough to mull over the last few days. Instead, it worked the opposite and gummed up his thoughts. Rounding a small bend in the road, he jerked his head at seeing a tall hooded figure fifty feet ahead on the sidewalk. The profile looked somewhat hunched and stood perfectly still, staring intently at something across the wide thoroughfare.

The streetlights suddenly began to flicker and then went off, leaving only the half-moon for light. He stopped a telephone pole length away from the stranger and surveyed the snow-covered landscape across the street, punctuated by a mammoth oak tree still clutching a few of its withered leaves. Scanning the gigantic tree, he expected to find an owl, turkey vulture, or perhaps a hungry raccoon, but the branches shivered alone in the light breeze. Further back the Buttonwoods Museum sat in darkness. Returning to the stranger, he remained puzzled why he did not move.

Internal bells began ringing and he tried to silence them. *So what if he's hooded? It's a cold winter night and who am I to define what acting weird looks like?*

He considered crossing the street, but feared what might be lurking on the other side that commanded such rapt attention. Turning around, he eyed the lights of downtown Haverhill. It would be a long, cold retreat and then what? Try and bum a ride to the hospital or go back to Salem and try again tomorrow? He took a deep breath and decided he had to press on and get to the hospital. Visiting hours may have ended hours ago, but he wanted to retrieve his clothes and wallet, hopefully still squirreled away in the bathroom ceiling, and find a quiet corner to sleep. In the morning, he would scan the parking lot for Mary's father's car before visiting Mary. He didn't know how to begin saying goodbye.

The moon slipped behind a cloud and the street turned even darker. *I'll just wait until a car approaches, and then make my move to get past this frozen flagpole.* Minutes ticked by and strangely not a single car appeared on the busy route, nor did the moon reappear. Add in the snuffed out streetlights, and it felt like an episode from *The Twilight Zone.* Christopher expected Rod Serling to begin narrating any moment.

The cold continued to infiltrate two pairs of cotton gym socks. No matter how hard he stamped his sneakers on the cement sidewalk, his toes were falling asleep while the dark figure maintained his trance.

The dark limbo grew unbearable. "This is ridiculous," he whispered, and stepped off the elevated sidewalk onto the road, wishing he had been able to channel Indiana Jones earlier and make off with Sergeant Mike's gun for protection. It was situations like this which made him anxious about hitchhiking south.

The salt and sand on the road made his steps sound like he had coarse sandpaper on the soles of his sneakers. The hulk remained motionless and apparently deaf as he approached.

"Cold night for a walk, my friend," a high-pitched voice commented which the breeze seemed to amplify as he passed.

He'd worked overtime for the past year dredging a deep moat around himself. "Only if you stop to chat."

"Clever reply, Christopher. Please give Mary my best when you see her in the morning."

His feet stopped moving on their own. "You know Mary?" he asked, turning around. *Better to start with that question rather than how he knows my name.*

"Yes, and it pains me how many don't recognize her unique innocence. Those who ridicule her today will come to regret it when they look back and understand how their tongues trampled her spirit." The hooded figure walked toward him to close the gap and Christopher blinked hard to find out he was terribly mistaken—the six-and-a-half-foot giant was a woman, although her features were impossible to scrutinize in the poor light. She reached into the side pocket of her long black coat and produced a small silver thermos. "I'm sure a little tea will work like antifreeze tonight." She unscrewed the plastic cup from the base with long ivory fingers.

Christopher accepted the cup and looked up and down the street still hoping for headlights. "What were you staring at across the street?"

She gave him a puzzled look like he was more of a simpleton than he faked sometimes. "Why, the Worshipping Oak, of course!" She began pouring the tea and a thin trail of white steam curled in the air between them. "Bigelow fan, right?"

He concentrated on keeping his hand steady. "Worshipping what?"

"When the first settlers arrived in Haverhill in 1642, Minister John Ward led services under that magnificent oak tree," she said, pointing. "Even after the Congregational church was completed two years later, they continued to worship under the tree in the summers." She finished pouring and smiled. "If you listen carefully, sometimes you can still hear the bell calling the congregation."

The moon came out of exile and Christopher got a better view of the woman's heart-shaped face. Her lips were plump and punctuated by a thin nose with a slight crook in the middle like his mother's, which she sustained in a sledding accident as a young girl. The woman's eyes looked black and contrasted against platinum blonde hair, most of which remained hidden under the hood.

Something about her face looked familiar in a troubling sort of way. "You'll have to excuse me as I nearly drowned a while ago, which put a kink in my short-term memory. Have we met before?" He reached for the notebook in his back pocket, but realized it wouldn't help much in the poor light.

The smile disappeared. "Sort of. You might say you bumped into me last year and I've been trying to get your attention ever since."

Christopher screwed up his face. "In Salem, Haverhill, or Billerica?"

"I'm not sure dreams have zip codes yet," she said with a faint smile.

Christopher bit his lip extra hard to make sure he wasn't dreaming in Danny's LTD. Not satisfied, he took a small sip from the plastic cup and it was the best green tea he ever tasted. He took another drink. "Wow, this is incredible."

She ignored the compliment and frowned instead. "I just don't understand why after nearly drowning, you would develop that strange habit of holding your breath and escape to the hinterlands of your imagination. From my perspective, the places you visit are somewhere between disturbing and cartoonish." She leaned down to look him in straight in the eye. "Isn't the twentieth century trouble enough for you?"

The cadence of her voice reverberated through him and he looked away so she couldn't read him. A few hundred feet ahead, he noticed a streetlight starting to pulse back to life and he decided to make a run for it so he could reference his notes.

She read his intention. "You've had a long day, so let me save you the bother. You will find the first three entries about me on pages seven, twenty, and thirty-two in your journal. Your notes describe dreams of running away from aliens, wild animals, and always a tall woman calling your name."

Christopher sucked in his breath and put his hands over his eyes.

"Look at me," she commanded.

He put his hands down and took a step backward. "Dreams are just made up stuff, that's all. Same with you," he said sharply.

She sighed. "You and your like underscore Proverbs: *Even fools, keeping silent, are considered wise; if they keep their lips closed, intelligent.*

He rocked side to side, not understanding the meaning, and looked her up and down even if it was impolite. The hem of her coat was so long it nearly touched the ground. "You said I bumped into you last year? How so?"

She reached up and slowly removed her black hood, and a cascade of platinum blonde curls which bordered on silver trailed down her back. Her index finger pointed to a small round bandage on her right temple. "I discovered your feet are made of pure New Hampshire granite after kicking me in the head." She looked at his feet. "I got you to the surface before things ran amok."

He couldn't explain why, but he had to reach up and touch the bandage with his finger. When he did, that terrible night came rushing back and he found himself underwater again.

Finally breaking free, he kicked toward the surface with his remaining strength and his bare foot hit something smooth and hard. With each new stroke, his arms began to weaken. Although the surface seemed only inches away, it stubbornly remained out of reach, like a mirage in the desert. His thoughts slowed as the darkness surrounding him began to shimmer with a bright light.

Suddenly, something grabbed him around the waist and propelled him upward with a tremendous rush. In the next instant, he felt cold air on his face and a hard slap between the shoulder blades. He gagged as the wind stung his face, and though he tried to tread water, he began to sink again. A ghoulish-looking Bobby Godfreye appeared beside him, keeping him afloat.

He felt dizzy and started to fall when a firm hand steadied him. "Take some more tea, Christopher. It will help."

He took three more sips and noticed the level in the cup never changed, no matter how much he drank. "My parents were religious and went to church every Sunday. My little sister talks to God like He's her best friend, which is surprising given everything that's happened. And me? Let's just say the seed landed on rocky soil, so if you're here to tell me you're my guardian—"

"Shhh," she whispered, as the moon disappeared again. "Don't say it out loud or even spell it."

"Why?"

"Because I failed. As with humans, there's consequences, but with the proper heart and discernment, a path back."

He moved quickly to try to get a better look at her upper back, but she matched his steps to prevent it.

"Okay, but I thought if *they* did exist—which I don't—you would be . . . ah, a guy."

"Pure intellects are neither male or female." She stood up straight and the improved posture made her a good seven feet tall. "Same with strength or any virtue."

He noticed a pinpoint of red starting to bleed through the white bandage. "I'm sorry I clocked you and didn't mean to aggravate it. But after a year, why hasn't it healed?"

She touched the bandage gingerly then slipped the hood back on as her stature diminished again. "Neither have you. Your panic proved to be a long detour into the wilderness for us both."

The tea started to come back up his throat. "That's . . . not . . . fair . . . I . . . was . . . drowning." He rubbed his throat trying to get the words unstuck.

She grabbed his hand; velvet felt coarse in comparison. "I'm talking about what's transpired since you woke up in the hospital. You've been treading water since then, kept afloat by the love you have for Kylie and Mary." She gave him a concerned look. "But the promise you made to your aunt about remaining silent, while also made out of love, is sadly misdirected." She looked across the street then back at him. "I have been pursuing you to warn you that red-eyed monsters surround you. If you persist in hiding behind your disabilities thinking it's a shield, or make foolish plans like you did earlier this evening, you will perish."

"You wanted to dump all of that on me in a dream? Seriously?" He studied the apparition and the deep worry lines cutting across her pale forehead. His mother used to tease how he attracted every nut in their area code. *No kidding!*

"Is there anything you don't know?" He took another sip of tea and swirled it around in his mouth, before noting how it stayed super-hot but never burned. "Enlighten me. If everything went as planned at World End that night, what did my future look like?"

"With free will nothing is ever cast in stone, but a path of strong possibility included bringing Kylie up, marrying Denise, having twins, elected to three terms as—" She stopped. "I've said too much."

"And my parents? None of this would have happened if they didn't take that flight."

She looked across the street again and remained silent.

A cold breeze kicked up and he looked away and then back again to see if he was imagining all this. "Then, what you're saying is as much as I've been trying to piece myself back together, like some modern day Humpty Dumpty, my future is messed up for good? If you're so special, why can't you just snap your fingers and make everything right?"

"Ah, you ignore divine intervention at your own peril, Christopher. Look at Paul as the best example. He was a nasty thug before Jesus knocked him off a horse."

"Nice story for someone your size. Can you downsize it for me?"

She thought for a moment. "Fine. Read the story of John Newton, a former slave trader who wrote 'Amazing Grace,' and consider how the Master Carpenter remakes a man *if* you let Him." She took his cup away. "'Let It Be' is a popular song for your age, but those three words can transform everything if you make them your response like a teenage Jewish girl did two thousand years ago."

He reached for his notebook and she touched his chest. "You won't forget what I'm saying as it's written in here by grace."

She pointed to the bloody patch on her temple. "I should take my leave now but," she sighed, "I still bear responsibility. While I do not want to interfere with the divine plan, I would like to make the road ahead a little less steep. Therefore, if you could ask for one thing what would it be? And no, I can't bring your parents back."

He exhaled and watched his breath hang in the air between them. "Is this like a genie sort of wish?"

The woman folded her arms and glared at him with a terrible frown. The hump on her back came alive and began to fidget.

"I . . . don't . . . know," he stuttered. "When I get nervous, things sometimes get jumbled in my head and I say stupid things."

Her expression softened and as she leaned over, he smelled lilacs. "I'm supposed to stay neutral in such rare offerings, but let me make a suggestion. The Information Age will accelerate and change the world with epic consequences. Say the word and you will become a pioneer in this technology revolution." She smiled. "Believe me, you won't need to keep tabs of things in that notebook anymore." She stepped back to gauge his reaction.

"How about Kylie and Mary? Can they be part of this too?"

She stood up straight. "Sorry, no add-ons. Free will, remember? Each must find their own path. So seize this opportunity for yourself and the global connections that come with it." She gave him a nudge. "Do not fear. You will have more than enough resources to assure Kylie grows into a well-educated and poised young woman, though often from a distance. Mary's path will continue to be challenging, but I can say no more." She gave him a wink. "Of course no promises, but in time your future may even intersect again with Denise's."

His ears welcomed the words like a spring shower after a brutal winter. The promise of a better tomorrow made his heart flutter, as his stomach rumbled anticipating exotic banquets on other continents. Yet at the same time, a small voice inside nagged, *"Remember Mom's warning."*

He searched the top of the curls for any signs of horns. "This all sounds intriguing, but I must say, out of character given your station. Didn't you just try and sell me on let it be?" He rubbed the back of his neck. "We've been talking for a bit now and I didn't catch your name."

"Just call me the Spark." She frowned. "The hour grows late. Quiet your mind and decide."

The wind ran away as the night held its breath and Christopher decided to do the same. After a long minute, the ember of his former self appeared pulsating with renewed vigor contemplating a future of money and prestige. *Perhaps if I pushed, she would throw in a supply of that wonderful tea,* he mused.

The St. Christopher medal suddenly felt hot against the center of his chest. In the same moment, he noticed how the edges of the ember looked ragged and a bit ashen, like charcoal briquettes his dad once bought that lit fast and bright, but quickly burned out. *"No staying power,"* he'd said, throwing them away. Focusing on the gray ash, he made out an array of thumbnail pictures and winced at one in particular. It was from last January before the accident. He was in Becky's kitchen covered in yellow paint and laughing as AJ mimicked Lori's sister scrambling around the floor picking up pennies kids threw at her.

He gasped for air and opened his eyes.

The dark eyes watched him. "So, you will take my recommendation?"

"Not so fast." He concentrated hard to line up the words on his tongue. "My mother used to read me *The Little Prince* when I was young. Her favorite line, which she drilled into me for years, was *'what is essential is invisible to the eye.'*"

The Spark nodded. "Yes, a lovely fable by Antoine de Saint-Exupéry, but I don't understand the relevance."

"I thought I was half the man I used to be, but now realize the better half survived, the one who would never abandon Kylie and Mary for any golden ticket. They give my world meaning and always will."

"You mimic the heart of Solomon in not asking for riches, power, or a longer life, which others would have sought. Nonetheless, you must understand, Christopher, nothing in life is guaranteed even with the noblest of choices, *for he makes his sun rise on the bad and the good, and causes rain to fall on the just and the unjust.*"

"The last year certainly proved that. I just want the wisdom to know the right thing to do and the strength to follow through."

The wind rustled through the branches. "*Behold, I am making all things new.* I see His handiwork and pray you have the grace to weather the coming storm. You also need to channel your inner courage." She hesitated and searched her coat pocket and pulled out a ten-penny nail, attached with a burlap string to a small crucifix.

"I carry this with me as a reminder there's nothing more brutal than a Roman crucifixion. Jesus knew what was coming; the whips and the thorns and the nails that would rip through flesh and bones. It was dark in the garden and his friends, the same ones that would deny and abandon him shortly, were asleep. He knew all this and could have slipped away to escape all the pain."

She untied the string and handed the nail to him as the moon slipped behind another cloud. "After the past year of hiding, may this nail give you the courage to open your arms wide no matter how bleak things look, how much it hurts, or how many times you fall. Beware too of the traitor, the one who holds a false lamp to camouflage the darkness around him. Everyone will be taken in by his guile, but not God, which sees all."

He turned the long cold nail in his hands. "You speak in strange riddles."

She thought for a moment. "When you were growing up, do you remember how much you and your friends liked playing Marco Polo?"

He pointed at his head. "My mind is a steel trap for what came before the accident, though I wish you could use an example that doesn't include water."

"But it teaches a lesson. Remember when you were 'it' and you had to close your eyes and use your other senses to locate the others in the pool? It's the same as your mother drilled into you. *What is essential is invisible to the eye.*" She pointed down the dark street. "But sometimes it isn't. Now get going, much is waiting."

He looked for her eyes and like Mary, she didn't grant permission. "Will I see you again?"

"Not with human eyes," she said, touching his chest. "I will always be at your side, but cannot intercede. You alone are the author of this story."

He nodded and looked across the street. "Will you continue to visit the Worshipping Oak too?"

"For a few more seasons yet. One year not too far ahead, a spring storm will bring it down."

"That's a shame after so many hundreds of years."

She shrugged. "Many will lament its loss and the fact none of the seedlings took hold. Too few understand we are the branches now." She walked toward the tree and he focused on the bulge on the top of her back which began twitching.

When she reached the other side of the road, Christopher started walking toward the hospital. A long parade of cars approached with blinding headlights and he resisted looking back. Not because he was afraid, but because he was terrified no one would be standing there.

CHAPTER THIRTY-FOUR

After retrieving his things from the hospital ceiling without incident, Christopher "adopted" an orphaned flashlight he found in the bathroom and had a wild idea. *It's the middle of the night. Why not retrieve my bike now?* No doubt, Ted the Sloth planned to deep six his uncle's prized Schwinn in World End or the Spicket River. But this required some physical effort with the ice a half foot thick, so chances were good he brought the bike home for storage. Not wanting another run-in with the apparition on Water Street, he used the ten bucks housed in the wallet to get a cab ride most of the way back to Salem.

Scrambling out of the cab, he apologized to the polite, middle-aged Greek driver for only having fifty cents to tip him. He attacked the remaining miles by alternating between running until he was out of breath, then downshifting to speed walking. No matter the speed, he fretted how the iridescent initials on the back of his jacket might become an unwanted beacon once he approached the Driscoll homestead. He considered removing the letters, but hated undoing all the meticulous handiwork. After much internal debate, he hit upon a nifty solution and simply turned the coat inside out. While he could no longer use the zipper, the heavy sweater underneath provided sufficient insulation.

With the snowbanks waist high and few sidewalks, he skedaddled into a driveway whenever a car approached. Distances measured in the mind are always half of what they truly are, and tonight proved no different. After he hoofed it for close to an hour, the address came into view and he hid behind a mountain of snow at a bend in the road. Peering around the white hulk, he sneered at the dilapidated brick colonial which the health department would have no trouble condemning if someone dropped a dime. A blue tarp covered half the roof with one end anchored to a front gutter partially detached from the house. The front porch leaned badly to the left as if trying to break away and gain its independence. Supposedly, the house wasn't always an eyesore. AJ never missed a chance to rehash how badly Mr. Driscoll had been played. Five years back, the family patriarch experienced a mid-life bout of insanity when he fell hard for a woman he met at some honky-tonk bar, while hauling printed-circuit boards to Newark. After he ditched his wife, the new girlfriend moved in and quickly maxed out his credit cards before taking off with all the family valuables. Now Jason and Ted rarely saw their father, as he worked long-haul jobs to recoup the losses and digest the embarrassment.

Surveying the house, Christopher could almost hear Mr. Godfreye lecturing the key to success is executing a well-thought-out plan. This would be especially critical since Fang, a mangy German shepherd was the reason the property didn't need a "No Trespassing" sign.

Christopher realized his bike might be imprisoned in the cellar of the house, but couldn't imagine Ted wrestling with the frozen bulkhead. Instead, his money was on the long detached barn fifty feet behind the main house at the bottom of a sloping driveway. Jason bragged how the barn was raised by local dairy farmers at the turn of the century, and the severely weathered shingles testified to its age. Christopher had never made it inside the barn, although he'd tried a number of times. While he didn't know what went on behind those thirsty shingles, the odds favored something illegal, given the amount of time AJ spent there and the reception he received whenever he tried to slither in. The last time he'd tried to get inside Fort Knox, Fang was tied with a rope to the bumper of a rusting white cargo van in the driveway. He'd tiptoed past the house and made it halfway down the driveway, before Fang came running full throttle. As he'd zigzagged away from the monster, he seriously underestimated the length of the rope. Fang tackled him like a linebacker and as he felt the dog's hot breath on his neck, the rope suddenly went taut. A bloodcurdling cry overtook his own screams. While Jason worked to prevent Fang from being promoted to guard duty in Hades, AJ slapped Christopher in the head for ignoring his warning about trespassing.

Now Christopher scanned the dark house and all looked calm as it should be in the middle of the night. "Well, I guess AJ didn't knock enough sense into me yet to stay away," he whispered. *But how to get in? It's not like I can just walk down the driveway.* Looking across the unbroken snowfield to the left of the barn, he noticed how the moonlight illuminated the icy crust. *Could I be so lucky?* He began to climb the snowbank and the snow crunched slightly, but held his weight. *Yes!*

Coming down the other side of the mound, the snow condensed only slightly. The mission would be truly stealth if the snow was just a tad more frozen, but that magic happened only with a perfect mix of conditions.

Making his way parallel to the house, he hugged a line of pine trees, grateful for their cover, but still concerned by the sound of his steps. At the last tree, he found himself only twenty feet away from the rear section of the barn, and debated whether he had the strength to shimmy up a tree if Fang came running with his long white teeth and bloody gums. A slight breeze cut across the yard and the trees swayed, continuing to laugh at his anxiety. Like Simo and Pial, he needed magic paints to make himself invisible. The logic side of his brain argued he should abandon this madness and just tell Sergeant Mike about the whole incident and let the police follow up. But he feared the other men in blue might not help a suspended cop, or assist a would-be shoplifter to locate a twenty-year-old bike.

Before he could think of another excuse, he crouched low and ran to the side of the barn and paused to listen for the rabid dog. Practically crawling, he made his way around back and found the double barn doors chained and padlocked. He lowered his head for a split second and then punched the air. Deciding to go for broke, he raced to the front of the barn and found the front doors with standard locks. Sitting like a duck in the open, he knew the right decision was to retreat, but he pictured the Schwinn glistening in the sun and didn't want to embrace defeat. Sure the bike would have to be disinfected after exposure to Ted, but he wanted it back and NOW!

He spied a window ten feet away and slithered over to it, knowing if Jason or Ted had insomnia and looked out their back door right now, he would be one dead numb-nut. The medical examiner would certainly make a note the corpse wore a winter coat inside out.

Some of the window putty fell out when he tried to push the rotting window open. To his surprise, it inched upward and creaked softly, inviting him in. He swung one foot in, half expecting to step on some devilish razor-sharp trap. Instead, his sneaker found a broad-plank wooden floor. Once inside, he tried to shut the window and it became temperamental and let out a sickly squeal, which to him sounded as loud as the sirens at the parade.

The pocket-sized flashlight he found at the hospital had an adjustable beam, and with one turn of the collar, it cast a large glow on everything in its path. Pointing the light, he discovered a rusting wood stove and some broken kitchen chairs. The scene repeated itself wherever he looked, as the flashlight uncovered a menagerie of junk and additional proof nature hates a vacuum and fills whatever space it finds.

He looked behind some of the larger items for the bike. In one corner, he discovered a stack of studded snow tires with a trapeze of cobwebs in the center. Thankfully, the aerial artists had the night off.

Continuing deeper into the barn, he came upon another garage door and pulled it up halfway before crawling under and finding himself in another large storage area.

Adjusting the head of the flashlight to cast the maximum swath of light, he pursed his lips in a silent whistle to see multiple automobiles in various stages of dismemberment. *Why are these being worked on here instead of at the salvage yard?* The flashlight found a Mercedes and two Camaros up on blocks, but not his sought-after prize. *Maybe my assumptions are wrong and Mr. Perch is learning to ride the bike at the bottom of World End.*

The flashlight hit the end of the building and outlined a large wooden door on casters. "How many chambers are in this house of horrors?" he mumbled. The urge to retreat grew, but he ran and tackled this door too. It let out small squeak as the bottom rollers moved in short spurts. A year ago, he would have needed only a few inches, but now he felt like a rhino and pushed the door wide open to pass.

When he finally made it through and pointed the flashlight, he froze. Sitting alone by the back door of the barn was a black Ford Mustang with a red pinstripe on its hood.

"Impossible!" he said much too loudly, and stumbled backward, more afraid of this automobile than of Jason, Ted, or whoever he encountered on the road to the hospital.

Could this really be Lori's car? He inched his way over to the driver's side and looked in, afraid to find a skeleton driver.

The white leather seats were thankfully empty and he took it as a sign he should disappear too. The rollers on the wooden door seemed frozen in place, but he continued pushing hard, wanting to leave no hint of a break-in. Perspiration collected on his forehead as the door finally relented and closed.

Making his way back though the barn felt like the glass house maze at the amusement park and he expected Jason or Ted to appear any moment with pitchforks. At last, he made it back to the window, the reconnaissance mission only moments away from completion. He started to climb out, when suddenly the spotlight on the back of the house came to life and he quickly threw himself back inside. When he peered over the sill, he watched Fang trot down the back stairs and sniff his way over to the edge of the driveway where he began to relieve himself.

Once the German shepherd finished doing his duty, he began sniffing the air and turned toward the barn. Christopher decided to abandon the super-stealth strategy and jumped up and closed the window, which cooperated.

Naturally, Fang saw it all and immediately started barking loud enough to wake half of Salem. Christopher looked around, wishing he could make himself small enough to hide in one of the snow tires even if he had to commune with a colony of spiders.

"Fang, get in here now!" he heard Jason yell.

The dog held his ground until Jason repeated the order but louder. The dog quickly surrendered and bolted up the stairs. Christopher waited for Jason to shut off the back light and in the process, caught sight of a marvelous lime-green treasure on the wooden deck by the back door.

He counted to three hundred before deciding Jason must have forgotten about the light and gone back to bed. Once he made it through the window, he felt his spirit yell *"Charge!"* As he sprinted toward the back stairs and the deck, he thought he saw the bike inch toward him in anticipation of the reunion.

CHAPTER THIRTY-FIVE

Fang heard his heavy footsteps run across the deck and started barking and throwing himself against the back door. Christopher, feeling like he was moving in slow motion, grabbed the bike and jumped on the seat before realizing he wasn't Evel Knievel and would never survive the jump off six steps. The miscalculation cost precious seconds, but it motivated his feet to move like Wile E. Coyote as he dismounted and carried the bike down to the driveway. By the time the front spotlights flashed on with the intensity of a federal prison, he had the bike in fifth gear and was pumping the pedals with all his might.

For the next two miles, he looked over his shoulder every ten seconds expecting a posse to be in hot pursuit, but the only thing that caught up to him was exhaustion. Panting hard, he finally gave in and slowed the pace as the sweat on his back began to flash freeze.

Up ahead, the Salem depot came into view and Godfreye's Superette glowed like an oasis in the pre-dawn darkness. He longed for a cup of tea, but knew it would never taste like the elixir he enjoyed last night.

Escorting the bike into the store, Christopher found the store owner already hunched over the counter cradling a humongous coffee mug and reading the *Eagle Tribune*.

Godfreye looked up. "My, you're up early," he said in a gravelly morning voice, before looking down again at the paper. "But if your goal is to be the first customer of the day, you better set your alarm clock an hour earlier. Nick Dunlap is here every weekday morning at four-thirty before heading into Boston. He doesn't talk much except for a few grunts, which is funny most mornings." He glanced up again and his eyes narrowed. "How many times do I have to tell you not to bring your bike in here? What do I have to do, put a sign on the door that says all patrons must wear shirts, shoes, and leave all recreational vehicles outside?"

Christopher deployed the kickstand and approached the judge. "I apologize, Mr. Godfreye, but wanted to ask if I could store my bike in the back room for a few days?"

Furrowed eyebrows met in the center of the store owner's forehead as he turned the page. "Do you mistake my store with one of those storage facilities that keeps popping up everywhere to handle the overflow of people's junk?"

"Of course not. My bike isn't junk and I promise it will be for a short time."

Godfreye took another sip of coffee and cocked his head. "Why do you need to leave it here? Doesn't AJ have room?"

"It's a long story."

He flashed a stop sign with his right hand. "Please spare me the details. This is my quiet time of the day before everyone starts yapping at me for the next fifteen hours. That said, I don't blame AJ one bit if he's giving you grief about riding a bike this time of year." He snuck a quick look at Christopher's sneakers. "Your late uncle had the sense to walk or bum a ride this time of year rather than risk ending up under the wheels of a car."

Christopher nodded, hoping to power through the rocky terrain. "So can I store it out back, please?"

The store owner grunted. "If I trip on it, you'll find it in the dumpster for long-term storage."

Christopher smiled and began wheeling it past the register.

"I heard through the grapevine AJ got his license back?"

He stopped, fearing a landmine.

The store owner cradled the mug in both hands and inhaled the aroma. "I need java like this on an IV drip this time of year." He pointed at the paper. "Well, at least the Sox begin spring training soon, which gives me hope to hang on."

"Maybe we'll get a January thaw in February too." Thinking of last year's made him bite his lip.

Mr. Godfreye shrugged. "If you ask me, a thaw is just a mean tease. We get a couple days with temperatures ten degrees above normal and people start thinking about beer, barbecues, and the beach. Then an arctic blast comes marching in or a nor'easter dumps a foot of snow and the whining gets so intense it makes me want to hibernate, or move so far south no one knows how to spell snow." He shook his head trying to dislodge the thought. "So AJ's good?"

Christopher hesitated. "Good doesn't come close."

An uncomfortable silence followed before Godfreye leaned over the counter. "Look. I've spent a lot of time on my knees thinking about what happened *that* night. There was more than enough wrong to go around, including a healthy portion for my son. But being angry or vengeful isn't going to bring my Robert back. I know AJ avoids me like the plague, but I wish he wouldn't. Tell him to stop by if he ever wants to talk and clear the air."

Christopher looked away and his eyes focused on a pail of red plastic umbrellas for sale and watched as they morphed into a dozen tire irons dripping with blood. The image made him dizzy and he looked out the front window, wanting to find pink cotton candy clouds in the morning sky, but the dark remained. *If the Spark was real, why didn't she meet me in a beautiful sunrise, instead of popping up in the cold darkness?*

"Going back to sleep?" Godfreye asked loudly.

He turned his back on the umbrellas. "No, it's just early."

"I take it you're more of a night owl. By the way, you didn't answer me. Does AJ have his license back?"

"Yeah, and he's driving a beat up Blazer which steers like a boat. He's saving up for something better later this year." He knew Mr. Godfreye liked to dabble at car auctions and kept a tab on all the classic wheels around town. He held his breath, knowing this was like ice fishing without a pole, and expecting a frozen fish stick to jump out.

"What's your cousin looking for? I have a knack for locating most anything on wheels; even those funny cars with propellers by the exhaust pipes so it doubles as a boat."

"Well, he and Jason have been talking. He loves Mustangs, but—"

"And that *but* should be in capital letters followed by the words: AJ will never drive one," he said, cutting him off. "I'm sure your cousin knows it would be pretty insensitive to own the same model as his missing girlfriend." He shook his head. "Poor girl, all this time and still no word." He sighed and began straightening a rack of cigarettes on a wall behind him. "I hope he stays away from Camaros too," he added, "for my sake."

An old pickup sped past the store with a loud muffler. Ted was out trolling for him.

"I have a shipment of marshmallow valentine hearts coming in next Tuesday," Godfreye said. "You can store it back there until then."

Christopher began wheeling the bike down the aisle when the store owner called his name. "Get yourself a cup of tea while I finish a few things up here. Then you can help me stock a few shelves. Storage comes with fees, you know."

He eyed an apple Danish display, but his stomach wasn't in sync with being hunted. The back of the store beckoned with three tall cylinders of strongly perked coffee. No wimpy exotic flavors were brewed here, just strong Robusta beans imported from South Africa. Police and nurses facing long shifts were regular customers, convinced one cup of the special brew would chase away sleep for a good twenty-four hours. Christopher anchored a tea bag in a cup of hot water for a good steep, before moving his tired bones and the bike into the safety of the cramped back room.

A few overstock cases of blueberry pie filling from last Thanksgiving made a perfect seat to rest and enjoy the tea. The sheetrock on the wall across from him had an interesting splatter diagram of ancient coffee stains, which the frugal store owner tried to hide with a poster of San Juan. Godfreye boasted how he planned to retire there someday. Christopher suspected the shrewd businessman wouldn't leave town until acquiring a bodega to fleece tourists.

After helping to restock the snack aisle, Christopher decided to head back to AJ's and catch some needed sleep. Passing Mary's street, he noticed a U-Haul truck backed up to her front door and decided to investigate. The yellow truck had a long metal loading ramp, providing a convenient bridge between the cargo bay and house. A young guy in his late teens, sporting a crew-cut and dressed in a burgundy sweatshirt and baggy jeans, staggered out of the house carrying a large cardboard box. He hesitated on the metal bridge long enough for Christopher to eye a Scrabble box peeking out the top. The game looked weird outside, its commute until now limited from the hall closet to the kitchen table.

A deep voice boomed from the back of the cavernous truck. "Rob, better cradle the bottom of that box!"

In the next instant, the cardboard gave way, and two dozen books tumbled out along with all the letters from the game. Christopher thought it would make a terrific picture for a contest.

"Are you kidding me?" a voice echoed from inside the truck.

"No harm, no vowel," Rob replied with a laugh, and started picking up the books.

A barrel-chested, thirty-something man, apparently immune to the cold and wearing a tight *Miami Vice* T-shirt and khaki cargo shorts, came running out of the truck. His tan work boots made a terrible clanging noise on the bridge.

"Everybody wants to be the next Seinfeld. Just hurry and pick it up, will ya?" he barked. "From what I'm told, the lady we're moving is a bit touched, so probably only spells one-syllable words anyways. She won't miss a letter or two."

"I don't know about that. Some of these I read in college lit." Rob held up a thin book. "This one has all the poems of Emily Dickinson."

The tough guy squeezed by him. "Mover by day and poet by night? Who knew? Just hurry up. It gives me the heebie-jeebies working a crime scene."

Boss man disappeared into the house and moments later a loud thud followed. "Get in here, quick! I need some help," he yelled.

The young guy went running in. Christopher let their conversation marinate for a bit and came to the realization Mary's father had expedited Mary's move to New York. He eyed a letter "Q" next to the back wheel of the truck. If it were a vowel, he might have left it there, but the letter was worth ten points, so he picked it up.

Cuss words filled the air as a queen-sized box spring appeared. The men groaned trying to maneuver it through the narrow doorway and into the truck. The older man hurried back into the house as Rob lingered behind.

"I know how heavy that is," Christopher offered, stepping forward. "Mary wanted to rearrange her bedroom last month and I threw my back out." He glanced in the cargo area of the truck, surprised how small the box spring now looked. "Then her father came home and made me move it all back, back sprain and all."

Rob's expression didn't change a fraction as he listened. "Who are you? The area welcome wagon creep?"

Christopher let it pass. Greetings like that didn't even register anymore. He was glad he wasn't wearing his coat inside out and pointed to the initials on the back.

The teenager took a pack of Newports out of the back pocket of his jeans. "Is the group home nearby?"

He took a deep breath. "No, this neighborhood isn't zoned for apartments."

The boss came bounding out of the house carrying a small maple nightstand and scowled at his co-worker. "Nothing like a little menthol to go with your cancer sticks, or should I say ours? I end up breathing all the secondhand smoke. Maybe I should start smoking too so I can have a cigarette break every ten minutes!"

"It's an addiction, Don." Rob took a deep drag and blew the smoke toward his boss.

"That's what I love about this world. Everyone's either a comic or a victim. But go ahead and keep taking those long tokes. Maybe it'll make you remember your money troubles and get your butt in gear so we're not here until midnight."

The teenager ignored the comment. "You woke up on the wrong side of the bed this morning, but I'll give you a laugh." He pointed at Christopher. "Check this dude out. It's not every day you see someone with their initials emblazoned in duct tape." He cocked his head. "What's *CM* stand for anyways?" He rolled his eyes. "Let me guess: Chump Man."

Christopher felt the edges of the frayed tape. "No. Christopher Maguire."

Rob nodded. "I think it would be really cool if you wrote out your entire name in tape. It might wrap around your jacket a couple times, but it would get folks to really take notice." He took another drag. "Then no one would forget your name. I sure won't."

Don came over and smirked. "Do you live here too?"

"No, I'm just checking on Mary."

Rob knelt down and Christopher smelled tobacco and backed up. "Well, you better split, Mr. Christopher Maguire, because you're a wanted man."

"I know Mary's father is really upset with me, although I wouldn't use the word *wanted*. Rejected fits better." He looked at the letter "Q" he was holding. Quagmire came to mind.

The teenager stood back up. "No, I think this dude wanted to scramble your brains for breakfast."

"Ah forget-about-it," Don barked. "This ain't Dear Abby! We have to get on the road if we're going to make it to Atlanta before spring."

The location ran faster than rapids in his brain. Christopher banged on the metal bridge and the noise surprised the movers. "Atlanta? You're . . . mistaken," he stuttered. "Mary is moving to New York."

"Is that what she told you?" Rob winked at his partner. "Then New York it is. Wonder what she told the other guy?" They shared a laugh and disappeared back into the house.

Christopher jumped up on the ramp and hurried into the cargo area to read the white address labels on the boxes. Sure enough, they were all headed to *Denton Place, 1412 Jefferson Street, Atlanta, Georgia.* He felt his knees buckle.

Rob came rushing down the ramp rolling a large green suitcase and waved him out. "Hey, CM, you're not supposed to be in there. We have enough insurance issues already."

"Sorry." He was headed for the metal bridge when the sound of loud exhaust filled the air. Rob pushed him back in the truck and motioned for him to be quiet.

"Hey, did that numb nut come around yet?" a strained voice shouted from the street.

Christopher waited for the mover's arm to hand him over to Ted. "Nothing to report, captain," Rob yelled back.

The truck sped off and Rob picked up the suitcase and placed it in the corner of the cargo hold before turning to Christopher.

"That creep is the numb nut."

"Why?" Christopher asked.

"Because I would have sold you down the river for a cup of coffee or a joint."

CHAPTER THIRTY-SIX

By the time Christopher dragged himself up the stairs to AJ's apartment, the sun had reached its zenith in the sky, which at forty-two degrees north latitude, amounted to a short hop in winter. Christopher knew he would be kidding himself to say he remembered the entire odyssey of the last couple days, but recalled enough to make his brain feel like a cement mixer. Around and around the images went, folding in on each other as they spun.

He opened the door and tiptoed into the kitchen. The volume on the television in AJ's bedroom filled the entire apartment, which meant the hangover from "Thirsty-Thursday" must have been intense enough to blow off work.

The rant from some shoot-'em-up movie sounded like a jackhammer, so he reached for the headphones and collapsed on the couch. Sleep quickly pulled him under like it had been pacing on a widow's watch anxiously waiting for his return. *Platinum hair and alabaster skin smelling of lilacs immediately embraced him. "Can I have a cup of that celestial tea?" he whispered.*

A hard rap on the top of the head made the dream evaporate. Opening his eyes ever so slightly, he found AJ standing over him.

"Well, look who dropped by! The half-wit boob who can't figure out if he wants to be an action hero or petty thief. Sounds like the pilot for a new *Marvel* series if you ask me, except its star is literally a washed-up loser."

Christopher kept squinting, hoping this storm would blow on through, and focused on his cousin's T-shirt with yellow pit stains. When they were teenagers, AJ used to strut around with a muscular build and come spring, douse himself with baby oil in search of a tan to complement the under-sized tank tops he wore. Unfortunately, the bizarre ritual landed him in the emergency room on more than one occasion, with second degree burns and looking like he had a bad case of the mumps. But after consuming the seven seas of beer and shunning fresh air like kryptonite, AJ was beginning to morph into a pregnant-looking opossum.

"Take the headset off," AJ yelled, and took a swipe at him.

Christopher moved fast enough to avoid the hairy mitt and hid the headphones behind his back.

"Isn't it time you grew up?"

The words stung remembering a similar scolding from the sergeant. He located the abused flap of skin inside his cheek and poked at it with his tongue. The blood tasted salty and his fingers fumbled with the buttons on the audiocassette player perched behind his back.

His cousin walked over to the window and held up his hands like a vampire shunning daylight. Gunfire from the television in the bedroom provided the right mood.

"You've really set Teddy off this time, cuz. He only wanted to teach you a lesson after giving him that fake twenty." AJ turned and glared at him for a second. "And how dare you use my ad to prank him like a fifth grader. If you had played it cool, you would have had the bike back in a few weeks. I mean, who needs one this time of year anyways?"

Christopher shrugged, which somehow lit AJ's fuse because he raced across the room and stopped only inches away from his face.

The air smelled sour as his cousin continued to sweat out last night's bender.

"I called out sick today, because I didn't have it in me to listen to Jason and Ted go on and on about you. All I can say is you better ask your cop buddy the penalty for breaking and entering charges. Maybe you should also inquire about protective custody because Jason wants to put you back in the hospital permanently." He slapped the back of Christopher's head. "I told them since we're family, I have first dibs. Maybe after I'm done here, you can share a hospital room with Morbid."

AJ tried to slap him again, but Christopher batted his hand away. "I think Ted broke one of my ribs, so I'm paid up."

"Not by a long shot. Jason knows you tried to get in the barn because he saw your footprints in the snow. How many times do I have to tell you that place is off limits?" He glanced at the door. "That stolen property better not be down in the garage because if I find it, the Caterpillar will use it as dental floss."

Christopher clenched his fists trying to figure out the knotted logic of how recovering his bike made it stolen.

His cousin backed away and put his hands on the hips of his gray sweatpants. "This mute act of yours is getting pretty old too. Though I have to say, when you do let your tongue out of its cage at the 400 Club—everyone may call you the Guvnor, but they're killing themselves laughing behind your back."

Christopher frowned. He started sitting with a group of "regulars" at the small bar late last summer. He would sit silent and nurse a beer, while they debated all sorts of topics like whether the Red Sox had a strong enough bullpen or why taxes only went up. Sometimes they discussed silly and mysterious things like crop circles and alien abductions. Then late one Friday night a couple months later, Debbie took a sip of her white wine and asked what *he thought* about their chitchat. It felt so good, and everyone listened intently, even if their eyes were glassy.

One evening after he explained in great detail why Bigelow made the best tea, he finally gained their respect.

"Fantastic logic! We should run this man for mayor," Johnny yelled, from three stools down.

"Mayor? How about Guvnor!" Sally replied. "He looks a bit British too." It was then decided by a quorum of four bar stools and two seated at a nearby table, that he be appointed the first and only "Guvnor of the 400 Club."

"I can still hear them laughing from here," AJ continued.

The grenade found its mark and the pain radiated behind his eyes. "I don't believe you. Especially Sump; he's my buddy."

"That drunken, know-it-all buffoon? I can see why he's taken a liking to you, because you suck up everything he spews. Everyone else figures you must be made out of those Styrofoam peanuts used for packaging. It's the only way to explain why you floated to the surface after falling in World End twice."

Christopher spied a dust bunny clinging to the leg of the coffee table and envied how it just hung around all day not being bothered. The Spark's words played in his ears when she gave him the nail.

"Beware too of the traitor, the one who holds a false lamp to camouflage the darkness around him. Everyone will be taken in by his guile, but not God, which sees all."

How could this warning point to AJ? His tongue was nothing more than a nuclear-powered potty-mouth.

"Are you going deaf too?" AJ asked, slapping his head again. "I bet you'd listen if Morbid was quoting that dead poet from a century ago. Come to think of it, maybe I'll swing by the hospital later and see when she's getting discharged. After all, we never did finish our date." He snickered. "And I'll be sure to promise an ending more exciting than whatever Disney fantasy my buddy planned before Captain Half-Wit arrived." He leaned down and searched Christopher's face. "Plus, she owes me something and you know what I'm talking about."

Christopher tried to get up, but AJ pushed him back down.

"She doesn't have the ticket," he yelled above the gunfire in the background.

AJ laughed and sat down on the recliner. "Like you'd tell me the truth given the stakes here." He studied him for a moment and his eyes narrowed. "Come to think of it, maybe you're trying to outflank everyone by playing hero at Canobie in order to win the jackpot for yourself." He waved a closed fist. "Given what you did to my car, your next bike should have training wheels."

The loose flap of skin in his cheek kept his tongue busy and he searched its ragged perimeter. He welcomed the radiating pain and it made him want to silence this bully and begin walking south to Florida. When he looked toward the recliner again, his cousin's hands were slicing the air.

"—and this is the thanks I get?" AJ asked.

The acidic voice in his head that made its debut at Sergeant Mike's house grabbed the controls. "I . . . paid . . . you . . . in . . . full . . . and . . . then . . . some," he stuttered.

AJ screwed up his face like he couldn't believe what he was hearing. "Why . . . do . . . you . . . say . . . that?" he mocked.

The path back to World End felt as deep and worn as the wagon wheels from the Oregon Trail, which can still be seen from space. There were a couple possible detours to escape AJ's wrath, but strangely, the usual fear and anxiety were absent. Whether this was from sheer exhaustion or the new strength he asked the Spark for, he couldn't say.

"Well?" AJ barked, expecting him to cave.

"I don't remember much about *that* night," he began. The words came out sounding flat, representing the usual headwaters of capitulation. He took a deep breath. "But I remember enough."

AJ snapped his head back, then sneered so all his stained and crooked teeth were on full display. "Be really careful, cuz."

Christopher grabbed his right leg as it began twitching. "The tire iron for instance."

AJ launched himself out of the recliner and grabbed him by the wrist. "Remember Mr. Snitch? Did you pack him with your things?"

Christopher pulled his arm away. After waking up in the hospital, he felt confused for days on end. One afternoon, AJ arrived carrying a small white Teddy bear with its eyes, nose, mouth, and ears stitched closed with heavy red thread.

"Say hello to Mr. Snitch," AJ whispered, putting him on the pillow next to him. "Every time you look at him, I want you to remember I can do the same to you if you breathe a word about what happened."

"I'd have to recheck my notes, but I don't think I ever saw it again after your mother took it home from the hospital."

AJ knelt down in front of him and searched his face. "After I threatened you within an inch of your life, you gave it to my old lady?"

"Your mother knew something bad happened out on the ice. I began to tell her the bits and pieces I remembered, but she stopped me, not wanting to know the details. She begged me not to say anything to the police. You were in enough trouble already with Lori's disappearance, and she was afraid things would only get worse." He rubbed his face. "The reason I haven't said anything was for her, not you. You're all she has left."

AJ retreated to the recliner and ran his hand through his hair, processing the information. Christopher glanced behind him at the Walkman and moved it into the corner fold of the couch.

His cousin noticed. "I have a good mind to rip your ears off and sew them back on upside down so you can never wear those headphones again. After that, I'll close up your mouth for good like I promised." Hearing his own words reignited AJ's anger and he came out of the chair and attacked him.

The lumpy couch was in cahoots with AJ and try as he might, Christopher was quickly pinned.

"So, college dropout, it's time for your oral exam. If you flunk, no worries, as I teach remedial learning for dummies, and will gladly beat the lesson into you. So tell me again, what do you remember? Here's a helpful clue. You were water logged the first time I pulled you out and after the second dunk, pretty blue. At least that's what I recall in saving your butt." He slapped his head. "Your answer, please."

Christopher wondered how many words he would get out before he tasted a fist, if he pushed. Looking up at the popcorn ceiling, he noticed a dark stain three inches across. Unfortunately, there were no signs the ceiling was beginning to bow.

"I still wake up with nightmares, frustrated I can't remember the details," he whispered.

"Atta boy. You keep thinking like that and you'll be promoted to the retard class in no time." AJ got up and moved to the worn recliner and lit a cigarette.

Christopher sat up and watched him take one deep drag after another. The growing ash reminded him of soot-stained snow.

"Some days I'm able to forget about what happened for a while, but reminders keep popping up. Like when I'm helping Mr. Godfreye at the store. I see these funny stick figures of a family drawn in red crayon on the wall in the storeroom and it kicks me in the stomach." He bit his lip and stared at AJ. "As much as you want me to erase everything, I can't. Neither can Mr. Godfreye. It's why he can't bring himself to repaint a wall his son drew on as a five-year-old."

AJ's mouth dropped open as the cigarette ash broke and fell on his lap.

"You were drunk that night and I should never have gotten in your car. That's on me."

AJ brushed the ash off his sweatpants. "Okay, enough with the ancient history."

Christopher watched as the wind-driven snow from that night blew the door and windows open in the apartment and swirled around them. "I remember you swinging for the fences with the tire iron."

"I said shut up," AJ spit back.

"The glass shattered all over Bobby and he had blood running down his face." Christopher looked away, trying to outrun the flashback, and his eyes stopped at the coat rack in the corner by the door. "I didn't remember very much after the ice broke—well, until I came off the meds."

AJ rolled his eyes. "You stopped your medications? So that explains the paranoia and hallucinations."

Christopher kept studying the coat rack cradling AJ's red ski parka. "Then I began remembering bits and pieces after the ice broke: being stuck underwater in the car, kicking something hard, a rush back to the surface, Bobby coming to my aid and you pulling me out. I remember Bobby begging for help, but you and Jason wouldn't let him on the ice. The last image I have is seeing red and white before the ice broke again. Then there's a cold shock and everything went black, until I woke up in the hospital."

"Okay, looney."

"I keep thinking about that splotch of red and white. I figured the red must be associated with the terrible gash on Bobby's head but—" He looked at AJ like he saw him in a new light and sucked in his breath. "You and Jason wore the same red ski jackets, right?" He pointed to the coat rack. "Except yours has white ski tags."

"So what?"

"Because," he began, carefully lining up the words, "Bobby was weak and instead of helping him, you must have pushed him under and held him there. I remember your white ski tags near the ice when you were talking with Bobby. He was there one moment and gone the next."

AJ rocketed upright in the recliner and looked over at his coat.

"But when the ice broke a second time the water washed away everything; the blood, the tire iron, the murder. You can't sew all that up."

AJ lunged out of the chair and got him in a headlock. "No, but I can squeeze all the air out of an inflatable Bozo."

Christopher punched his cousin repeatedly in the side as the vise tightened around his neck. Just before he blacked out, AJ let go and limped back to the recliner and lit up another cigarette.

"Okay, now it's my turn," he said with a weary look. "Family is supposed to have each other's back when they're in a jam." He took a short puff and blew the smoke his way. "Your aunt shouldn't have to plead with you to help circle the wagons."

The back of his neck ached and he massaged it with his fingertips. "But I didn't know what I was promising when she asked me. Now that I know—"

"Things got out of control that night, okay?" AJ said, interrupting him. "Godfreye and I were friends until he stole what was mine."

Christopher jerked his head. "Lori belonged to you?"

AJ took a long toke and exhaled the smoke in small circles. "Look. If Bobby knocked on my door today, I'd greet him with some Phil Collins. *"Can you feel it coming in the air tonight, oh Lord, oh Lord,"* he started singing badly out of tune. *"Well, if you told me you were drowning, I would not lend a hand.* Then I'd whack him in the head again." He took another puff. "But listen carefully. I . . . didn't . . . kill . . . Bobby," he said slowly. "The ice broke and put an end to our disagreement."

"But I remember—"

"You remember nothing. It's all a hallucination since you were drowning. For your sake, you better drink that Kool-Aid fast."

"So what happened to Lori then?"

AJ cocked his head. "If you're insinuating something like the cops keep trying to do, I suggest you swallow it fast before I knock it down your throat. We're not in a confessional here, but as far as she's concerned, let Bobby be a lesson to you. He must have thought he could make it up to me by helping to rescue you." He took another drag. "But the water proved to be a better judge, jury, and executioner than I could ever be. Lori is just as guilty as him and can rot wherever she is."

"How about Jason?"

"What about him?"

"Did you give him a Mr. Snitch too?"

"Don't have to because Jason acts more like family than you ever did. I suggest you get back on your meds fast before your twisted thinking gets you hurt." He took one last toke and deposited the rest of the butt in the empty beer can. "Enough chewing on this cud. Let me make it crystal clear for the simpleton—which to be clear, is you. Bring any of this up again, and I'll tie a honey-baked ham around the two-hundred-pound vegetable sitting in front of me. Then I'll ship you down to the Everglades so the gators can enjoy a New England boiled dinner."

He got up from the recliner and headed for the hall, but stopped and turned around. "The funny thing is no one this side of sanity would believe a single word you say about those new memories. People already think you panicked and held Bobby underwater so you could save yourself."

Christopher rocked side to side on the couch and waited for AJ to slam the bedroom door. Then he reached for the Walkman and stopped the recording.

CHAPTER THIRTY-SEVEN

"Be careful what you wish for," his mother used to say with a wink after Sunday dinner. Then she would disappear into the kitchen and he and Kylie would try and guess what mouth-watering creation she whipped up for dessert. His favorite never changed: mile-high apple cream pie which he washed down with a tall glass of ice cold milk, not the fake powder junk his aunt tried to substitute.

Be careful what you wish for. Tonight his mother's words echoed, as he huddled inside the cab of the Caterpillar, listening to the recording of him and AJ and taking notes. When he promised his aunt to remain silent about what happened on World End, the worst part involved AJ beating up Bobby. But as Paul Harvey said: "*And now you know the rest of the story.*" This meant he witnessed attempted murder if the ice really did break like AJ claimed, which he questioned. Christopher chewed on the pen cap and mulled over whether to tell Sergeant Mike, despite all the hurtful things said between them. Looking through the notebook, he reread the entry about finding the Mustang at Jason's and wondered if it was connected.

"*Be careful what you wish for, especially if you've got to crack a few eggs to make an omelet,*" his mother also said. She loved mixing proverbs and came up with some weird combinations that would make Yogi Berra smile. He closed the notebook and decided to borrow the spare key from Lori's wallet and break into the barn again. If the key fit the

Mustang, he would call in the cavalry. If not, he would avoid getting everyone all riled up and signing his death warrant with Jason and AJ. Timing was crucial before Jason moved the car, so he decided to do it tonight. He knew this might be his last ridiculous stunt, but first, he had to get the key.

Sneaking upstairs, he found AJ passed out in the recliner. Beer cans littered the floor around him as he apparently tried to drown himself and Bobby again. Christopher watched his chest heave for a couple minutes, before slipping off his sneakers and skating across the floor in his gym socks. He glanced back once before sneaking down the short hall into the dark bedroom. Turning on his flashlight, he quickly made his way over to the closet and uncovered the dashboard memento. The glove compartment door surprisingly opened on the first try. As he grabbed for the wallet, he suddenly heard the kitchen faucet running. Switching off the flashlight as the sound of heavy footsteps approached, he crawled into the closet knowing this might soon become his tomb if discovered.

AJ stumbled into the dark room and collapsed on the bed. Christopher held his breath and waited, sure his heartbeat was loud enough to wake up the drunk and also be picked up by seismic monitors. Minutes passed and AJ launched into a snore-fest. He decided to abort the mission, but his fingers attempted a coup and continued working on extracting the key from the wallet. Once he felt the smooth metal in his hands, he decided to continue with the plan and began an agonizing slow motion crawl out of the closet and toward the hall.

It was after midnight when he finally made it outside. The air felt cold, but moist, and he noticed a ring around the moon. "Yeah, there's a storm brewing, all right," he whispered, and headed down the stairs.

The hike back to the barn seemed longer than the night before, and he figured this was due to the nagging feeling his luck was in serious overdraft. He tried to counterbalance the negative thoughts by arguing that so much bad stuff transpired in the past year, perhaps a bit of good fortune still remained on the balance sheet. Even so, he knew this visit would be different. Last time, he came to retrieve something rightfully belonging to him. Now, he hoped to solve a mystery that flummoxed people a lot smarter than him.

Ninety minutes later the outline of the barn appeared and he stopped at the same snowbank as last night. One deep breath followed another, each paired with a reassuring thought. *Jason and Ted would never imagine I'd come back. I have my bike so why would I?* Before any hesitation took hold, he started up the snowbank.

The first hint the sequel would be more difficult started below his feet. The snow looked the same, but the bright sun of the day worked its magic. Consequently, the crusted surface lost most of its tough-skin properties and his right foot broke through up to his shin.

Slowly retracing his route along the pine trees, he broke through the top layer every few steps. Snow soon found its way into both sneakers, forcing him to stop and clear them out while listening for Fang, who no doubt slept with one eye open while the other dreamt of mauling him.

Sitting in the snow and picking the ice crystals off his gym socks, he wondered why the Spark didn't show up to light his path, or at least bring a mug of that delightful tea to sustain him.

"How about helping me a bit, instead of being mesmerized by an oak tree? No wonder you failed as a guardian angel," he whispered to the ringed moon.

Not a whisper of wind responded and he wondered if the apparition was nothing more than an exhausted mind with a touch of frostbite. With a low moan, he jumped up and remembered to turn his coat inside out. After a couple more steps, he decided to abandon the methodical approach and make a wild dash for the barn. As he ran, the snow quickly repacked his sneakers and he fell three times.

He was panting hard by the time he reached the barn window, which tonight proved fickle and refused to open more than a few inches at a time. Pieces of window putty began to rain down on his hands and he feared the panes themselves would dislodge before the window finally surrendered. When he began to climb in, he thought he detected a faint bark and, as he lost focus, his trailing left foot caught the window sash and made a terrible bang which reverberated like a cannon in the silence.

Five minutes later the house still sat dark and his heart stopped galloping. Finding the hole in his right cheek, he felt the ridge of a large canker beginning to form around the wound. Pressing the tip of his tongue hard into its center, he felt pain radiate to his ear and used it to concentrate. After adjusting the flashlight, he made his way quickly to the next door. The flywheel began to squeal when he pulled up on the handle, so he slowed down the process and measured progress by inches and crawled under when it was barely high enough.

Spying a couple of plastic milk crates nearby, he placed them under the door to keep it from shutting. Looking around, he was surprised half the cars from last night were replaced by new entries. An old forest green Pontiac Grand Prix sat against one wall with a bent front axle. His eyes scanned its long nose and he remembered his dad owning one and how it took half a day to wax the beast. Peering in the driver's side window, he noticed the seats were split open like a fish being gutted. On the dashboard were the tools AJ boasted he wielded with the precision of a surgeon: hog ring pliers, a seam stretcher, upholstery shears.

Why would AJ go to the trouble of redoing the seats with the rest of the car in shambles? he wondered. A Volkswagen Jetta sat behind the Pontiac, its rear quarter heavily damaged. The seats were butterflied open too and a box of sandwich bags sat perched on the dashboard. Christopher watched enough police shows to know they weren't used to store lunch.

The last sliding door repeated the same rusty welcome, but behind it the flashlight only found piles of automobile parts and nothing else. His stomach dropped like it did when he rode the roller coaster and cold sweat made tiny pinpricks across his back. *Did I imagine the Mustang like the angel too?*

The flashlight zigzagged in a wild fashion around the barn before stopping at a long train of tires stacked six feet high. He ran over and peeked around the front end of the tire wall and discovered a green tarp covering a vehicle.

Squeezing into a narrow space, he lifted up the end of the tarp and found *Mustang* spelled out on the left corner of the trunk. Pins and needles raced up and down his back as he debated whether ignorance was better than knowing.

"Be careful what you wish for," his mother whispered again, this time with urgency. *"What about cracking those eggs?"* he replied, inserting the key.

The lock clicked as he turned it clockwise and he used his left hand to keep the trunk from springing open.

"You have to be kidding me!" he said, much too loudly. His hand trembled as he kept the lid closed, fearing Mary's dead sister might be waiting on the other side. The air felt heavy and if the man in the moon was watching, he would see a ring around the barn now.

Gritting his teeth, he opened the trunk.

Thankfully, only a spare tire caked in dust greeted him. Using the flashlight, he searched the compartment and discovered a dark canvas bag in the upper right-hand corner. He stretched to reach it, and the contents came spilling out.

A pair of white ice skates tied together.

He picked them up to examine. The leather looked cracked and thirsty, while the blades were peppered with rust. On the inside of the right shoe tongue, he identified the owner in black magic marker: *Lori Martin.*

The ice skates were the only thing Lori took when she disappeared in the Mustang and led to a number of ponds, lakes, and rivers being searched by divers. Whenever he and Mary watched television on the weekend, she would search all the channels for figure skating competitions. He enjoyed watching all the complicated moves, especially skaters pulling in their arms to spin like a top. Through it all, Mary would sit quiet and watch as if expecting Lori to take the ice next.

And now he found her skates.

His mouth started to water like he was going to be sick. Spitting into his gray handkerchief, he shut off the flashlight to conserve its power and knelt down next to the car hoping the nausea would pass.

Lori's skates, Lori's car, he thought. After listening to the recording of AJ repeatedly, he heard his cousin's words come back.

"We're not in a confessional here, but as far as she's concerned, let Bobby be a lesson to you . . . The water proved to be a better judge, jury, and executioner than I could ever be . . . Lori is just as guilty as him and can rot wherever she is."

"I need to talk with the Sergeant," he whispered, looking at the Mustang and realizing Lori must be dead. "AJ and Jason are both involved, just like he thought."

Christopher hid the ice skates in the well of one of the stacks of tires and quickly put the tarp back over the car. A dizzy feeling overcame him and he stumbled out of the small enclosure and accidently kicked over a coffee can filled with sheet metal screws. They sounded like a dozen cymbals scattering across the floor. He wanted to stop and listen for Fang, but nothing could drown out the sound of Mary crying for her sister. *How could he tell her what he found?*

The flashlight began to flicker and he quickly slid the first door shut and made his way to the second, held up with milk crates. He crawled under and began to stand up when a terrific force threw him against the metal door and the clanging noise echoed through his scrambled brains. In the confusion, he dropped the flashlight.

"Do you have him?" a voice called out from the darkness.

"Yeah, and I like to kill varmints in the dark, with one swing of my axe," a gruff voice next to him replied.

An intense light suddenly blinded him and he held up his hands to shield his eyes.

"I thought we had a rat problem, but it's only a hairy vole," Jason commented, dragging him to his feet. His blond hair looked wild and he pushed him hard into the garage door again. "What are you doing in here?"

Christopher never thought of what he would say if caught. Nothing plausible came to mind and his ears were ringing from kissing the metal door twice.

Overhead shop lights buzzed to life casting a surreal glow, and Christopher looked for a hint of kindness in his cousin's best friend. Winning the lottery would be easier.

Jason motioned to Ted. "Go call AJ and tell him to get over here quick."

"Why should we wake him up?" Ted slammed the electrical panel shut. "He'll just make more excuses for him. Why don't we wait a bit and teach this bobble-head a lesson he'll never forget?"

Jason fished in the pocket of his ratty-looking blue robe. "You heard me. Make the call."

Ted groaned and disappeared.

"You've done some stupid things in your sorry life, but this one takes the cake," Jason said, pulling him along.

What should I do? he thought. *Offer him a tea bag and then tell him I found Lori's Mustang and her ice skates? Then ask where they dumped the body?*

Jason threw him into a small closet and locked the door.

CHAPTER THIRTY-EIGHT

Cold dusty air mixed with the claustrophobic darkness. Christopher surveyed every inch of the coffin-like quarters including an antique lock on the door. It seemed fitting a skeleton key was required, making him wonder if Lori had been imprisoned in the closet too. He found a cardboard box in the corner containing a dozen or so metal cans that smelled like they contained motor oil.

Time slowed and he cradled the St. Christopher medal in his hand thinking how he let Kylie down by not making her the priority. He should have tried harder to accompany Becky to Florida, or simply bummed a ride with the moving van to Atlanta and figured out how to bridge the remaining distance. Then there was the matter of whoever he encountered on the road to the hospital. If the Spark wasn't a figment of his overworked imagination, why didn't he accept her offer of a better path? It seemed more feasible to find a way to work Kylie and Mary back into his life from a financially successful future, than trying to climb Everest without an oxygen tank. He couldn't remember the last prayer he said, and confident if he could check his notes, there would be no entries. The acidic voice in his head laughed. *"C'mon, man, He will see right through this desperate move. There's no atheists in foxholes, right?"*

Christopher pushed the doubt away and bowed his head. "Please help me, Lord." He bit his lip. "I'm not asking for it to be easy, nothing important ever is. Just give me the strength to see things through." He thought of the Spark's words and spread his hands in the small space. "What I'm trying to say is, I'll do my best, and leave the rest to You."

The sound of footsteps approached and the closet door swung open. The fluorescent lights backlit a menacing figure.

A long arm reached in and pulled him out of the small prison and immediately punched him in the stomach. He collapsed on the floor.

AJ grabbed him by the hair and pulled him back to his feet. Writhing in pain, Christopher noticed a heavy dungaree coat replaced the red ski parka.

"You imbecile! What have you done now?" The words sounded slightly slurred.

Jason appeared carrying a long black flashlight that resembled a nightstick. The sorry-looking robe had been replaced with a hooded sweatshirt, but he still had bed hair. "From what I can tell, it looks like he toured the entire operation." He balanced the flashlight on the hood of a car and grabbed Christopher by the throat. "I should have finished you off at Canobie. You would make a fun whack-a-mole in the arcade."

Ted entered stage right carrying a pair of ice skates. He held them by the laces at arms-length like they were infected with bubonic plague.

"Looks like he was trying to plant these in the tires."

AJ immediately became bug-eyed and rushed over to grab the skates from Ted. He inspected them for a moment and his lip began to quiver.

"Where did you find these?" he asked, glaring at Christopher.

"In the trunk of Lori's car." He couldn't tell if he was seeing guilt or surprise on AJ's face.

His cousin curled his lips in a peculiar way, like he didn't believe him. "In her car? Where?"

Christopher pointed. "Behind that door and the wall of tires."

AJ bolted ahead and Jason tried to intercept him. "Look, man, before you go in there, you have to know I'm being set up."

AJ pushed him away and Jason grabbed Christopher by the arm and followed close behind.

Within seconds, AJ ran behind the wall of tires and attacked the tarp. It came off with a swishing sound, revealing Lori's Mustang underneath. AJ stood with his mouth open for a second before scanning the front and back seats. Then he turned and ran after Jason, who abandoned Christopher to seek safety on the other side of the tire fence.

"I can explain," Jason said with outstretched arms.

AJ nodded and pulled on his hair with both hands. He started to stagger like he might pass out.

Jason came around the tire wall, thinking he knew his life-long friend well enough, but got suckered by the ruse. AJ waited until he was less than ten feet away, then pounced and tackled him. They wrestled on the wooden floor until Jason broke free and jumped up and grabbed a mallet off a shop table.

Ted hovered in the background, looking horrified he might have to intercede.

"You said Lori met with Bobby after she broke up with me!" AJ yelled, staggering to his feet.

"She did. They had a beer at the 99 Restaurant on Route 28."

"How do you know?"

"Because she had the next two with me." He shrugged. "C'mon, man, we all flirted with her. She was like a bright light attracting all the moths."

"So, I guess that makes me the bug zapper then." He picked up a rusty shovel and practiced swinging it.

Jason watched, unimpressed. "Give me a break. You talk like you owned her. How long did you go out? Six months?"

"Doesn't matter. Friends don't—"

"Blah, blah, blah. You keep singing the same tired tune," Jason said, interrupting him. "And it sounds especially off-key coming from the guy who put the moves on Debbie when we were having issues last year. The truth is Lori and I . . . well, we had a thing."

AJ looked like he was about to cry. "I can't believe what I'm hearing! You watched me take out my wrath on Bobby and it was you all along?" AJ pointed at the car. "And I've been working in here and her car was on the other side of the door?" He rubbed his forehead. "Tell me what you did with her."

Jason pointed the mallet at his best friend. "Nothing! I came home a few days ago and some sick Secret Santa snuck her car in here to frame me." He looked at Christopher and then shot AJ a hard look. "Mighty funny, I find your cousin here."

"Why didn't you call the police?" AJ asked.

Jason turned the mallet slowly in his hands.

"Because they will find his DNA in the car," Ted answered for his brother.

Jason shot him a look to shut up. "Like I said, we went out a few times."

AJ heaved the shovel, but his aim was poor and the spear flew over his friend's head. "I can't wait to see the cops grill you like they did me. Once I tell them—"

"Be careful, buddy," Jason said, cutting him off. "Remember, I was at World End that night too and unlike your cousin with molasses for brains, people will believe me if I start talking." He stroked his chin. "I'm thinking you knew the cops were getting ready to arrest you, so you planted the car here, but forgot the skates. You knew I was planning on going to Foxwoods tonight, which gave you an opportunity to finish the set-up before you called the cops. But if you bothered showing up for work yesterday, you would have known I decided to cancel my trip. Problem is, your boy got caught. You can beat him like a drum and act like he did this on his own, but I know who's pulling his strings." He pounded his palm with the mallet. "Don't tell me what you did to that beautiful woman, because I don't want to be charged as an accessory after the fact. Just give me the car keys so I can get rid of the car."

AJ clenched both fists. "I don't have the keys! Say another word and you won't have to buy those whitening strips for your teeth anymore. Thinking I'm behind whatever happened to Lori and setting you up to take the fall is a sick fairy tale not even my deranged cousin could dream up."

Jason looked away.

"Look. The cops have closed the whole mess on World End," AJ continued and pointed at Christopher. "He's living proof we lost one and a half men that night. Just remember before you go spilling your guts, you were kneeling right there beside me when I—" He stopped short and glanced at the Mustang. "But go ahead and talk, because that car is the Ace of Hearts and will trump whatever comes out of your mouth. Especially with your DNA in the car."

"Won't they find yours in there too?" Jason ran his hand through his wild hair and put the mallet down. "You're always bragging about being a big picture guy, but it's the small details that will kill you. Don't be stupid. The cops would love either of us to talk. That way, they get two pounds of flesh out of each of us." He shook his head. "Last year, I just wanted you to cool off before I told you about Lori and me. Then things got carried away out on the ice and yeah, we dodged a bullet." He pointed to the middle section of the barn with all the cars. "We have a good thing going here and no one suspects anything. A couple more years and we can winter in the Caribbean. So help me dump the car and let's put this sorry mess behind us."

AJ put his hands on his hips and stared at the car.

"All we need is for Sponge Man to tell his cop buddy or his special needs girlfriend," Ted added.

Christopher rushed at the punk, but Jason grabbed him.

"Once the Mustang is at the bottom of the Merrimack River there's no story, just rantings from a couple of town losers living on the fringe," AJ said. "This is just a glitch to manage through."

Jason spit on the floor. "You call this a glitch? This is what I'm talking about! Ignore the details this time it will get us thirty to life. Your daffy cousin has been looking around here and soon there'll be others with badges and guns."

AJ shrugged. "I'm not finished with you about messing with Lori, but we'll deal with that later. In the meantime, I'll take care of my mentally challenged relative."

Ted waved him off. "How? He saw everything!"

"Saw what? The only coke he knows comes in twelve-ounce cans." AJ walked over to the Mustang and thought for a moment. "Okay, we still have some time before morning. We'll fill the car with all of Christopher's stuff before we dump it. That way, if they ever do recover it, he's a suspect too." He shot Jason an ugly look. "I can even say he told me how obsessed he was with Lori and they met for drinks before the ice capades at World End." He walked over to Christopher and smiled. "Before we dump the car, though, maybe I'll show it to Morbid so she will cough up that lottery ticket for me."

Christopher struggled to get away from Jason, but couldn't break free.

"I'll hotwire the car and we can stop by your place and load it up with his stuff," Jason explained. "But I still want you to take care of him. It's a problem."

AJ nodded. "Lock him back up in that sick closet your father used to punish you in. Tonight I'll reward him with a nice cocktail of all the meds he's been fasting from," he said, winking at Christopher. "If he's running low, we can make up the deficit."

"I . . . won't . . . swallow . . . it," Christopher stuttered.

"Who said you would have to?" AJ said, leaning in close. "I take care of those who cross me. Just like I did with Bobby *before* the ice broke," he whispered. "Now, it's your turn."

A shiver ran across Christopher's head, but he didn't let on.

"So, we get him messed up. Then what?" Jason asked.

"Have him walk the plank at the Lawrence Dam. By then he'll be out of his mind and drooling. He'll end up a pitiful case like my old man." A sudden smile spread across his face. "Take it from an upholsterer: a stitch in time saves nine—and us."

CHAPTER THIRTY-NINE

When the most sought after car in New England left the barn after being hotwired, some of the exhaust fumes remained behind and snaked their way into the closet. Christopher pictured Jason hunched over the steering wheel, looking frantically in the rearview mirror as he followed the Blazer on back roads across town. *Guess the Mustang could use some invisible paints too.*

The fumes mixed with the darkness, making the air feel thick. He faked a cough to fight off the growing claustrophobia, hoping to learn if Ted remained behind to guard him.

Two more loud coughs produced no additional clues from the other side of the door.

"Ted, are you there?" he finally called out, trying to sound calm.

Only the cold silence replied. He fought the urge to kick it up a notch and scream, but knew Ted would enjoy hearing him freak out.

Stretching out his hands, he surveyed the tiny prison again and sat down on the box of oil cans. He tried downshifting his thoughts in order to counter the solitary confinement and AJ's threats, but after a few minutes stood up again. Mumbling voices saying nothing discernible filled his ears as if he were standing in the middle of a bus terminal. No matter how much he shook his head, the gibberish wouldn't stop.

He used to think overcoming fear could be cured with one heroic act, like climbing out of a foxhole to save a comrade. The image of the unidentified man in Tiananmen Square single-handedly blocking a column of tanks shot across the blackness. Where did he find such courage and was it sustainable in the days and months that followed?

Surprisingly, he found himself thinking about his late uncle Aram. He endured hell in Vietnam, only to be ambushed by the enemy every day for the rest of his life. Sometimes he beat the Viet Cong back into the shadows, but most days they captured and tortured him.

He took the notebook out of his back pocket and fingered the smooth plastic cover, realizing the strength he prayed for was not something granted, but earned every day. Neither was it a solo journey. His aunt proved that in serving as combat medic to her husband and providing trauma care for wounds which never healed.

Remembering what he could of the past year, he realized instead of embracing Aram's courage and perseverance, he chose to mimic his uncle's eccentricities in order to be left alone. And here he was, locked away in a closet and very, very alone. *Ah, be careful what you wish for!*

He also realized the world would continue to spin no matter what transpired. The last year proved that in spades after losing his parents, the separation from Kylie, Bobby's death, Lori's disappearance, and his own sense of self in limbo. Today was no different. Down the street, Mr. Godfreye busied himself in preparing his infamous brew. By midday, the store owner would be watching every time the door opened, expecting him to waddle in and ask for a cup of hot water and play the straight man to the grieving father. By dinnertime, Mr. Godfreye would forget he never stopped by. Then tomorrow he would hear how he flipped his lid and walked the plank.

His left foot began to fall asleep and he slumped backward against the wooden wall and the Mustang door and trunk key in his back pocket stabbed him. He took it out and turned it in his hands, grateful Jason and AJ never found it.

The closet door felt old and badly blistered, and he used the head of the key to scrape off some of the paint. Pin-the-tail-on-the-donkey came to mind and he tried to force the tip of the car key into the door lock, but it was badly oversized. He needed something with a finer point and found the ten-penny nail in his pocket which the stranger gave him as a reminder of the ultimate act of courage and sacrifice. He thought of his mother and how she tried once to jumpstart his faith by telling him if he was the only person on earth, Jesus would still have hung on the cross for him. His former self rolled his eyes, but now in holding the nail which fused flesh to wood, the sense of unworthiness felt suffocating.

The nail went into the keyhole only a quarter of an inch. Even so, he pushed, hoping to break the lock, but his hand slipped and the nail went flying as his fingers smashed against the handle.

He yelled out in pain and punching the door, rattled the frame. Putting his head on the door, he let out a long groan. No reply came, so he knew Ted was not stationed outside as he wouldn't be able to swallow that laugh.

Christopher fell asleep for a microsecond before waking with a start. He punched the door again to feel the wood quiver, and tracing the frame, his left hand explored the top hinge. The head on the stainless steel pin was not properly seated and stuck up a good quarter inch.

"What would Sergeant Mike do?" he asked aloud. "He'd assess the environment and use whatever resources were available." Kneeling, he read the wooden floor like Braille and quickly found the nail. Using the car key and nail in combination, he worked to pry the pin out of the hinge. The effort proved a frustrating failure as both tools continually skidded out of the slot.

"You're not going to beat me," he whispered to the door, beginning to break a sweat. Positioning himself underneath the hinge, he used the head of the nail like a plow and pushed with all his strength. The pin began to move slowly, but the small success proved short-lived as the nail skidded off the target and he dropped it again. This time, he located it right away. After multiple tries the pin finally surrendered.

Dropping to his knees, he turned his attention to the bottom hinge, where he found the pin only with a slight lip. When he tried to wedge the nail into the space, it slipped and dug into the back of his other hand. The bleeding made for slippery work, so he wrapped his hand in his handkerchief and continued the attack.

Ever so slowly, the pin began an agonizing journey northward. He was drenched in sweat when he finally succeeded in extracting it.

With the hinges untethered, he tried to pull the door toward him. Not surprisingly, it wouldn't budge as the lock still held it in place. Picking up a quart-sized can of oil, he hammered at the edges of the door, which produced an impressive noise, but the jail keeper survived the assault.

"I've come too far to give up now!" Crouching on the floor, he ran his injured left hand along the edge and felt a new crack growing. Next, he sat and braced himself against the back wall and kicked at the weak spot with his left foot. The door shuddered badly.

"Now I get why sneakers are stupid in winter," he yelled, "because if I had steel-toe boots like AJ, I'd be out of here with one kick." Taking a deep breath, he pretended Mary was on the other side coaxing him on, promising to reward him with a big mug of Bigelow tea and a plate of her mouth-watering peanut butter cookies. He kicked past the point where his foot and leg ached as sweat burned his eyes. The door took all he had like a fighter up against the ropes, absorbing the blows and confident to outlast his strength. A bright yellow light splashed across the blackness and he knew he was near the end of this round and gave another flurry of quick kicks. Suddenly, the door began to splinter and a dim shaft of light appeared. He stopped to reposition himself and wipe away the sweat before attacking again. Two dozen kicks later a large section of bottom door fell away. Pushing himself out feet-first, he had a breech birth.

Christopher rolled over and lay face down on the wide-plank floor wanting to rest for a moment, when he felt a tap on his back. Looking up, he expected to find either Ted with a mallet or the Spark with some tea, but he was alone in the surreal fluorescent lighting. He slowly stood up and stumbled toward the garage door. Pulling it up halfway, he caught sight of Fang standing next to a Chevy Nova, no more than ten feet away. Their eyes met for a split second and Christopher managed to slam the door shut before the man-eating wolf arrived. The door shook as Fang threw himself against it, apparently trying to copy his escape from the closet. Running to the back of the barn where the Mustang exited, he found the rear entrance locked. Freedom meant dealing with a big head, little eyes, and plenty of teeth.

He surveyed the piles of orphaned tires: black walls, whitewalls, racing tires, some on rims. Grabbing the smallest one he could find, he rolled it up to the garage door. Next, he looked in his coat pocket and found the dog bone he always carried—which might become the appetizer, if he ended up as the main course.

He bit off a small piece of bone. At the 400 Club, he used to gross out his friends by dunking one in a beer when things got boring. After they made fun of him, he would offer small pieces and say it tasted like chicken. "Doesn't everything?" Sump would laugh.

Cracking the door open a couple inches, he started to whine softly.

Fang must have sensed the change and stopped barking to listen. He slid a small piece of the bone and the dog chased the morsel and returned. He repeated the process a few more times and practiced sliding them like a puck in air hockey to gauge the distance and best angle. With the last piece, he took a deep breath and sent it flying far away from the front door.

Fang took off after the bone and Christopher hurled the door open, grabbed the tire, and made a run for it. Halfway to his goal, Fang returned like the great white shark in *Jaws*, but without John Williams's famous score.

The dog lunged and Christopher used the tire as a shield, but the force of the ninety-pound fiend sent him headlong and almost to the floor. At that moment, he knew if the door was also padlocked from the outside, he wouldn't need to walk the plank tonight, because Fang would finish him off. He reached for the door handle and it turned, just as Fang's claws ripped the left shoulder of his coat. Instinctively, he elbowed the beast, and the dog fell away for a micro second and he slammed the door shut. Fang threw himself against the door and as Christopher backed away, he noticed the half open window to the right. As he lunged to close it, Fang arrived and snapped at his midsection. Luckily, enough of the window putty remained in place to keep the window from breaking.

Panting and sweating out of every pore, Christopher turned around and surveyed the main house. It sat quiet as an orange sherbet sky kicked off another surreal day.

He had a wild idea of breaking into the house to use the phone, but started running down the street and nearly collapsed before reaching a telephone booth a half mile away.

"What's your emergency?" a woman's voice asked after he punched 911.

"I have a few, but right now it's at the Driscoll barn at 32 Flint Street. They're hiding drugs inside the car seats. Better be careful though because there's a vicious dog guarding the place."

He put the receiver down and smiled. There would be an-all-you-can-eat buffet of arms and legs for Fang to gnaw on for breakfast in a few minutes.

CHAPTER FORTY

Christopher counted to fifty after hanging up the phone before he heard the first siren in the distance. He had no desire to be caught in the coming dragnet and ran to the next driveway and crouched behind a stack of firewood. Sure enough, two minutes later, a police cruiser came bounding over the hill, straddling the middle of the road with blue lights flashing and passed him doing seventy. He recognized Officer Petersen, fresh out of the police academy and tasked with keeping the town safe during the midnight to eight shift. He watched Petersen try and maneuver a sharp curve and the rookie's motivation almost got the better of him as the cruiser fishtailed.

He moved on before backup appeared, although it would have been convenient to ask one of the policemen for a ride back to the station so he could walk across the street to Child World. When he reached Route 28, he stuck out his thumb and incredibly the first vehicle stopped. Opening the passenger door, he recognized the red-haired mechanic as a regular at Godfreye's.

"Good morning," Christopher said, getting in.

The man yawned. "Not until I get some coffee in me. I take it you're headed there too?"

"No, but if you could drop me off at Child World on the way, that would be wonderful."

"Didn't know they opened this early." He glanced at the blood-stained handkerchief wrapped around his hand. "Nasty cut?"

"I used to have a matching outfit."

The ride was ultra-short and Christopher jumped out next to the sign marked for employee parking. The sergeant told him one could mark time by surveying the mix of vehicles in the lot. Minivans and newer sedans arrived first thing in the morning and by mid-afternoon a few souped-up cars from high-schoolers needing gas money peppered the lot. The mix would change again during the holiday season when older cars driven by the stoics would take over the midnight shift to restock shelves. They were the ones willing to sacrifice sleep for some extra money.

This morning there were few cars in the lot given the toy shopping drought after Christmas. He was disappointed not to see Sergeant Mike's tan Chevy Citation.

"As long as it gets me from point A to B, any set of wheels will suffice," the sergeant would say whenever the conversation turned to cool cars. Christopher thought he preferred a conservative ride after being flashy all week in a police muscle car.

"Moving up to grand larceny?" a voice boomed from behind.

Christopher turned and caught sight of the security manager jumping out of his Buick. The London Fog coat looked weird with his Elvis sideburns.

Mr. Security nearly ran up to him. "What are you doing here?" He gave him a once-over like he already broke into the store.

"I'm looking for Sergeant Mike. I know it's very early, but I'm willing to wait." He didn't want to take the chance of being near his aunt's house if AJ found out he escaped.

"Well, you'll be waiting a long time."

He bit his lip and then saw a smirk appear on the manager's face. "Why? Is he off today?"

"Yeah, and tomorrow and the day after that too. I fired him."

Christopher felt his right eye begin to twitch and focused on the retail crime fighter's blue nylon lunch bag. He guessed him to be a liverwurst or deviled ham spread man and probably cut the crust off his Wonder Bread too.

"For the life of me, I can't figure out why he risked his job to protect you," Elvis continued. "If you were related to him I would understand, but from what I hear, you're nothing but his nut-case, man-boy neighbor." He pointed a stubby finger at him. "Just know this. If I see your shadow inside the brick building behind me, I'll arrest you for trespassing."

Christopher listened intently as the words washed over him. "I think you meant faux brick," he said, pointing at the store.

"What?"

"That's not real brick, Chip. The contractor uses a special stamp on the wet cement to make it look real. I watched a show about it last week," he said with a wink. "They advertise all sorts of interesting stuff in the middle of the night. Come to think of it, I saw the matching thermos that goes with that lunch bag of yours. I'm sure Spaghetti-O's would go nicely with the deviled ham spread I smell."

The Elvis wannabe looked down to make sure his lunch hadn't been pilfered. "Go ahead and make fun all you want. You're still a nobody. Now get out of here before I call the police and have you arrested for vagrancy."

Fat chance as every cop in town is trying to tame Fang, he thought. Nevertheless, he turned and the security chief watched his retreat.

Christopher didn't try to thumb a ride, as he had more than enough steam to quickly hike the two miles to the sergeant's house, while keeping a lookout for a Blazer and Mustang. He found his friend in his driveway loading cardboard boxes in the trunk of the Citation. The memory of the ice skates entombed in the Mustang flashed in his mind.

Sergeant Mike glanced at him as he came up the driveway, but ignored him and continued arranging the boxes.

Christopher came up alongside and waited for a greeting that never came.

He noticed a black turtleneck sweater sitting on top of one box. "Moving stuff?"

The sergeant nodded. "I've enlisted my wife in the Salvation Army, or should I say what's left of her. After I drop this stuff off, I'm headed out to visit my kid sister."

"Sister? You never mentioned you had one."

He shot him a blank stare. "No? I thought you had uncovered all my deep secrets by now." A smirk took over the corners of his mouth. "Well, most of them."

Christopher watched as the sergeant went over to a keypad on the house and typed in four numbers. The heavy gauge steel door opened slowly and the sergeant grabbed two more boxes and transported them to the trunk.

The air between them felt colder than expected. "Where does your sister live?" he asked.

"Tulsa, and she's been hounding me to meet my nephew Gus. I decided to interfere before he begins nursery school." The sergeant screwed up his face. "Little Gus? What were they thinking? My brother-in-law is named Gus too, so my guess is he wanted a junior because misery loves company. They should have just named him Sue. At least then he could listen to Johnny Cash after he gets beat up at school."

Christopher let the long explanation blow by his ears. "The reason I'm here—"

"It would be tolerable if we could call him by his middle name, which is Timothy," the cop continued, "but his father won't hear of it. I can't believe he finally found his spine." He looked at Christopher and frowned. "Other than that, I have no strong opinion on the subject."

He's still angry because I never apologized, he thought. "I ran into your boss at Child World. He told me he fired you. Because of me?"

The sergeant waved him off. "Now there's a guy who deserves a special name and I can think of a few that would fit perfectly." He glanced at Christopher's coat and laughed. "And I would love to see it spelled out too. Mothers would have their kids sucking on bars of soap if they said it out loud."

"Look. I'm really sorry about what happened."

His eyes grew large, surprised by the apology. "Well, I'd be sorry too if I wanted a career tracking toy crimes. Thank goodness I only have another couple weeks left on suspension. Maybe I can talk some sense into my sister and brother-in-law in the meantime. If things go bad, I'll be back by tomorrow night." Sergeant Mike looked at the boxes. "You'll be okay, though. Just don't let AJ push you around so much."

Christopher felt his stomach jump and he slowed his breathing to focus. "The other night you kept asking me about World End."

The sergeant sighed. "I'm really in a rush today, Chris. Suffice it to say we all have demons as pets. I get that. But when you grow tired of feeding yours, or letting it walk you, call me."

He grabbed the sergeant by the arm. "I was telling the truth about having trouble remembering what happened that night. But you were right that there were . . . ah, other complications too. My dad used to tell me it didn't matter if you were rich or poor, smart or stupid; all anyone can offer is their word." He took the notebook out of his back pocket and held it up. "But he also believed *the truth will set you free.*"

"Those are strong sentiments. When I'm back we can talk some more."

"There's no time." He reached in his pocket and handed a cassette tape to him. "It starts out happy enough. Mary and me horsing around, but listen to the conversation that follows."

The sergeant held up the cassette and shook his head. "You and your doublespeak drives me nuts. Maybe if it was July, I wouldn't mind sitting for a spell and draining a six-pack while you explained yourself." He handed the tape back to him. "Do you want me to call AJ? I don't have time to drive you home."

Christopher backed up. "Don't you understand? I figured it all out! If you don't believe me, call the station. I told them to raid Driscoll's barn."

The cop's hands went to his hips. "I heard it on the scanner. You were behind that?"

He expected the sergeant to grab him by the shoulders until he detailed the rest of the story. Instead, his friend surprisingly turned away and started to rifle through one of the boxes like he was looking for something. Christopher noticed his ex-wife had very nice clothes; a bunch of silky-looking shirts with price tags from Jordan Marsh. *She bought but never wore any of these clothes? That's strange,* he thought.

Christopher shook his head to refocus. "So, did they find the drugs in the car seats?"

The cop stopped rummaging, but didn't look at him. "Well, they knocked on the door and the kid—ah, what's his name, came to the door like they woke him up," he said to a box.

"Ted was home?" *How did he not hear Fang?*

The sergeant looked at him, confused. "Everything appeared fine. There was no reason or warrant to search the premises based on some anonymous crackpot, which turned out to be you." Sergeant Mike finally looked at him. "You never cease to astonish me with your drama and I'm impressed how much effort you put into each performance. I'll never forget the other night with my gun."

The sergeant took the cassette back and glanced at the front and back. "Let me guess. You recorded *Mister Rogers' Neighborhood* and plan to get your jollies thinking how I'll listen to it for hours."

The words burned. "You're the sorriest cop I ever met. You don't know what you're holding!"

"Sure I do," he said calmly, "more fantasy and grand delusions." The sergeant turned around and threw the tape in ones of the boxes. "I think it's time for you to move along. I have a lot to do."

"I found Lori's Mustang in the barn along with her skates. Now AJ and Jason are planning on ditching the car and throwing me off the Lawrence Dam."

The sergeant ignored him and fiddled with a box.

"Did you hear me?"

The sergeant didn't answer and Christopher tried to retrieve the cassette, but the cop pushed him away. "I've had enough of your fantasies. Now go!"

He ran down the driveway and never looked back because the sergeant never called.

CHAPTER FORTY-ONE

Bands of wispy cirrus clouds streaked across the pale blue sky, demonstrating the immensity of beauty without boundaries. A gentle breeze from the south sweetened the air with the wet fragrance of melting snow. Christopher snuck along the cement block foundation and stopped at a rear door leading into AJ's double bay garage.

He could hear movement inside and tried to peek through the left corner pane on the rusted steel door, but a thick layer of filth prevented it. Grabbing a handful of snow which had the consistency of an Italian ice left out of the freezer too long, he gently rubbed some against a section of the glass, which only accomplished smearing the dirt. After another application, he discovered it didn't matter how much he scrubbed the glass as there was another curtain of dirt on the other side too.

Backing away, he crouched down in the snow. *Being here is a really bad idea. Spying will only result in me getting killed earlier than planned. But if I can't count on Sergeant Mike, who will believe me? Becky is too far away and ill.* He decided Mr. Godfreye was his best hope and would require a painful confession.

Hugging the building, he began making his way back toward the road, when he heard a cry. It was only a short burst, but the tone was familiar enough to make him stop in front of a rusted Ford pickup. Looking up, he saw a garage window left open to vent exhaust fumes when the doors were closed. *If I can get on the roof of the truck, I might be able to see in.*

Carefully climbing into the bed of the truck, Christopher found himself standing in a half foot of soft snow. The sides of the bed were so rusted, he was afraid they might collapse with his weight if he used it as a bridge to the roof. When he raised one foot to brush off some snow, he noticed it had the consistency of Play-Doh. *Perfect for making a snowman.*

Kneeling down, he rapidly rolled the snow into a compact ball and placed it against the rear of the cab. Then he removed his coat to get better leverage and stepped on the snow stair and pulled himself up on the roof of the pickup.

Crouching low, he peered into the window and swallowed a yell before it escaped his throat. Mary was on crutches and AJ had her pinned against the Mustang as Jason paced in front of them.

"This is going from bad to worse," Jason yelled at AJ, pointing at Mary. "What are you going to do? Drug her too?" He held up a police radio. "Luckily, Ted got rid of the cops, but we've made them suspicious. He said he heard the dog going nuts in the barn, but doesn't want to check it out in case they come back."

"You and your brother are nervous Nellies," AJ shot back. "How could anyone guess Morbid's first stop after breaking out of the hospital would be to take a taxi over here?" He opened up his dungaree coat and pointed at the gun wedged in his belt. "We won't have to waste any of our expensive inventory on her. She'll follow her boyfriend anywhere, even over the dam." He glanced at Mary. "We won't have to weigh her down once that cast gets wet."

Jason shook his head. "You're nuts."

"No, you both are!" Mary cried.

"Look at it this way," AJ continued, ignoring her. "If we don't take care of this quickly, our employer will make sure we're the ones going for a long cold swim."

Jason waved him off.

AJ grabbed Mary by the arm. "Christopher must be getting mighty lonely by now. But before I let him sign your cast, do you remember what you told me the other night?"

She looked at the floor. "You were scaring me. I said a lot of things."

He knocked on her forehead lightly. "You promised to show me the ticket."

Christopher read Mary's confused look as she began fiddling with the ends of her hair. "I don't remember saying that."

"But you did, darling." He grabbed one of her crutches and pretended to strum on it like a guitar.

The steady drip of the melting snow from the roof matched the rhythm of Christopher's pulse. *Even if I call nine-one-one, they have a police scanner.*

"I'll make you a deal with you," AJ said, waving the crutch. "Give me the ticket and I'll tell you where your sister is."

"You know where Lori is?" she asked, breathless.

Christopher held his breath.

AJ shrugged. "If I don't, why do you think I have her car?"

"Stop leading her on," Jason yelled, coming to a standstill. "I'm beginning to think you belong in the closet with your cousin too." He glanced at his watch. "We're wasting time here. We were supposed to have dumped the car in the river two hours ago."

"Hey, Mr. Detail man! No wonder you lose so much at blackjack. You're always wanting another hit and don't know when to stand. We'll hold off until tonight. In the meantime, we better focus on making that scheduled delivery this afternoon. If we don't, Morbid will have more brain cells than both of us combined."

"You really know where Lori is?" Mary asked, leaning on one crutch and looking like Tiny Tim's sister.

AJ caressed the door of the Mustang. "Don't believe me?" He reached into the front seat of the car and pulled out a plastic bag and handed it to her. "Recognize these?"

"You're a moron!" Jason added.

AJ ignored him. "Give me the ticket and I'll take you to Lori," he purred.

Mary looked in the bag and collapsed on the floor. "These are my sister's skates!"

Jason shoved his friend. "That's enough. I've been telling you all along she doesn't have the ticket. C'mon, man, like you said, we have work to do."

AJ shoved him back twice as hard. "How do you know? No one else has come forward." He opened the car door and put out his hand. "No ticket, no Lori."

"But I don't have it with me," Mary replied, and began sobbing.

Christopher had heard enough. He jumped off the roof of the truck and fell into the soft snow. He ran toward the front of the building, ready to jump off the dam if they would leave her alone. Drowning didn't scare him anymore. *Been there, done that.*

Passing the backhoe, he noticed how the melting snow ran down the long nose of Goliath.

He stopped midstride and smiled. "It's time to show folks just how crazy I really am."

CHAPTER FORTY-TWO

After scaling the stairs two at a time, Christopher made a beeline to the pine drawer in front of the hot plate; a catch-all for bent cigarettes, empty BIC lighters, pens without caps, and a couple personal checks branded with "Insufficient Funds" in red. Despite the seedy neighborhood, it wasn't hard to locate the fat stubby key. Quietly retracing his steps, he slid into the cockpit of Caterpillar. As a boy, he spent hours moving sand, dirt, and rocks in Tonka trucks while squinting into the sun pretending to be the master earth mover.

The key quickly found its home, and the guttural sound of the diesel rousing itself awake erased his childhood bravado and made him realize how ill prepared he was for this undertaking. While he had mastered the toy model with distinction, this machine dwarfed his hubris. As much as he studied AJ fooling around with the man-made dinosaur, he needed to practice filling in World End to gain any competence. Now, one wrong move would result in an out-of-control rodeo for this spur-of-the-moment plan.

He eased off the choke and the engine stopped racing, although it continued to tremble excessively, perhaps aware of the madman at the controls. Looking through the cracked windshield, he was happy to see how the left garage door lined up perfectly and knew only seconds remained before AJ came out running. He pushed a lever, and the front loader hydraulically extended its open mouth, eager to sample New England rocky road.

He buckled himself in and slapped the steering wheel. "Hope you're hungry, buddy." He held on tight and gave it the gas.

The sound of wood buckling, concrete collapsing, and glass shattering made for a terrible symphony. His world rocked back and forth and it wasn't until his head slammed against the side window that he thought about stopping. But the unleashed beast had a mind of its own by now as a blue Pontiac Grand AM came into view. Glancing to his left, he watched the rear bucket take out a windshield and almost decapitate a gawking AJ.

All that kept the Caterpillar caged was the rear wall. He noticed a mystery lever next to the seat and yanked it upward. Without a seat belt, he would have been launched like a torpedo through the windshield as the beast pitched violently forward before falling back. Heavy smoke, dust, and the smell of diesel filled the air. Christopher turned off the ignition and unbuckled the seat belt, before feeling the wetness on his forehead. Touching it, his fingers came back red.

An arm reached in and pulled him out. "You idiot!" AJ screamed, and pistol-whipped the back of his head.

A flash of bright light danced across his eyes as he stumbled backward. "Mary!" he screamed, looking frantically around, afraid he might have killed her in the mayhem.

"Over here!" she replied.

He turned and saw Mary pop up from behind the Mustang, which miraculously sat untouched in the next bay. He started in her direction, but AJ grabbed him by the arm.

Jason, looking dazed, stumbled past them as they wrestled.

"Where are you going?" AJ yelled after him.

"This is a family matter, buddy, and I want no part of it." He slithered toward the new enlarged opening. "This place will be crawling with cops."

"Hey, you can't leave me with that car!"

Jason waved him off. "She's all yours, like you always wanted."

AJ watched him for a half second before pulling Christopher over to the Mustang and throwing him beside Mary. He opened his coat and pointed at the gun tucked in his belt. "Let me say this real slow so you both understand. Open your mouth when the cops show up and I'll shoot you both on the spot."

Christopher was turning to put his arm around Mary, when he felt AJ grab the notebook out of his back pocket.

"Hey, you can't take that. It's all I have to—"

"Shut up!" AJ said, quickly leafing through the book and stopping to scan the last page. He shot Christopher a dirty look. "I promise to make the last entry."

Christopher watched AJ throw a black tarp over the Mustang and noticed for the first time how AJ's work boots were tied with a double knot. It made him think of Aram and how no one could explain why his shoes were tied together with a similar knot, which was why he tripped. *Did AJ have a hand in that too?*

The sound of sirens grew and AJ rushed to hide the ice skates and the notebook in a cardboard box on a side shelf. Then he took the handgun out of his belt and put it in a tool chest drawer. Moments later, the garage was bathed in flashing blue lights. A muscular patrolman with silver hair walked in surveying the devastation.

He adjusted his hat and studied the backhoe covered in debris. "I can't wait to hear this one."

AJ walked toward the officer, stabbing the air in Christopher's direction. "Yeah, it's a real tragedy, Officer, as my cousin Christopher has lost his mind. He stole the keys and ran the backhoe smack into the garage, nearly killing me and my girlfriend." AJ pointed at Mary's cast. "Morbid—ah, I mean Mary, just got out of the hospital and he's behind her broken leg too." He shook his head. "I rescued Christopher from nearly drowning last year, but he was under too long and ended up brain damaged. He's been staying with my mother ever since, but she has cancer and went to Florida for treatment. Given my cousin's anger issues, we could have put him away, but since he's family, I took him in. Today, I found out he's not taking his medications, and when I made an issue of it, this is how he showed his appreciation." He looked around and sighed. "But this is too much! You better take him into protective custody before I finish what World End started."

The cop listened and nodded in empathy before reaching for his handcuffs. Christopher lined up the words to tell the cop about the Mustang, but glanced over at Mary. She held a finger to her lips and he knew she was right. Better to talk at the station than risk getting shot here.

"Sarge?" the cop suddenly called out. "I thought you were . . . uh, still on leave?"

Christopher looked over and saw Sergeant Mike dressed in his police uniform. He had Jason by the arm.

AJ rolled his eyes. "Can't you ever stay out of our business?"

The sergeant ignored the dig. "What have we got here, Ned?"

"Looks like a wing-dinger of a domestic." He gestured toward Christopher. "Seems that one over there had a hissy fit of sorts when he wouldn't take his medicine."

The sergeant deposited Jason in front of the patrolman. "Well, something tells me you'll want to interview this clown too." He walked over and inspected the blue Pontiac minus a windshield. "What a shame. Hope you have glass coverage," he said in AJ's direction.

Christopher watched AJ lick his lips like he did whenever he got nervous. "Let me guess, you're selling insurance on the side." AJ looked at the damaged car. "I just finished the seats on it too," he groaned.

The sergeant smiled. "Yeah, your mom tells me how talented you are with a needle and thread." He looked toward the other bay and pointed at the black tarp.

"I'm not much of a connoisseur of cars, but I do love Corvettes. Maybe because it makes me remember dating your mother back in the day. By any chance is that one over there?"

AJ gestured to the patrolman. "Look, I don't need this harassment and my cousin looks like he needs stitches for his head. Can we get going?"

Ned glanced at the sergeant. "I think we're done here for now."

"But I won't be able to sleep tonight wondering what's under that sheet," Sergeant Mike said. He walked over and pulled off the black tarp, revealing the Mustang underneath.

The patrolman's eyes grew wide and he let out a whistle. "Well, I'll be."

The sergeant looked at Christopher for the first time. "I'm very disappointed you never told me your cousin bought a Mustang. You know very well we've been looking for one just like this for over a year now. Heck, I'm surprised it's not pictured on milk cartons."

Christopher cleared his throat. "But I did tell you—"

The sergeant waved him off and frowned at AJ. "Remarkable gumption on your part to risk bringing it here. Where have you been hiding it?"

AJ shrugged. "You got it wrong, like always. You'll have to ask Jason about the car as he drove it here." He positioned himself near the tool chest.

Jason shot AJ an ugly look. "It's not like it sounds. Someone left it in my barn trying to set me up."

The sergeant rubbed the back of his head. "This story is getting more fantastic by the second. So someone left the grand dame of all missing vehicles at your place and instead of calling the police, you park it here?" He looked at AJ. "Why would you let him do that?"

AJ shrugged. "I just found out this morning he had the car. I let him drive it over here so I could call the police before he got rid of it."

"He's the one that planted it in my barn with the help of his dim-witted cousin that I caught," Jason yelled.

AJ snickered. "Says the man whose DNA is all over the inside of the car."

"They know where my sister is too," Mary added in a surprisingly strong and steady voice. She hobbled over to the cardboard box and pulled out the white ice skates and handed Christopher his notebook.

"Don't listen to the psycho. She showed up here with those skates," AJ shouted, giving her an evil look and fingering the drawer.

"That's a lie. I saw it all from up there." Christopher pointed to the window above. "You said you knew where Lori was and offered to take her there." He held his notebook up. "It's all in here."

AJ waved him off. "Give me a break. I was just trying to get her to show me the lottery ticket."

Christopher looked over at Mary. The crutches were too big for her petite frame and her white wool coat looked ruined with splotches of grease. She seemed lost and staring into the back seat of the Mustang like she expected Lori to appear any moment. He walked over and took her hand, which felt cold and clammy, and followed her line of sight. His eyes surveyed the white leather with fine black stitching on the edge of the seat cushion. As he let his eyes linger, tiny letters came into view.

betray . . . me . . . and . . . your . . . prized . . . locks . . . will . . . cushion . . . my . . . ride . . . forever...

Christopher blinked hard and the letters disappeared back into the stitching. It was like finding hidden images in a picture; you had to let things distort before the secrets popped out. He eyed a screwdriver on the floor of the back seat.

Officer Ned took out his handcuffs. "Turn around," he ordered Jason.

Christopher jumped into the back seat of the Mustang. Grabbing the screwdriver, he counted seventeen jabs before the sergeant stopped him. Even so, the stab marks weren't that impressive, until the sergeant tried to pull him out and he used the screwdriver as an anchor. The resulting tear connected some of the punctures.

The handcuffs felt tight on his wrist and he held his head back so the blood from the gash on his head wouldn't run into his eyes.

"See, I told you he was nuts!" AJ said.

"Read the stitching!" he yelled to the sergeant who remained behind in the car. "Betray me and—"

"Wait a second," the sergeant said, cutting him off. The tone was urgent. When he got out of the car, he held up a long ponytail of dark hair.

"Lori!' Mary screamed.

The sergeant dropped the horrible find and reached for his pistol in one fluid movement.

Christopher caught a micro-second of hesitation on Sergeant Mike's face before a terrific sound echoed through the garage.

The sergeant fell against the Mustang and grabbed at his shoulder.

Another shot rang out from Officer Ned's gun and AJ bounced off the tool cabinet before collapsing on the cement floor. Blood quickly overwhelmed an oil stain underneath.

CHAPTER FORTY-THREE

The train tracks across the street from Godfreye's were encased in ice from last night's freezing rain. Christopher kicked at a piece with the heel of his sneaker until the ice turned white from the beating and began to splinter.

Looking south, his eyes followed the shimmering rails in the late afternoon sun, and he thought how they threaded their way past the silent mills of Lawrence on their way to Boston and beyond. He still marveled at the skyscraper-sized smokestacks of red brick dotting the North Canal Historical District five miles away in Lawrence. They stood as monuments to the fearlessness of the workers in the nineteenth century and their ingenuity in designing a model industrial city. He wondered if the million-plus bricks remembered the last time they felt the heat from the great furnaces that pushed billows of smoke skyward. Memories tended to favor the firstborn. The library and city archives were filled with images of the construction and dedications of the mills, but their last gasp, not so much. In the same manner, the first hello, slow dance, and kiss perpetually glowed in one's memory—or in his case what was left of it. But the lasts were either too painful to remember as Barbara Streisand sang, or more frequently, not recognized when they occurred. For instance, he couldn't recall much about the last dinner he had with his parents, or the last time AJ raced him around the yard in a wheelbarrow before it became too childish.

Christopher decided if he ever encountered the Spark again, he would beg to stand in one of those great chimneys in order to catch the scent of Mary's lilac perfume when she turned on a fan in Atlanta. He was willing to wait in one of those dark chimneys forever to feel near to her again.

The sound of crunching boots on the icy terrain made him turn around.

"What are you doing over here?" Mary asked. "Waiting for the future or hoping your past will catch up?"

"Hoping to become a hobo and ride a box car to Atlanta." He tried to smile, but it quickly collapsed.

"Well, that will be a long wait. The trains don't run on these tracks anymore."

Christopher figured she must have stopped to say goodbye to Mr. Godfreye because her eyes and cheeks were the same color.

"I only have a few minutes," she said, scanning his face quickly before looking away.

Christopher didn't acknowledge the time limit and studied Mary's unbuttoned overcoat, which revealed the same impeccable black dress she wore for her sister's funeral yesterday. St. Joseph's beautiful fieldstone church was packed with mourners and it pained him to keep a respectful distance given her father's wishes. He planted himself in the back pew, feeling guilty by association ever since the police found a knife with Lori's blood in the box spring of AJ's bed. It was the one place he never searched.

Although Father Flaherty must have notched a thousand funerals over fifty years of priesthood, he was visibly moved by the tragedy. Stepping off the altar, he stood in front of a portrait of Lori and read from the book of Psalms: *"If You take away their breath they perish and return to dust. When you send forth Your spirit, they are created, and You renew the face of the earth."*

Where did AJ bury her? he kept asking himself since AJ took the secret to the grave.

Mary touched his arm and he almost jumped. "My father wants to get on the road before dinner. He gave me strict orders not to see you, but that wasn't going to happen."

He nodded, thinking how her grief-stricken father didn't realize by moving Mary so far away, she was joining a sad trio: two lost daughters and a wife. A lump grew in his throat as he already missed her. Not wanting to upset her, he bit his lip and looked across the street and caught the Superette sign light up with dusk approaching.

"I'll call you when I get settled," she said with a sniffle.

He blinked hard as his eyes filled with tears and noticed how her lovely neck became pink and blotchy like it did whenever she got upset. She scratched a hive on her throat, upsetting a ruby necklace on a thin silver chain. It looked familiar, yet strangely out of place.

He pointed. "Is that a new necklace? I never noticed it before."

She took a step closer and held it up for him to see. "My sister and I bought matching ones when we went shopping at the Methuen Mall a few years ago. It's a reminder we're always in each other's heart." She gave a sad smile.

Christopher heard a loud buzzing noise and glanced again at the store. A few of the light bulbs in the middle of the sign flickered on and off. For a split second Godfreye's became *God eyes*.

The Spark's warning echoed in his ears. *"Beware too of the traitor, the one who holds a false lamp to camouflage the darkness around him. Everyone will be taken in by his guile, but not God, which sees all."* He blinked and she continued. *"What is essential is invisible to the eye, but sometimes it isn't."*

He was still staring at the necklace when Mary handed him a package of peanut M&M's. "These may be made by Mars, but have two a day to remember I'm still on earth," she smiled bravely. "Lucky for you, they're marked with my initials."

He hugged her tightly, never wanting to let go.

CHAPTER FORTY-FOUR

After he'd been hiding in the woods for hours, the garage door opened and the Chevy Citation slowly backed out. Christopher waited until the taillights disappeared down the street before bolting out of the thick brush, sprinting across the yard, and then up the short driveway to the garage door. Retrieving his notebook, he used the flashlight to illuminate the marked page and entered the four-digit code. The steel door opened slowly, and strangely without an overhead light coming on, which worked to his advantage. The cellar door was immediately to the left and he held his breath, hoping it wasn't locked. To his relief, the handle turned and he hit the button to close the garage door and dashed inside. Afraid to turn on the light, he used the flashlight to survey the conventional-looking cellar. A long gray workbench occupied the back wall and had an impressive array of tools neatly displayed on a red pegboard above it. To its left, two racks of metal shelving held enough paint cans to service the entire neighborhood, followed by a white coffin-like freezer.

That would be pretty gruesome, he thought, and made his way over and opened the freezer lid slowly. The light inside flashed on and highlighted an impressive array of frozen steaks, chicken, hamburger, and sausages, but no human parts. Christopher moved on and investigated the furnace area and a number of boxes under the stairs which held Christmas decorations. If he tried to explain the rationale for this break-in was due to the Spark's riddled prognostications, which fueled his wild imagination of linking Mary's necklace, the double-locked cellar door, the new women's clothing, and the extra-large refrigerator, Sergeant Mike would have him committed for sure.

Needing to make a hasty retreat before the sergeant came home, he stopped to consider whether he should he wipe down the freezer handle in case of fingerprints. Reaching for his handkerchief too fast, he dropped the plastic yellow flashlight on the cement floor. Bending down to pick it up, he noticed how its beam traveled across the floor and highlighted what resembled large door hinges to the left of the workbench. Puzzled, he walked over and examined how the triangular metal pieces were meticulously painted to blend in. Then he noticed how the tools on the pegboard were secured in place with thick plastic rings. *Do you have to cut the rings if you want to use a wrench? That's a pain.*

He tried pulling the bench toward him like a door, but it refused to move.

"Okay, I've officially gone bonkers," he said out loud and turned to leave.

"Hey, I'm hungry!" a tiny voice said.

Christopher spun around, expecting the Spark to be sitting on the workbench, but no one was there.

"If . . . that's . . . you . . . I . . . have . . . questions," he stuttered.

There was a long silence. "Who's there?" a female voice boomed like the *Wizard of Oz*. The voice came from *behind* the workbench.

Christopher felt his heart jump into his throat. "Where are you?"

A shorter silence followed. "Pull out the drawer in the middle of the bench and kneel down."

He obeyed and the top half of a familiar face looked back. He could make out a small room behind her.

"Lori?"

"Who are you?"

Christopher illuminated his face with the flashlight. "I'm . . . a . . . friend . . . of . . . your . . . sister." He rubbed his throat, trying to help unstick the words. "How can . . . I get you out?"

She backed away and put her hand over her mouth. "You're here to rescue me?"

Please don't use that word, he wanted to say, but nodded.

"He has a key and always takes it with him. How did you find me?"

"It's a long story. I'll go and get the police."

Her eyes filled with tears and she looked giddy. "Hurry!"

Christopher made it halfway across the cellar before a cold thought stopped him in his tracks. *No one will believe me!* The sergeant was being hailed in local and national news for solving Lori's murder, reopening the case of Bobby's death, and breaking up a cocaine ring. Plus, he took a bullet in the shoulder. They only spoke once in the last few weeks and the conversation had been very strained. The sergeant refused to acknowledge the cassette tape or his assistance.

He went back to the workbench and reopened the drawer, but didn't look in this time.

"What's the matter?"

"The police won't believe me," he started.

"Why not?"

"The sergeant is a hero for solving your murder by pinning it on AJ and he's dead now. Plus, everyone thinks I'm nothing but damaged goods." He pulled on his chin. "If I push, he may spare me because I'm all my aunt has left." Christopher looked through the slot at Lori's glassy eyes, "But not you."

She backed away. "I'm already halfway to dead. Now I know why he's been so full of himself lately. Michael said he cracked some big case and that's how he got hurt. Since then, he's been complaining I'm like a dog and he's tired of having to always be around to take care of me. Last night, he said he doesn't need me to fill in the hole from someone named Becky, because there's a pond filled with them now."

Christopher pictured his aunt and for the first time recognized the resemblance.

"Call the FBI or State Police and tell my dad. He'll fight for me."

He didn't have the heart to say her father would like to build a similar prison for him. *Who could help him?* Denise came to mind.

He leaned in. "Before I go, I want you to know Mary held out hope the longest. She's on her way to a group home in Atlanta and left me some M&M's to remind me of her." He backed away. "I miss her terribly."

"Peanut M&M's?" Lori asked, making it sound like one word.

"Yeah, you know how she much she loves them because—"

"Do you have them with you?" she asked, urgently.

He felt his pocket, thinking she must have a craving for chocolate. "Yeah, they're yours if you want them."

Suddenly the garage door sounded.

"Hurry up and give them to me," she begged.

He slid them through the opening.

She backed away. "Now hurry up and hide!"

CHAPTER FORTY-FIVE

As a boy, he enjoyed playing hide and seek and finding the most imaginative locations to disappear. Now as Christopher scanned the small cellar, he looked for the most basic shield before the lights came on. The chain on the garage door opener rumbled as it closed and he squeezed behind a single stack of boxes next to the cellar stairs.

Fluorescent lights overhead came to life as he half crouched. His heart raced and he concentrated on taking shallow breaths, until his eyes identified a fatal error.

His yellow flashlight sat horizontal on top of the furnace with the light on and pointed toward the workbench. Christopher tried to slither ever so slightly to retrieve it, but the stack of boxes in front began to wobble.

The sergeant came rushing in carrying a large white pizza box in his right hand as his left was still in a sling. Taking a silver key out of his baggy dungarees, he inserted it into what looked like an electrical plug outlet on the pegboard and pulled. The entire workbench swung open, revealing a ten-by-twelve-foot cell containing a metal bed, stainless steel toilet, and sink. Fluorescent lighting overhead was protected by a steel grate.

Lori sat on the bed wearing a black silk robe. Christopher leaned to the right to get his first full look at Mary's sister. The beauty from the pictures Mary showed him remained, but Lori looked very thin.

The long dark hair must have been sacrificed for the Mustang grand reveal as she now wore a short bob cut.

The sergeant held up the box. "I got us some beach pizza for dinner. Becky and I used to love Tripoli's at Salisbury Beach. I'll sure miss this when I move south."

Lori looked at the floor and her mouth moved ever so slightly like she was chewing gum.

The sergeant opened the box and smelled the pie. "Man, this sure brings me back."

Lori stood up and Christopher sucked in his breath, noticing the iron bracelet around her ankle married to a long chain.

She reached up and pulled a thin string and the fluorescent lighting went off, casting the room in a shadow.

"What are you doing?" the sergeant asked. "You were on my case all afternoon how sick you were of my cooking."

"I am," she said cooing. "But," she said with some hesitation, "I want to show my appreciation that you braved the cold to get me a pizza."

The sergeant laughed. "Like I told you yesterday, I'm not taking you south with me, honey." He took a bite of pizza. "But that doesn't mean you can't try and change my mind." He smiled at her. "That's how we got involved in the first place. Remember? You were tired of all the silly boy games."

She smiled. "Come over here."

He put the box down and Christopher watched as Lori pulled him down on the bed and passionately kissed him.

He began a slow motion crawl to retrieve the flashlight and froze when the sergeant jumped up.

"What's that I taste? Chocolate peanuts?"

Lori followed him. "What are you talking about?"

The sergeant pushed her away and turned on the light. He began searching the cell and scratching his throat. "If I find—"

Lori followed him. "How would I get peanuts in here?" she asked, interrupting him. "It's not like you let me go shopping! Maybe the pizza is contaminated."

The logic worked and he grabbed the box and inspected the pie.

Lori stroked his arm. "Sit a minute and calm down."

He pushed her away and started to wheeze. She clung to his waist and he dropped the rest of the pizza and wrestled to break free.

"What's the matter with you?" he yelled, and grabbed at his neck and staggered out of the cell. "I need the EpiPen."

Lori pursued him, but the chain went taut like it did with Fang. "Stop him!" she yelled.

The sergeant stopped in mid-stride, no doubt wondering who she was pleading with, and saw the flashlight on the furnace.

Christopher threw a box of Christmas decorations as an opening salvo and then tackled him at the knees.

The sergeant fell like a top heavy maple and hit the cement floor hard. Wrestling with AJ had never ended well, though it taught him to absorb the first blows and work hard not to get pinned. The element of surprise was in his favor as the sergeant seemed stunned by the attack and could only defend himself with one arm.

Christopher succeeded in getting on top and tried to use his weight to keep the lower half pinned. The success proved short-lived as the life-long cop used his training, and the urgency of the moment, to roll hard to the right and overpower him.

The sergeant stared at him with eyes he didn't know and smelling of some mystery perfume he must have made Lori shower in. "I knew you were an imposter," he wheezed.

The sergeant wrapped the sling around his neck and pulled it tight. Christopher knew the Spark's warning was right. He might have the right heart, but it didn't guarantee the outcome. As the noose tightened, he stopped kicking and trying to gasp for air and held his breath, hoping the sergeant would fall for the trick given his condition. Long seconds passed.

Pial walked past the white men plowing their fields. His heart was beating hard, but he was confident he applied the paints with faith this time. Fear did not infiltrate his heart.

The old man who killed his brother was asleep on the porch. Pial took a piece of rope and quickly bound his wrists and feet and the man did not stir. Next, he proceeded across the yard and down to the barn. When he opened the door, the mare greeted him. Her long nose felt hot, and he sensed its frustration of being held in captivity for so long. Applying the green and red paints under her eyes, Pial led her past the porch in silence. The thought crossed his mind of dragging the murderer behind him, but he realized his mission was pure. The killer would get his punishment tomorrow when his father and the others returned with sharp tomahawks.

The river was ahead and he kept his eyes on the other shore and the horizon beyond. The water stung like a million bees, but he did not allow it to become an obstacle.

Christopher gagged and opened his eyes. The skin surrounding his neck was on fire and he grabbed at the tight cloth around his throat. The cries of a woman thundered behind him.

"Get up quick!" she yelled. "If he gets the EpiPen, we're both dead."

He staggered to his feet and rounded the staircase and caught sight of the sergeant pulling himself up the last three stairs.

Christopher stumbled badly but caught up with the sergeant as he reached for the thin yellow box sitting on the window sill over the sink. He grabbed a kitchen chair, which was the venue for so many interrogations, and whacked the sergeant's arm. The box went flying across the floor and Christopher scooped it up and ran down the hall to the bedroom and locked the door. A white phone sat on the nightstand and as he picked the receiver up, the hollow pine door came crashing down.

The sergeant looked gray and Christopher knew he would go for his gun.

He held up the box.

"I'll give it to you if you promise to let Lori and me go."

The sergeant wheezed badly and leaned over. "I would never hurt either of you."

Christopher threw the box on the bed and made a run for it and the sergeant caught him by the arm. "Wait a second so I can show you how to use my gun. You were so anxious before."

The cop looked in the box and growled. "Where is it?"

Christopher held out his arm as the sergeant pounced on him. This time he concentrated on the syringe and absorbed ferocious punches to keep his fingers locked. A terrible punch to the temple ended the effort.

The sergeant grabbed the syringe and standing up, placed it against his thigh. Before he could push the injector button, Christopher managed to kick it out.

"Time for you to join AJ," the sergeant wheezed, moving to the floor. Christopher crawled to the other side of the bed, waiting for the bullets to find him.

Instead, he heard a thud and peeking around the corner, he found the sergeant unconscious on the floor. The needle was in his leg and the gun in his hand.

Christopher listened to the sergeant's shallow breathing and dialed 911.

CHAPTER FORTY-SIX

Dressed in a black business suit and clutching a leather portfolio binder, Denise already looked like a lawyer.

"When I called the police chief yesterday, he offered to send over an officer and make sure everything goes smoothly."

Christopher smiled. "That's the third time you reminded me since we landed. Maybe I'm not the only one with short-term memory problems."

She shrugged. "Considering everything you've been through I understand why this may not raise your blood pressure. But Evelyn is a wild card and Kylie doesn't need to see her freak out."

He glanced at the sidewalk leading up to the mahogany front door. "I will take it slow and easy. My aunt has been avoiding me for the past year and I don't see that changing much today." He touched her arm. "Thanks again for everything. If it wasn't for your father's legal help, I'd still be fighting to get Kylie home."

Christopher rang the doorbell and when the door opened, not surprisingly, it was Becky who greeted them. She wore a bright red kerchief on her head and a very brave face.

After hugging them, she led them into an airy room with green floral print furniture.

"I want to say a few things before you tell Kylie the news," Becky said in a low voice before sitting down on the couch. She reached up and took her nephew's hand and pulled him down beside her. "We've been through a lot, but we're still family."

Christopher nodded. "Of course. It's just—"

"Please let me finish," Becky continued. "Your perseverance led to surviving World End, saving Lori from a monster I thought I knew, and removing a terrible stain from my son's memory." Her eyes filled with tears. "I wish there weren't others." She took a deep breath. "But I've learned the hard way how an overused strength can become a weakness. My focus on family led me to extract a promise from you I should never have asked. It was wrong and I will be forever sorry. Without it, AJ might be in prison, but alive."

Christopher hugged his aunt. She felt so thin.

"But there's a lesson here for you too," she continued, looking him in the eye. "Your perseverance can make you pig-headed about what's right for Kylie, even with the law on your side. You have to realize Evelyn and I wanted nothing but the best for you and Kylie after the loss of your parents. Did we make mistakes? Absolutely." She sighed and took a deep breath. "Especially my sister. Evelyn can be just as stubborn as you. We should have talked more and worked through the fireworks. That's what families do." She pointed to her kerchief. "I'm tired of all the loss and want to preserve what's left."

Christopher nodded. He began to reach for the new ultra-thin notebook in his back pocket, but something told him he would remember this. When he sat back on the couch, he glanced over at Denise sitting in a wing chair. The legal pad was at her side and she was holding back tears too.

Becky pointed toward the hall. "Okay, I've said my piece. Kylie's out on the lanai. Denise and I will stay here and catch up, while you break the news to her. I have an overnight bag already packed. We will forward the rest of her things tomorrow."

He hugged his aunt again and made his way to the back of the house. Kylie was sitting in a lounge chair reading a book and didn't hear his approach.

"It will be at least another month before you can wear shorts in Billerica," he announced.

The little girl looked up and her smile eclipsed the Florida sun. He rushed over and gave her a tight hug.

"I thought Evelyn was going shopping, not to the airport!"

Christopher smiled to keep from wincing. "Denise drove me here."

Kylie continued smiling. "She's so nice."

He nodded and pointed to her textbook. "You're hitting the books on a Saturday?"

She nodded. "I love my teacher Miss Haley. She makes learning so much fun. My best friends Krista and Shelley are a blast too. We're in the same reading group."

He sat down in the chair next to her and let the sun warm his face. "Do you miss home?" he asked, trying to hold back from gushing the big news.

A frown crossed her face. "I miss Mom and Dad a lot. I think," she hesitated, "that living in our house would make me even sadder because I'd always be expecting them to come home. It would make me think about," she looked away, "all that awful stuff."

He wanted to argue it was the memory of them engrained in the DNA of their house that meant so much to him, but held his tongue.

She reached over and grabbed his hand. "I love Auntie Evelyn and Becky and all my new friends; but you're my brother. I want to be with you."

He reached under his shirt and took off the St. Christopher necklace and put it back on her. "Thanks for lending me this as I faced some pretty rough waters." He bit his lip and pondered her words. "I always thought I was supposed to be the strong one and carry you to the other side. I realize now, it's your love that delivered me."

Christopher gave his sister a kiss on the cheek and standing up suddenly felt taller. "Let's go out for lunch and then you can give me the grand tour of the neighborhood. Maybe there's a house for sale nearby."

"You mean you would move down here?" she screamed, jumping to her feet.

He smelled the warm air. "I'm thinking we've both seen enough of winter."

The faint sound of a carpenter cutting wood with a Skil saw pierced the quiet morning and the Spark's words came back. *Consider how the Master Carpenter remakes a man if you let Him.*

CHAPTER FORTY-SEVEN

The buzzer reminded him of a prison as the door clicked open authorizing him to enter the facility. A middle-aged woman fitting the description of Mrs. June Reardon sat behind a white reception desk. Her blonde hair was stacked high in a bun like Mary described and it did look like she might be hiding a soup can up there.

Mrs. Reardon flashed half a smile and pointed to the register, instructing him to sign in. Christopher scanned the page and noticed the last visitor was two days ago. He scribbled his name quickly then reached in his pocket and placed a tea bag on the opposite blank page.

The smile turned upside down fast. She stood up like he just unloaded contraband. "What on earth is that?"

He thought she looked pretty stylish in the oversized cream-colored sweater and black leggings, so Mary was being a bit tough on her. "I just wanted to thank you for taking such good care of Mary, that's all." He pointed at the tea bag waiting to be adopted. "I thought you would enjoy a cup of Bigelow green tea from my special stash."

She looked both unimpressed and ungrateful. "Please take a seat and I'll let Mary know you're here."

Christopher nodded and selected a rocking chair by the window and started scanning a copy of *The Atlanta Journal-Constitution*. He tried reading a few articles, but the anticipation of seeing Mary made the words run together. So he focused on the pictures instead and noticed how few politicians ever smile in Washington.

Ten minutes passed and despite the air conditioning, sweat began to form under his Red Sox hat. His favorite coat felt strange too, now devoid of all duct tape. Mrs. Reardon didn't seem to have any curiosity why he wore winter garb. His guess was she never traveled to New England where the snow can still threaten well into April.

Suddenly, a door to the right of the reception desk opened and Mary came strolling out smiling. Her hair was pulled back and she wore a crisp pink polo shirt and blue jeans. The southern sun certainly agreed with her and cultivated a crop of fresh freckles on her nose.

He bolted to his feet much too quickly and the rocking chair made a terrible thud as it hit the back wall. Mrs. Reardon looked up from the computer terminal with a frown.

Mary gave him a tight hug and held on. "You'll have to tell me if she asked about Kylie's birthday party seeing as she screened all your letters before Lori put a stop to it," she whispered in his ear. "I wonder if she ever changes the can of soup in that bun of hers. Upstairs we have a running bet. I'm thinking it's chicken noodle, but everyone else believes it's chunky vegetable."

She let him go and he was surprised when she looked him straight in the eye and held on.

"Can I check out where you live?" he asked.

Mary shook her head. "Sorry, it's against the rules to have men upstairs." She glanced around the room. "But it's not much different than down here. Most everything is sterile white. The only hint of color is in the kitchen which needs updating. You should see the putrid yellow old stove. Miss Dee laughs and tells me no, that's what we call harvest gold, my dear." She laughed softly. "No wonder they decided to paint everything else white." She inspected her fingers and Christopher noticed her nails were long too. "These hands were never meant for peeling vegetables."

Mrs. Reardon coughed and pointed down the hall. "Why don't you two use the visitors' room down the hall." She held up the tea bag. "You can also have this back if you like. I'm more of a coffee person, to tell you the truth."

He waved her off. "You'll be a convert once you try it." He glanced back at Mary. "Do you know where we can get a nice bowl of chicken noodle soup for lunch?"

Mary struggled to contain the laugh and a small chirp escaped.

They strolled down the hall and into a sunny sitting room. Pink azaleas were visible through the window.

"I checked and Lori's flight left on time," he said, sitting down on a white cotton couch.

She sat down next to him. "Are the streets really blue in San Juan or are you just trying to lure me away from harvest gold and soup in a bun?"

He laughed. "The Spanish loaded their ships with the bricks for ballast and replaced them with gold for the journey home. There were so many, they ended up paving the streets with them. It was very kind of Lori to invite me for part of the sisters' big reunion vacation."

"I still wonder if my father really agreed to it." She touched his arm. "Did you bring the Walkman, like I asked?"

"I didn't dare come without it." He took it out of his coat thinking how it felt like a piece of him; its cover scratched, the internal workings sometimes freezing up, but still soldiering on. "What's so special about this anyway?" he asked, handing it to her. "You have one just like it too."

"True, but this one's been through a lot. Plus, I used it to—" She stopped and studied the back of the unit. "Lori and I talked about Florida." She glanced up at him. "Did you really mean it?"

He nodded. "I used part of the settlement to buy a nice house in the same neighborhood as Evelyn and Becky. Kylie has the best of both worlds now. She lives with me and has two doting aunts three streets over." He took her hand and it felt warm and soft. "The house is huge: four bedrooms, three baths, and a kitchen without a hint of harvest gold. I offered to let Lori stay until she finds a place of her own. I know she and your dad don't see eye to eye about much of anything, and it's not getting any easier with your new stepmom. Lori's looking for a new start and you deserve the same." He squeezed her hand. "We'll take things slow, but I want you in my life forever."

"Emily Dickinson said *'forever is composed of nows.'* That's how I want to live. My father doesn't understand."

"We will deal with it," he said, interrupting her. "My aunt says it all comes down to communication. From what I know of Lori, she is a force to be reckoned with. She's in your corner and will make your dad come around."

Mary looked at him again. "I'm not looking to be saved, you know, just loved for who I am." Her eyes glistened and she started fiddling again with the audiocassette player.

"I put fresh batteries in," he offered, "in case you want to record a funny farewell to Mrs. Reardon."

Mary pried the lid open and quickly removed the batteries. Then she pulled hard and the battery case popped out, tethered by wires.

"What are you doing?" he asked, confused.

"Open your hand," she commanded.

He didn't know what to expect, but stretched out his palm as directed. She shook the Walkman twice and out popped one green M&M.

Christopher laughed. "All this for one stale chocolate-covered peanut?"

She ignored his comment and placed the autopsied unit in his hands and glanced quickly at the door to listen. "You don't understand, silly. This is a *very* special keepsake and proves why you should never doubt me."

"You're right and I apologize for the hundredth time." He began to reassemble the unit when a folded piece of white paper tucked deep inside the machine caught his eye. He figured it must be a quality inspection tag like they insert in everything nowadays, except this one looked bigger. Reaching in his coat, he took out the nail the Spark gave him and fished it out. Without unfolding it, he realized it was a lottery ticket.

He sucked in his breath and Mary steadied his trembling hand.

Christopher looked at the folded ticket and then at Mary. She was smiling and studying his reaction and didn't retreat when he found her eyes. Truth be told, he found himself in a state of confusion after Lori was found and everything around him exploded. One night, in the middle of a long walk, he stopped by Mary Queen of Peace church in Salem to rest. By chance, he sat in a hard pew, next to the ninth station of the cross.

Christ falls for the third time.

He studied the image of a fallen Jesus bearing the weight of a large cross and suddenly felt the rocky soil within him fall away. Thirsty for guidance, he opened a prayer book in the pew and the Spark illuminated a passage.

> *I prayed, and prudence was given me;*
> *I pleaded, and the spirit of wisdom came to me.*
> *I preferred her to scepter and throne,*
> *and deemed riches nothing in comparison with her,*
> *nor did I liken any priceless gem to her;*
> *because all gold, in view of her, is a little sand,*
> *and before her, silver is to be accounted mire.*
> *Beyond health and comeliness I loved her,*
> *and I chose to have her rather than the light,*
> *because the splendor of her never yields to sleep.*
> *Yet all good things together came to me in her company,*
> *and countless riches at her hands.*

Mary drank in his expression. He smiled and handed the unread ticket back to her as a gift, which surprised and pleased her.

"I love you, Mary, and will never doubt you ever again," he whispered.

A brilliant smile beamed on her face. "I know I have trouble expressing myself sometimes, but don't give up on me. I love you too."

Christopher reached over and caressed Mary's cheek. The long sweet kiss that followed proved richer than any payday on earth and crazier than he could ever pretend to be.

ACKNOWLEDGMENTS

Some epiphanies require time and distance. After editing *A Difficult Crossing*, I wondered why I kept thinking about the famous *Pale Blue Dot* photograph of earth, which Voyager 1 took after traveling thirteen years and 3.7 billion miles. Digging through some old mementos, I realized the connection underscored the fact that I've been wrestling with this story since the space probe launched in 1977.

Let me explain. Every town has a few residents that march to the beat of their own drums. Growing up, I remember two in particular. One was a middle-aged WWII Army veteran, thought to be suffering from shell-shock. He was regularly spotted riding his bike or enjoying a smoke and a cup of tea after procuring some hot water from a friendly merchant. And yes, he carried his own tea bags and sometimes taped his first name on his coat. My dad used to give this gentle soul a ride when he occasionally hitchhiked. I was in college when I first began drafting a fictional account, wanting to recognize both his service and his sacrifice. That maiden voyage proved short, but I promised to try again someday.

Thirty years passed before I attempted to make good on that commitment and discovered time and distance had changed my perspective. While I continued to admire the soldier, I found myself compelled to include another fixture in town from the same era. Around thirty years of age, blonde, and very thin, this woman wandered up and down the main drag of town dressed in a skirt and heels no matter the season. There were many rumors about her life, but none substantiated. She could be found most days at the mall and other fast food hangouts, checking phone booths and vending machines for abandoned coins. Sadly, she was known to everyone as "Morbid Mary," for reasons I could never determine, other than the cruel nicknames lavished on the misunderstood. This silent woman suffered ridicule for many years, including some from my circle of high school friends—a fact that still troubles me.

What I found intriguing in rebooting the project was not chasing a Forrest Gump "life is a box of chocolates" outlook, but rather, the bittersweet portrayal of two characters living on the fringe; one by unforeseen circumstances, the other by nature and nurture. In reflecting on the past, my brother Jude eloquently summed up the town's reaction to the pair: "If it was raining, many would stop and pick up the veteran and throw his bike in the trunk. But with Mary, they just aimed for the biggest puddle." Striving to construct a meaningful story, I decided to link the two characters, and also throw in a healthy dose of my own apprehension if faced with similar challenges. With that in mind, I delved into crafting a hero's journey across a winter landscape, with greed and obsession as the catalyst to highlight the courage and commitment of two living on the margin. This second attempt was entitled *A January Thaw* and culminated in reaching quarterfinalist status in the highly competitive "Amazon Breakthrough Novel Contest" in 2009.

Eight more years passed before I returned to the manuscript, fortified with lessons learned from publishing *Chasing Mayflies*. I decided the bones of the novel were good, but the story line needed to be expanded, the characters deepened, and the response to grace elevated. The image I carried was from a trip my wife and I made to Savannah, where I took a picture of a majestic angel with a broken wing. While we all suffer brokenness at one time or another, if we look within our families and communities, we find stoic examples of the physically and emotionally challenged that respond with extraordinary resilience, and are embraced too seldom.

While inspired by real people, I must doubly stress—especially to those with long memories from my hometown—that this novel is a complete work of fiction and the characters represent archetypes to highlight deeper truths. With that important disclaimer, I do have a final footnote to share. The noble WWII veteran passed away in 2005 at the age of eighty-three. His obituary highlighted his service to country and how deeply his family loved him. Mary—if that was even her first name—remained a frustrating mystery, as I prepared the final edits prior to publication.

Sometimes heaven's gifts arrive unexpected and with dramatic flair. At an anniversary dinner with my wife a few months back, I broke open a fortune cookie and read: *An old love will come back to you.* The next morning, my brother Joe directed me to a Facebook group he discovered, where people were reminiscing about the old days in town. One post included a spirited discussion about Morbid Mary, and I finally learned my "old love's" true name. While the group debated whether this mostly silent woman suffered from a developmental disability and if she moved south to a warmer climate, what gave me pause—and hope—was the regret so many shared on how they treated her so long ago.

I could say that every time I hear about Voyager 1, as it continues hurtling toward its date with a star 40,000 years in the future, I will think of these two special souls. That's certainly true; but more often, I will think of them as I navigate the area roads where they made their brave stand. I am blessed for what they ultimately taught me and only wish I had truly known and befriended them.

In completing this journey to publication, I am deeply indebted to family and friends for their love, friendship, and support in what proved to be my own difficult crossing at times. Special thanks to my wife and best friend, Robin, for sustaining me during a marathon measured in years. Words cannot begin to acknowledge my love to my daughters, Heather and Taylor, for their encouragement, keen insights, editing, and marketing skills. Special thanks also to Heather's husband, Michael Beaudoin, for his creative flair in cover and website design. I also want to recognize and thank my literary agent, Kimberly Shumate, for her early support for this and two other novels. I remain very privileged to be part of the eLectio family and owe a debt of gratitude to the entire production team. The constant support, professionalism, and friendship of Publisher Jesse Greever and Chief Operating Officer Christopher Dixon at eLectio Publishing have been nothing less than phenomenal.

I sincerely hope you enjoy *A Difficult Crossing*. I look forward to hearing from you at **vincentdonovanbooks.com.**

CPSIA information can be obtained
at www.ICGtesting.com
Printed in the USA
FSHW01n2258231018
53118FS